A man o...

Fearless. Loyal. Brilliant. Ruthless. Bold words are always used to describe English war hero Captain Chase Eversea, but another word unfortunately plays a role in every Eversea's destiny: *trouble*. And trouble for Chase arrives in the form of a mysterious message summoning him to a London rendezvous . . . where he encounters the memory of his most wicked indiscretion in the flesh: Rosalind March—the only woman he could never forget.

A woman of passion . . .

Five years ago, the reckless, charming beauty craved the formidable Captain's attention. But now Rosalind is a coolly self-possessed woman, and desire is the last thing on her mind: her sister has mysteriously disappeared and she needs Chase's help to find her. But as their search through London's darkest corners re-ignites long-smoldering passion and memories of old battles, Chase and Rosalind are challenged to surrender: to the depths of a wicked desire, and to the possibility of love.

Romances by Julie Anne Long

SINCE THE SURRENDER
LIKE NO OTHER LOVER
THE PERILS OF PLEASURE

The
Surrender

Julie Anne Long

AVON
An Imprint of HarperCollinsPublishers

AVON BOOKS
An Imprint of HarperCollins*Publishers*
10 East 53rd Street
New York, New York 10022-5299

Copyright © 2009 by Julie Anne Long
ISBN 978-0-06-134161-8
www.avonromance.com

First Avon Books paperback printing: August 2009

Avon Trademark Reg. U.S. Pat. Off. and in Other Countries, Marca Registrada, Hecho en U.S.A.
HarperCollins® is a registered trademark of HarperCollins Publishers.

Printed in the U.S.A.

10 9 8 7 6 5 4 3 2 1

For Dom

Acknowledgments

Much, much gratitude to my insightful, delightful editor, May Chen; to my agent, Steve Axelrod, for wisdom and Olympic-class pragmatism; to Kim Castillo, for cheerfully brilliant assistance; to the hard-working crew at Avon, who made the book you're holding possible; and to all the lovely readers who help make writing such a joy.

Since The Surrender

Chapter 1

*B*anished.

  Chase Eversea—Captain Charles Eversea—took perverse, righteous pleasure in the word. *Banished* from Pennyroyal Green, Sussex, his home, and his family, all for muttering six little words into the foam of his ale at the Pig & Thistle just four nights ago. He certainly hadn't meant anyone to *hear* them. He hadn't even meant to say them aloud. But out they'd come, and in all honesty, he couldn't think of a soul who would blame him given the circumstances.

It was his brother Colin's fault.

But then, historically in the Eversea family, things usually were.

Chase scowled with gargoyle ferocity up at the unprepossessing door of a boardinghouse on a London street that straddled a frayed edge between respectability and dissolution—which, granted, some would have said neatly described *him* these days. Inside, a distant Eversea cousin, a certain Mr. Adam Sylvaine was allegedly lodged, and Chase had been summarily, uncompromisingly dispatched—in other words, *banished*—to determine whether he would make a suitable new vicar for Pennyroyal Green. A task for which *he* of all people was surely unsuitable.

He suspected this interview was merely a ruse perpetrated by his family to rid Sussex of him.

As if inspired by the sheer thunder of his mood, the dense summer sky opened and unceremoniously dropped its load of rain.

He stood as water drilled upon his hat and spilled in rivulets over his shoulders and eddied about his boots, turning him instantly into an incongruous glowering fountain around which pedestrians were forced to dodge. It amused him to be obstructive. One would have thought the sky was spitting hot fat, for God's sake, the way this lot carried on, scurrying with arms flung up over their heads.

A young man hunched against the rain inadvertently intercepted his scowl and froze, startled, like a pointer flushing game. He unfroze and bolted seconds later. His feet a blur. Surreptitiously crossing himself as he fled.

Chase snorted. Once upon a time he could quell uprisings or blacken the mood of a regiment with that scowl. He could do the converse with a smile: inspire dispirited soldiers to uncommon battlefield valor. Melt petticoats from women.

He rationed smiles these days as though the war was still on.

But he smiled now at the retreating man. And though it wasn't precisely a *pleasant* smile, a woman dashing by arm in arm with a man, her bonnet in danger of becoming a sodden ruin, slowed as if the curve of it had snared her like a net.

And thus she sacrificed what remained of her bonnet

to gaze at Captain Charles Eversea, who pretended not to notice, and seconds later she was tugged into motion again by the man whose elbow linked hers.

The rain ended almost as quickly as it had begun, as summer rains do, leaving everything soaked and steaming. Chase sighed and leaned hard on his walking stick to propel himself forward again. He still *needed* the damned stick for the first step after motionless, and the fact of this was always a touch paper to the fuse of his temper, and his temper propelled him the rest of the way up any given hill or flight of stairs so quickly his limp was nearly imperceptible and the pain nearly forgotten.

Nearly.

It was as constant and varied and part of him as thought now. It ebbed and swelled, it tormented, it simply was.

A bit like his bloody family, he thought sourly.

Chase took another step and found he could go no farther. Something had hold of his coat.

"Guv!" the thing spoke. In breathless cockney. From somewhere near his hip.

Chase glowered down. A pair of very blue eyes peered up at him from a filthy boy's face.

"I've a message fer ye!" The grubby fist *not* gripping Chase's coat extended and opened, revealing a square of foolscap that appeared to be folded into eighths or sixteenths.

Chase stared at it suspiciously, then tweezed it up between his fingers. It was warm and damp on the outside from the messenger's clutches. He had little hope of finding the inside unsmeared from rain and sweat.

He whipped his coat out behind him and shook the

thing open in one hand, and then, without turning his head, his hand shot out and snatched the collar of the boy's shirt just as the urchin tried to dart away. The collar nearly came off in his fingers, so he clamped his hand on a bony shoulder and spun the lad around.

"I'll have that back."

The boy blinked. "*How* did—"

"I'll have that back," he repeated with even-toned menace.

A distracted person might not have felt the nimble fingers nick the button from his coat, which was what the urchin doubtless had been counting on. Chase was seldom *truly* distracted, regardless of the concerted effort he put into distracting himself.

"Just a button," the boy tried.

"Just *my* button."

It was an absurd negotiation. He should just cuff the little street rat, as this one had obviously been all but bred for the hulks or gallows. The boy had yet to grow into his ears; they projected horizontally from his very round head. Thanks to dirt, his hair was an indeterminate color, probably blond, and his expression was surly, but his robin's-egg-blue eyes were frightened and not unintelligent. Rain had made narrow roads in the grime on his cheeks, striping him like a small animal in native camouflage. Perhaps offering a foreshadowing of what he might look like behind bars.

Bloody London. He'd scarcely arrived and he was being *robbed*.

Chase blackly, fixedly, stared a threat until the dirty fist extended and uncurled again.

The urchin stared in nervous wonder at his own hand. As though it had betrayed him. The button winked in the grimy palm. Good brass one, that. Worth four shillings at the least.

Chase took his button.

"I would have paid you," he told the messenger-thief ominously.

"Took yer time abou' it, din't ye." It was a far less confident squeak this time. He tried to dodge away.

Chase, undecided as to whether he wanted to turn this one over to the Charleys, kept his hand clamped on the boy's shoulder as he shook open the seamed message to see if it was indeed a message or just a means of robbing him. It was an odd sensation—having a captive. Let alone a small filthy boy captive. Chase hadn't done anything quite so decisive as *prevent* someone from doing something in a very long time.

He read:

Captain Eversea—Meet me at the Montmorency Museum in one hour near the Italian pastorals. It's a matter of utmost urgency.

P.S. Pastorals means cows and the like.

No signature.

The Montmorency *Museum*?

Italian *pastorals*?

Worst of all:

Cows?

He stared at the word in rank disbelief. It all but throbbed before his eyes.

Cows were the reason he was here in the first place. If only bloody Colin could have stopped *talking* about cows that night at the Pig & Thistle—

He frowned and thought about the Montmorency. Chase had never seen a reason to go beyond Covent Garden into Bloomsbury, so he'd never visited it. If he recalled correctly, it had come about when a wealthy, eccentric (was there any other kind?) naturalist had cocked up his toes and left his vast collection of *things*—sarcophagi, embalmed insects, scrolls, furniture—to a surprised and not entirely grateful British government, which had done a decent job of sorting it all out and then had stuffed it into a centuries-old residence purchased from an aristocrat—that would be Montmorency—who had long ago abandoned it for a more fashionable address.

Hardly the ideal setting for an assignation, if that's what this was meant to be.

The script was indeed very feminine, but it wasn't one he recognized. Generous loops bloomed atop long lean letters joined with profligate flourishes, all tilting impatiently forward. It was made by a heavily inked pen. The margin of the paper was jagged. It appeared to have been ripped in haste from a book. The better to imply "utmost urgency," he supposed.

"Bin followin' ye aaaaall the way from St. James Square," the urchin volunteered cheerfully, suddenly. As if they were old friends. "Ye're quick fer a gimpy cove."

Chase slowly levered his head up and fixed him with a black stare. The cheeky expression gave way to a far-more-appropriate-to-his-circumstance unease.

"Who gave this message to you?" He barked the question.

"A liedy." The urchin was startled into answering instantly.

What in God's name was a lie— Oh.

"Who is this 'lady'?"

A stubborn hesitation. "*She* gave me a shilling. Said ye'd give me a shilling, too."

A mind on a singular track, this one. A shilling was a princely sum for a street rat. And this woman had promised the urchin *his* money?

Confident woman. Or a foolhardy one.

Or this was all some sort of elaborate ruse.

"Who is *she*, and how did you know to give this to *me*?"

Urchin tried to shrug, but his shoulder was under the governance of Chase's hand. He managed only a twitch.

"Dinna ken 'er name. The liedy knew yer 'ouse number—and ye were walkin' out of the door, puttin' on yer 'at, so"—with one hand, the urchin cockily mimed a gentleman tugging on a hat, complete with a self-important expression—"and so I followed ye and followed ye until ye stopped. *Finally*."

Chase had taken a hack part of the way from the family town house and walked the rest, because he didn't like his leg to think he ever intended to coddle it, given that he'd spent the better part of five years in Sussex healing (and drinking, and counting on Colin to distract him). A boy on foot could move more nimbly than a hack through some crowded streets.

Urchin was dogged, he had to admit. He'd earned his shilling.

"But how did you know *I* was the person she sought? Did she give you a description of me?" And what would that description have been? *Tall, self-important, scowls and limps?*

"Nay. Jus' the 'ouse number. Took a chance, din't I, that ye were the gentleman 'twas meant for?" Urchin was pleased with itself. "And I were *right*. Often am," he added complacently.

Chase was struck by the fact that this sounded just like something he would have said.

"What did she look like? This lady?"

Urchin frowned. "Old. Like you. Posh voice. Like yers. Not fat."

Chase scowled his disapproval of this entirely inadequate description, which made the urchin flinch again. "And?" he snapped.

"And she had a—" Urchin stopped.

"A what?"

"A p-pretty hat." Urchin looked embarrassed and faintly awed at his inability not to obey Chase's command. "Feather up top." He waved his hand over his head.

A posh, well-dressed, not fat *young* woman had apparently impulsively sent this street rat in search of him?

He thought back over the "liedies" he'd consorted with in the five years since he returned from the war. In truth, few of them could accurately be described as "ladies." He had great difficulty imagining any of the *actual* ladies of his acquaintance sending a cryptic, anonymous message by way of a boy who smelled like the bottom of a boot.

Chase fixed the urchin with his best truth-extracting stare.

Urchin blinked as though he'd had scalding water flicked into his eyes.

"Why should this woman send *you*?"

"I were *there*, weren't I?" Urchin sounded matter-of-fact. "In the courtyard of the museum. I 'olds the carriage horses heads when carriages pull up, and down she come from the hack. Some gives me blunt when I do it; others naught."

It was a time-honored scheme: performing a useless service and then expecting someone to feel guilty enough to pay for it.

"Those that pay you pay you to *leave*, most likely."

Urchin's grin was a quick and brilliant surprise. "Dinna care *why* they pay me. So into the daft big museum she went, then out she come right quick, looks about fer the 'ack, but 'tis gone, right? And I've *no* blunt to show fer it. But she sees me, asks if I want to earn a shillin'—a *shillin'*!—and went in again and came out with this message and sent me to find ye."

"She came in a hackney?" he repeated sharply.

"Aye. No coat of arms. She'd 'ired it."

An interestingly intuitive response: it was precisely what he had wanted to know. He searched those clear eyes looking for evidence of lies or knavery.

The boy twitched like an insect caught by one wing. His gaze slipped sideways.

A liedy. He had been foolish for a woman only once in his entire life. It was both the truest and least honorable thing he'd ever done. *And* the most carnal, as fate would have it.

Ironic, given that honor had at one time been the thing that defined him. It had of course been quietly catastrophic. In that moment, he hadn't felt he had a choice in the matter.

But now he did. He narrowed his eyes at the message, and at the messenger.

Was she pretty? Was she alone? Did she seem afraid? Is this a trick? What kind of trick? Is this a trap? What kind of trap?

What the hell.

He would discover the truth of all of this for himself.

Against his better judgment, Chase produced a shilling and held it out in two fingers just as he released his grip on the boy's shoulder.

"Now get out of my sight."

Urchin snapped the shilling away like a fish taking bait as Chase released him.

"Fare thee well, guv!" he bellowed cheekily over his shoulder, and went skipping off on bare feet through the fetid London puddles.

He felt surprisingly little guilt as he turned his back on his cousin's boardinghouse. He wished now he'd arranged to have a horse saddled for him before he'd set out from the Eversea town house this morning rather than dividing the trip between hack and foot. But he walked as often as he could, as far as he could.

At night he suffered for it, or drank.

He would need a hackney to get to the Montmorency, however, and decided he would take it all the way there, a concession to the leg.

The district he stood in now wasn't precisely Seven Dials, but from the looks of things, it took Seven Dials as an inspiration. Only a few businesses hung their signs on the street. Shirts and drawers festooned lines slung between window ledges of adjacent sagging boardinghouses. Soaked and heavy from the cloudburst, they would dry to stiffness in the heat. He hadn't yet seen a hackney. Likely because no one wanted to come here and no one could afford to leave via hackney even if they wanted to.

He walked a bit. Past a cheese shop, a milliner, a cobbler, a pub. Another pub. Another pub. Like most parts of London, alleys tributaried from the street he walked. Deep at the end of one he saw the flash of white buttocks busily pumping between a dress furled up in a pair of fists. A man being serviced by a prostitute.

Lovely.

About then he realized he was being watched.

Or, rather . . . hunted. The feeling was *singularly* different.

He knew in a blinding instant why: he'd given a coin to a street rat who had taken note of his slightly uneven gait and his clothes and thought, A charitable gentleman with a limp, a walking stick, and a pocketful of shillings? Easy prey.

There were two of them, Chase sussed out. Flanking him. A man on one side of the street, a man on the other. Moving toward each other in his peripheral vision, closing in on their objective.

Fat leftover rain clouds aimed precise celestial sun shafts down on him; the ground steamed from the short cloudburst. With it came the smell of London street soup: piss and manure and mud and food and somewhere, in the distance, something fresh and green. Grass, trees. Just not anywhere near where he currently stood.

The celestial light was ironically quite helpful: it showed him that both had knives. Palmed; having been slid down into them from their coat sleeves. The sun nicked light flashes from the blades.

Spendid.

Chase calculated he couldn't reach his boot pistol in time. He cursed the fact that he'd only brought the one with him on this outing, when force of habit and sheer love of weaponry usually meant he had another loaded and tucked into his coat.

His blood was an exhilarating tsunami through his veins.

Time, as it always had in moments at the precipice of danger, slowed for him: seconds stretched out luxuriously, like a tightly woven blanket pulled wide, revealing to him every minuscule move his stalkers made.

Only two of you?

If they had seen his smile then, they might have had *grave* second thoughts regarding what they were about to do.

They did not. He was diabolically glad.

They were even with him now, parallel to each other, close enough for him to see the color of one's eyes: brown as manure.

The first one lunged.

Chase brutally whipped his walking stick across his torso. The man folded double, allowing Chase to drive his elbow down between his shoulder blades, once, twice, again, piling him into the ground. And when the man toppled, Chase drove his foot into his groin, then spun to crack his walking stick across the plunging forearm of the other man. He held him fast; inches away from his face, aimed at a point between his eyes; the knife point trembled.

Strong brute.

But Chase only needed to hold him just long

enough. He slackened his hold a split second, long enough to surprise the man into thinking he was winning, to relax almost imperceptibly. Which is when Chase seized the wrist holding the knife and bent it back and back and back until the man rasped a hoarse scream, his fingers splayed, and the knife tipped from it.

Ugly-beautiful thing went winking in the sun to the damp ground. *Thunk.*

Very good knife, that.

He kicked the man hard in the knees and down he went, hard. With a bit of a splash. Gazed up at him, stunned, from the ground. Chase slid his pistol out of his boot, cocked it without ceremony and pointed it into the man's face.

"Optionally," he said, as though they'd been in the midst of a negotiation, "I can crush your windpipe with the heel of my boot, and you can die slowly rather than quickly." He was scarcely breathing heavily.

The brown eyes, flat and soulless in a pitted face, reflected more astonishment than terror. "S-S-Sorry, guv!"

Chase's laugh was mad and incredulous; it scalded his throat. *Sorry I attacked you with a knife, guv! Sorry! 'Twas all just a misunderstanding!*

Terror officially replaced astonishment on the man flattened below him.

Chase explained patiently, "I think I see your error. Did you think I was a 'gentleman'? You'd be amazed at how many gentlemen were made savages by war. I've killed better men than you without blinking. I'd think twice the next time you to come for one of us. Some of us might have even developed a taste for it."

The other man was spared a soliloquy and a gun in his face because he was rolling about on the wet ground, tucked up like a hedgehog and gasping something about his baubles.

Chase assessed him curiously for a moment, the way one might regard an animal needing to be put out of misery. And then he locked his pistol, knelt awkwardly—his leg was nearly ready to buckle beneath him, and somewhere beneath his fury pain sang its relentless, familiar tune—and collected that devil's knife, too.

Quite good, they were. He'd been an artillery captain; he was still able to admire a decent weapon regardless of context. Who knew when he might need them?

He fished about in the man's pocket and found a sheath and managed to tuck both knives into it.

When he pushed himself upright with the stick, and righted his hat, which had tipped down over one brow, with one hand, Chase looked more like the urchin's cocky imitation of a gentleman than he would ever know. He nodded curtly and nonspecifically to the cluster of people who'd stopped to gawk, and hailed the hackney clip-clopping by, oblivious to the seconds-long ruckus that had just taken place and unaware that a gent armed with knives and a pistol was about to board it.

Chase pulled the door open. The hackney was empty, but a great cloud comprised of the smells of all its previous passengers rushed out.

He was suddenly aware that his body was sticky with sweat and rain dampened. He settled into the seat, produced from his pocket a soft handkerchief embroidered by his sister Olivia with his initials and three tiny *flowers*, of all things. He hadn't had the heart to tell her he didn't *want* them on his handkerchiefs, since Olivia felt she'd needed practice with flowers, when what she really needed was to stop charmingly rebuffing every man who'd attempted to court her since that bastard Lyon Redmond had disappeared. He dragged the handkerchief over his face, slid it behind his neck, stuffed it back into his pocket.

Well, then.

He was shaking a little: from nerves, from exhilaration, from all the ways that life had changed in the past five years. Rolling along in that carriage, he suddenly felt restless and strangely disembodied, separate from everyone and everything else in the world, a member of no country or family.

A humorless smile stretched his lips. Then faded.

He supposed he did resemble prey now.

He sighed, stretched his leg out and propped his heel on the seat across from him. Then drove his knuckles hard into it, kneading it, to stop the twist of pain. He did it again. And closed his eyes. And waited.

And breathed.

And breathed.

The third breath was more of a sigh.

"You ought to marry, Chase!" his brother Colin had taken to urging with an intolerably enigmatic air, as one initiated into a sacred secret order, when he wasn't talking about cows. As if marriage were the Rosetta stone, the thing that finally gave meaning to the merry chaos of Colin's life.

"*I* ought to throw this pint at you," he told his brother. "Ha ha." Thanks to Colin, Chase had learned that one really *could* speak through clenched teeth. He would be damned if anyone would tell him what he ought to do.

But *that's* not what had gotten him banished. Colin and Madeleine had just laughed and laughed. *That* time.

Unbeknownst to his family, Chase had written to inquire about a position with the East India Company in India, requesting that his reply be directed to him in London.

Now, he left his quieter leg where it was, lifted off his hat and tapped it against his hand to dash the remaining water from its brim, slid his arms out of his greatcoat and gave it a shake. Pinhead bright droplets flew everywhere. He smoothed his hair with his hands and jammed the hat back down.

Thus concluded whatever grooming he would do for his assignation at the Montmorency.

He pulled the grubby message from his pocket and read it again. He hesitated then, half-whimsically, gave it a sniff.

He could have sworn he detected the faintest scent of . . . roses?

Chapter 2

The Montmorency Museum reminded Chase of an abandoned mistress, perhaps a French one: elegant but aging resentfully, reluctant to receive visitors. The French architectural influence was there in the mansard roof, in the small, fanciful dome arcing over the center door, in the curving bay windows flanking it. The courtyard the urchin had described was surrounded by an uninviting spike-topped iron fence. It wasn't precisely swarming with eager visitors, either.

Chase got up the wide marble steps with the help of his temper and walking stick and pushed the enormous doors open.

He paused, nonplussed. The place was vast and marbled and as hushed as a sickroom, and lit with a certain amount of drama: daylight must have once poured into the half-circle windows built high into the walls, but buildings had mushroomed up around it in the intervening century since it was built, and good wax candles burned in a brigade of small, elegant sconces stretching back and back through a warren of halls and rooms. And when he inhaled, he discovered that the place smelled like the tiny, ancient church in Pennyroyal Green, with all those ancient wood pews polished by linseed oil and centuries of Sunday best-clad Sussex arses and candle smoke soaked into its walls.

Which of course reminded him of the duty he'd shirked in favor of this misadventure.

He shrugged off his conscience much more easily than he'd fought off his attackers and stepped forward.

A clerk of some sort, his posture buckled with boredom, was stationed behind an exquisitely simple desk. He'd propped his cheek in one hand and was disconsolately fingering the pages of a book with the other, reading without seeing. Another, much larger, book lay open next to him, quill and inkwell nearby. A guest book. Its sheer size and volume was a trifle optimistic, Chase thought. As though the Montmorency expected legions of visitors.

He leaned forward nosily: only four names were written on the page in front of him, three male, none he recognized. The fourth was a woman's name: *Mrs. Smithson*. He *did* recognize the handwriting and the color of ink. She'd written her message to him here at the Montmorency. He nearly rolled his eyes: Mrs. Smithson. Very cunning, indeed. Quite the *subterfuge*.

"Where might I find Italian paintings?" he said to the clerk.

The man shot upright as though a puppeteer had jerked strings from above. His book went tumbling to the floor. He blinked at Chase. He had a pink handprint on his face.

Chase realized then that he'd inadvertently barked a command rather than a question. Habit of intonation. He immediately forgave himself.

The man recovered. "Paintings of Italians, sir, or paintings of Italy, or paintings painted by Italian artists, or paintings of—"

"Cows."

The man didn't even blink. Admirable. Chase peered: he saw the telltale powder marks beneath the skin. Yes, as he'd suspected: this one *had* been a soldier.

"Italian cows, sir? Or cows in *addition* to the Italian paintings? Or—"

"*It*alian cows." Chase made it a drawled challenge.

The clerk reared back, accepting the challenge. His eyes rolled ceilingward and he cocked one eyebrow, presumably to aid concentration, as he mentally prowled the museum corridors.

Somewhere, an ancient clock tocked out seconds. *One . . . two . . .*

"The East Wing!" A triumphant pink flushed the man's face. "Go straight back and bear right at the puppetry exhibit. The room is small, and adjacent to a room filled with sixteenth-century bedroom furniture."

Oh, God. The news that there *was* a puppetry exhibit was very unwelcome.

"You'll find paintings by Italian painters of Italian landscapes, and in these you'll see cows and other farm creatures, should you care to look at those as well, sir."

This was said without a trace of irony. He was no doubt accustomed to all manner of daft questions and specific requests from the aristocracy.

"My thanks," Chase said sincerely, because he was always genuinely pleased to encounter anyone who knew their job, and he invariably enjoyed testing people as much as he enjoyed being tested.

The man nodded acceptance. "If you would sign the book, sir?"

Chase signed his name and rank: *Captain Charles Sylvaine Eversea,* taking an immodest amount of space on the page.

He surreptitiously thumbed through a few pages and found a ragged quarter inch of paper remaining in the seam where a page had been torn from the book. And scarcely any names on the other pages.

"Are all of your visitors required to sign the book?" Chase asked.

"Aye, sir."

How on earth did the Montmorency justify its existence if no one came to see it? But then again, it was only Monday, the start of a new week, and perhaps the ton was still recovering from drinking the night before.

And then he went where the man pointed. The clerk peered down at his name as Chase left.

And went still as a stone.

Linseed oil and beeswax couldn't completely banish the must of aging wood and upholstery, of old things moldering together in a crowded and dim space. Chase passed a room filled with Egyptian antiquities: saw sarcophagi propped along the wall, and tiny ancient glass bottles shining dully behind the newer glass of cases, slabs of stones with Egyptian letters etched into them, fragments of the stories of other people's lives or perhaps codes of law. Another room made his soldier's heart leap: here was armor, suits hammered both for horses and men. Italian armor he recognized quickly; another suit, he knew, hailed from the twelfth century.

The Everseas owned several suits of the stuff, all apparently bequeathed by ancestors, all positioned strategically throughout the house and kept gleaming and oiled by the servants. They'd damaged one suit in an attempt to extract his brother Colin from it when Colin was thirteen years old, but to be fair, his brothers had all dared him to get *into* it. Judging from the armor, the men in the Eversea clan had been much smaller centuries ago. Doubtless they'd been forced to grow larger in order to defend themselves against the Redmonds.

The thought amused him.

He would treat himself to a look around this room one day. To make up for the fact that he would have to walk by . . .

Puppets.

He tried not to look, but there they were. Rows of them lined the walls on specially built shelves. Little bodiless hand puppets with their heavy heads and tiny little hands. Some suspended on hooks, like torture victims.

And then there were the marionettes.

When he was younger, his uncles had told them—because he and his brothers begged them to, as it was the nature of little boys to be gory—stories of medieval torture, about how accused criminals were strapped to a table and strategically stretched and stretched and stretched until their limbs popped from their sockets and dangled uselessly.

This is what Chase thought of when he saw marionettes.

Rattling, wrecked, unnatural things with screamy falsetto voices provided by invisible people yanking at strings. Evidently, people throughout the centuries had considered this entertainment. The first marionette performance he'd seen gave him a nightmare when he was six years old, and he had avoided them as much as he could ever since.

If he'd ever told a soul how he felt about marionettes, he'd known he could expect his brothers to pool their allowances to buy him a marionette for every birthday; that he would likely never be able to go up to bed at night without wondering whether one was stashed beneath his blankets; that he would have been surprised by a puppet show now and again when he went to the loo, which meant he would have screamed and pissed *everywhere*.

The Eversea boys were endlessly inventive. Chase was intelligent and excelled at self-preservation.

He'd never enjoyed watching Punch swinging his stick at Judy, but marionettes were by *far* the most loathsome. And there was an enormous one perched up high in a chair, presiding dourly over this wing of the museum. Doubtless centuries old and priceless and a fine example of Czechoslovakian craftsmanship and all that, but it had bulging eyes painted white and dotted with minute blue pupils, outsized grim ruby lips, and a nose like a petrified potato: enormous and misshapen. A deliberate wart sprang from it. Its face was carved into a scowl. Its legs and arms dangled impotently from a body covered in a white shirt and lederhosen.

Chase spared this atrocity a killing glance, then pretended it wasn't there at all, though he thought he felt its eyes on his back.

And at last found himself in what appeared to be the East Wing, because cherubs and angels swam into view.

* * *

There *was* a woman standing alone in this room.

She was apparently riveted by a painting covering about three-quarters of the back wall. Tall. Slim. An air of suppressed vigor, as though stillness was an unnatural state for her. Her pelisse fell from her shoulders in the sort of effortless line only certain modistes seemed able to achieve—he had sisters, he'd kept a mistress or two, he recognized the difference; perhaps they paid crews of seamstresses to massage the fabric into languid compliance. She wore a hat with a feather in it—a subtle hat, a subtle feather—brown and fluffy but not at all fussy. *Pretty hat*, the urchin had told him, and he'd been right. From bonnet to boots she was, in fact, dressed in rich shades of brown, from chocolate to the dark gold trimming the pelisse. The overall effect should have been one of camouflage, given the old wood and muted light surrounding her. But she was the sort of woman who had no hope of remaining unnoticed regardless of where or how still she stood. She had presence.

Given his gait, he, for that matter, had little hope of remaining stealthy.

He stepped forward. The floor gave an irritated squeak against the press of his walking stick.

She didn't turn.

She appeared to be *drinking* in the painting.

Chase casually paused before a painting called *The Miracle,* at least according to a brass plate affixed to the frame. The artist was an Italian whose surname was nearly as long as the painting itself and primarily comprised of vowels. He supposed it would be considered pastoral—there were trees clustered in a

meadow, with two muscular black cows and two improbably fluffy sheep arranged beneath them—and in
the sky were two winged cherubs so fat that surely the
miracle in question was how they had gotten aloft at
all. They would have needed to have the wingspans of
albatrosses, not those foolish wee flaps sprouting from
their shoulders, he decided, irritated. One of the cows
was looking up at them with what he fancied was an
expression of surprise and alarm. Which was precisely
the expression *he* would wear if he'd suddenly noticed
two fat cherubs bearing down on *him*.

Now, a fine James Ward picture of a horse, or an
Antoine-Jean Gros battlefield scene, even if it depicted
Bonaparte doing something fraudulently benevolent
with lepers, something practical, visceral, something
of actual *life* . . .

Though doubtless Colin would have been enthralled
by that cow, he thought sardonically.

He threw a quick sharp glance sideways. Interesting: the feather in the woman's bonnet was quivering
as though someone had sighed over it. Had she turned
so quickly to look at him that he'd missed it? It seemed
unlikely.

Her face was still aimed at the painting; her back
was still aimed at him. She seemed rooted to the spot.

He began to *need* to get a look at her face.

From somewhere in the museum he heard what
sounded like . . . was it a giggle? A female sound.
Ethereal. A trifle eerie, but then the whole damned
place was. Doubtless a member of the cleaning
staff taking inordinate glee in her work, since no
other woman had signed the book apart from "Mrs.
Smithson."

He craned his head toward the painting that trans-
fixed Mrs. Smithson: it was large, blue of sky but otherwise comprised of glowing celestial shades of pink
and gold and pearl, and crowded with all manner of
things, trees and livestock and whatnot, and it had
cherubs, too. A bloody swarm of them, like bees. His
sister Genevieve, an expert on painters of nearly every
provenance both popular and obscure, would likely
know the reason Italians seemed to want to put them
on everything. Maybe he should ask her when he returned home.

If he *deigned* to return home.

He was gentleman enough to wonder how he ought
to approach an unescorted woman of apparent quality
. . . when she finally moved. Subtly, yet discernibly: a
restless tilt of her head, a slight roll of one shoulder.

She might as well have driven a boot heel between
his ribs.

His breath left him in a single painful gust, and he
stared, struggling for equilibrium, and tightened his
grip on his walking stick to brace himself against the
force of memories blowing him back and back through
the years, to Waterloo, to Brussels, to all the other times
he'd seen her do precisely that.

And, inevitably, to the last time he'd touched Rosalind March.

Roses. He should have known.

Chapter 3

Mrs. Rosalind March had known Captain Eversea was approaching even before she heard the floor squeak. She'd forgotten he had a way of disturbing the atmosphere of a place, like any proper thunderstorm. The little hairs on the back of her neck stirred with it. The backs of her arms were cold with nerves.

He'd come. Triumph!

She supposed.

But now she was uneasy. She decided to allow him to approach her. Or, rather, this is what she *told* herself. She preferred this to the version where she hadn't the nerve to speak to him, despite the fact that she'd been impulsive enough to send for him.

"Your . . . messenger . . . gave me inadequate directions to this rendezvous, Mrs. March. Or should I say, Mrs. *Smithson*."

The words contained all the warmth of a commanding officer chastising a subaltern and were steeped in irony. But . . . oh. The voice. How had she not been prepared to hear his voice again? Deceptively gentle, dark and velvet textured: it lulled like opium smoke when the conversation was casual and close—during a waltz, at one's elbow during a dinner party.

In command, he could make a single word crack like a pistol shot.

His voice was a weapon.

The irony in it was because he understood precisely *why* she'd chosen her messenger: if *she'd* sent for him, he very likely would not have come.

Quite rightly he associated Rosalind March with trouble.

"And good morning to you, Captain Eversea. Very good to hear you once again exerting yourself to charm."

She held out her hand for him to bow over.

As ever a gentleman—in the little niceties and rituals that bound together his class, anyway—he didn't hesitate, didn't twitch a brow: he bent, took her fingers lightly in his.

Hardly a touch at all.

She glanced down at his fingers and knew a vertigo comprised of a rush of years: she'd seen his hands cleaning weapons, absently knuckling away the black powder from his lips after he'd loaded a musket, hoisting weapons to his shoulders in drills, lifting up the heads of dying soldiers to offer water. She'd seen them lift brandy snifters, clap her husband on the shoulder in camaraderie, help silk-clad women in and out of carriages.

She knew the weight and heat of them pressed against the small of her back during a dance. She knew how his bare fingers felt threaded through her hair, cradling her head, to tip it back to—

She withdrew her fingers from his quickly. Her rib cage tightened, fortifying herself against a tide of memories.

She pointedly looked into his face, and not at the hand gripping the horse-head-topped walking stick, his Waterloo souvenir, which he was grinding into the floor as if to punish it for being necessary. He'd always seemed etched from something more enduring than mere human flesh; he'd always seemed somehow more distinct than anyone else in any room. She was not surprised to find his face even harder now. Time and sun and pain and long nights involving God only knew what manner of male diversions had engraved lines at the corners of his eyes, sharpened and deepened the angles and hollows of his long face, made an implacable thing of his mouth. From the looks of things, it would make a veritable creaking noise should he attempt to turn it up into a smile now.

His eyes . . . his eyes could still cut diamonds. Could light a mine shaft.

They were blue.

No: "blue" was an inadequate word for what they were.

She turned from him to gaze at the painting. *Rubinetto* was painted in the corner in tiny, uneven black letters. She'd spent a goodly portion of her courage and strength on that oh-so-casual greeting, and she needed a moment to marshal more of it.

"Hideous," he said, with absolute authority. He meant the painting. He was frowning punitively at it.

Wonderful. It was no comfort to discover he was precisely as he ever was.

She'd always heard his character described in absolutes: *Courageous. Loyal. Trustworthy. Brilliant. Unyielding. Relentless. Disciplined.* Perhaps unsurprisingly, his judgments—regarding everything—had the permanence of monuments once he made them, and he usually made them with breathtaking speed. Her husband, Colonel March, had loved him and trusted him unquestionably. Captain Eversea's bloody-minded certainty *inspired* absolute trust. His instincts in matters of warfare and men were invariably correct, and she supposed this meant he possessed an innate goodness that nevertheless seemed to have nothing of softness or easiness about it.

But all of this also meant that forgiveness was *far* too ambiguous a concept for Captain Eversea. She'd given up self-recrimination as superfluous long ago. But she knew his weaknesses as he knew hers, and for this she knew he would never forgive her.

Or himself.

It made what she came here to do that much more difficult.

"I suppose I ought to ask you how you fare before I ask for your help, Captain Eversea." She no longer stifled her impulse toward directness; she no longer felt the need to charm him or anyone else. *I'm not that girl anymore, Captain Eversea.*

There was a silence, which she fancied contained surprise.

And then, wonder of wonders—one side of the mouth lifted. *Creeeeak.* It was a smile. Of sorts.

Beautiful mouth.

Best not to look at it.

He ignored the question of how he fared, probably thinking it superfluous. "Why do you need my help, Mrs. March? And why are we . . . here?" He gave the word "here" the intonation he might give the words "French prison." He cast another baleful glance at the painting, then returned his gaze meaningfully to her, as if accusing her of subjecting him to it.

She hadn't considered where to begin or what to say. She hadn't said the words aloud to anyone else outside of her family, and they sounded terribly unreal in her ears when she did. She took a deep breath.

"My sister is missing."

He was instantly brisk, which was bracing. "The loud one or the blond one?"

"The blond one." Jenny *was* loud; she saw no point in disputing it. "Lucy. Jenny is married two years this month. Her baby is a year now, and has a tooth—"

He made an impatient sound, which she knew meant, *Relevant information only, please*, and reminded her afresh of why it was difficult to *like* him. Death-defying height of his cheekbones notwithstanding.

"Forgive me for boring you with superfluous details, Captain. Lucy was arrested for a petty crime and was to be held at Newgate for her trial. Instead she has disappeared from the prison, and has been missing now for a week, and no one seems to know what became of her."

It was as close to a military brief as she'd ever delivered. She felt a bit cheated: she enjoyed details.

But *his* eyes had gone brighter, and the choke hold on his walking stick had eased as she spoke. Bloody contrary man was happiest in the presence of contrariness.

He'd always liked her best when she was tart.

"What on earth did Lucy do?" He sounded bemused, not appalled, which was comforting and reminded her of why she'd actually *liked* him. He was an Eversea, after all, and their history was downright woolly with black sheep. Not to mention the fact that his own colorful younger brother had recently enjoyed a certain celebrity as London's most popular criminal, replete with a very jaunty little tune about his exploits sung on streets and in pubs and on stages simply *everywhere*, and who had gone on to escape from a very public hanging.

"She was accused of absconding with an expensive bracelet, fashioned of carnelian and onyx set into—" Another impatient noise from the captain. She inhaled her irritation. "She fastened it about her wrist in the jeweler's shop, and stepped forward to admire it in the sunlight in the shop doorway, and then she took a few steps *outside* into the sunlight—just for a moment, mind you—to get a closer look, as it was dimly lit inside the shop, you see. The shopkeeper saw the incident rather differently, and a certain amount of . . . unpleasantness . . . ensued. She meant no harm."

"Ah."

And what a disbelieving syllable *that* was.

Still, it didn't contain a shred of judgment.

Rosalind said nothing, because the disbelief wasn't entirely unwarranted, and she was an essentially frank person. Apart from the fact that they were both very pretty, her sisters did her no credit, and no one knew this better than he did, unless it was Colonel March, who had taken them on when he married her, because she had made it a condition of their marriage. It was a risk on her part to insist upon it, and could only have been blind infatuation on the colonel's part that he'd agreed to it. But the colonel, who could marry as he pleased and was financially quite comfortable and no stranger to risk, had seen her and been smitten and took them all away. They'd grown up with the specter of destitution, of want, hovering always. She knew Lucy's probably futile social ambition made her more reckless than she ought to have been, and she knew precisely why that bracelet had called to Lucy.

That, and the fact that she was a trifle feathery in the brain.

She would greatly have preferred that the bracelet not called Lucy out of the door of the *shop*, but that was neither here nor there at the moment. She would have very much preferred to have an *uncontroversial* sister, but she loved both of them indiscriminately, and she'd never once failed to take care of them. Since her husband's death, they were her only family.

She wouldn't fail Lucy now. Still . . .

Loss. The prospect of it blew a cold breath on the back of her neck. If she entertained the possibility of it for longer than a few seconds, it would weaken her, and she needed her strength. She fought the urge to rub her chilled palms down her pelisse, and then she did. She never, never, *never* lost without a fight. All her life she'd always done precisely what she'd needed to do.

"And why did you contact me, Mrs. March?" Another brisk question.

This is where all the nerve and strength she'd earned in intervening years since they'd met was required.

"Because I think William Kinkade might know something about what became of her."

His face closed so abruptly she actually felt a jarring sensation in her teeth. As though she'd dashed her head against something unyielding.

She'd expected this. She'd forgotten, however, just how *delightful* it felt.

Kinkade had served with Chase, and had been as close to him as her husband.

"I am certain he would speak to you about the matter, should you be so kind as to ask him about it."

His face remained as immovable as the statue of William III in St. James's Square. Eyes inscrutable.

"He's *deuced* difficult to see," she continued, her voice considerably calmer than her stomach, which interestingly, suddenly seemed to contain spinning windmill blades. "I've requested to speak to him through letters to his office but I received an official reply stating he knew nothing at all concerning the whereabouts of Miss Lucy Locke. I attempted to meet with him at his offices—I appeared there one day. I was told he was unavailable. I have not yet been to his home, which would be a somewhat desperate measure, I grant you, but it would be the next step I take in my attempt to contact him. I have not yet been to the hulks, but why would they take her there? It has been a week. She is gone. Surely *someone* knows what became of her."

Her voice had become increasingly taut with her own fear.

Her ears began to *ring* with his silence. The room was peculiarly still and close, both as a result of the skillfully sealed old building and the fact that Captain Eversea always seemed to use more than his share of air.

She had the odd sense he was both watching her and listening to her, and he was taking in two very different sets of information with his eyes and ears.

What do you see, Captain Eversea? Do I look as different—and as the same—to you as you do to me?

"Lucy fell in with a crowd that included him," she

continued, as if the conversation actually consisted of two sides. "Or rather, she moved rather on the *fringes* of a crowd that included him. Wealthy, fast, not all of them . . . wholesome. This I discovered later." She faltered on that last word. It had taken courage to say it to that steely face. "She . . . admired . . . him greatly, I know. She said something to me that led me to believe that he might know—"

"'Deuced'?" Chase said so suddenly and sharply she gave a start. "Did you say 'deuced,' Mrs. March? Next you'll be smoking cigars and drinking brandy and throwing your legs up onto furniture and spitting."

"Surely not spitting."

A beat of silence.

And then, oh so reluctantly, both corners of his mouth turned up and he was smiling. His entire dazzling, difficult self was in that smile. He looked twenty years younger than the thirty and then some he must have been, and her heart, the bloody traitor, did a hard flop in her chest, like a supplicant flinging itself at his feet.

She'd once worked so hard to earn his smiles.

And then she'd needed to learn to withstand them, the way one needed to learn to adjust to giddy altitudes.

What an *idiot* she'd been once.

Her jaw set, her spine straightened. She didn't need or want his approval now. She needed his help.

They both knew she didn't deserve it.

The light of the smile faded naturally, and he simply looked at her. She endured his not entirely dispassionate scrutiny, her chin up. He could look and look all he liked, but he wouldn't find her—that girl who'd never dreamed that the unspoken role of the wife of a colonel was to be, in a way, *all* women to the men—mother, sister, lover—by proxy. The girl who'd been too young and far too busy merely surviving to develop her own *very useful code* to live by, the way Captain Eversea had. She'd fumbled her way through, utterly in the dark, and had finally lit her way by flinging charm indiscriminately and everywhere, like fairy dust. Astonishingly, the charm had both dazzled and camouflaged, and everyone was too blinded by infatuation—which she'd admittedly rather enjoyed—to notice she was frightened and out of her depth and often bored and resentful when she should have been grateful and gracious and all that was mature.

No one had noticed, of course, except Captain Eversea.

In the end, however, she'd inadvertently spun a trap out of her own charm.

For herself and for Captain Eversea.

"You do still consider Kinkade a friend, Captain Eversea?"

"Of course. I'll see him tonight at Lord Callender's do. But why on earth do you think Kinkade had anything to do with it?" He'd come to some conclusion in that moment of studying her. His tone established distance: it was cool and inquisitional.

She refused to panic. "Because he works in the Home Office, and he would be able to see and review the petitions for freedom for condemned felons. And though Lucy has not yet been tried, he's intimately acquainted with the people who work for the prison, with the Charleys, with the magistrates. Surely he can help discover what became of her. She has high social aspirations—Lucy does—and I fear they were encouraged because she is pretty and flighty and it amused these people to encourage them, not because they feel any real regard for her. When I went to see her in . . . " She cleared her throat, as she would never say the word easily. " . . . in *prison*, she said, 'Fuss not, Rosalind. Billy is going to help.' She sounded nervous."

Silence.

"You're basing Kinkade's involvement in a disappearance on the hopeful surmise of an infatuated girl?"

His tone would have been flat but for the maddening whiff of incredulity. How *dare* he. Lucy was her sister—not a "disappearance." But in his way he was making it very clear that she was implying an insult to Kinkade's character and that this was dangerous ground for her to tread upon, indeed.

"She wouldn't tell me anything else. She seemed . . . afraid. Downcast."

"Anyone who isn't a looby would be afraid and downcast in Newgate."

Temper licked at the edges of her words. "I think she might have been afraid of him. Of Kinkade."

"I cannot imagine how this could possibly be true." Quick and detached and bored.

She stifled an actual *growl*.

He sensed it, and seemed to like it: his gaze sharpened into something like a dare. Challenging her to raise her game.

Her earlobes were hot; this, she knew from unfortunate experience, was a prelude to the rest of her face heating like a branding iron. "I think she was either protecting me or herself by not telling me more, because I did ask her to expound, as I am *not* precisely a fool. She *isn't* careful by nature, but she was being careful then, which is why I think I need to take her seriously. And I shouldn't need to explain this to you, but I *know* her, Captain Eversea. I all but raised her. I know her as well as you know your own brothers and sisters. And I sense when something is very amiss. Tell me, would you know if one of your sisters was afraid, no matter what she said to you?"

She knew precisely what his brothers and sisters meant to him.

Still, appealing to sentiment in Chase was generally as rewarding as spitting into the wind.

She hadn't the faintest idea what *she* meant to him, if anything. The girl he'd known hadn't been careful by nature, either. Sending for him impulsively was precisely the sort of thing that girl would have done, too.

He turned his head abruptly toward the painting.

A brown bovine that could feed a small village should it ever be roasted on a spit gazed from its center with large placid eyes back at the glowering Captain Eversea. Its tail swished upward, as if in preparation for doing what cows so often did. The cow mingled with a sage-looking horse, its great soft head drooping over a fence over which trees studded with some unidentifiable orange fruit loomed—she couldn't be certain they were oranges, despite the fact that they were round—and flowers, red and blue ones, sprinkled the ground, peeked through the fence, trailed up the tree. Cherubs, a veritable cloud of them, hovered over the pasture. The sky was blue, but a peculiar blue, as though it might be twilight rather than daytime. This surmise was borne out when she saw the half-moon in the sky. An angel was on high, and she had her harp out and was strumming away up in the corner, her expression dreamy, her bosom startlingly robust and benippled for one so celestial.

Every creature seemed rather pleased with, or at least not at all adverse to, whatever was happening in the picture, and Rosalind knew a peculiar moment of envy.

"Why did you arrange for me to meet you *here*?" His tone was still interrogatory. "And why . . ." Suddenly, surprisingly, he sighed. "Why *cows*?" The last word he imbued with a puzzling hint of despair.

He turned back to her.

"Because the last time I spoke to Lucy—they were taking her away from me—she told me to go to the 'the Montmorency Museum.' And she said this after I asked her to explain what she'd just said about Mr. Kinkade. *Twice*, she said it. Repeated it. 'The Montmorency, Ros! The Italian room!' And her—"

"Perhaps she thinks you would benefit from a well-rounded education in the arts."

"—tone was very . . . portentous. I inquired of the man who keeps watch at the entrance to the museum—"

"Helpful gentleman. Knows where everything is kept. An orderly mind." Implying hers was not.

Oh, he was *brilliant* at this. She would *not* allow her temper to get the better of her. She had little hope of preventing this. Even now heat was creeping up her neck, and she knew her face would be a scarlet bloom within seconds.

"—*and* he tells me that Kinkade has made three bequests to this museum recently, and the paintings you see in this room are among them, and I thought perhaps . . . I thought perhaps . . . perhaps you knew something of his interest in art, of Kinkade, and perhaps somehow I would discover what this might have to do with Lucy . . . so I sent for you."

She suddenly heard now how absurd and fragmented all of this sounded.

"Only a man of sterling character would have both the good sense to rid himself of this painting should he have the misfortune to possess it and the generosity to donate it to a public institution on the very slim chance that someone *else* might actually enjoy it."

Rosalind narrowed her eyes to dangerous crossbow slits. Her cheeks were officially scorching.

Captain Eversea hadn't changed color at all.

He stared back at her, so certain of himself, so immovable, she was surprised he didn't slip his watch from his pocket to review the time out of sheer boredom.

Still as inflexible as the bloody Rock of Gibraltar. As the cliffs of Dover.

He waited, as one would wait to ascertain that the enemy was indeed dead after one has just shot them at close range. And then he said, "I understand your concern for your sister, Mrs. March. I wish everything good for you and your family. But I can see nothing of merit in your suspicions. I fear I cannot help."

She knew he meant he *would* not.

And she knew why.

I would undo what happened if I could, she would have shouted at him.

Except, God help her, she wasn't certain this was true. Even now. Even for Lucy.

He was done with her. As if in a dream, she saw him touch his hat by way of farewell. Saw those vast shoulders begin to turn.

And before she could reconsider the wisdom of it—before she could think at all—her hand was on his arm to stop him.

It wasn't a gentle touch.

He halted, surprised. Drew in a short sharp breath. His eyes dropped to her hand, and for an instant he went so still she felt his stillness reverberate through her. For all the world as if he were a sword she'd just driven into the ground.

In an instant she knew her mistake: even through his fine wool coat, the arm felt as hard and unyielding as the man. The sort of arm that could hold up the earth. *Had* held up the earth, at one time, in the eyes of some people.

He flicked widened eyes up to her face. He dropped them again quickly. Oh, but not quickly enough. Not quickly enough to disguise it:

Want. In its rawest form. And something so very near vulnerability she wanted to . . . protect him from it, to apologize for it, to . . .

In short: it was exactly what she'd seen in his face five years ago. On that day. In that moment.

When he looked back up at her a moment later, his face *had* changed color. Whiter now, tense at the mouth. He was *furious*. Furious with her for reminding him that he was a flesh and blood man. Just a *human* after all.

And furious with himself for allowing her to see what he knew she'd just seen in his face.

She had no way of knowing what her own face gave away. She knew she hadn't blinked in what seemed like years.

A few frozen seconds later she slowly, slowly took

her hand away, as though a sudden move might inspire him to snap it off in his jaws.

And like a wild animal slipping a tether, without another word he turned and abruptly left her.

His boot heels came down hard on the museum's marble floors, swift and measured as a march, creating a unique rhythm with his walking stick. It seemed like part of him now, that stick.

She cupped with one hand the hand that had touched him, as though comforting it. She looked down at it. Shaken, her thoughts a kaleidoscope, her face aflame, she watched him until he disappeared through the arched doorway toward the museum entrance.

She stared long after he was gone.

Unable to move quite yet. *Unwilling* to move, until the echo of his presence faded.

She marshaled a half smile.

Even cliffs are vulnerable, Captain Eversea, she thought. The sea gets at them, eventually, reshaping them inexorably, giving them no choice at all in the matter.

He hadn't reckoned on the woman she'd become.

The sea, she thought, had nothing on Rosalind March.

Chapter 4

The filthy urchin was waiting outside the museum. Chase flicked a look at him the way one might flick a hot cigar butt and strode two steps north across the courtyard, ignoring him.

Then stopped and turned back to him.

"Where can I get a strong and nasty drink in this godforsaken part of London?"

"The Mumford Arms." Urchin promptly held out his palm for coin. "Past where they set up the fair, like, on fine days, the opposite side o the square, then down Black Cat Lane."

Chase ignored the outstretched palm and set out over the courtyard with leg-punishing speed, slamming down the walking stick. He crossed the entire courtyard without seeing it, then plunged into the inexorably wearing streets. A dozen or so yards up he saw the beginning of the square, marked by a great patch of balding grass and scattered clumps of appealing but unkempt trees.

Damned urchin shadowed him. He could hear the running smacks of his footsteps behind him on the pavements as the bare feet tramped through the puddles left behind by the earlier rain.

And now it was talking.

"I saw ye fight them rough coves!"

"Did you," he said flatly.

"Proper amazin', it was! " Out of the corner of his eye Chase saw the urchin miming kicking and swinging a walking stick as he ran. "Nivver seen anything like it! Ye're a right divil! They'll be talkin' 'bout ye fer *years*, I ken."

Chase ignored him.

"D'yer see the liedy, then?" Urchin pressed cheerfully. As though he had a vested interest in all of this.

"Oh, I saw the 'liedy,' " Chase said grimly.

He in fact seemed to be running from the *liedy*. He slowed for that reason, to prove to himself that he was not.

A mistake. The thought of her caught up to him and in an instant she swamped his senses. *Rosalind*. Her name raced over his spine and tingled his scalp like fingers pulled through his hair during lovemaking. He lifted his hat and swept his hand back through his hair, then jammed his hat back down when he realized what he was doing.

What a bloody ridiculous, infuriating *metaphor*.

He strode forward again, just as violently, walking but not seeing. Vividly in his mind he saw her small white hand resting on his arm.

She still nibbled down the nail of the little finger on her left hand.

Why should the very fact of this make him ache peculiarly in the chest?

He inhaled deeply, exhaled gustily, and continued walking.

The low wrought-iron spiked fence surrounding

the square unfurled dizzyingly forever, keeping the mythical Mumford Arms out of reach. This was an illusion of the weather and his mood, he knew. Limp, untended late summer flowers, battered by the rain, leaned through it like convicts through bars.

Which made him think of Lucy Locke, Rosalind's sister.

It was *impossible* to picture Lucy in prison. Lucy was pretty, had bubbles for brains and a bosom that belonged on the prow of a ship. He could well understand why Kinkade would be happy enough to include her among his friends, but he'd never once mentioned her to him in correspondence. It was patently ridiculous to think that Kinkade would have anything to do with Lucy's disappearance, particularly anything nefarious, and even more ridiculous that a bad painting of cows and cherubs would be at *all* related to it.

But Rosalind was afraid for her sister.

He found this, for some reason, unbearable.

His hand squeezed the top of his walking stick so tightly the horse head bit into his palm.

The last time he'd heard anything of Rosalind March was years after the war, from a fellow soldier: he was told she'd searched through the bodies on that blood-soaked battlefield calling for her husband until she found him, grievously wounded. That she'd visited the hospitals wherever they sprang up in Mont St. Jean and Quatre Bras: cottages, barns, the streets, homes of the wealthy—that she heard the last words of dying soldiers, held hands, changed dressings. Her husband, like so many extraordinary men, had been wounded badly and died slowly, and he'd heard that she was with him when he breathed his last breath.

So she had courage.

It didn't matter.

He would never betray yet another friend for her by believing for an instant that Kinkade was somehow dishonorably involved in the matter of Lucy Locke's disappearance.

She should have known better than to ask.

Well, she *had* known better. Which was, of course, why she'd done it with a cryptic anonymous message sent via the street rat dogging his heels. And this, he told himself, was *hardly* courageous.

Clever, he conceded. But not courageous.

He fought the corners of his mouth as they began turning up into a smile.

She certainly knew him.

"I didna lie about the liedy, did I?" Urchin said triumphantly. "Earned me shilling!"

Chase forbore to agree or disagree.

"Will yer buy *me* a strong nasty drink?" urchin tried.

"No."

"Oive 'ad gin before," it boasted.

"I don't doubt it. It's poison, you know. Don't drink it again. You'll . . . grow bubbies like a girl if you do."

This horrified the urchin into silence, which Chase had known it would. He hoped he'd *flee* from horror.

No such luck. Chase strode on, he and his good leg and his bad leg and his walking stick and his new filthy dogged little shadow.

In the distance, beyond the square, a figure was standing on tiptoe to hang a lit lantern on an iron hook in preparation for the evening's business. Chase assumed this was the Mumford Arms, and this inspired him to walk even faster.

"Is she yer woman? The liedy?"

"No!" he snapped. He stopped again abruptly, and the urchin stopped abruptly. Chase breathed, and sighed out roughly, in and closed his eyes again, this time to try to orient himself in his storm of memories.

Like the night she became a person to him. Not just Colonel March's late-in-life folly.

At first Chase had been at best amused by the very *fact* of Rosalind March, the colonel's new wife. She laughed too much and danced too long and with kitten-like bravery flung herself in play and flirtation at people who could just as easily squash her as be charmed by her. Like the smoldering, reputedly dangerous Captain Eversea.

Everyone had loved her.

Chase had been indifferent. He preferred far more sophisticated flirtations, and in Belgium sophisticated flirtations were *routinely* directed at the handsome captain and frequently concluded in a bed.

For in those weeks before the bloodbath outside of Brussels that ended the damn war, there were endless glittering frivolities hosted by Belgian aristocracy, all of which were stuffed to the brim with English aristocrats who had come to watch war as though it was puppet theater, and Chase was compelled to dance with all of the wives, including Mrs. March. The young Mrs. March was in particular captivated and flattered by Lady d'Aligny, a Belgian countess who was young, pretty, excruciatingly sophisticated, and could be ironic in five Continental languages. The two young women spent a good deal of time in hushed, bright-eyed conversation together behind painted silk and ivory fans—Rosalind's fan a gift from Lady d'Aligny. They engaged in a ceaseless exchange of teas and drives and dinners.

Chase wasn't convinced the d'Alignys weren't spies; he was wary of the impulsive Mrs. March's friendship with them; he considered her little better than a child.

He'd been in search of the punch bowl at one of the d'Aligny soirees at their magnificent *palais* when he'd heard Rosalind's voice mingled with a man's near the flung-open doors leading to the terrace. Their words had the unmistakable lilt of flirtation. He shamelessly hovered near one of the pillars flanking the double doors to listen and watch.

Rosalind and the soldier shared a low laugh, and when it faded, the soldier said, "It's funny, but Colonel March is such an arrogant old sod that he—"

"Sergeant Maris."

Her words were soft. But they dangled icicles. *Very* disconcerting from Mrs. March. She of the gossamer charm and too-easy laughter.

Chase had straightened alertly.

"What . . . makes you think I would tolerate hearing such a thing about my husband?" Her voice was soft and even.

There was a short silence. Broken finally by a short surprised laugh from Sergeant Maris. Who clearly hoped she was jesting.

But when she said nothing—simply seemed to actually be waiting for an answer—he began to stammer. "But—But . . . Mrs. March—I thought—but he's so—"

Chase remembered how very, very gentle her tone was. It was the *compensating* sort of gentle employed by people who had great respect for the power of their own tempers. She was gentle because she was *furious*.

He had been fascinated.

"You thought wrongly, Sergeant Maris," she continued in that gentle, gentle tone. "He is my husband and your commanding officer, and as such he will have your respect at all times and you will refer to him with respect at all times. I have enjoyed our conversation because until now you have been all that is respectful. I shall forgive you this one transgression and I shall not share our conversation with my husband. If I ever hear you saying such a thing about him ever again, I will make very certain you are flogged."

All said nearly apologetically. All said quite softly.

But she impaled that soldier with a stare.

For a long moment he seemed helpless to move away from it. Finally he slunk tentatively, awkwardly, away from her, bowing and muttering apologies, as if she were indeed armed with a pike.

She had stared after him, pupils flared, delicate jaw set, cheeks pink. Apparently lost in thought. And then at last she took a deep breath and seemed to sigh it out.

She flicked her eyes up. They flared in surprise when she saw Chase.

She knew instantly he'd witnessed all of it.

She went very still, and an interesting variety of emotions chased each other across her face, as if in that moment she could not decide whom to be.

And then she gave up; she'd been caught. She shrugged one shoulder. Then, chin up, held his gaze for an inscrutable moment or two, awaiting his reaction, his verdict.

He hadn't been able to help it: he smiled crookedly, and brought his hands together in slow, silent applause.

Bravo, he mouthed. She'd done almost precisely what he would have done.

She bit back a smile. White teeth sinking briefly into her full, soft bottom lip: he remembered that image for a long time after.

And then she gave a deep, theatrical, sardonic curtsy, which deepened his smile, and she glided away toward one of her sisters, who'd been flirting a little too overtly with another soldier for most of the evening, which is what they did most evenings. Rosalind March, he'd realized then, was forever looking after her sisters.

A détente of sorts had been reached between them. And as he was her husband's closest confidant, they were ever thrown together—at balls, and dinners both large and private—and détente evolved into a friendship.

If one could call careful politeness stretched over a hum of sensual awareness friendship, that is.

Chase found himself cataloguing the minutest things about her.

The head tilt, the shoulder roll—she did that when she thought no one was watching; he knew it was her way of shifting the mantle of grace and gravity thrown over her the moment she became a colonel's wife. She wore it willingly but it had never fit comfortably, and Chase was certain he was the only one who noticed the strain. The faint birthmark on her collarbone, roughly the shape of a fan. The quickly disguised flint in her green eyes whenever someone made a foolish remark, betraying a surprisingly impatient mind. The affectionate deference with which she always addressed her husband. The myriad subtle colors in her hair, from . . . well, *flaxen*, for lack of a less dramatic word, to a shining honey-brown, the bitten down nail of the little finger on her left hand, a sign of worries Rosalind March never betrayed in any other way, and—thanks to a conspiracy between candlelight, a chilly room, a dropped shawl, a silk bodice, and a strategically timed glance—the precise outline of her nipples.

He knew that she generally smelled faintly of rosewater.

One night Chase had danced with her and discovered she smelled both very faintly of rosewater and her husband's shaving soap, much the way a woman who had just been kissed—or considerably more—by her husband might before she'd gone down to the soiree.

Jealousy had been a shocking machete swipe through his torso.

He'd been unable to speak or even, for an instant, breathe.

He'd given her saturnine silence for the duration of the dance. He'd taken perverse pleasure in deflecting her conversation the way a window deflects pebbles hurled by a lover at midnight.

He knew it was childish. He knew it was unforgivably rude. Perhaps even cowardly, a word he would have called anyone out over should they have had the grave stupidity to direct it at him, and not even his brothers were quite *that* stupid.

He'd read *La Morte D'Artur* when he was a child, for God's sake. And though he'd enjoyed the questing and the battles, he always found the Arthur and Lancelot and Guinevere business—the drama! The anguish! Good *God*—impractical and *surely* avoidable.

In truth, he didn't know what to do.

He was at the mercy of something he didn't understand. And in that moment, he'd felt like a child, not like a battle-hardened soldier.

He'd watched hurt darken her pale green eyes.

Then anger.

Then wounded pride.

When the last gave way to comprehension, he knew he was in trouble. The girl was cleverer than he preferred. Than *she*, for reasons of her own, preferred anyone to know.

And after this, any easiness between them was gone as if it had never been.

She began to watch him, too, in just the same way. And for the same reasons. Silence separated them. Fascination bound them.

Entirely his fault.

He knew himself, and he knew her, which meant he should have known how it all would end.

He shook himself back to the present urgency: his search for the Mumford Arms.

"Rosewater," he muttered darkly and kept walking. He might as well blame the rosewater as anything else.

"Wot's rosewater? Can ye drink it?" Damned urchin was still behind him.

Chase shot him a dark look. "You'd have to be foxed to drink it. It's . . . something girls wear. To smell like girls. To smell like . . . flowers."

The boy's face crinkled in incredulity. "I ken no girls what smell like *flowers*."

"I don't doubt it for a moment."

"I dinna like girls at *all*."

"That makes you a clever lad, indeed."

The urchin glowed in male solidarity, not at all discouraged by Chase's discouraging tone. "D'yer ever drink rosewater?"

"I've never been quite that foxed, no."

"D'yer drink whiskey before?"

"Yes."

"Rye?"

"Yes."

"Gin?"

"Yes." He could do this all day.

"Brandy?"

"Yes."

"Blood?"

"Once or twice."

"Cor!" The boy gave a thrilled leap straight up and then frisked sideways. Chase gave him a blackly quelling look and the frisking stopped and the urchin ran to catch up. "Blood!"

"Inadvertently, mind you," Chase said sternly.

"In a vertinly? A vertinly is a tankard, like?"

"'Inadvertently.' It's a word that means 'not at all on purpose.' It was just that after the battle of Waterloo the whole of the battlefield was covered with soldiers dead and dying, and the canteens of water were nearly all empty, and all the dead and wounded soldiers lay over the field for hours, for nearly a day, with nothing to drink or eat. There was many a soldier would have fought that battle all over again for one sip of water, whether or not blood was in it. So, yes: I wanted to live. And the water I found in a well tasted of blood, and more than one of us drank of it."

The urchin was all palpable, speechless awe.

It occurred to Chase that this was the first time he'd

recited this part of his story in detail to . . . anyone. He
began to understand why his father and his uncles enjoyed telling stories to their boys: in making a legend,
one could gild horror. So they could be reminded more
of the courage than the carnage at times when the cost
seemed too high. And he could remind himself of a
time when he felt essential.

"Ye were lamed at Waterloo?"

"You could say that."

"Can I see it? Your leg?"

"No."

"Wot 'appened?"

Chase recited without missing a stride. "I woke with
a great weight upon me, and I couldn't see at all; 'twas
black before my eyes. I thought I was blind. I could
hear moans and screams all around me, cries and words
from men in English and French. I wiped at my eyes
and discovered I wasn't blind: my eyes were just filled
with blood from a wound to my scalp. I'd been shot
here." He pushed up his hat and his hair and pointed to
the white scar as he walked.

The boy squinted in fascination up at him, and
hopped twice to get a closer look. "They didna get yer
brains?"

"No, they did not get my brains. Just my scalp, and
the scalp bleeds rather a lot when it's nicked, just so you
know in case you ever sustain a wound to the head."
The boy put his own hand up to his forehead, as if to
test the structural integrity of his own scalp. "I wiped
the blood from my eyes with my hands so I could see,
and I discovered the weight was the body of a French
soldier. He was dead, laying right atop me, and his eyes
stared right into mine."

He spoke to the boy as if he were a man, which is what boys preferred, he knew. He preferred it, too: unadulterated truth. He wasn't the only one to wake to pain beneath a dead man on that day. He wasn't the heroic Colonel Eversea in that moment. Just another English body battered in its duty to its country.

This boy stopped in his tracks, momentarily paralyzed by the gory glory of it all.

Chase took the opportunity to accelerate his pace.

The boy, bloody hell, ran to catch up.

"D'*yer* kill 'im?" he said breathlessly. "The frog atop ye?"

"I must have done. It was my job to kill French soldiers before they killed us."

"I would 'ave killed *'undreds*!" Urchin leaped and pointed an invisible musket at a passerby. *"Boom!"* The passerby jumped and scowled at the boy, one hand over his heart. The boy grinned.

The man shot by the phantom musket sent a commiseration-seeking look toward Chase. Who ignored it, as he was in need of commiseration himself.

"Ah, but it was not so easy. French soldiers were very good fighters, and we took no pleasure in the killing, but we did take pleasure in doing our jobs for our country. When the fighting was done, the hospital wagons took all the wounded soldiers they could carry, French and English, back with us to the hospitals and we were all the same then. All of us fighting men."

Chase knew the notion that the enemy could be admired was far too philosophically abstruse for the typical bloodthirsty ten-year-old boy. He hoped the urchin would grow bored, halt the stream of questions and abandon him to the luxurious, painful, confusing rush of his memories.

She looked older now. Not worn. Her fine features were more . . . distinct. Less girlishly soft now, more refined by circumstances. She was twenty-five.

Her skin. He remembered her skin had been unutterably soft.

He knew a sizzle of desire so shockingly fierce his breathing struggled. Oh, God. Even as his mind turned memories of her round and round with suspicion and wonder and resentment, his body felt it was *owed* her.

His leg chose that moment to remind him that it wasn't what it once was, and he clenched his teeth against a burgeoning wave of pain and strode onward, hardly missing a stride.

Nor did the urchin.

"D'yer ride a fine 'orse? 'Ave a great gun?"

"Yes and yes. I was captain of the Artillery."

"D'yer see 'er? The colonel's wife? When ye were dyin' on the ground?"

Dying on the ground? He supposed he *had* been dying on the ground.

"No." It was painful to admit.

Oh God, what he wouldn't have given to see her. He'd thought he heard her. He thought he'd smelled her, the rosewater and sweetness amidst the earth of mud and horse, the acrid tang of blood and sweat and gunpowder. Which is when he knew he'd been dying, because he knew this was impossible. He'd thought perhaps someone had flung open a window in Hell and let in the scent of Heaven.

He'd known then that if she was the last thing on

earth his senses conjured, the loss of her—the fact that he could never have her—was inexpressible.

"Why didn't you see 'er?"

"I was no longer in the colonel's command on the morning of the battle."

His leg gave another throb then, helpfully reminding him of the ignominy—and shocking pleasure—leading to *that* turn of events.

And now she wanted his *help*.

She was delusional if she thought a terrible cow painting had anything at all to do with her sister.

"Oh." The boy lost interest in this line of questioning. He was onto a gorier one. "So why d'yer limp?"

"My leg was shot open. They wanted to take it off with a great saw and I wouldn't allow it."

"Blimey!" the urchin breathed. "Was it bloody and did it hurt? Did your bones show?"

"Quite bloody and it hurt and no one told me whether my bones showed and I couldn't see whether they did. But they sewed me up, and I stayed in Quatre Bras in a little farmhouse with a kind family until I could walk again, and then I came home to England."

Before that he'd refused to allow any of his own grievously wounded men to die alone. He heard confessions; he pretended to be the loved ones called for in a fever haze, sat beside them when they could no longer speak at all and ensured that they died knowing their captain valued them. But soon he'd become too ill to do that, and then everything beyond that had been a blur of fever and pain.

Shrapnel still, to this day, was working its way to the surface of his skin, the way memories did. Waterloo was still embedded in him, and with it, Rosalind March.

Silent waves of nearly tangible adulation poured from the boy. Chase might as well have just concluded a delightful fairy tale with "and they all lived happily ever after."

"I want to be a *soldier*," Urchin finally said with hushed awe.

Chase snorted and walked on, and the boy scrambled after him like a page in the wake of a royal coach.

"I can work fer ye, like," he said breathlessly. "Tell you where to find nasty strong drinks and carry messages fer ye and the like."

Interesting definition of a job.

"You cannot. I am not in search of an employee at the moment. I'm in search of a whiskey and a wom—a nice ale."

He'd just then decided to add a woman to his objective.

"Though yer jus' wanted a nasty strong drink." Shrewdly observed.

"I'll find one, mark my words," Chase said grimly. He stopped abruptly. "Where the hell *is* this bloody pub? Did you tell me the truth about its location?"

The boy ignored the salient question. "Will ye teach me to fight?"

"No." Chase thought it all too likely that this one would learn to fight all on his own. He looked down at the dirty boy. His eyes were so blue, Eversea blood could have caused them. Perhaps they were simply blue in contrast to the grime in the rest of his face.

He stared at him for a tick.

"Do you have a name?" he heard himself ask, and regretted it immediately. This one seemed to want words as much as shillings, and he wanted nothing more to do with him.

"Aye. It's Blade." This was accompanied by a chin jut.

"It's not. What is your real name?"

"Liam." Liam seemed in awe of his own inability to *not* answer Chase's questions.

Chase looked away from Liam toward the mirage-like Mumford Arms. "Do you have any brothers, Liam?" he asked gruffly. Thinking this was how *he'd* learned to fight.

"Loads of 'em."

He turned back. "Sisters?"

"Loads."

Chase sighed. "How many *actual* brothers and sisters do you have?"

"One sister." Glumly admitted. He made having a sister sound like a character flaw.

Chase knew it was unfair, using his captain's voice on a child. Still, he had no patience for prevarication.

"Your mother? Your father?"

The boy shrugged. A lift of one bony shoulder, nearly Gallic in nature. It could mean anything.

Chase suddenly felt leaden with weariness. He was weary of the boy, of the questions he'd indulged, of himself, of the day, of yesterday, of tomorrow, and more than anything, he longed for the aforementioned strong, nasty drink . . . and, yes, definitely a woman. Too many new things and too many old things were happening to him all in one day, when in truth he wanted to be left alone again.

He roughly fished a coin out of his pocket and held it out. "Go, Liam," he said brusquely.

The boy stood stubbornly.

"Go."

He'd said it quietly, but the word contained the dark, impersonal force of nonnegotiable command.

And Liam was someone who seemed hungry to obey someone, anyone, who seemed certain about things.

Certain about things. Ha.

Liam hesitated, fingering the coin, knowing he was being *paid* to leave.

And then he obeyed.

He spun and ran off, deliberately landing in a puddle to splash another passerby who turned and swore at him. Liam, as if by rote, thumbed his nose, and dodging horse carts and costermongers and walkers of the innocent and not so innocent variety, dashed off to God knew where.

Hang the bloody Mumford Arms, wherever the devil it might be, Chase decided. He wanted the kind of oblivion that took away pain and gave great pleasure, and knew just where to find it.

Chapter 5

Rosalind lingered after Chase was gone, much as one waits out aftershocks in the wake of an earthquake. He'd always tended to leave rooms feeling emptier than they'd been before he entered one. Good heavens, the Montmorency was unnaturally quiet. But it soon occurred to her. . . .

By way of noise, there was the hiss of wax dripping into already melted wax from one of the wall sconces. And that was *all*. Not even the ambient creak of wood, the usual sound of a building responding to the vicissitudes of weather and age. Not even the distant echo of a footstep on marble. No voices. Clearly the thick old walls allowed in no noise from the inelegant street outside. And scarcely any air, either.

Then again, the Montmorency seemed to lack a certain universal appeal, hung back as it was from the street, as if in lowered-head recognition of the superiority of other museums.

She took one last look at the painting, at the great placid cow and the angel with her forward-spilling bosom, and sighed. What on earth could this have to do with *Lucy*? Lucy with her too-ready laugh and yearning for luxury and her constant, restless *aspiring* for something she thought would make her happy, when only starting life over again with plenty of *things* to begin with would have done that. Lucy, her baby sister, not at all a baby anymore, but a very pretty woman who'd never been given a reason to develop any real sense, and this in part was her fault, Rosalind knew, because she had taken upon herself the burden of being sensible enough for all of them. She should have kept a closer eye on Lucy, but she'd been in Derbyshire since Waterloo, wallowing, savoring the rare solitude. Waiting with a curious near-detachment to see what shape her life would take in the wake of the war.

She smoothed dampened palms down the elegant shape of her pelisse.

Maybe she *was* mad. Flailing for clues the way someone plummeting to the ground flails the air for holds of any kind on the way down. She hated her sudden uncertainty, but she'd felt the tug of Captain Eversea's usual certainty as he spoke. It was tempting to surrender to it, to conclude she was of *course* misguided. Deluded, even.

And this is why she hadn't told him about the letter she'd received a week ago. Because she could imagine his expression *then*.

Unsigned, comprised of one vague, offhand sentence. It frightened her, coming as it had just after she'd begun inquiring into Lucy's disappearance. But when she held it up to the cold light of Captain Eversea's surgical reasoning, it, like everything else she considered a clue to Lucy's disappearance, seemed circumstantial. Worrying about Lucy doubtless made her easier to frighten.

She sighed and turned to leave the museum.

Which is when she saw, out of the corner of her eye, a man dart across the room next to her.

* * *

Shock congealed a scream that would have tattered her throat.

An embarrassing rasp of sound *finally* emerged from her. Her heart crashed so punishing against her breastbone that she touched the wall for balance.

She could have sworn the man was wearing . . . a doublet. And a cloak that he'd swished elegantly aside as he walked.

And . . . *puffy drawers.* Stuffed hose, in other words.

She was certain she would have heard another human being anywhere near her. Had another *living* human being in fact been near.

Her wits reconvened with the aid of a few deep breaths, and she found herself cleaved by two impulses: to investigate, and to flee.

Curiosity, that wonderful panacea against all things frightening, moved her two steps forward into the room before she fully realized what she was doing. She stopped, and wondered dryly if courage by nature required a deficit of sense.

Then again, despite all the other things she might have been, she was not, nor had she ever been, a coward.

She paused, and listened, and tried concertedly to *feel* whether anything was amiss. Whether another human was present.

Once again she heard and sensed nothing at all.

She was emboldened to inventory the room with her eyes. It was stocked with furniture allegedly plucked from King Henry VIII, according to the brass wall plaques—an enormous, complicatedly carved bureau, fashioned of a cacophony of shining whorled woods and propped on fussy gilded legs—surely one needed a ladder to reach whatever one kept in the top drawer. A crown? A writing desk as fussy and shining as the other furniture, the wood as patterned as the pelt of a jungle cat, an inkwell and quill atop it—looked ready for its owner to settle in and record the happenings of the day: *Flogged serf for insolence. Devoured hart haunch. Ravished mistress.*

The ravishing, she decided, must have taken place in the canopied and curtained bed the size of a barouche that occupied the center of the room. An uncompromisingly, arrogantly masculine bed, curtains titillatingly drawn about the mattress upon which surely hundreds of bouts of sweaty royal ecstasy had ensued. As arrogant as Captain Eversea, that bed. As potent in its confidence.

Before she truly was aware of what she was doing, Rosalind was near enough to touch it, apparently spooled forward by its sheer magnetism.

In truth, she hardly felt entitled to be in the presence of such a sensual thing. She stared for a moment, biting her lip. Then she stretched out a hand tentatively, furtively; she drew it back abruptly. And then she drew in a sharp breath and boldly seized the decadent velvet of the curtains and slowly, deliberately, wound her fist in them. She drew in a shuddering breath. Her eyes fluttered closed in deference to her senses.

And she remembered.

Not once had she . . . *yearned* for her husband's touch. He'd made love to her with the enthusiastic and unimaginative rigor one would expect of a sinewy old soldier, and she could not truthfully say she'd loathed it, because there was much to be said for gratitude and ease and a warm body stretched alongside hers at night.

But had he survived the war, she would have spent the remainder of her days alongside him carrying the burden of a tamped, ferocious . . . hunger. An awareness, a sense of infinite sensual possibility she never would have dared acknowledge or indulge again lest the regret prove more than she could bear.

Not regret over the indiscretion. Regret that she may have died never knowing whether desire that incendiary had anything to do with love.

Chase's legacy to her. She could not say she was grateful for it.

But that tamped hunger needled her now, like a limb wakened from sleep.

When she tossed her head to shake off the torpor she could ill afford, she caught a glimpse of herself in a mirror: it was brilliantly polished but a trifle warped, framed in a network of gilt branches and satyrs. Her wavy reflection gazed back at her, and she could see, abashed, how very white her face had gone when she saw the man.

Ah ha! She must have seen her own reflection in the mirror, she thought, with a sense of Eureka. Not a *man*, for heaven's sake. Not a bloody *ghost*. The movement of her pelisse as she turned—she must have mistaken it for a cape. She *was* a bit light-headed, after all, having downed just one cup of tea and crumbled a piece of toast into powder by way of breakfasting this morning, though she would eat heartily enough tonight.

Once she was convinced she was alone, it was suddenly difficult to shake the impression she was invading someone's admittedly posh privacy. She began to back from the room.

"Sorry to intrude," she muttered whimsically.

"Oh, it's no intrusion at all," came a pleasant voice from behind her.

This time her scream had no trouble at *all* emerging.

The Velvet Glove fit every man who crossed its portals like its namesake: deliciously snug. It was lit just enough to ensure that intriguing shadows filled corners, and carpeted and upholstered in silk, satin, and velvet in shades of rose and cream and beige, colors and textures evoking the wonders of nude women. Its carpets and chairs and settees—and mattresses, of course—were as lush and inviting as the lap of its proprietress, the Duchess. Her real name was Maggie Trotter, but this knowledge had mostly been lost to the annals of time. No one could recall how she had come by her aristocratic appellation, but then again, a good deal of forgetting went on at the Velvet Glove.

Chase was hoping to continue that fine tradition this evening, with the aid of a strong hasty drink and a woman.

"Captain *Ever*sea." The Duchess greeted him with the hushed reverence usually reserved for royalty. Chase wasn't unduly flattered, as every man who crossed the Velvet Glove's portals was given much the same greeting, but it was still undeniably pleasant. "It has been far, far too long. A year? Two years?"

Chase couldn't recall, so he ignored the question.

"Duchess." He bowed low, because this was part of the ritual, and then he kissed her cheek, because he liked her. Her flesh was dusty beneath his lips, and she smelled of powder and rouge and a variety of other female unguents. "Always a pleasure. You're looking radiant." The radiance was in part a contrivance of rouge and lamplight, but age, and her profession clearly agreed with her. "The coronet suits you," he added.

She nodded regally and touched her hand to her complicatedly coiffed and hennaed hair, where a coronet did indeed precariously perch. "Thank you, Captain Eversea. It's new. And real. Well, mostly real. A gift from an admirer."

"Of which you have many."

"Naturally."

"You may count me among them."

She tilted her head and looked at him for a tick of silence.

"You'll forgive me, Captain Eversea, if I observe that your compliment sounded a trifle rote. Might I suggest that you're a bit distracted this evening? Or perhaps you're in *need* of distraction?"

Chase laughed.

And when he laughed, all the female heads in the place turned so quickly and in unison they nearly created a wind.

That's when he realized that something was amiss: his was the *only* male laughter he'd heard since entering. The Velvet Glove's front parlor, in his experience, was usually decorated with entwined male-female duos or even trios, giggling and whispering, flirtations punctuated by the clink and gurgle of spirits endlessly poured and imbibed, and the creak of the stairs as some man was led up, often speedily.

But now all he heard was low, desultory female conversation and, of all things, the pop of a faro box. The girls were seated around a table, and apart from the fact that their *wares*, as it were, were virtually as visible through their diaphanous clothing as delicacies were displayed in a shop window, they might have been matrons at a game table at Almack's. One of the girls dangled her slipper from her toe in boredom. Another had her chin in her hand and was nibbling her bottom lip thoughtfully, examining her cards, brow furrowed.

"Good evening, ladies," he said solemnly.

They each promptly struck a pose designed to reflect their best angles, card game forgotten. Some had decided a pout flattered them best. Two of them decided upon smiles. He turned to look at the Duchess, a brow upraised, and angled his chin toward the girls by way of asking a question.

"Oddly, it's been quiet of late," she confessed, her voice lowered as though a crowd were indeed present and would overhear. "There must be a great shooting party in the country, or some such."

"There might well be. I can tell you that *Sussex*, at least, was quiet when I left it. I've just arrived in London and haven't been to White's, so I haven't been freshly apprised of any shooting parties that may have sent the men away or scandals that might be keeping them at home rather than out at brothels. I'm expected at a soiree at Callender's tomorrow, so I know a few diverting friends will be on hand then. Perhaps I'll discover a thing or two."

"Freshly arrived in London and you came straight to see us. I am flattered, indeed."

"As you should be," he agreed, which made her laugh. "Any unsavory rumors concerning your establishment floating about that might deter visitors?"

"No more so than usual. None that our usual crowd would spend a moment believing." The Duchess ran her brothel as tightly and cleanly as Captain Eversea had run his regiment. "The crowd has only been a bit thin for nigh on a week or so. Perhaps a day or so longer than that? Please do tell Lord Kinkade that Marie-Claude is pining for him. He is her favorite visitor."

"Visitor." What a polite euphemism for someone who routinely vigorously pressed Marie-Claude into a mattress.

Chase suddenly wondered whether *he* wanted to press Marie-Claude into a mattress. She was one of the girls who had decided a pout suited her. It certainly did. Her pillowy mouth could tempt a man into writing her into his will, into doing rash, reckless things for her if she would only do certain things with *it*.

"I'll . . . tell him."

The Duchess noticed the direction of his gaze. "What can we do for you this evening, Captain Eversea?"

The "we' had a whiff of appealing decadence, and she knew it.

Chase acknowledged that with a leap of a brow and half smile, and tried to imagine those four lovely girls transferring their attentions from faro to the needs of his body. But it was like trying to grasp hold of a reflection in water: the harder he tried, the more scattered and turbulent it became—the image wouldn't take shape.

He was suddenly freshly angry with Rosalind.

Because not even forty women clamoring to pleasure him for forty nights could assuage the particular need that had led him here.

He'd come here to forget. But now it was clear that he first needed to make himself remember.

All of it.

"I'll have whiskey," he told the Duchess. "And keep it coming, please."

Chapter 6

What the *devil!*

Rosalind's head swung like a weathervane in a windstorm, searching for that voice. And then she saw him.

Or . . . it?

Gooseflesh rose on her arms. At the top of a ladder pushed against the wall near that enormous marionette was a . . . man. But at first glance he seemed indistinguishable from the puppet. His hands were so gnarled and brown they appeared carved of wood, his cheeks glowingly ruddy and as hard and round as if he were using them to store nuts; in contrast, gravity softened and drew his jaw ever downward. Now, as she took him in, the laps on either side of his face made him look like the marionette's cousin.

His eyes were large, a peculiar crystalline shade of blue, and pouched in folds of skin. He was smiling, a weary sort of smile. The sort a marionette couldn't accomplish on its own.

He wasn't made of wood, after all.

She realized her hand had flown up to cover her overtaxed heart. She lowered it abruptly, embarrassed and more than a little irritated. She was beginning to resent the havoc this odd museum was wreaking on her nerves.

The man's eyes shone with amusement. "My apologies, madam. I didn't mean to frighten you. I thought perhaps you were addressing me when you apologized for intruding, since no one else is about."

An easy enough mistake, since she *had* been talking to no one in particular, just like a looby. In truth, she likely would not have seen the man at all if he hadn't spoken or moved. And this unnerved her, too. As though crossing the portals of the Montmorency Museum put one at risk of becoming an exhibit.

Waiting for her reply, the man applied himself to what appeared to be puppet maintenance. He tested the puppet's arm joint as tenderly as he would touch a cherished human, not a lump of wood deliberately carved to be ugly.

Rosalind's heart slowed as she watched the soothing ministrations.

"Oh, no, please accept *my* apologies," she finally managed. Her voice was a bit thready. "I'm not usually such a ninny. It's just that it's so very still here and I . . . I thought I was alone. I was musing aloud."

She quite deliberately did not mention the ghost. Or the hallucination. Whatever the man in puffy drawers might have been.

He nodded, as though this made perfect sense. " 'Tis a quiet place, the Montmorency. One might be tempted to muse aloud."

Good heavens. An understatement.

"Are you a caretaker here at the museum, then, sir?"

He straightened the marionette's trousers over its skinny wooden legs with a tug. "Aye, but of the puppets, mainly, madam. My family has been puppeteers for centuries. And I do a bit of carpentry for the museum now and again, too. You were admiring the painting?"

He'd been watching her? Wait: watching her *and* Chase?

Had he been *listening* to them?

The fine hairs at the back of her neck stirred in distaste. She disliked being watched when she wasn't aware of it, particularly in light of all that had happened recently. But she had to admit that in all likelihood she would never have seen the man if he hadn't moved or spoken to her directly, such was his camouflage.

"I was *looking* at the painting," she conceded.

He smiled faintly, appreciating her careful distinction.

"And Captain Eversea? He was looking, too?"

He must have heard her address Chase. She stared at him.

"Yes," she finally said, cautiously.

"What drew you to the painting?" The question *seemed* idle; he turned away from her as he asked it, and was now testing the mobility of the marionette's neck. He took it in both hands and gave it such a twist that Rosalind's hands flew to her throat. She dropped them instantly.

"It . . . reminded me of my sister."

Apparently satisfied with the head, the man retrieved a cloth from his toolbox, hiked the ugly marionette's shirt and gave its smooth wooden chest a bit of a polish with some sort of pungent oil.

Rosalind was peculiarly tempted to avert her eyes. She was relieved when he pulled the shirt down again.

"Isn't that interesting?" he mused. "The painting reminds me of my daughter."

She was not about to tell him why it reminded him of her sister.

He was not further forthcoming regarding his daughter.

They regarded each other mutely for a moment.

Then he turned decisively back to his work. Next he applied the cloth to the lumpy wooden face of the marionette. She winced when he dug his fingers into its carved nostrils and twisted.

"Do . . . do *you* like the painting, sir?" She suddenly wondered what this craftsman thought of the Rubinetto.

He wiped his knobby hands on a cloth tucked into the waistband of his trousers.

"No."

The word was inflectionless and immediate.

He backed down the ladder, each rung giving a squeak beneath his weight. He bent for the handle of a toolbox on the floor, gave her a short bow by way of farewell, and walked past her, deeper into the museum, without looking back.

By his second whiskey at the Velvet Glove, Chase was remembering the day English intelligence confirmed that the d'Alignys were spies for the French.

Lady d'Aligny, they'd said, was the niece of a high-ranking French official who had the ear of Napoleon and had been the source of information regarding tentative English troop positions. Doubtless she'd flirted the information strategically out of an English soldier, and Chase wondered whom he would need to order flogged. Or worse.

He wasn't naive enough to feel any particular sense

of betrayal where the d'Alignys were concerned, merely a fatalistic disappointment. War was war, and Englishmen were even now secretly, comfortably, moving through French society, mingling within Bonaparte's inner circle, making friends, betraying those friends, and sending intelligence both useful and trivial back to Wellington.

And of course dancing with French wives.

It had ever been thus in war.

Colonel March had been philosophically, humorously grim. A battered old soldier, whip-lean, bent just a bit at the shoulders from an old wound, the colonel's eyes were sharp but not jaded. Without his hat, Chase suddenly found his friend's hair strangely poignant. Soft as cobwebs. Only a little of it left.

"We can't suddenly refuse all of their invitations, of course, because it will reveal what we know and put our own men in danger," the colonel had said. "They set the best table in all of Belgium. Better to know, aye?"

"Yes, sir. But what of Mrs. March? She's a particular friend of Lady d'Aligny."

"I'll tell Rosalind to curtail her visits and impress upon her the reasons for it. She'll be . . . greatly disappointed." The colonel hated to disappoint Rosalind. "But she's a sensible girl."

It wasn't the first word Chase would have chosen to describe Rosalind. But the colonel didn't see his wife as clearly as he saw her.

Or perhaps he saw her only precisely as he wanted to see her.

So instead he'd considered it *his* duty to watch Rosalind, though he had scarcely spoken to her in weeks.

Two days later he'd just made an early departure

from a meeting with the colonel and two other officers, Kinkade included, when he saw her hurrying through the foyer of their house so quickly her dress sailed out behind her. She glanced furtively about the foyer before ducking into the narrow passageway leading to the kitchen, which opened up onto the servants' entrance.

Chase instantly recognized she meant to surreptitiously leave the house.

In her hand she clutched a half-crumpled sheet of foolscap.

In two strides he was within a few feet of her. "Good day, Mrs. March. Where are you going?"

She visibly started. Halted in her tracks.

And then her shoulder went back stiffly in resignation. She turned very slowly. Her eyes flared hotly when they met his.

His question *had* been very direct.

But then, he was generally very direct, as she knew.

"You seem to be everywhere, Captain Eversea. And yet we speak very rarely these days, don't we?"

Impressive gambit, indeed. An attempt to put him on the defensive.

"Are you reluctant to answer my question, Mrs. March?"

A hesitation. He could sense the tick of her thoughts.

"Is my destination *truly* any of your business, Captain Eversea?" She'd tried for imperiousness. She was the wife of his commanding officer, after all.

But he just smiled a slow, grim, entirely comprehending smile that soon had her fidgeting nervously with the sheet of foolscap in her hand. She was clever but young, and doubtless inexperienced when it came to lying, simply because it didn't come naturally to her.

Otherwise she would have known her evasiveness was tantamount to confession.

"It most certainly is my business if you intend to visit with Lady d'Aligny after the colonel has requested you not to do it."

She went visibly still. To her credit, she didn't deny a thing, or lie about where she intended to go. But he saw a wounded flicker in her eyes. The message rustled; her hand was shaking.

Somewhere out in the garden a bird gave voice to a series of trills.

"But she's my friend." She'd tried to measure out the words evenly. But he'd heard the pain in her voice, and his fingers curled involuntarily into a fist. She held up the message, as though displaying evidence of friendship. "She invited me for tea. She misses my company, she says, and I miss hers, and it's been but three days since I've seen her. Surely just for tea . . . " Something approaching stubborn defiance began to harden her lovely features. "Surely there could be no harm in tea, Captain Ever . . . "

She trailed off at the cold, implacable expression on his face.

"She's not your friend, Mrs. March. She's using you. This is war. The colonel doubtless has made his wishes known to you with regards to the Lady d'Aligny. Don't be a child."

He'd said it firmly. But gently, gently, too. As though the message she held was a loaded and aimed pistol and he was attempting to talk her into lowering it.

She dropped her eyes to the message quickly, her fine brows diving. Trying to disguise her hurt and disappointment and confusion.

He'd seen all of it, anyway.

And in that instant he felt her hurt so acutely it might well have been his own.

And, absurdly, *that* was when he became truly furious at the d'Alignys.

And what kind of soldier did this make him when suddenly the welfare of Mrs. March meant more to him than the d'Aligny betrayal?

She lifted her head again. They regarded each other wordlessly for a moment. Her pale eyes seemed unnaturally bright. Two faint spots of pink had appeared high on cheeks.

"How do you know she's *not* my friend? Perhaps she cares for me because she enjoys my company, and not simply because I might do her the good fortune of betraying the British army to her in some useful way. And I swear to you, I never have."

This was so desperately, staggeringly naive and surprisingly, maturely ironic that for a moment he didn't know how to respond.

"I know you never have, Mrs. March. Your husband would ensure you were never able to, and he would never put you in that position or use your friendship with Lady d'Aligny in that way. I fear your loyalty to Lady d'Aligny is admirable but misguided, Mrs. March, and you must abandon it."

It was no pleasure to disappoint her, to watch her struggle with a betrayal. Perhaps the first she'd ever known.

But suddenly her eyes glinted bright as flints and the high color in her cheeks blazed.

Ah. And here was the temper Mrs. March tried so valiantly to disguise.

"Despite what you might think, calling me Mrs. March again and again does not impose a greater distance between us . . . Captain Eversea. One might think you're attempting to remind yourself that I *am* a *Mrs.* . . . March."

He froze.

A brutal warrior, was Rosalind March. She'd identified and aimed straight for his weakness as no one before had. She'd rendered him speechless and momentarily helpless for the first time in his life.

Unfortunately, his weakness was also her own.

She knew she'd gone too far. She stared at him. Her mouth parted just a bit in shock. She'd frightened herself with her own recklessness.

He couldn't yet speak. He was gruesomely ashamed that she was correct.

And furious to be laid bare by a woman.

He would never forget her dress that day: white muslin, covered all over with tiny, whiter dots, the neckline edged in fine lace. The sleeves were puffed and short. Her arms bare. Maypole strands of hair had escaped at her nape and fell in loose twists to her jaw. Her lips were generous: lush, pale pink, the bottom fuller than the top. A band of satin, cream-colored, tied beneath her waist, it reflected light, as did her skin.

That her mind and soft voice should cut him so startlingly to the bone seemed wrong, incongruous. She was all softness.

At last she jerked her eyes away from his gaze.

But she'd drawn back a veil between them that could not now be dropped. The moment was a precipice for both of them.

Still, she'd tried a conciliatory laugh. It was a failure: short and nervous. "Oh, fear not, our valiant captain. I consider myself duly warned. I shall obey. You needn't fuss so." Her hand came up then to touch him, lightly. Meant to flirt, or to soothe, or to placate, he supposed.

He snatched it in midair as though it were a striking cobra.

He hadn't even given her time to gasp. Her green eyes were dark, her pupils enormous with pure astonishment. She was too *surprised* to be too frightened of him.

Yet.

He held her wrist fast, and perhaps too tightly.

Impressions set in: God, but her skin was unthinkably fine. Soft. So soft. How could it survive this war unscathed?

How could destiny allow anyone but him to touch it?

A ridiculous, traitorous thought. But it owned him. And it ached in him. Mocked him.

In seconds he was mesmerized by the fact that he was touching her skin outside of any social context that would allow him to properly do it. He ought now to speak or at least release her.

He seemed unable to do either.

The silence began to pulse.

Rosalind swallowed. He watched, fascinated. Her pupils were huge, turning her pale green eyes to ash gray. She was riveted by something in his face. Her swift breath fluttered the few stray tendrils clinging to her jaw.

It was Rosalind who broke the silence with a whisper.

"Why are you *afraid* of me?"

A more sophisticated woman would have turned the

words into an innuendo or a taunt. But she wasn't that kind of woman, not yet. She was genuinely confused and hurt by whatever was between them; he heard it in her voice. And he heard fear there, too.

But she couldn't disguise the fascination. For what red-blooded woman wouldn't be fascinated to discover how much power she held over a man like him?

Chase was suddenly aware of how very alone they were in that passageway. It seemed as secret, as separate from the house, as their feelings were secret from the world.

You ought to afraid of me, Mrs. March.

Because I'm afraid of myself.

Because he wasn't one to waste words, and because she knew the answer to her own question, and as patience wasn't his forte, he said nothing. Instead, as if in a dream, he watched himself slowly turn her hand over. And slowly raise it to his lips.

And then in her palm place a kiss that surely must have seared her, must have branded her, with its sheer carnal tenderness.

There's your answer, Mrs. March.

Her breath snagged audibly. Her arm gave a minute jerk.

And as he was in no way a coward, just a military man without a compass or a map in this particular terrain, he lifted his lips from her palm and looked into her eyes to assess the consequences of what he'd just done.

But he didn't give her hand back to her.

She didn't attempt to retrieve it from him.

Color had rushed into her throat, her cheeks, over the tops of her breasts, flushing cream skin to pink. Her eyes were brilliant, shot through with emotions too complex and varied for Chase to decode. Her lashes lowered in confusion, but she lifted them swiftly again, a force of will, and with them up came her chin. Bravado. She wanted him to know she wasn't a coward, either.

Still they said nothing.

And as the silence was growing absurd, and as he still had her hand, Chase raised her arm again slowly enough to make it a dare, to give her ample opportunity to pull away.

She did not. She was mesmerized.

And his fingertips, like a scout, led his lips softly, softly, along the faint blue vein of the underside of her arm, to the crook of her elbow. The scent of roses was stronger there, in the bend.

That's where he placed his next kiss.

Uncompromisingly adult, hot, leisurely—it was the sort of kiss he'd give a practiced lover after they'd exhausted each other in bed. He touched his lips to her, opened them to touch his tongue to salt, sweetness, silk. His lips lingered long enough to feel the skittering of her pulse. The heat of her skin hinted at the rush of blood through her body; he savored this, knowing what he was doing to her, knowing that her nipples had gone hard, that she was likely sweetly, deliciously, dampening between her legs. He savored what he was doing to himself. His skin, every inch of it, felt feverish. His cock stirred, swelling. He did nothing at all to disguise it.

He was out of his mind.

Her breathing was rough now. She was frightened or aroused. Both, most likely.

He slid his hand from her elbow up to her wrist

again and held it loosely in the circle of his thumb and forefinger.

Giving her the option to take it back from him.

He met her eyes. *Willed* her to take her arm back from him. To slap him. To say something, *anything*, but preferably something idiotic or contemptuous enough to cure him of this, to stop him, to stop the both of them.

But she seemed to have gone mute as well as pink.

He flicked his eyes toward her bodice: her nipples were sharply peaked beneath the fine muslin of her dress. And his eyes lingered there, and he was certain they spoke silently and eloquently of the things he'd like to do to them. Lick. Touch. Suck.

He didn't care whether she saw him staring.

She noticed him noticing. Her hand gave a tiny spasm then; it was an attempt to free it.

He released her at once.

She lifted her hand. He waited for the slap.

But her hand hovered an instant, seemingly frozen in time. And then, as if hardly daring to do it, it moved for him, landed softly against his jaw. And she dragged the tips of her fingers along his jaw gently, as though daring a wild beast to snap at her.

He stared at her. His heart beat in painful, martial thumps.

She'd done it as a test, he knew, bloody woman. To see if his expression would change when she touched him.

And God help him, he was certain it did, because he saw in hers something that unnerved him. Behind her defenses, her pride, her desire . . . was what looked like sympathy. She understood.

When her fingers rested against his cheek, he turned his face into her hand. Unable not to. Hating himself for it.

She cradled his cheek for an instant. And then she slid her hand behind the nape of his neck, very softly. Her hand was cool, smooth, achingly feminine. And placed the other on his chest and dragged it slowly up to rest against his shoulder. Making her intent very clear.

In this way, she'd made herself complicit in the betrayal of her husband. She had her own sense of honor, then.

She wouldn't allow him to entirely blame himself.

In a swift instinctive motion Chase's arms folded her into his body, and her body molded to his with staggering instinct and perfection. One hand settled at the nape of her neck, sliding up the downy short hairs to cradle her head. One at the small of her back.

He pressed his body, his aching cock, hard and deliberately against her, felt her legs open to press her own body harder, closer to him, closer. So close doubtless they were both hurting each other, themselves, and it was the sweetest imaginable pain.

He tipped her head back in his hand. Her arms wrapped around his shoulders, around his head.

The kiss was a sensual clash, quick and angry and imperfect, because they were angry at each other and at themselves and were strung tight with a need they could hardly fully unleash. She tasted inexperienced; she tasted immeasurably sweet; she was tense and quivering. His fingers dropped from her nape, snagged in the lace of her bodice, dragged it down until he found the satin of her breast, and then her nipple, ruched and hard, and he took it between his fingers and rubbed roughly; she gasped an oath into his mouth and ground herself harder against him.

Sweet Christ.

He had evil, traitorous thoughts: did his dear friend the colonel merely hike his wife's night rail at night and ground away at her? Did she have any idea of the kind of pleasure that could be had from her body? Did she have any idea what he knew, of how he could make her feel?

Her *body*, in its lush awkwardness, instinctively knew. He moaned into her mouth.

Chase knew this kiss was a mistake for a million reasons beyond the obvious, but mainly because in it he sensed dizzying possibility, something that stung like a deep clean saber cut, something that could have been pleasure or pain or both. It was fraught with a thousand things he knew he could never possibly articulate because he'd never needed the vocabulary for them. The taste of her, the way her body blended into his, was entirely new.

With astonishment, he realized he was shaking.

Falling. He fell and fell. Her lips were a cloud, her tongue satiny and hot, touching his, testing his, twining and taking, and desire gripped him with talons. And he knew, somehow, he could not fall forever, in the way that a man strung from a noose could not fall forever.

He needed to end this. It was within his power to save himself and her.

He did end it. Somehow.

And then somehow she was out of his arms.

For an instant he was relieved.

In the next instant he felt a heaviness, a sadness, that

nothing about this grim war had yet induced in him.

It was silent again. That silence was the sound of his life transformed forever.

Betrayal sounds like this, he thought, and was then grimly impressed with his newfound sense of melodrama.

From the corridor, in the distance, through a cracked door, they heard bellowing. It sounded like Kinkade, who must have left the meeting. Chase only heard the last part. " . . . and if you touch my bleedin' boots again, Crimway, I'll make ye wear yer arse for a hat, d'yer hear?"

"I love my husband, Captain Eversea." Her voice was low and steady.

"I love him, too." His voice was quiet.

She inhaled sharply and exhaled a sigh. Steadying her pulse, he knew. And then she nodded once, shortly: *Good.*

It took her longer to gather her composure, because she was just a young woman in the midst of a war, and he was probably only the second man she'd kissed in her entire life, when he could be a quarter of an hour or more remembering all of his lovers.

He saw her retreat into herself with a straightened spine, her expressive eyes going distant and impersonal.

Well, then. At some point during this war she'd turned into a colonel's wife after all. It was entirely possible, Chase thought, that he had something to do with it.

A different voice, this one Sergeant Wilkerson's, floated toward them. " . . . and dinna tell *me* how to polish a—"

Ah, the tortures of war.

To the sounds of profanity and inanity, she'd left him.

Two days after he kissed Mrs. March, Colonel March informed Chase that he'd been assigned to a different regiment.

A quiet meeting. Swift and succinct, an order delivered. And that was all.

The reassignment might very well have been coincidental: Chase was well regarded and needed, and redeployments were not uncommon. But he knew better.

He would never forget the look on his friend's face. Not cold, or angry, or regretful.

Impassive.

Which was much, much worse than any of those things.

Chase would never know for certain how Mathew knew. Did Rosalind tell him?

And here everyone had thought Captain Eversea was a bloody hero. He supposed even *he* had begun to think he was a bloody hero.

He hadn't the faintest idea who he was now.

And he'd sat for a moment in a sinking silence. And then, unable to speak, he simply nodded when he was dismissed. And bowed.

After *that*, having his leg shot open felt rather superfluous.

It was the last time he saw either Colonel March or Rosalind March.

In the Velvet Glove, he threw back another whiskey. It burned less going down, which meant memories and pain were dimming, too.

Chapter 7

And while Chase was drinking to remember and then forget her, Rosalind discovered that the same wild, filthy street boy she'd enlisted to track down Chase was perched on the museum steps when she exited, licking his fingers free of the last bits of a pasty. She shuddered thinking of how much dirt was going into his mouth along with the pasty and sailed past him.

He stood immediately and began trailing her.

Uneasy, she picked up her pace, and when she reached the gate, craned her head down the road, looking in vain for a hack.

"D'yer see the gimpy cove 'ere at the museum, then?"

Rosalind felt her eyebrows fly up imperiously. She whirled on him and sent a look down her nose like someone aiming down a gun barrel.

"You will refer to him as Captain Eversea."

Liam stared at her, nonplussed. And then the cheeky little bugger grinned. "Sound just like *'im*, ye do. Captain Eversea."

Rosalind was reluctant to be charmed. "He's very good at giving orders, yes."

"Ye saw 'im, then?"

"I did, and I thank you for completing your task. I appreciate a man who can keep his word."

The boy flared his narrow shoulders like a peacock spreading a tail, flattered. She'd suspected he would be.

She began to wish she could shoo him away as if he really *were* a peacock.

"D'yer know Captain Eversea woke up with a dead Frog atop 'im at Waterloo?" the boy offered conversationally. "They shot 'is leg open, and 'e didna know if the bones showed or not, but they didna take 'is leg."

Oh, God.

For a moment she couldn't speak at all. She stopped, absorbing the force of the words.

"I knew," she said softly.

Even as she'd diligently, dutifully, frantically looked for her husband on that battlefield that day, she'd known that any of those broken bodies could have been Chase's. His was the face she saw in her mind's eye even as she'd called for Mathew, and she'd lived with the knowledge of that ever since.

"So is Captain Eversea yer man, Mrs. March?"

"No!"

For some reason, Liam seemed to find her vehemence amusing. He was all wicked grins.

She said, sternly, "That is, I am a widow. I have no ma— I'm not married."

"Ye'd be the *colonel's* widow."

She looked sharply at Liam. "And how do you know this?"

"Captain Eversea, 'e told me ye were the colonel's wife."

"Seems you and Captain Eversea had a fine chin wagging, then," she said dryly.

"We did!" Liam agreed happily. "'E said 'e needed a nasty strong drink and a woman."

"*Did* he."

"'E must have been tired from the fight."

She froze mid-step. Then slowly turned to face Liam. "Fight?" she said faintly, after a moment.

"Two nasty coves wiv knives, they jump 'im, right? Right after I gives 'im yer message. And 'e—"

And here Liam reenacted the outstanding aspects of the attack, complete with kicks and twirls and descriptive details like "right in the baubles!" and "*Crack!* 'in the gut then, right, wi' 'is stick!"

Rosalind watched, riveted in shock.

"Captain Eversea, 'es a right Abram cove! 'E's got *bottom*, 'e 'as! Not a mark on 'im!" Liam concluded, panting a little. "Two knives 'e walks away wiv, an two men on the ground gaspin' fer air, fair near death."

She listened, stunned, and frowned darkly at him, an unfair way of shooting the messenger. The boy looked confused by the frown.

So Chase had been in a violent fight, during which he had brushed two men from him the way one might brush lint from a coat. And then had appeared at the museum as though naught had happened.

She had two thoughts, and the first—how dare anyone try to hurt him?—she batted away in favor of the more important one: *this* was the man she'd hoped to persuade to help her, after he'd coldly declined to do so? He'd always been formidable, but fresh evidence that he remained precisely as formidable as ever was hardly a comfort.

Freshly daunted, she sighed. Kinkade, on the other hand . . . a good soldier, one of Chase's closest friends during the war, and nothing like Chase in terms of stubbornness. Then again, no one was. Personally persuading Kinkade to help her was likely her best chance.

"Is your story true?" She fixed the boy with a lie-defying stare. "The fight?"

"Ask the captain yerself," he said cheerfully, sounding only slightly wounded.

Liam swung for a moment on the bars of the gate that would be locked in another half hour or so. He was just about slight enough to slip through them. He began to try, just to see whether he could, then decided against it and followed Rosalind out of the gate the orthodox way.

Rosalind watched, thinking how children considered nearly anything a toy, experimented with, tested. It was a regret, a piercing one that she nonetheless refused to linger over: She would have loved to have a child.

Don't ask it. Asking, she knew, was in a way a commitment, a true acknowledgment of someone else. She did it, anyway.

"What is your name, young man?"

A hesitation, as he apparently decided whether to tell her the truth. "'Tis Liam."

"I am Mrs. March. Liam, would you like to earn another . . . " She fished about in her reticule.

"Do it fer ha'pence, what e'r it is, if you promise me work again."

She looked at him sharply. "Good heavens. A man of business, are you?"

"Aye," he agreed happily, as if this was the first time he'd ever heard the term, and with the air of someone who would be using it again and again. "A man of business."

Rosalind paused in her reticule rustling and peered up the street. She still saw no hackney, and the lowering light and the ghost in the puffy drawers in the museum and the very idea that two men with knives had come at the all-too-mortal but immortal-seeming Chase Eversea—all of it, truth be told, was making her feel exceptionally nervy.

"Girls." Liam sighed. He put two fingers in his mouth and whistled so shrilly she clapped her hands over her ears.

Within a minute the clatter of hackney wheels was audible, and then the hackney itself wheeled into view, the horses stepping with a certain amount of weariness, lamps already lit in preparation for evening.

Liam turned to her. And raised those fair eyebrows up in his dirty face.

"Very good skill," she approved coolly.

"Aye," he said with airy aplomb, and held out his hand for the ha'pence, and she put it in.

"Do you like to work, then, Liam?" she said briskly.

"I likes ter eat."

So matter-of-factly said, so free of self-pity and full of amusement.

Rosalind's breath stopped. She frowned again, startling him, as if the frown could drive away encroaching, weakening, inconvenient sentiment. He was so bold and cheeky and *dirty*. Especially his feet.

His feet were so small.

She jerked her eyes away from them. "I need to know where Lord Callender lives," she said as the hack drew nearer.

"In Washington Square. Everyone knows where Lord Callender lives," Liam said pityingly. "'E gave me a 'a'pence. 'Ere at the museum, 'e come out. More than once, 'e did."

It sounded like a hint. She gave him another ha'pence, and this time she surrendered a smile. "I've been in the country, Liam. I am not so sophisticated as you."

He scrambled to hold the heads of the horses as she boarded the hack, looking even smaller by contrast to those horses, by contrast to the lowering shadows. His mother, whoever she was, ought to have gathered him in for the evening and locked the door against the dangers London presented around even the most benign corners.

But Liam seemed to view London as his playground. She doubted he *had* a mother.

"Gi' me regards to Captain Eversea."

The sheer cheek of the boy! The last thing she saw was his grin shining in his dirty face as he scrambled to shut the door for her.

A miracle the door shutting hadn't cost her yet another ha'pence.

Five glasses of whiskey later, Chase was surprised to find himself alongside Marie-Claude on a bed upstairs at the Velvet Glove. She was stroking his thigh, but it was having the opposite effect than she intended: it was making him sleepy.

How had this happened? Oh, that's right: one glass of whiskey had turned into four, then five, that's how.

"Rosalind?" he murmured.

"If you wish, monsieur," Marie-Claude said.

He tipped backward on the bed, unable to remain

upright. He gave a short laugh. Good God. She couldn't fool him: *she* wasn't Rosalind.

Suddenly this seemed like a terrible dilemma, but then, he'd had five glasses of whiskey.

He closed his eyes. Ah: *there* was Rosalind. In his memories.

Marie-Claude's hand had crept over to his cock and began to stroke.

He gripped her wrist as abruptly as he'd stopped Rosalind's hand so many years ago, surprising her.

"Sorry," he slurred politely. Not while Rosalind was in his thoughts.

How on earth did he manage to get up here to begin with? His memory didn't seem to extend back as far as climbing the stairs. He'd spent it all on remembering Rosalind.

He sighed. Whiskey was generally a mistake, in his experience. Solved nothing.

At least nothing as incurable as Rosalind March.

You ought to marry, Chase. Suddenly Colin's words echoed in the sodden cavern of his mind. Chase gave a short, sharp, ironic laugh that made Marie-Claude jump. The truth was—and he could thank whiskey for revealing this to him, at least—if Colin had known just how those words sounded to him—if he'd had *any* inkling of the regret, the inconceivable longing they called up in him—he never would have said them again.

Colin wasn't a *complete* ass.

Chase plucked Marie-Claude's hand gently from him and stood, but he had to do it in stages: first he got his torso up, and when his head stopped swimming, he levered the rest of himself up, and when the room stopped turning, he turned, and this was how he noticed for perhaps the first time the bad and yet decidedly erotic painting hanging over the bed.

A dark-haired angel was blowing something rather more anatomical than a trumpet.

Everyone in the painting—the angel and the lucky recipient of her attentions—looked quite pleased with the turn of events.

She looked quite familiar, this angel. Chase stared and stared at the painting. Marie-Claude thought he was mesmerized for another reason altogether.

"You want that I should . . . " She gestured illustratively.

"No, thank you, Marie-Claude," he said absently.

He paid her for her inconvenience—probably absurdly too much—leaving her confused. He would go home and sleep. And he made his way back down the stairs, using the walls and his walking stick for balance, and still thinking.

Bloody hell.

He was certain he'd seen that angel before, but at the moment he couldn't recall where.

When Rosalind finally returned home, the lamps flanking the door of her narrow, stucco-fronted row house—borrowed from her sister Jenny's husband— were lit for the evening, and despite everything, she knew a surge of pleasure. The house had a bright red door, which she quite liked, and the window box was filled with bright, thriving-against-the-odds late summer flowers. A maid came in but once a day to do a few maidly things, like fetch in the coal and tend the fires and do the marketing. Servants had done for Rosalind during her marriage, which she thoroughly enjoyed; she'd decided to do for herself in London. She preferred it. Solitude was still an untold luxury after years spent as a colonel's wife, and before that as surrogate mother to a pair of challenging sisters.

She'd just inserted her key into the keyhole when she saw the sheet of paper lying folded at her feet.

Her hand froze on the doorknob.

A chill bloomed in the pit of her stomach. And then she sighed, plucked the thing up, got inside, *slammed* and firmly locked the door.

She forced herself to casually move about the room, lighting the lamps, a show of bravado, before she deigned to give the thing attention. She shook it roughly open.

I thought I warned you, Mrs. March.

Bloody hell.
The first one had said:

I wouldn't if I were you.

She stared at it, deciding how she felt.

For God's sake, if one is going to send a threatening letter, she thought, one ought to make it a good and proper one. With intimations of death and destruction, or perhaps specific threats of harm to loved ones. Not *these* pallid things.

Apparently, *angry* was how she felt about it.

The sheer *incompetence* of the threats was irritating, not to mention the fact that someone seemed to want to frighten her—*her*, Rosalind March! Who'd known poverty and marriage and spies and Waterloo and an illicit, bone-melting, life-altering kiss from arguably England's most fascinating man! It was laughable, truly.

Still.

She carefully refolded the message and packed it into the humidor, which is where she'd impulsively decided to store the first one. It was in fact less a humidor than a place to store buttons these days, but it still smelled like her late husband Mathew's foul cigars, which made it a talisman of sorts, she'd decided.

She closed the humidor lid, locking the messages up like a pair of prisoners.

And then she marched upstairs and from beneath her bed pulled a latched wooden case. The hinges had a good long creak when she pushed up the lid, as though the thing were yawning after satisfying sleep. It hadn't been opened in years.

The pistol still gleamed in its velvet nest.

The stock and barrel were of blued steel, the delicate network of engraved silver vines untarnished. Beautiful thing. A big pistol. A *proper* pistol—not the sort of pistol one could slip into a reticule or a boot. She knew Captain Eversea kept an appropriately compact one in his boot at all times, though given what the boy Liam had described, it hardly seemed necessary. Trust Chase to handily use his walking stick as a weapon.

But *she* wouldn't be making a move without this pistol from now on.

She latched the case and set it aside.

And then she opened up the trunk she'd brought with her to London and lifted out a dress of pewter-colored lutestring—a kind of shimmering silk. Cut low at the bosom, trimmed at the neckline in sleeves in a lighter satin, it was simply but elegantly cut, unobtrusive in its timelessness, and still quite flattering to her trim figure. Like the pistol, it hadn't been unwrapped in quite some time. She was glad she'd impulsively brought it with her to London.

Ironically, the pistol and the dress were complementary colors.

Tentatively, with a wry quirk of the mouth at her own expense, she laid a hand flat against the back of the gown, at the waist, remembering the last time she wore the dress: at a d'Aligny ball. All the men had vied to dance with her. But the only one she remembered dancing with—the waltz—was Captain Eversea. She remembered how his hand had fit just so, right there above her waist, where her hand rested now.

It was the night he'd simply stopped talking to her. The night she realized and truly understood for the first time the magnitude of her own power as a woman and her power over Chase.

Likely Chase didn't dance anymore. And she wasn't that girl anymore.

But the dress, and the gun, were talismans.

My battle uniform, she thought dryly. The uniform she would wear to Callender's tomorrow night to confront Kinkade.

Chase awoke the next day and lay very, very still, trying to decide whether he preferred being shot to how he currently felt. Something inside his head was struggling to *hatch*.

Why did he always forget that whiskey was a terrible idea?

A brisk knock sounded on his door. The sound was visceral agony, but he was too incapacitated to groan.

"I have coffee, Mr. Eversea!" sang the housekeeper cautiously, damn and bless her eyes. "A lot of it," she added a moment later when she heard nothing. "You needn't eat anything. 'Tis just coffee." She wheedled a few moments after that.

He almost smiled. Moving his lip muscles caused him grave pain, so he decided against it.

"Mr. Chase?"

She sounded worried. He would need to make a sound to reassure her.

"Guh," was the sound he finally made.

Was he dressed? He rolled his eyes—which seemed to have been replaced by hot sandy lead balls in the night—very carefully down to his torso to investigate. He was wearing all of his clothes. Including his boots. And his coat. He wasn't even under his blankets.

He waited another moment to absorb this.

"In," he rasped.

She swung open the door, bearing an urn of coffee steaming such thick black fragrance it was purely a miracle he didn't double over and cast his accounts. She deposited it on the writing desk near the window, paused to regard him prone there on the bed, shook her head, and left again, gently closing the door behind her.

It took him long seconds to recover from the pain of the sound of the door being closed.

Why had he gotten into this condition? Ah. Of course.

Bloody Rosalind March.

Encounters with Rosalind, he decided, would inevitably end with pain and inconvenience. He ought to have known better.

But a memory he'd nearly drowned with whiskey swam to the surface of his brain. That angel in the painting at the Velvet Glove . . . he could have *sworn* it was the same angel in the Rubinetto painting at the Montmorency.

And this he wouldn't have known if Rosalind hadn't driven him to drink impractical, rather juvenile, amounts of whiskey.

Perhaps it was destiny.

Then again, whiskey and destiny often felt one and the same to the man drinking the whiskey.

Bloody Hell.

He opened one eye to a slit, through which he could see that the housekeeper had also arranged his correspondence on the coffee-bearing tray. But given that he couldn't quite speak just yet, he wasn't certain he could remember how to read. Correspondence would have to wait.

Getting out of bed was his project for the next hour or so. He managed, at last, treating his body with ginger respect. He drank the whole pot of coffee in shifts, downing more of it the better he felt, his hands trembling a little less with each cup. Next, he bathed ruthlessly in the bedroom basin, scrubbing his face and beneath his arms and down his back and between his legs, all the muskier and sweatier places. He shaved himself with a trembling hand and suffered only one nick.

He'd have a proper bath before the Callender do tonight.

In a few hours his head merely ached rather than

pounded, and he thought he might be able to eat. And so he made his way down the stairs, his boots and walking stick announcing his resurrection to the household staff, and carried with him his correspondence

The house, he discovered, had been pitilessly cleaned while he'd been indisposed. The furniture and mirrors and silver didn't so much shine as glare. His eyes shriveled in their sockets in torment and he clapped a hand over them.

He took himself and his correspondence rapidly off to the much darker library.

He threw open a window: The air smelled fresh enough, apart from the usual smells of London life carried erratically in by a breeze: dirt and coal and horse and every now and then a dash of salt and brine blown in off the Thames.

Which he could appreciate now that all smells didn't make him want to cast his accounts. It was time to address his correspondence.

The first letter was a very welcome one from Kinkade.

Glad you're in London, you old recluse. Callender's first, old man, then drinking, and God only knows what then.

Yrs,
—K.

Ah, Kinkade. It was reassuring to know that *someone* still lived in a world of "God only knows what then." Judging from how he'd felt this morning, he suspected he would have difficulty living in that world now.

It was still difficult for Chase to imagine Kinkade

donating the Rubinetto to the Montmorency. Because he *did* know a bit about Kinkade's taste in art.

He recalled one typical evening sitting about a fire surrounded by bored soldiers. Kinkade had handed him a sheet of foolscap. "What say you, Eversea?"

In the margin of a letter he'd received from his brother, with the burnt end of a sharpened stick Kinkade had sketched a nude, improbably buxom woman with nipples erect as cannon fuses.

"I think her breasts might be too small," Chase critiqued dryly.

Kinkade had taken him quite seriously and set to work again with the sharpened stick, refining, tongue between his teeth in concentration.

Tedium was as formidable an enemy as the French during the war. Some men kept journals. Some soldiers, like the Earl of Rawden, the poet known as the Libertine, had written poetry. Some gambled. Kinkade sketched the occasional nude woman, and was generous about passing the sketches around to the men and cheerful about accepting criticisms and suggestions, which he seldom incorporated, as he had his own vision. He signed them *O. McCaucus-Bigg*.

A new soldier was always puzzled by this, given that this wasn't Kinkade's name.

"O. McCaucus-Bigg?"

"Braggart, are you?" Kinkade would roar. "Not as big as mine, laddie!"

A good joke, suitable for thirteen-year-old boys and bored sergeants and subalterns.

In short, unless Kinkade had suffered a conversion to which Chase hadn't been privy, his tastes in art didn't run to cows and cherubs and his possession—

and subsequent relinquishing—of that painting, if he had indeed donated it to the Montmorency, was puzzling. Perhaps he'd had the paintings foisted upon him as part of an inheritance. Doubtless they came with an interesting story, because Kinkade, thank God, was invariably entertaining.

Chase pictured Rosalind gazing at the painting with that fixity of concentration so singularly hers. Such a cool color, her eyes so like spring. It had always struck him as odd that they could *burn* so when her temper or her intelligence lit them.

He stared out the window. Saw Rosalind. Not London. And sighed.

Genevieve would likely know about Rubinetto. He wasn't certain whom else to ask.

If only he hadn't seen that damned angel at the Velvet Glove, he wouldn't feel *obligated* to ask.

He shook his head roughly free of Rosalind—though it was a bit premature for the rough head shaking, and his stomach lurched in protest—then fished out his next piece of correspondence. This one bore the Eversea seal. He hesitated, burning with self-righteousness.

And then he sighed, capitulating, and broke the seal.

Colin's handwriting. Chase braced himself.

Dear Chase,

The new calf is doing very well, and Madeleine sends her regards. We hope you enjoy your stay in London and look forward to your report about our cousin the potential new vicar. Don't forget to visit him. We need to know if he's a bore.

P.S. You really ought to marry. It's marvelous for the nerves.

P.P.S. We've named the new calf Charles, after you. His bollocks are impressive. Thought you'd be pleased.

Chase stared. His bloody, bloody brother. He was torn between laughing and crunching the message in his fist and hurling it across the room. Colin had no *right* to make him laugh.

It was Colin's fault he was here at all. Colin—who'd survived duels, horse races, ill-advised gambling, nearly drowning, plummeting from the trellises of married countesses, the war, and the gallows—in other words, who was historically *great* fun—had become, of all things, a farmer after he'd married. It was all he talked about: cows this and sheep that and drainage ditches and crops. Night after night Chase, who relied on Colin to distract him from himself, sat across from his brother and waited for him to cease being insufferable.

But four nights ago at the Pig & Thistle, when Colin had begun to pantomime how he'd assisted with the tricky birth of a calf, complete with exuberant thrusts of his arm to illustrate just how his hand had gone *up* the cow and imitations of distressed cow noises—for the love of *God*, distressed *cow noises*!—while his new wife Madeleine leaned forward, glowing with as much pride and held-breath suspense as if Colin were recounting heroics at *Salamanca* . . .

Well, it was more than anyone should be expected to endure. And what Chase had muttered—quite rightfully—was:

"I cannot bear it any longer."

Colin hadn't even slowed his narrative. But even through his lovely ale haze, Chase saw Colin's green eyes flick toward his wife, like a smuggler telegraphing a boat off the coast with lanterns—the sort of thing married people do, in which volumes of information are exchanged, decisions reached, and nothing at all said.

He could imagine what had happened next: Colin had told his brother Marcus, who was throwing darts in the Pig & Thistle to impress *his* new wife. Marcus had told their sister Olivia, because the two of them were thick as thieves. Olivia, seeing a way to interfere, had briskly gone to their mother, *not* to Genevieve, who was far too sympathetic and would have come to him with commiseration and warning. And his mother had told their father, Jacob. Who'd sent him to London, because "it would do him good."

Bollocks, is what Chase thought.

In all likelihood his family couldn't bear *him* any longer.

A bird trilled in the garden. It reminded him uncomfortably of the day Colin had been scheduled to hang: the silence in the town house, the oblivious birds singing arias in the garden.

He laid his brother's letter gently down.

Damn, but the town house was quiet without the rest of the Everseas in it.

He told himself righteously that he preferred it that way.

He reached for another piece of correspondence.

From the seal, he knew precisely what it was. Anticipation was present, but not powerful; he suspected he knew what he'd find inside. He slid his finger beneath the wax, broke it, and learned that the East India Company would indeed welcome an officer of his talents, as he was exceptionally well regarded and came highly recommended, and that the India-man *The Courage* sailed for India in a fortnight and they would expect to see him on board.

He held it, bemused. It was what he was made for, after all: life as officer of the Crown. Odd to see his future succinctly sketched in just a few lines. Satisfying to be reminded of his strengths when his first day in London in years had been one long reminder of his weaknesses.

He fingered a blank sheet of foolscap, deciding what to do about one of those weaknesses now.

Likely there had never been any question that he would do it.

He wrote to his sister Genevieve:

Dear Gen,

Rubinetto. Italian Renaissance painter of landscapes . . . if you can indeed call this painting a landscape. Has cows, trees, and cherubs. Also busty angel. Very ugly and confusing. Located at Montmorency Museum. Please advise via messenger straight away.

Yrs,
Chase

He sprinkled sand over and pressed it closed with a disk of wax and the Eversea seal. He would send it by messenger rather than post, which ought to alarm his family, but since Colin had become so dull and everyone else seemed to be sinking into the routine of marriage, Pennyroyal Green doubtless needed a bit of stirring up. Which was really the reason he'd done it.

Not even *he* believed that.

Ah, Rosalind. He smiled half bitterly, mocking himself. Barely a tip of the lips. See what you've made me do for you, despite myself?

He need do nothing more, he told himself.

He pushed himself hard away from the desk, as if to disassociate himself with that letter and what it meant, and took himself downstairs for some more coffee. He would need to fortify himself to prepare for the "God knows what then" that would follow Callender's ball this evening.

Chapter 8

_____∽◯◯◯◯∾_____

Carriage after carriage had rolled up to the Callender town house to disgorge passengers until the square was quite clogged with motionless conveyances and frustrated horses. New arrivals had no hope of getting anywhere near the house. Philosophical drivers were swigging from flasks and conducting cheerful, ribald shouted conversations to each other across the tops of barouches and landaus and hacks; party guests threaded gingerly and philosophically through it all, prepared to walk miles if necessary. A small price to pay to attend what promised to be a legendary crush.

Rosalind peered out the window of her hack. From a distance the house was so extravagantly lit it appeared aflame; closer, she discovered it buzzed like a hive of angry bees, the result of hundreds of voices all shouting at once to be heard. She congratulated herself on her timing: entering the party unnoticed depended upon a substantial crowd already being present.

Her hack, like so many others, was forced to stop a good distance from the house. She walked the rest of the way to it, gown clutched up in her fingers, as London streets generally featured a variety of shoe-ruining liquid and solid surprises. But the night was pleasant and still, with a bit of a breeze, and she completed her journey without splashing her shoes or hem or sweating unduly and promptly, surreptitiously attached herself to a large laughing group of men and women who shouldered their way past the footmen.

Surely no one would look at her twice, she thought, when the woman next to her was sporting what appeared to be an entire pheasant wing dyed red protruding from a tightly wound turban. The group was laughing uproariously about something, so Rosalind laughed merrily, too, her head thrown back to show her teeth and disguise her face, her fan already out and whirring the air in an attempt to dizzy the gaze of the footman who impassively—but accurately, she would have surmised—studied everyone to ensure no interlopers breached the entrance.

And thus the shiningly groomed human tide swept her through the door, no footman set dogs upon her in order to drive her out, and she was inside the Callender town house, pushed genteelly this way and that like driftwood by all the other humans.

Music, lively, lilting, and accomplished, poured up from the ballroom, and down the stairs she went toward it with the rest of the partygoers. Feeling increasingly rash and giddy.

When she saw the swarm of people—brunette heads, blond heads, redheads, beplumed and coroneted and complexly coiffed—she was dizzied and mesmerized, as if she were standing on a cliff's edge staring out onto the sea. How in God's name had she thought she could find Kinkade in this crowd, when she hadn't seen him in five years, and when one crisply dressed man here blurred into another? Below her, white smiles were as ubiquitous as strings of pearls, and overhead a chandelier of swooping ropes of crystals and dangling crystal bagatelles presided like a new kind of moon. She'd been too long in the country. The glitter hurt her eyes.

Everyone was shouting in order to be heard at all. It was overwhelming.

She did, however, love beautiful gowns. And here they abounded.

Her eyes greedily took in virginal whites and subtle jewel tones, intricate beading and embroidery, somberly dressed matrons and widows. She assessed jewels and coiffures. She had no doubts about her own simply pinned-up hair, which was quite good, shiny and thick and enviable, and she saw no need to feel modest about it. And as her senses began to accommodate the spectacle, her heart remembered how it felt and she began to wish she could dance. The way she hadn't since Belgium. Since her innocence, such as it was, had been lost to war and the d'Alignys and to Chase.

Since she hadn't precisely been invited, however, it was likely her hostess would quickly note her, should she reel her merry way across the ballroom.

But surely no one would mind if she at least tapped her foot? She tucked herself between a large laughing group and a corner occupied by a regal pillar. Her slipper patted the floor, her shoulders began to sway, her fan waved beneath her chin, and then she saw Kinkade.

She sucked in a gasp and pressed herself against the wall.

He wended through the crowd with a nod here, a greeting there. She knew why she'd spotted him: he seemed scarcely to have aged at all since she'd last seen him, where Chase had hardened. Though the omnipotent chandelier might simply be casting everyone in flattering light. He was still lean and angularly handsome. His face turned toward her and his eyes flashed silvery for an instant, and for a heartbeat she thought he'd seen her.

But no: his expression didn't change. He heartily greeted another man but kept moving. He seemed to have a specific destination and was heading determinedly toward it alone.

He would disappear unless she followed him, and she might not see him again.

She watched the back of Kinkade until he turned up a staircase. Deeper into the family quarters, no doubt.

She hesitated. The stairs weren't precisely guarded by Scylla and Charybdis, she told herself. She could lie easily enough if she were caught.

And so she waited, tapping out a few bars of the music with her slipper.

And then up the stairs she went, too.

Chase gamely plunged into the ball crowds scaling the front stairs of the Callender house in pairs and groups and managed to insinuate himself through it, sparing smiles for acquaintances who shouted greetings he couldn't hear over the noise, and offering up lingering smiles for the ladies, because why shouldn't he, and it was a pleasure to freeze a few in their tracks and know that their eyes remained glued to his back as he passed.

"Captain Eversea. Very good to see you in London, sir." The Callender footman had an impressive memory. But then, so did Chase.

"Thank you, Morton. I'm happy to be here."

But he was less and less certain this was true.

A cascade of screechy feminine laughter cut through the roar of voices. Someone was clearly already drunk and in decidedly high spirits, and more than one woman would lose consciousness and need to be hauled out to the garden for a wrist patting tonight or the Callenders would consider the evening a failure.

His thoughts must have shown on his face, because he detected what appeared to be a flicker of sympathy in the footman's eyes.

"If you'd like to join Lord Callender and Mr. Kinkade, sir, and a few other gentlemen, they've gone up to the library. I've had instructions to send you there—and I should tell you I was requested to repeat this verbatim, sir—'Should you deign to show your misbegotten visage at all this evening.'"

Dancing was something he did only awkwardly these days if he did it at all, and he took no real pleasure in it, so heading straight for the cigars and conversation riddled with horses, women, carriages, guns, politics, money, war, epithets, and the like, sounded like a perfectly agreeable way to at least begin the evening.

He chose the second set of stairs, the one leading up, knowing he would likely find the library on the second floor. By the first landing it was mercifully, significantly quieter; by the third landing the hum of voices and music were made ghostly by distance.

He made a right turn: he'd heard masculine voices and a scattering of laughter of the unfettered, ribald quality one hears near battleground campfires, and toward it he went.

The library floor was thick with oxblood-and-cream-colored carpets imported from Persia, and it silenced his footfall. He'd taken two of those plush, silent steps when he stopped abruptly.

Interesting.

He thought he detected the scent of . . . roses.

He frowned. It was faint. But it was enough to send a sizzle of awareness and suspicion down his spine.

But doubtless hothouse roses were crammed into a vase here in this library.

" . . . and I said, gaslight is the way of the future, old man." Sounded like Ireton.

Chase saw immediately this was a robust library, the work of a serious collector. Tall, elegant shelves lined not only the walls but ran at angles to each other, too, with narrow passages left between, so that he needed to weave among them to get closer to the fire and to his friends, whom he could hear but not see yet. Each shelf was stuffed full of books that looked as if they might even have been read at one time or another. Gold glinted dully from lettered spines as his boots and walking stick sank into the carpets.

He stopped abruptly. The scent of roses was suddenly stronger. And potently familiar.

He knew. He knew before he saw her.

And at first he simply stared and thought: *Impressive*. Because apart from the dull sheen of her dress, nothing sparkled about her—no jewelry, no combs, no coronets—but the lyrical shape of her body elevated to stunning the simplicity of her gown. The shade of her dress blended her with the shadows on the rugs and shelves. She could easily have passed for a ghost. But really, he—or anyone, for that matter—might just as easily have missed the woman lurking among the rows of shelves.

Apart from the scent of roses.

Despite himself, his body surged in response. She was slightly bent, arse outthrust, bosom spilling forward, peering intently through a parting she'd made between two large books. Oh, God. Ironically, the line of her was achingly beautiful. Chase imagined drawing a leisurely hand from the nape of her neck, down her lean spine, over the nip of her waist and sweet curve of her arse, savoring the perfect symmetry of her. The muscles of his stomach tightened.

But Rosalind March was *spying*.

What the bloody hell should he *do*?

He was neatly cleaved between yet again protecting her—from being caught, and hearing what he knew she was likely to hear—and from protecting the men from being spied upon. He knew what sorts of things would be talked about among old soldiers. Very little of it would be suitable for a woman's ears.

He could pick all the voices out now. Kinkade, Ireton, Lawton, Kirkham, Callender. Rising, blending, tumbling over one another. Much laughing. Profanity. He heard the clink of crystal and the *glug* of brandy, the *snick snick* of cigars being clipped, and seconds later the first tantalizing puff of smoke as good cigars were sucked into life.

If he didn't join them in a moment, he would officially be spying, too.

Bloody hell. Stopping Rosalind was the best way to protect everyone.

The thick carpet took the weight of his feet and his walking stick. The leather of his shoes obliged him by not creaking. The men were too temporarily deafened by spirits and laughter and the loud ballroom orchestra to hear him, and besides, why should they be straining their ears for people *creeping* up behind them?

Not even Mrs. March heard him. So intent was she on peering at the men.

In a few more steps he was so close to her he could smell her: not just roses, but something soft and warm. Soap, the herbs she'd stored her dress in, something uniquely her. He could see one tiny white hair sparkling amidst the shining dark of her coiffure. It caught his breath. She was not yet thirty years old, but it wasn't as though the war and her flighty sisters wouldn't have left its mark upon her.

All the little things about Rosalind had always spoken strongest to him. He could not have said for certain why. They seemed to tell the story of her truthfully.

He was scarcely an inch away from touching her now, and he stopped and waited for her to sense the heat of his body.

In seconds she stood bolt upright.

Which slid the silk length of her body up a tantalizing length from his hard torso. Not at *all* unpleasant, regardless of their circumstances.

Her gloved hand went up to her mouth to cover her choked gasp. She angled her chin in an attempt to peer over her shoulder, but he was so close he'd made it impossible.

Her throat moved in a swallow. Her eyes were wide with fear; her nostrils flared.

Neither of them could speak—they could scarcely breathe, for that matter—without risking discovery.

" . . . she said to me, I'll ride you into tomorrow, and by God if she didn't!"

"Which one was this? Mildred?" This sounded like Callender.

"No, no, the little one! Cassandra! On the pirate stage."

On the *what*? No woman should be listening to this.

But Chase's torso was warming deliciously from the beautiful warm woman pressed against it, which was distracting him from the conversation.

" . . . took me upstairs after that, she did."

No man should have to worry that a woman was listening to this.

" . . . charge a subscription. Exorbitant. Exclusive. Very clever, I've decided. Now I've begun to think I'll sell shares in the . . . " This was Kinkade.

The line of fine, fine hair trailing fernlike up Rosalind's white nape mesmerized him. Her pulse thumped visibly in her throat.

It was all he could do not to lean forward and lick it.

" . . . where the hell are you going to get the capital, Kinkade? You're up to your ears in debt, aren't you?"

Her arse was now brushing against the official beginnings of what promised to be an impressive erection.

Sweet Mother of God.

" . . . she made the most brilliant mermaid . . . "

What on earth? *Mermaid?*

The conversation made no sense but sounded fascinating, and combined with the sensual woman in front of him, who had just purposely—he was certain of it— slid her arse ever so slightly across his now quite hard cock, he felt enmeshed in a druglike dream.

Rosalind's head angled again; she wanted to see him. He could see that her lips were parted a little; her breath was shallow now. Her eyelids lowered to slits; her dark lashes quivered against her cheekbones. Against him, her ribs moved.

He swallowed, too. He had ducked his head so his own harsh breaths would be muffled by her shining hair. Which is when he saw that the fine, clinging fabric of her dress explicitly revealed the planes of her arse: round and smooth and taut as a peach.

Of a certainty she wasn't wearing anything beneath that dress apart from stockings.

" . . . Ireton had to run for it! He was caught! Thought he 'twas in Covent Garden!"

A roar of laugher from the men.

Because it seemed, in the moment, a sensible and entirely unavoidable thing to do, slide a feathery finger along the crease of her buttocks as revealed by that dress.

Rosalind froze in what he assumed was shock.

Too bad, Rosalind, he thought. He did it again: the same feathery touch, originating at that sweet, wickedly erotic spot at the base of her spine, following the sweet crease of her buttocks.

And then again. Coaxing. Teasing.

Until her arse made a wee, deliberate circle against his erection.

Oh, God. He pushed himself hard against her, which might have been a mistake, but he hardly had a say in the matter: it was all his body's doing.

What had he started?

She'd started it by being here at all, was his unworthy conclusion.

His palms slid down to cup then saucily squeeze her arse, and her head tipped back into his chest, affording him a splendid view of her breasts, rising and falling, rising and falling.

He relinquished her arse and gently wrapped his fingers around her forearms to lift them. Her arms went unresisting.

And then he deliberately placed her own hands over her breasts. Then dragged them lightly down over her peaked nipples in a circle.

Just a suggestion, Rosalind. An incredibly *wicked* suggestion. *A way to participate in your own pleasure.*

For he was a planner, and he had plans for *his* hands, and for her pleasure.

" . . . found 'im at Tatersall's for my wife."

Chase began to furl up the front of her dress. Slowly, slowly, lest it rustle unduly; mercifully it glided easily up over her silk stockings and her smooth skin. He held it bunched in one hand. And then he slid his palm over the silken and—*oh, God*, lovely wet curls between her legs.

She was *rigid* in shock. But her whole body would be pliant in seconds. He knew what he was about.

His finger slowly, lightly, traced the seam between the soft folds. Snagging in those fine silken curls. Leisurely, leisurely, twining in them, as he circled against her arse.

She was still rigid. But her breathing had gone staccato.

" . . . that horse couldn't run to save its life!" someone objected. The voices of Chase's friends came to them from another world now.

He traced that sweet damp seam as though he were drawing her into being. Leisurely, as though they were in no danger at all of being caught. Torturously leisurely. Again.

And then again.

Her skin pulsed to his touch.

Lightly again. And this was when her legs slipped wider, and his finger slid through velvety wetness.

He nearly swayed from it.

His breath now gusted against her throat, and she tugged her own bodice down roughly, giving him a view of the pale rose bead-hard nipples she'd taken between her own fingers.

He was fairly certain he'd never been this aroused in his entire life.

" . . . best idea you ever had, Kinkade."

The musk of desire surrounded them now. Her knees began to buckle.

He wrapped her tightly with one arm to hold her upright, and his body took her weight, and he slipped a finger deep into her.

" . . . and I said, 'Those shares will be worthless when they have the Stockton and Darlington railroad completed . . . ' "

She turned her head into her shoulder and bit down on her soft bottom lip, and he saw again white teeth in her bottom lip like that night at the d'Alignys'. Her swift breath was hot, moist against his shirt. Her eyes closed tightly. And when he saw her fingers on her own breasts, circling, languidly circling, his own arousal was such a drug, such a madness, he suddenly became certain he could take her here, plunge into her here, behind this bookcase.

His finger slid into her . . . and out. And in, and out. He traced hard, repetitive filigrees over her hot, satiny flesh. He wanted her to acknowledge what she wanted, to ask for it definitively with her body. And she at last began to move against his hand, and together they found a swift and primal rhythm that would end beautifully and inevitably and hopefully soundlessly.

He began to feverishly imagine tipping her forward just a bit more to achieve the angle he needed to penetrate her. He liked imagining whether she thought he would, because suspense was a whetstone for his desire, and now it was urgent.

He took his hand reluctantly from between her legs and began to slide her dress up from behind.

And her body suddenly stiffened to the pliancy of a plank.

He went still, too. Puzzled.

And then . . . fiercely, darkly suspicious.

Her thighs were ever so slightly parted, and before she could jam them closed he slipped a hand through the space between them: something bulky and dully shining was strapped to her thigh with a pair of satin garters—one pink, one white.

She clamped her thighs closed on his hand—or tried to—but his hand had already wedged itself in there.

He traced the contours of the thing. For an instant the contrast between the silky give of her skin and the lethal, unyielding metal of the weapon was astoundingly erotic, and his absurdly high state of arousal prevented its significance from penetrating instantly.

An instant later desire evaporated in shock and fury.

What the bloody hell did she intend to do with a *pistol*?

He froze.

And she did, too. Her desire had completely given way to fear. As well it should. *Bloody woman.*

With feather-delicate fingers and a heart thudding from nerves and thwarted lust merging into anger, he did what he could have done in the dark, anywhere, with any pistol: he ascertained it was locked.

It was.

He dropped his hands from her silky thighs, and the now crushed dress fell like a blind drawn, and he landed his hands hard on her shoulders.

Rosalind's mouth was sandy with terror.

Despite that, she felt . . . thwarted. There was a cold fluttering in her stomach; she deeply, irrationally resented missing the shattering release she knew would have been hers. She *should* have felt inappropriately indignant at being thus handled, despite how thoroughly—how *wantonly*—she'd participated. How on earth had it begun to make perfect sense: why *shouldn't* Captain Eversea take me behind the bookcase in the library?

The way all kinds of rashness made sense when he was near.

If only he hadn't raised her dress up so *high*. He might never have seen the pistol at all.

Sweet merciful God. What was she *thinking*? Thank *God* he'd hiked her dress up that high, or God only knows what she would have done. And if a woman couldn't hide a pistol up her thigh, then where *could* she hide it?

Chase turned her around to face him. Slowly.

She didn't *want* to turn, but it wasn't as though those hands of his gave her a choice. She was eye-level with his cravat now. She risked a look higher up.

His eyes glittered with all the warmth of a gun barrel.

He mouthed the words broadly: *Go. Down. Stairs.*

He stared at her until she did what he seemed to want her to do: she nodded vigorously in comprehension.

Quietly, he added.

He didn't add *or else,* but it was rather implied by his expression. She wondered what he intended to do.

Chase couldn't just leap out from behind the bookshelf with his fading erection.

She waited.

He backed slowly, slowly, away from her, edging along the wall toward the entrance of the library again. Just the way *she'd* entered. One careful backward footstep at a time. He seemed to be listening hard, and Rosalind, breathless with nerves, listened, too; but none of the voices fell in volume or ceased chattering; nothing about the rhythm of their seemingly impromptu male gathering suggested they might know someone was spying or creeping backward or anything else.

He reached the entrance.

And then all at once Chase plunged forward with a hearty, "Gentlemen!"

Rosalind gave a start.

"Wondering when you'd turn up, E'ershea!" Someone was drunk and had lost the ability to pronounce certain consonants.

"Chase!" said someone else in round aristocratic tones.

Rosalind began to inch backward in just the same way Chase had. One light, *gingerly* light, backward footstep at a time.

"Captain!"

Much manly clapping of backs and clasping of hands seemed to be taking place. Slurred, profane, affectionate greetings, the sort she was accustomed to hearing among soldiers, were exchanged.

She crept farther back; the wall was cold against the half-moon of her back exposed by her gown.

The corner around which she could disappear, and the hall, were so tantalizingly close.

Chase was talking. "Took a wrong turn in the house, gentlemen, and bumped into an old friend here, which is part of the pleasures of London. I cut it fine, I fear, and I thought I might have time to linger for a chat, but fear I must be on my way. On to another engagement."

A chorus of protest rose up.

"Surely there's no other place worth being tonight?" This was Kinkade's refined voice; Rosalind recognized it, and damn it all, she wanted to talk to him, but she didn't dare now.

She heard absolutely nothing from Chase by way of response, but he must have either winked or made a rude and illustrative manly gesture—she could simply picture it—because the men burst out laughing and hooting.

"You're right, Eversea, *that's* a place worth being at *any* time." This was Kinkade, sounding sincere. "But thank you for gracing us with a moment of your presence, Captain. And do ride her once for me."

Bloody hell. He was *leaving*? She thought he'd intended to stay with the men and was simply sending *her* away.

This was when she bolted.

The voices faded as she dashed down the hall, skirt gripped in her hands, face aflame, stomach a block of motivating ice-cold fear. Lit sconces were a blur as she rushed by them.

Her hair began to loosen; there was so much of it and the pins could only be counted on to hold it for so long, and down it came, a strand at a time.

She nearly skidded when she turned the hall corner. If she could only outrace him—*surely* she could outrace him now (and what an unworthy thought *that* was)—she wouldn't have to face his wrath.

She hadn't the courage quite yet.

At last, there were the stairs, mercifully. She placed her hand on the cool, beautifully polished banister. She saw her face distorted in its shining surface as she launched herself down the marble steps, her slippers clacking down hard, her borrowed dress bunched carelessly in one fist to free her feet. She watched her slippers carefully, lest she fall. The flash of her toes hitting marble dizzied her.

And she came to a sudden abrupt halt.

A crowd clotted the foyer and the main door, of course.

Damnation.

She plunged into the crowd with all the grace of a diver. She made a valiant go of it, gamely wending her way out of the door of the town house, weaving skillfully as a polo player through the silk and muslin and long-coated men, shaking off the long coats that snagged on her as she shoved past, taking a plume in the eye just once, leaving in her wake more than one indignantly squeaked *"Oh!"* as she elbowed through.

She saw the door. The brace of footmen. The tiny rectangle of dark outside. She felt the breeze of the night air.

And she was jerked to a halt by a large, hot hand gripping her elbow.

An experimental tug told her she wouldn't be freeing herself with any ease.

She turned her head over the shoulder and flinched when she met angry blue eyes and a positively horizontal mouth.

She gave another fruitless tug.

Where had he come *from*? Bloody fast, he was. "Abram cove," indeed.

"Duck your head," he commanded. Low and cold, right in her ear, the tone brooked no argument.

He hurried her—*marched* her, rather—out of the door, clearing the way with his own height and his walking stick and willingness to step on toes, until they were once again into the blessedly cool-by-contrast night, his own head tucked into his chest to hide his face in order to protect her reputation.

She could feel the ever so slightly uneven gait as he dragged her down the stairs.

Nauseatingly hard, swift heart thuds sent blood ringing in her ears.

Why are you afraid of me? she'd asked him so many years ago. What an unforgivably green girl she'd been. Her taunting of him, her flirtations, her testing, had been because she was afraid of *him*—so much stronger, more certain of himself, was Captain Eversea. So seemingly *impervious* to her.

Her attempts to disarm him had been like so much hissing of a kitten.

She should have known better then. He'd had his limits. They'd both paid the consequences.

She should have known better now.

All she'd done for him, truly, was cause him grief, and between the two of them, they'd nearly shamed each other yet again.

Her extremities were cold with fear despite the sultriness of the night. She couldn't anticipate what he intended to do to her. Hers was a child's temper compared to his.

He'd gotten her through the ball crowd, and they were on the street now, wending through the great diverse clog of hackneys and carriages of all vintages and quality. His gloved fingers were not quite digging into her arm, but still, it was *not* entirely comfortable.

"Where are your lodgings, Mrs. March? Are they close? Did you take a hackney here?"

Why were they going there? Was he merely escorting her home?

Hope and wild relief surged through her.

"Three streets over. Across the square. I've a small—" She was surprised when she heard her voice. A thin, frayed thing.

His anger and tension made it difficult to speak.

"I've a house. Very close."

Chapter 9

The walk was unpleasant, fast and silent.

Gaslight newly installed in the district lit soft patches of cobblestone and left chessboards of darkness and light along the street. His arm was rigid; he was alert as a panther prepared to spring. His gait was only a trifle uneven. She half sensed he would welcome another attack, for at least he could spend some of his anger.

She turned toward the house, got up the stairs, and her hand trembled. She fumbled endlessly with the key, and still his hand remained where it was, gripping her arm.

She got the door open. She turned to him, with a naively hopeful, "Thank you, Captain Eversea. I bid you good—"

He pulled her into the house, closed the door with a certain amount of *feeling.*

And released her elbow at last.

She rubbed at it while he whipped off his coat and hat and arranged them with swift neatness in a stack on the table where her mail and invitations would have collected, had anyone been about to collect mail or invitations for her.

"Why," he said, that soft-smoke voice *far* too reasonable, "the bloody hell are you wearing a pistol strapped to your thigh?"

Something had happened to her lungs. They seemed disconnected from the rest of her body. She couldn't breathe. Then again, she couldn't think or speak, either.

She could hear *his* breathing now, which could not bode well.

"I will ask again: why are you wearing a pistol strapped to your thigh, Mrs. March?"

"I—"

Suddenly he was on his knees before her, and before she could gasp, his hands roughly yanked up her dress. He swiftly looped her garter with a finger and sliced it with a frighteningly sharp knife that seemed to come from nowhere. The silk gave like butter under its blade and came away in his fingers.

He did the same with the other.

The gun fell heavily into his hand.

The tips of his fingers rested where the gun had been, on that satin, vulnerable skin between her legs. He left them there, her dress hiked to just above where her legs made a vee, parted just the width of the gun.

She was terrified, shivering.

And it was all she could do not to open her legs and invite him in, *Oh please*, *please*.

He looked into her face, his hand still hot on her bare thigh. His fingers spread, savoring her skin, tormenting her. Teasing her. Frightening her.

His eyes flared hotly at what he saw in her face. He dropped his eyes, steadying his own breath. And deliberately he slid his fingers down, down, away from her.

Leaving a hot trail over her skin. Snagging briefly in her stockings.

And then he yanked down her dress.

And sat back in a chair.

All done in seconds.

She was speechless.

And he said nothing at all.

A moment passed while they both gathered composure. The breathing in the room seemed unnaturally loud.

The fire was a wan thing, and she wished she could poke it up a bit, but she hesitated to move just yet.

She could not have guessed what passed through his mind in that long stretch of wordlessness. Still, she did know when a tentative peace arrived, when the worst of his anger had ebbed. It was palpable.

"Tea?" she suggested tentatively.

His mouth quirked.

She stood. In the tiny kitchen she filled a kettle and put it on to boil. The maid had left a fire burning low.

When she returned to the sitting room, he was still studying the pistol. "Mathew's," he said.

She found her voice. It emerged subdued. "Yes. It was Mathew's. I intended it for protection."

"Protection." He said this flatly. "Protection." His head came up; he stared at her incredulously. "What if it fired while you were dancing a quadrille, ricocheted off the punch bowl, severed the chain above the chandelier, which then fell and crushed the cream of London society?"

It was certainly one possible scenario.

" 'Cream' is a subjective term, wouldn't you say?"

Two blue marble eyes stared at her.

"I didn't intend to quadrille, as I wasn't precisely invited to the ball."

So she wouldn't be able to charm him this evening. The eyes continued boring into her.

"Weren't you?" he said dryly. "I suppose that means you weren't invited upstairs for brandy and cigars with the gentlemen, then, either."

"What if *your* damned ever-present boot pistol shot off your foot during a vigorous . . . "

Oh, bloody hell.

She was about to say "quadrille," but his quadrille days were likely behind him for good.

Her eyes squeezed closed. When she was a child, she'd had a beautiful Spanish shawl, a bit tattered, handed down from girl to girl in the family by an aunt. She used to pretend its shimmery folds could make her invisible.

She rather longed for that shawl now.

She opened her eyes, as she would need to do that at some time anyway.

He was watching her, and damned if he didn't look amused. " 'Damned'?" he repeated softly.

She felt herself blushing again.

"A vigorous *what*, Mrs. March?" That low voice dragged over her senses like a silk scarf. Unfair. Unfair. "*What* do you imagine I do vigorously, these days?"

He had a talent, a positive diabolical *skill*, for knowing when she was uncomfortable and then fanning her discomfort into something approaching excruciating.

Because now she was picturing precisely what she was certain he would do vigorously and well. She imagined she could still feel five hot places left behind by the press of his fingers on the inside of her thighs.

She imagined the slide of his long, warm fingers inside her. Her skin pulsed as if he were touching it still.

If he hadn't found her pistol, she might have . . . he might have . . . they might have . . .

Well, she might have slept better this evening than she had in years.

She was suddenly terribly afraid of how quickly she'd capitulated, how quickly her sense had surrendered to sensuality. It unnerved her to think that anyone could have that sort of control over her.

He was watching her closely. Eyes as darkly fascinated as though he'd watched everything she'd just imagined take place right before his eyes.

"Should the pistol have accidentally fired, likely it would have killed me before it killed anyone else," she reassured him. An attempt at lightness.

The light instantly abandoned his eyes. "Yes."

Less a word than a hiss issued between clenched teeth. As if a slow child had finally arrived at the proper solution to a problem.

Ah, so it mattered to him whether she inadvertently killed herself.

"But the pistol was locked—"

"I knew that straight away when I touched it, yes." Dryly ironic.

While I was touching you, were the unspoken words.

"I know how to load it, how to fire it, how to shoot *well*, Captain Ev—"

"For God's sake! My hand has been up your—" He shook his head roughly. "You know my name is Chase. Please use it."

Far be it for her to argue a fine point. She'd clearly

demonstrated she wasn't prim enough to object to that sort of informality.

"Very well. Chase. I'm a very good shot. I haven't been sheltered. I'm not . . . *fragile*. I am not so foolish about weapons. I understand what they're for. I thought it unwise to leave home without it, and I needed to put it somewhere. I could hardly put it in my bodice or my reticule. It's quite a seriously good and solid pistol."

"But why bring it at all? Why were you spying on him? Did you intend to threaten him for information? Kinkade? Did you intend to brandish it in the ballroom and make accusations?"

"No! Do you really think I'm that. . . . stupid and reckless?"

Silence.

Oh.

The last time he'd saved her from her own recklessness could have ruined his career; it nearly had. It *had* changed both of their lives forever.

And even now, the pain of that moment, the shame of it, his doubts about her character, and yes, the blame, flickered in his eyes.

A bit of the interesting tension ebbed, and a sense of bittersweet crept in. And she wondered if they ever would mention it, or if it would lie between them forever.

She was chastened.

"I promise you, I would never do anything so rash. I have no wish to do violence to myself, to the cream of London society, or to Mr. Kinkade. My God, Chase. Lucy is at stake. I only wished for a chance to speak to Kinkade, since I've failed to speak to him so far. Since he's *refused* to speak to me so far. My intent in carrying the pistol was to protect myself."

"At a ball? What are you afraid of?" he demanded. "Rosalind?" he said, his voice harder, when she didn't answer him.

It sounded like a warning.

She inhaled and stood, watching him carefully.

She moved over to the humidor and lifted out the two letters. They both smelled faintly of cigar now, which meant they smelled faintly of her former husband. She hesitated to hand them to Chase, because doubtless he would remember it, too.

Ultimately, she did hand them to him.

"I received this one yesterday. It was waiting for me when I returned home from the museum. The first one arrived a week earlier."

He read them, silently.

"They're silly, really," she added quickly. "Quite deliberately ambiguous. I don't know why anyone would think they would frighten me. If someone truly wanted to do *harm* to me, I imagine they would simply go right ahead and harm me."

They of course *had* frightened her, since she'd strapped a pistol to her thigh with garters before she went out in public.

She watched his face. Nothing about his expression reflected that he thought they were silly. It in fact grew stonier the longer he looked at those two short sentences.

Which both assuaged her fear and did not.

"They were written by the same person," he finally said. "The handwriting is masculine, if I had to guess. Same paper used each time."

He rustled it between his fingers. His voice was abstracted. There was a pause.

"Cowards," he said musingly, "who hope to frighten a woman this way, should be shot."

"Hence my pistol."

It was meant to be a jest.

He didn't laugh.

He looked up at her. "I wouldn't, if I were you." A ghost of a mischievous smile. Which faded as their eyes met.

"That one arrived shortly after I began inquiring about Lucy. The other arrived yesterday. They're very noncommittal as threatening letters go, aren't they?"

"In a way that makes them more sinister."

He'd just said aloud what she hadn't wanted to.

And then he was quiet, lost in thought, willing those letters to impart greater meaning to him.

The teakettle began to whistle, which made her jump.

She bustled over to it. The sequence of the familiar task soothed her: she unlocked the caddy and spooned rich-as-turned-earth China black tea into the pot—bone china, delicate but not fussy, a single brilliant red rose painted in the center of it. She poured boiling water over the tea leaves. Watching the lovely fortifying blackness stain the water was meditative; it drew her back to other times she'd shared tea with Chase and her husband in Belgium. A time that, on the surface, seemed more peaceful. But she knew Chase took his tea without sugar or cream; she remembered this still. And she knew this because she'd once silently hoarded the homeliest of details about him as though they were guineas. For that reason, the time in Belgium had, in truth, been as peaceful as a polite stroll over planks lain over lava.

Thankfully, she wasn't that girl anymore.

She arranged the pot and two cups on a tray and carried them to where he sat, apparently still musing, and settled the tea and cups down with a pleasantly domestic *chink* of porcelain on the small table between them.

She poured for them.

Chase looked at the tray. His head swiveled to his cup. But he didn't pick it up. He seemed riveted.

She took a sip of her own tea.

"We ought to marry," he said firmly.

She choked, and tea sprayed everywhere.

She spent the next few seconds coughing inelegantly from shock.

Water poured hotly from her eyes. Chase shifted forward, clearly poised to leap into action should he need to take the precaution of giving her a good thump on the back. His hand came up in preparation for it. She waved a *No, no, I'm quite all right* arm at him.

And she *was* all right after a moment.

After a *long* moment.

Though she needed to sniff, and wipe at her eyes, and she was certain there were blotches all over her face, and she hoped she hadn't stained her borrowed gown.

Silence fell.

He didn't apologize. But why should he? He hadn't known that a proposal would make her choke.

He'd gone unnaturally still. He actually seemed to be waiting for her to reply.

"I . . . well, I suppose I . . . I *beg* your pardon? We ought to . . . marry?"

A hesitation. "Yes."

She stared at him. Something moved in his eyes, something she couldn't quite read. Had he surprised himself?

He held perfectly still.

"Each . . . *other*?" She was thunderstruck.

"Yes."

His inflection—or lack thereof—was maddening. She hadn't the faintest idea what to think, or what he was thinking.

Stupefied silence on her part ensued. Inscrutable silence on *his* part ensued.

Her face began to itch a little; coughing had shaken her coiffure irrevocably loose and tea had glued a few stray hairs to her cheek. She brushed absently at her face.

"Why?"

Another brief hesitation. "I daresay you didn't dislike what happened in Kinkade's library," he began. The unspoken being: *and what happened between us so many years ago.*

Oh. Oh, God. Her face was so lividly hot she wouldn't have been surprised if fragrant steam spiraled from it.

Unthinkably ungentlemanly.

And quite true.

Appallingly, he wasn't finished. Apparently her scarlet face was answer enough to his first question— *no*, she hadn't "disliked" it—*like*, *dislike*, what pallid words from the usually absolute Captain Eversea, and for how she felt about what happened in the library.

"And I shall need to marry at some time."

She stared at him, and suppressed a startled laugh. Only Captain Eversea would issue a proposal as though it was an *order*. A solution to a particular problem. But *which* problem? Was he proposing to her out of a sense of honor—because she'd tempted him into sliding his hands up her thighs and he'd succumbed and would clearly have succumbed to much, much more and would have partaken happily? Out of a need to protect *her* honor? Out of honorably resolving whatever had happened between them in the past?

She said it delicately, as though handing him something aflame: "Chase . . . is this about what happened between us in . . . Belgium?"

"No." Flatly, immediately said. Accompanied by a warning flicker in his eyes and that familiar sensation that she'd run headlong into a wall.

Ah. So they weren't to talk about that, then.

She stared at him. This was a man of absolutes, and there was nothing more absolute than marriage. And he invariably felt the need to make things . . . *right*.

But . . . everything seemed wrong, suddenly. Where to begin?

"What on earth makes you think we'd *suit*, Chase?"

Ah, well. Apparently she wouldn't begin diplomatically.

He did stir a little, restlessly. He took in an audible breath.

"I cannot imagine who could possibly suit me, if 'suiting' you means 'shares my pursuits and temperament.' I'm far too difficult and set in my ways. I'm not certain 'suitability' is grounds enough for marriage anyhow—for how well does anyone truly know anyone they marry? I suspect we should suit in some ways and not in others."

The "some ways" were quite obvious to the two of them.

She was stunned to hear it recited so honestly and baldly. Then again, this was quite like him, too.

She stared at him. He stared back, evenly, that fascinating face maddeningly impossible to read. And even as her sense of romance, such as it was, felt *mortally* wounded, her body, even now, responded: with a prickling in the nipple area, a tingle at the back of her neck, a hum between her legs, as though it were offering up helpful suggestions to her as to where Captain Eversea should touch her next.

She felt a pressure rising in her chest. Incredulous hilarity? An urge to flee?

Swelling disappointment she recognized.

Because with his even-voiced suggestion Captain Eversea was shredding to bits the vestiges of tortured romance that had clung to her memories of him. She'd been denied that sort of thing as a girl; she'd spent sleepless nights wondering whether they ought to buy coal to heat the house or buy a fish for stew, since heating and eating were both luxuries. Poverty and practicality had dictated she marry a wealthy infatuated colonel the instant the offer was made. But it wasn't as though she'd ever truly envisioned a happily-ever-after with Captain Charles Eversea. And yet . . .

She'd *been* wanted before. She'd been worshipped before.

And now she wanted to be loved. And to love in return.

She looked back at this undeniably beautiful man

and found it difficult to associate that soft word—love—with him.

Desire, certainly.

There might be vulnerability in him, there *might* be feeling, rather than simply pride and *want*. But she sensed it was something she'd be forever reaching for in this unyielding man.

Difficult and set in his ways, indeed!

He was still talking.

" . . . and here we are, unmarried and of marriageable age and familiar to each other—"

"*Familiar* to each other?"

He was looking again at the tea. He *had* noticed she'd remembered how he took his.

"—and as I said, I shall need to marry eventually, and I might as well do it now rather than later. There's no reason why you shouldn't marry again. I can protect you from . . . " He lifted the letters and their implied threats. " . . . and from yourself. And I've a reasonable fortune of my own."

And here is where his recitation ended. His case, as he saw it, seemed to have been made.

And once again he assumed an attitude of waiting.

She was dumbstruck.

She flailed in silence for words. Haltingly, they emerged.

"As . . . deeply flattering and romantic as that sentiment is, Chase, and despite what . . . well, what happened earlier this evening, which we *cannot allow* to happen again . . . and as *appealing* as the case you have made for your . . . character . . . it isn't reason enough for us to marry."

A pause.

"Isn't it?"

His voice was odd. She couldn't tell whether he was amused. Or relieved. Or simply curious about what she had to say next.

His eyes had a peculiar glint.

She disliked being unable to read him, and once again it felt as though he had the upper hand, which seemed grossly unfair given that she had just rejected him.

It occurred to her that he expected an answer to what she'd taken as a rhetorical question.

"No. It isn't."

He said nothing. He briefly transferred his gaze to his knees, seemed to find them fascinating for a second or so. Then he returned them to her face, with an attitude of waiting. He seemed to be holding himself very still, unnaturally so. There was something stoic about his posture.

Oh, God. She would rather die than hurt his feelings—*did* he have feelings?—or his formidable pride. She tightened her hands around the teacup. Her knuckles were white.

And as it so happened, his continued silence forced more uncomfortable truths from her.

"And as moving as your . . . proposal? . . . is, I'm not certain I want to marry anyone. It's the truth, I swear to you. I've forgotten how to be coy. I haven't the talent for dramatics, like Lady d'Aligny or . . . the girl in Sussex rumored to have once threatened to cast herself into a well over an argument with a suitor—"

"Violet Redmond," he supplied, surprisingly gently. Everyone had heard that particular story about Violet Redmond.

"Violet Redmond. And I'm not *old*, I know. I'm not precisely on the shelf. I do know I should feel free to marry again. You needn't tell me any of those things, for I'm a grown woman, and a widow. I'm not interested in falling on my sword or martyring myself or anything quite so dramatic and foolish. If I wished to marry you, I would do it."

She was quite finished.

She sat back, clutching her teacup. Very little tea floated in there now among a few stray leaves. If she'd known how to read them, would she have been warned of a marriage proposal and thus not spluttered tea everywhere?

He waited. As if he was very certain she intended to say more.

She waited, because she was certain she'd said all she wanted to say.

As it turned out, he was right.

His silence drew it right out of her. She'd seen him do this to subalterns. He'd always known when there was more to a story. There really was no defense against Captain Eversea when he was deciding to be patient. His patience, in its rarity, was in some ways more potent than his impatience.

"It's just . . . I have never been allowed to decide what *I* want. I've only ever done what I've needed to do to ensure my sisters and I are cared for—food and shelter and whatnot. I've only responded to needs of the moment without a thought beyond that. And though I know I am not unlike *other* women in this regard, I might very well be unlike other women of your acquaintance. And now . . . now I've an income from my late husband, modest though it may be. I come and go as I please. I was grateful to Mathew and I loved him for the kind person he was, for his strength of character. I find I am in a position now to determine what *I* want. And I don't know what or who that might be."

The confession left her feeling awkward and exposed.

Not because she was ashamed of it, but because it was the first time she'd ever said anything of the sort aloud. It was like trying a new language, worrying about pronouncing the words correctly. She half resented him for forcing her to make it.

Odd what the man could accomplish by simply being silent.

"So I must decline your proposal. Though I thank you for your . . . gallantry? . . . in issuing it."

"You're welcome," he said immediately. The reflexive manners of the Everseas.

His eyes were fixed on her face, but his thoughts were somewhere else altogether. On *her*, but not on this moment. His face was abstracted. He didn't look crushed, in truth. He didn't appear to even be listening to her.

She began to feel a bit irritated. "You needn't look so relieved."

"Do I look relieved?" He sounded surprised.

"A little."

But relieved wasn't the proper way to describe how he looked. It was rather a mix of things, and she couldn't have deciphered one from the other. Undaunted was definitely one of them. Surprised might have been another one.

And not precisely crushed was another of them.

She wondered fleetingly if he'd surprised *himself*.

But he wasn't a rash man or a reckless man. He wasn't his brother, serenading countesses or plummeting from trellises or whatever the broadsheets said he had done. She'd known Chase to more than once make decisions, difficult ones, brave ones, *right* ones, in a dangerous heartbeat. Which made this all the more puzzling.

She returned his steady gaze.

Like sunlight bouncing off a quiet lake: such an *unfair* blue, those eyes. Her heart squeezed with the pleasure, the struggle, of simply looking into them.

"I'm off to India in two weeks," he said conversationally.

She gave a start.

"To serve there as an officer with East India Company. It's what I do best, I suppose—serving my country. It's what I was made for. I sail on *The Courage*."

He'd be gone again. As quickly as he'd returned to her life. She knew a swooping moment of regret.

Followed by an acceptance that bordered on profound relief.

"Well," she said gently, "I don't want to go to India."

He nodded curtly. "I suppose that settles it."

As if everything she'd just said *hadn't* settled it.

He glanced down at the tea, frowning a little, as if deciding whether he wanted any. He didn't reach for it.

Speaking of settling, a choking silence settled like dust. When it became well nigh unendurable, she gave a short laugh to disturb it. It was meant to sound casual and balm over the hideous awkwardness, but it did the opposite.

She'd underestimated him, however. Despite the awkwardness, when he spoke next, his voice was natural. And naturally he issued a command.

"I cannot allow you to run about with a pistol strapped to your thigh."

She almost bristled at the "allow."

But she reminded herself that it was how he spoke, and how he felt things: he was all duty and commands and protection and right and wrong. Whether it had to do with how he felt about *her* or with his sense of responsibility mattered little at the moment.

All that mattered was Lucy.

"I am not so foolish as to decline an offer of assistance or protection, Chase, should you choose to extend one. I do value my life. If someone wishes me harm, I should feel safer with you keeping a watch. I should be grateful for your help. I should like to see my nephew grow up. I should like to see Lucy again. I couldn't *bear* it if I couldn't see Lucy again."

He was quiet. What was going on in that mind? Ought she to ask? She suspected she didn't really want to know.

"Your nephew is nearly a year old now?" he asked.

"Yes," she said, startled.

"He has a tooth?"

He'd remembered.

His eyes crinkled a little at her surprise. Not quite a smile, but close. Just when she'd thought he hadn't listened to her at all. All of these little surprises were wreaking havoc with her already precarious equilibrium.

"Will you speak to Kinkade for me?"

Chase sighed. "He's a busy man, Rosalind, and he's hiding naught from you. He answered you as best he knows. Imagine your question, your inquiry about your sister, multiplied by a thousand, and you'll know what he sees every day. One heartfelt petition begins to look like another. Hundreds if not thousands of crimes large and small are committed in London every month."

"But not by *my* sister." She said this with quiet defiance. "Whether or not she did could very well be beside the point."

They both knew this.

The entire government was *fueled* by the connections between people. People lived and died, prospered or declined, rose or fell, all based on the webbings of relationships between them. She'd been the wife of a respected colonel, but he was dead now, and she had only a modest income and no family connections of her own.

She fully intended to use the only real one she had: Chase.

"And frankly, Chase . . . I don't know whether this scandalizes you or not . . . I don't care whether she did steal it. I will deal with Lucy when I find her."

He was thinking. Tapping one hand rhythmically against the arm of his chair.

"He'll do it for you, Chase. He'll exert more effort to find her. For you, if not for me."

"Tell me, Rosalind," he said suddenly. "Who arrested her?"

"A Charley in Covent Garden. The shop where Lucy . . . *tried* the bracelet is in Covent Garden. I believe she was there to meet friends to go to the theater, but I don't know why she was alone. She should not have been."

The unspoken words were: *and I should have been with her.*

"She's a grown woman, Rosalind. As much as we want to protect our siblings, they *will* do things that get them thrown in Newgate."

Dry humor from the man whose brother had been rather a national sensation as a result of what *he'd* allegedly done. Chase knew firsthand what the inside of the prison looked like.

"And the Charley turned Lucy over to the magistrate?" he asked.

"And then apparently she went from there to prison, because that's where I next saw her."

Tap . . . tap . . . tap went his hand. Like a metronome for the torrent of his thoughts.

And finally he breathed in, then exhaled at length, and nodded.

"Very well. I'll call on Kinkade about Lucy tomorrow. But you *cannot* come with me. I'd like to obtain *unvarnished* truth, and he'll only give that to me, not to you. I will call on you the moment I know anything at all. And you may count on me for protection and assistance—as you call it—until I depart for India."

His way of issuing commands generally inspired her to rebel.

"Thank you," she said instead, all quiet dignity. "You have my deepest gratitude."

And my shredded garters.

There they were, limply surrendered, in his fist. She glanced at them.

He followed the direction of her glance. And instead of returning them to her, he quite deliberately put them in his pocket. Like a trophy, she thought.

"You may learn things about your sister you don't wish to know."

"I am usually difficult to surprise. I shall rely upon your inimitable discretion and powers of interrogation."

"Wise of you," he confirmed.

He stood suddenly, launching himself to his feet with a press of his hand on the shining gold stallion head atop his walking stick.

She stood, too, smoothing down the skirts of her dress, surreptitiously studying them for any signs of spluttered tea. She brushed a few hairs away from her cheek, where they clung, glued by tea splashes. She wondered if she had any tea in her eyelashes.

"Difficult to surprise," indeed. It was a lie, given how thoroughly he'd just surprised her. She'd reached for words in that moment, any words, like a shipwreck survivor scrambled for flotsam.

Desiring someone—and oh how she found she desired this particular someone—and surrendering the rest of her life to someone were two entirely different things.

She was afraid to do either of those things, truthfully. It was so much easier to do neither of them.

She was glad that he would be leaving for India.

He placed his hat upon his head and turned again. Eyes unreadable above the snowy fluff of his cravat. Mouth an even line. Demeanor more peaceful than she would have preferred given that she'd declined his proposal of marriage. Skin shining from his ruthlessly fresh shave. Entirely self-possessed and trustworthy and solid. He looked down at her for a moment, thoughtfully, and she thought he might say something about his rejection, and prayed that he wouldn't, because the awkwardness was so newly papered over with conversation.

But he surprised her again: he delicately looped a finger through a strand of her hair clinging to her lips from the spluttered tea, a hair that she'd missed, clearly.

She stared up at him, then was held fast by that blue field of his eyes as he drew the hair gently, slowly, across and away from her lips.

And somehow this was enough to light, one by one, very rapidly, every cell in her body until she felt as softly, brilliantly ablaze as that chandelier in the Callender's ballroom. He drew the hair through his thumb and forefinger, the whole length of it, and carefully, reverently, placed it back where it belonged with the others framing her face.

Looked at it a moment, as if to ensure it stayed where it belonged.

Smiled with just one corner of his mouth.

He'd only touched her *hair*.

And suddenly she couldn't breathe for wanting him.

"I shall endeavor to endure my disappointment, Rosalind," he said softly.

She wished she knew whether the amused irony in his voice was for her or for himself.

And with a bow, he was gone.

Chapter 10

C hase slept very badly. Pain lightninged through his leg at intervals all night, and thoughts and plans paraded endlessly through his head like soldiers heading into battle.

He woke feeling as though he'd survived a debauch but without the pleasant memories to go with it.

A moment passed before his memory ran in parallel with consciousness. And when it did, he lay heavily, feeling freshly killed. Eerily very much the same as he had so many years ago after he'd kissed Rosalind March.

Rosalind March had been born, he decided with grim humor, for the express purpose of humbling him.

Then again, every time he'd felt freshly killed, he managed somehow to get back on the battlefield.

He was inclined to blame Colin again. When his brother had urged, *You ought to marry, Chase!* somehow he had never considered the possibility that he'd be soundly rejected once he decided that, yes indeed, he *ought* to. Colin made it sound as though it was something anyone could do: "You ought to go to Brighton!" That sort of thing.

Why in God's name *had* he proposed last night? He

would never ascribe it to impulse: impulsive was the last thing he was; all of his decisions were reasoned. But then again, his reasoning was always swift and informed by instinct, and he was invariably *right* . . . and invariably obeyed.

Which was why he was quite surprised when he'd been rejected.

Last night's proposal could only have been his way of responding to instinct, but he didn't know what this particular instinct was in service *of*. Solving the problem of saving Rosalind from herself? Resolving guilt surrounding an indiscretion that had haunted him for years? Or ensuring that she would be in his bed forever?

None of those things alone seemed quite right.

He sighed. She wanted to determine what *she* wanted.

It seemed a thoroughly reasonable thing to want.

Since in that moment he'd only, in truth, considered what *he* wanted. And why shouldn't she want it, too? Again: he was generally so *right*.

And then listening to her, perversely, he wanted desperately for her to have whatever she wanted.

Which might not, of course, be him.

Which was not at all what *he* wanted.

Though her *body* seemed fairly certain it wanted him. And this could very well be the key to convincing her that he was what she wanted after all.

His body was quite, quite certain it wanted her. More than it wanted its next breath.

Above all he wanted her to be safe and happy forever.

Which struck him as an extraordinarily selfless thing

to want, and quite surprising, since it might very well mean he wouldn't get what he wanted, and he generally did get what he wanted, because he made certain of it.

And thus he awakened with a hangover comprised of frustrated logic, thwarted lust, and a lingering disbelief that he'd issued a *marriage proposal,* for God's sake.

But as promised, he'd sent word to Kinkade late last night asking if he might call upon him in the morning, because this was apparently what she truly wanted from him.

Kinkade had sent word back to him promptly— Kinkade always kept absurd hours—directing him to a pub on the outskirts of Covent Garden. Doubtless Kinkade intended to spend a day with an actress lodged above it, which would mean that all he had to do was tumble downstairs for a bit.

Chase's head throbbed with contradictions and complexity and difficulty. These were, of course, his favorite things.

Perversely, despite the disappointment and frustration, he had hadn't felt more charged with purpose in years, and he went downstairs so early and sober that he startled the maids.

At breakfast he found a reply from his efficient sister Genevieve, apparently delivered by a frantic messenger.

Dear Chase,

Thank you for your typically effusive letter. Urgency a bit alarming, but only to me, as Mama is accustomed to alarming things from the men in

the family. V. pleased to discover edifying your-
self with art. The painting does sound hideous. I
have never in my life heard of Rubinetto and do
not recall this particular painting being a part
of the Montmorency collection, although they
possess other respectable pictures. Please ask
someone to translate his name into English for
you, as I blush to do it in this letter. Do you al-
ready know? Are you teasing me? Is our cousin
the vicar handsome? This is very important. Do
not come home until you know.

Much love, your sister,
Genevieve

Despite the fact that he'd been *banished*, Chase
smiled.

Of his sisters, Olivia was fiery and Genevieve gentle,
but he sometimes suspected the fiery ones suffered the
most, and that the gentle ones merely needed just the
right gust of wind from life to become fiery. He worried about both of them.

Rubinetto, he knew, meant "cock."

He poured nearly an urn of coffee down his gullet
and finally got out the door.

He'd thought the fresh air would enliven his mind
and spirits, but the air was as dense as a sweaty blanket,
which did nothing for his mood. His clothing would
likely be glued to him by the time he reached Kinkade,
and he wished he'd thought to bring a fresh shirt to
change into before he called upon Rosalind.

He wanted to throw off the entire *world* like a sweaty
blanket.

Still, he walked. Swiftly, scarcely limping at all.

But his Covent Garden destination took him once again past the ragged square outside the Montmorency Museum, where the day became much, much worse:

Because a puppet theater was erected in the square.

He slowed, as one would, should one encounter a carriage accident with bodies strewn everywhere.

Punch wasn't just having a go at Judy. As luck would have it, this was a more elaborate affair. On a stage, two marionettes were engaged in a spastic dance—their arms somehow linked, their legs kicking somewhat in unison, which he supposed indicated a talented puppeteer, otherwise they would have ended in a knotted heap of rattling limbs on the stage, but which didn't matter in the least to him. That anyone would *wish* to be a puppeteer astounded him.

He suppressed a primal shudder and began to turn to go back the way he'd come.

But then, by God, if he didn't hear, in a pair of horrible puppety falsetto voices:

> *"And if you thought you'd never see*
> *The end of Colin Eversea*
> *Well come along with me, lads,*
> *come along you'll see*
> *The pretty lad is mighty glad*
> *That you were right—he's free!*
> *Everybody!*
> *Oh, if you thought you'd never see—"*

Obediently, *everybody* did indeed launch into song.

Chase struggled not to clap his hands over his ears. He did pull his hat down a little more snugly.

For *God's* sake. It never, never ended.

Granted, it was an insidiously infectious tune. While Colin was in prison and his release had seemed likely, Chase and his brothers had invented their own verses, mostly concerning his sexual prowess, his body odor, his intelligence. Things of that sort. He imagined performers throughout England found it a pity to waste a perfectly good melody simply because Colin hadn't been hung by the neck until dead after all, as scheduled, and had carried on writing verses.

Chase wondered, in a moment of flailing horror, whether there would be numerous new iterations as Colin grew older.

He could think of one now:

> *If you thought you'd never see*
> *The glamorous Colin Eversea*
> *Up to his shoulder in a cow—*
> *Come along with me, boys! Come*
> *   along with me!*

The crowd cheered and clapped their approval of the song, and the marionettes bowed and curtsied in their revolting loose-jointed way, batting wooden-lidded eyes, sweeping wooden arms across their wooden tums in bows.

He stopped short of stampeding away through the crowd; he did take two determined steps through it, hoping his height and breadth would inspire people to part for him. A hat had appeared and seemed to be traveling through hands, no doubt initiated from behind the puppet stage, and the clink of coins cheerfully volunteered joined mingled laughter and cheers.

People snugly wedged him.

He eyed the crowd like a battlefield to assess the best way to clear a path, and was contemplating bringing his walking stick down on the instep of the man next to him by way of beginning when the puppety voices began squeaking out another song.

It felt as though they were dragging their puppety claw fingers down his spine.

He tossed a glance over his shoulder, unable to resist it. And discovered the song came with a gay little dance, more like a reel this time. Two puppets were approaching and retreating from each other on the stage.

> *"High diddle diddle*
> *The cat and the fiddle*
> *The cow jumped over the moon*
> *The little dog laughed to see such a sight*
> *And the dish ran away with the spoon."*

That silly child's rhyme about intrigue in old Queen Bess's court? The masses certainly *could* be cheaply entertained.

He tried again to move. He was still solidly wedged. He turned his shoulder, thinking he might begin to sidle, but the bulk of a gentleman seemed to magically spill into the space he'd created.

A crescent moon, painted gold, suddenly dropped down over the stage, twisting on its wire, shining like a curved blade in the sun. Five silver stars followed—*bounce, bounce, bounce, bounce, bounce*—and then came the inevitable cow. This was a marionette, a big, bulky, soft-looking animal, and it was to jump over the crescent moon by whomever was jerking its strings.

Chase was desperate to get away before a puppety dish and spoon joined the party.

With an effort of will he squeezed between two large women and a round man in a blue coat who were rooted like trees by the show and oblivious to the one person in the crowd pointing away from the stage. It was unworthy of him, but did it: he brought the stick down—lightly, but warningly—inside the boot of a man standing there. The man shifted a very little.

And in this rugged fashion—wending, elbowing, employing his walking stick—he managed to reach the outskirts of the crowd when a second verse started up:

> *"High diddle diddle*
> *The cow's in the middle*
> *And the angel's playing a tune*
> *All the lords laugh*
> *At the gels on their backs*
> *All underneath the half-moon."*

Chase froze.

Very reluctantly, very slowly, he rotated back toward the puppet theater. The hair at the back of his neck prickled alertly. He pulled his hat farther down over his eyes to shield them from the sun and stared at the stage.

The rest of the crowd was smiling and clapping, delighted by this new verse.

The clapping finally died away and the clustered audience dispersed, trailing away one by one or in happy, cheaply entertained pairs, still laughing, some still singing.

At last just he and marionettes remained in the square.

He could clearly see the little puppet theater again from his distance of about fifteen feet.

The puppets remained on the stage, side by side as if in peculiar puppety solidarity against this solitary large and mortal human made of meat and bone gazing at them. Apart from a breeze that lifted the edge of the female puppet's frock, they were entirely motionless, which meant they were being *held* motionless through the will of someone holding their strings—otherwise the breeze would have swayed their fragile limbs, too, and they would have dangled in a grisly way, like freshly hung felons. Behind those clunky wooden lids edged in bristly little lashes, two pairs of large, flat turquoise eyes . . .

Stared at him.

He studied the puppets, taking in the details to keep his flesh from crawling. The male puppet had a nose as formidable as an oar. Not quite the crescent moon that Punch's chin and nose created as they curved up and down to meet each other; still, quite phallic, and quite a deliberate deformity. Not at all amusing, as far as he was concerned. Their complexions were smooth, with a matte luminosity, carved and polished in an exaggerated parody of human features—long chins, huge eyes. Their faces were painted in brilliant colors: bulbous crimson cheeks and huge, pouting crimson lips, enormous turquoise eyes, each with a black pupil square center. The female puppet's bright yellow hair was fashioned of something fine, perhaps silk thread, and wound up on her head in a style that his sister Genevieve would have approved of and would never have been able to achieve on her own.

Neither of the puppets blinked.

For a good thirty seconds Chase stared them down as though they were enemy spies. The peculiar prickling sensation at the back of his neck amplified. As if bristly little marionette eyelashes brushed against it.

Brrrrr.

He whirled on his heels and crunched off over the cobblestones the way he had come, thumping down his walking stick. He thought he could feel their wooden gaze on the back of his neck.

The cow's in the middle.

Just a bastardization of a nursery rhyme, surely. But he hadn't any children, and he could not be expected to know the current verses.

Cows are *whimsical*, he told himself. And ubiquitous. The cow had jumped over the moon, after all, in the first verse, a verse everyone knew. Unsurprising that it should do things in the second verse as well.

The angel's playing her tune.

And angels . . .

Well, angels were simply everywhere and in everything, too. Fireplace carvings, cornices, hymns, altar cloths, stained glass windows.

Paintings. Brothels.

Underneath a half-moon.

There was indeed a half-moon in that painting.

All of those things were in that hideous painting at the Montmorency Museum. The one allegedly donated by Kinkade. The one Rosalind was fascinated by.

All the lords laugh at the gels on their backs.

The image struck him as sinister, though this could

have everything to do with the fact that it was sung by puppets.

The crowd clearly didn't see it that way. But they weren't viewing it through *his* particular lens.

Chase drew even with a portly man, who was buffing an apple against the front of a grayish shirt as he walked. He recognized him from the puppet crowd. The man stopped and slowly, deliberately, opened his jaws to guillotine the apple. Chase said, "They're quite good, aren't they?"

The man clapped his jaws shut with a start and looked up to find the tall Captain Eversea gazing down. He grinned disarmingly. Not the usual response to him, Chase reflected, but perhaps the puppets had put the man in a good mood.

The man jerked his thumb behind him, but declined to turn his head back toward the theater. "Them puppets? Dead right! Funny, ain't they! D'yer 'ear the bit about Colin Eversea?" The man inhaled ominously— Chase reared back in preparation—and then came out with bellowing joyfulness: "*Oh*, if ye thought ye'd *nivver* see—"

"I. Heard. It!"

The man blinked in astonishment.

Chase cleared his throat; he hadn't meant to bark. "That is, *yes*, I heard it," he hurriedly added with what he hoped was convincing cheeriness, " 'La la la, everybody *sing*!' I in fact stopped to watch the puppets because I heard the song. One of my favorite tunes."

He was struck by the fact of this: he *had* stopped because of the song.

He had the sense he should squirrel the thought away and examine it in privacy.

Or perhaps Rosalind was affecting his powers of reasoning.

"Was there for 'is 'angin, Mr. Eversea's. They did a whole show fer it, the puppet theater did, 'ad a little puppet scaffold, wi' a wee noose danglin'—"

"Very skillful, indeed," Chase interjected hurriedly. A song commemorating the event was one thing; he found a pantomime of Colin's near-hanging a trifle less whimsical. "I'm sorry to have missed it. Do they sing Colin Eversea's song very often? The puppets?"

"Nivver 'eard 'em sing that particular song before today. 'E's free now, Mr. Eversea is, wasna guilty a'tall! Imagine that. Wonder what 'e's about now?"

"I wonder, too. Do you, sir, know anything about the puppeteers?"

The man's shoulders heaved up and down in a shrug, and as if he could wait no longer, his hand catapulted toward his mouth and he cleaved the apple in half. His next sentence was muffled by masticated fruit. A fine spray of juice accompanied his words, drizzling over Chase like a Sussex fog.

"Nah. I dinna know. I jus' watch, and gi' a penny when I'm able. They pass the 'at around a' the end, like." He held the remaining half of apple out to Chase with an eyebrow arched in question. Chase demurred with a slight shake of the head. The man shrugged again, just one shoulder this time, and, to Chase's relief, swallowed.

"Are they here often, then? The puppeteers?"

"Two, three days o' th' week when the weather is fine." He beamed approvingly up at the sun beaming agreeably down upon them.

Helpful information. "Thank you, sir."

"It's Martin, and perhaps I'll see ye again."

"I'm . . . Mr. Charles. I'll be here tomorrow, if the weather is fine."

"Splendid!" Mr. Martin was pleased to meet a fellow marionette admirer, and they parted with an exchange of civil bows, Martin jauntily whistling the tune about Chase's brother, and Chase knew he was doomed to hear it in his head all day.

Colin would have been immensely amused.

Martin paused to click the heels of his big boots before heading cheerfully into the Mumford Arms, just as someone else was being heaved out of it. Someone who, from the way he rotated like a lopsided wagon wheel on his two feet, arms windmilling gracelessly before he landed on the ground, had been in there all morning.

Chase took one final look over his shoulder.

All traces of the puppet theater were gone, and the square was empty apart from a black cat slinking alongside one of the weathered buildings, weaving in and out of rain barrels as if for the sheer pleasure of being thin enough to do it.

Chapter 11

The Final Curtain was an ominous name for a pub, Chase thought, but as long as they served strong drinks they could have called it the Devil's Arse for all he cared. It was clearly filled with ambitious actresses and opera dancers and men with cash to spend upon them. They could have easily eliminated half of the chairs; the women, it seemed, preferred to sit on the laps of men.

Kinkade was standing in the rear near an empty table, as though guarding it. Perhaps in deference to the fact that he hadn't reminisced with Chase in a good year or so, he hadn't an actress in his lap. Chase was quite, quite touched.

"Injure your leg dancing again, Eversea?" Kinkade said by way of greeting, when he saw Chase threading over to him.

"Injure your mirror by looking into it, Kinkade?"

And thus the bonds of affection were re-established to the happy satisfaction of both men.

"Here." Kinkade kicked out a chair for Chase to settle into.

The pleasures of whatever had happened the night before showed in the shadows and sagging skin beneath Kinkade's eyes and his gray face. He no doubt had enjoyed a *proper* debauch last night. Which was a contradiction in terms, Chase supposed. Nevertheless.

Chase took the chair while Kinkade remained standing, because his scars from the war were on his back, and sitting too long made him uncomfortable.

He'd always thought he looked more appealing to the ladies when he stood, anyway.

"How was your assignation, Eversea?"

"Surprisingly satisfying." Not entirely a lie.

"Are you going to share the name of this woman?"

"I don't intend to share her at all," he said cryptically. This, he suspected, wasn't entirely a lie, either. He patted the table loudly; a barmaid who seemed made of more bosom than anything else wended her way over to them.

"Ale, luv," he decided. "The dark."

He knew a brief yearning for the magical stuff on tap at the Pig & Thistle. Perhaps the Final Curtain had something drinkable.

Kinkade was disdainfully sniffing a cigar. "Foul thing. Gift from a friend, but now I suspect it was more of a fobbing off than a thoughtful act. Reminds me of Colonel March. Remember that foul blend of tobacco he insisted on smoking? A singularly acquired taste. You could smell the man from across a room."

Chase remembered too clearly. "I remember. I couldn't persuade him to any other kind, though. Quite set in his ways, March was. A good man."

Such a pointless platitude. Then again, platitudes were an effective way to keep residual guilt at bay and to prevent the man in question from entering the conversation.

"Speaking of those days," Chase continued smoothly. "Kinkade, I heard about Lucy Locke. Is it true she was arrested? An unfortunate incident involving a bracelet? I imagined you'd know something about it, given your position in the Home Secretary's office."

Kinkade was lighting his cigar, his back to him. Still lean despite his rigorous lifestyle of drinking and eating to excess, clothes tailored nearly to a skin fit. The look of a rake, but he was closing in on too old to be a rake and in a year or so his dignity would suffer for it. With surprise, Chase saw that his friend's hair was thinning; he could see pale scalp through the blond.

Kinkade turned around. His face was pensive. He blew out the smoke.

"Shame, that. Naught I could do."

"Truly?"

"Well, the fact is, old man, Lucy Locke has stolen at least once before, and I saw her do it. She begged me not to say a word. Deuced awkward, too, given that she stole from the hostess of a party we were attending."

Chilling news. "What did she steal?"

"'Twas but a bauble. She'd secured an invitation to a party at the Burkes'—Washington Square, you know the place. Large party. Lucy was being taken about the ton by Delilah Moreton, who likes to surround herself with girls as pretty as she is regardless of whether they possess brains. An aesthetic thing, I suppose. Found Lucy in Lady Burke's chambers palming something from her night table. Turned out to be a comb." Kinkade pointed to his own hair, as though this needed further illustration.

"The thing you won't be needing to use in a year or so."

"Oh, well played, old man!" Kinkade was delighted. "Virile! 'Tis *virile* I am. The balder atop, the harder and longer lasting below. Proven fact. *This* comb was the sort ladies use to hold up their hair, like. An expensive furbelow. Ivory."

"What were *you* doing in Lady Burke's chambers?"

Chase was acquainted with Lady Burke. Occasionally she forgot to shave the hair from the mole on the side of her chin, and it seemed to sprout seasonally, like wheat. Other than that, she was quite attractive in a sparse way, and an acerbic and informed conversationalist, which made the hairy mole all that more startling.

Kinkade hesitated.

"Might have been I was looking for Lucy," he confessed. "Juicy gel, that, and you can't deny it, Eversea. I defy you to. After the dinner, I saw Lucy gliding up the stairs, trying to be sneaky about it. I'd had a bit to drink, you see. More than a bit. Saw her go up and seconds later I confess to succumbing to impulses ungentlemanly and followed her. Thought I'd . . . oh, steal a kiss. Get in a bit of intimate conversation, as they say."

"How *very* unlike you." Chase's ale arrived. He slid money into the barmaid's palm and she winked at him.

"Isn't it!" Kinkade was in full, astonished, mocking agreement. "I generally confine my animal impulses to . . . places one should confine such impulses."

"Admirably constructed sentence."

"Thank you."

"Had she gone upstairs to steal?" Lucy Locke was a bit of a featherbrain, but he'd never thought of her as larcenous. He tasted his ale and winced. Dreadful stuff.

"Couldn't be certain. I think she was having a look around. She's a mushroom, no other way to say it, always wanted to see how the trees lived. We all saw it, poor gel. If not for her face, she would never have been invited to places, and she hadn't the wit to parlay her looks tactically. Unlike her older sister, who bagged a colonel and charmed a regiment and kept us all in line while we were at it, didn't she? When Lucy saw the comb, doubtless she couldn't resist it, as she never could have afforded it, and she could be one up on the rich gal. 'Twas small enough to tuck into her bodice, and that's where she put it. But I suspect she had the habit on her, I think—stealing. A bit of a problem, when one isn't an aristocrat." Dryly said. "If you get caught, that is. And she had gambling debt, too. Mayhap she was looking for something to pawn."

Chase didn't relish telling any of this to Rosalind.

"What did you do?"

"I told her to put it back, and she bought my silence by allowing me to retrieve it from her bodice. She'd had it well and truly tucked in there, too. Took my time about it."

Was Kinkade serious? "Your suggestion or hers?"

"Do I detect a whiff of righteousness, Eversea?" Kinkade gave a sniff.

"That stink is your cigar, Kinkade."

"Of course. Well, it was my suggestion, of course. I'm not a fool, I think on my feet, and she was too frightened to think at all."

Kinkade sounded a little too pleased with himself.

Something unfamiliar crawled along Chase's spine,

a sensation subtle and new and difficult to identify. The idea of a frightened Lucy Locke, featherbrained as she might be, allowing Kinkade to root around in her bodice, wasn't playful. It was repellant. It smacked of a casual abuse of power, rather than flirtation.

Chase wondered if he was getting old.

He tasted his ale again. It was still awful. "Do you know where Lucy is? Mrs. Rosalind March tells me that she's gone missing, of all things. Can't imagine it would be easy to get out of Newgate without anyone *noticing*."

"It's a wonder she went to Newgate at all, old man. If she was there—well, they've no record of it. I've asked, I assure you. I can't find anyone who claims to have seen her there."

This was unexpected.

"But Mrs. March says she visited her sister in prison. And an unpleasant visit it was."

"So her letters to me have said. No one has a pleasant visit with anyone in Newgate. But Eversea, there are hundreds, thousands, of felons to track. Many of them are women. When prisoners die they're shoved under with quicklime at Newgate right quick. The place reeks of it. Well, you've spent a little time in the godforsaken place, thanks to Colin, so you know. She might have been recorded under a wrong name. She may have been moved by mistake. She might have been inadvertently transported—a ship sailed to Botany Bay only two days ago. And then there are the hulks. There are actually women kept in some of them, awaiting transportation. Such are the prisons now. Mistakes have been made before, though it's miraculous that we make them as seldom as we do.

It's unfortunate, I grant you, but then again, so is rampant crime."

Somehow he was hearing this as through Rosalind's ears, and it struck him as shockingly callous. If someone had spoken so *rationally* about the disappearance of one of his sisters, he would likely be choked with fury. He did understand Kinkade's point of view.

Nevertheless.

"But Lucy Locke is your friend, Kinkade," he said evenly.

A moment of silence. Kinkade's silvery eyes regarded him levelly. "Define 'friend,' Eversea."

It was lightly said. But a tense ambiguity swam beneath the words. Chase disliked it, because in his experience, *nothing* about Kinkade was subtle.

"All right. She was an acquaintance, then."

"I've many of those, and many are pretty, but she's the only one ever arrested for theft, a simple fact. I cannot lay claim to any strong feelings of loyalty, and I *did* make inquiries about her whereabouts, but beyond that I don't know how I can help Lucy. How on earth did you hear about Lucy from Mrs. March anyhow?"

"Quite by accident my path crossed with Mrs. Rosalind March here in London and I inquired after the health of her sisters."

It wasn't a lie.

Kinkade was quiet for a moment. "What of the other sister?"

"Has a husband and a baby."

"Felicitations to her," Kinkade said absently.

Kinkade gave his cigar a prurient suck, as if hoping it would taste better the more he smoked it.

"Is she still something to look at?" he asked thoughtfully after a moment. "Mrs. March?"

"She is no gargoyle." Chase wanted to protect Rosalind, to keep her from conversation.

"Rosalind March . . . " Kinkade mused. "Do you remember how we were all in love with her?"

"No," Chase said flatly.

"I suppose you couldn't see her quite that way—the way the rest of us saw her—as you were quite tight with the colonel. A dear friend of his family, and all that."

Chase again thought he detected irony. But then, he was hearing the words through the filter of his own conscience.

"Let me remind you, Chase. She was a vision. Beautiful thing. Young, a corker, so lively. Lucky old dog, Mathew, rest his soul. Odd, we saw a good deal of the top of her breasts in those dresses, but I always wondered about her legs most of all. Had a birthmark"—Kinkade gestured to his collarbone—"here. I loved her voice. Used to love to hear her laugh. Was like hope, like spring thaw, that laugh."

"Positively Byronic of you, Kinkade. My heart sighs."

"I cannot tell you the number of times I imagined her tits."

He knew he was supposed to laugh, but his back teeth ground together as he beat back a surge of something black and ferocious. And he was uncomfortable with the fact that he was suddenly uncomfortable with Kinkade, who was simply being precisely who he was and who he always had been, and yes, Rosalind March's tits were worthy of any man's fantasies.

He settled for smiling a smile he knew didn't reach

his eyes, and he was certain Kinkade noticed. Chase shifted in his hair, accommodating a twinge in his leg, and hoped his friend would ascribe any tension to that.

"Did you draw them?" he tried.

"Them" being the tits.

"In my mind, ever night, after every ball. But I never got around to recording my imaginings in charcoal for posterity, if that's what you're wondering. Nor did I save any of my other pictures."

"Fear not, Kinkade. I don't need to look at pictures when the Velvet Glove is but a wish away. By the way, the Duchess sends her regards."

"Did she? How kind of her." *Puff puff* went Kinkade on the cigar.

And then Kinkade swallowed the remainder of what seemed to be his third ale of the day, and winced.

"Pig piss," Chase commiserated. "Marie-Claude is pouting for you, apparently. At the Velvet Glove."

"Marie-Claude pouts for effect. Her heart isn't broken, and I suppose I regret if her purse is growing slimmer. But one grows tired of the same thing day after day, doesn't one? Covent Garden, brothels, gaming hells, horse races. One needs *variety*. Originality. To make life worth living. One must ever seek out new ways to not die of boredom."

Interesting sentiment from a man who hadn't seemed to change at all since the moment he'd met him, apart from the fraying head of hair.

"I suppose it's why I'm going to India," Chase said. "With the East India Company."

"I heard you'd planned to do that. You call *that* variety, Eversea? Shackled to the army. Shackled to a woman," Kinkade made a *tsssking* sound. "Why is it so many of our gender seem to need to be *shackled* to something? You're a *gentleman*, Eversea." He sounded indignant. He spread his arms wide, which was meant, Chase supposed, to remind him that the world was his oyster, his birthright.

"Structure, belonging, purpose, brotherhood, travel, excitement," Chase said. "A test of what you can endure. Honor," he told Kinkade, ironically amused. "Those are reasons."

"I'd frankly rather know how much pleasure I can endure, rather than how much sleeping near farting soldiers in the mud I can endure."

"You were the worst offender, if I recall correctly."

"You recall correctly," Kinkade said solemnly.

"You were a good soldier, Kinkade."

"Motivated by interest in survival."

"Not just."

Kinkade seemed to consider this. At a table near them, a woman shrieked and slapped without conviction at a hand creeping up her dress, and the man belonging to the hand laughed and laughed.

Then Kinkade gave a short nod. "Very well, then. Not just." He inhaled, with what sounded like impatience or discomfort. He contended with his own old wounds, less grave than Chase's, but the scars on his back made standing or sitting for long periods of time difficult. He took a seat, turned it backward, straddled it.

"Some men are made by the army, Kinkade."

"And some are destroyed by it. And one might substitute 'women' for 'army' in that sentence and it would just as easily be true."

He had the distinct sensation that Kinkade was . . .
not precisely taunting him, but definitely, deliberately,
touching on sensitive places. Testing him?

Although he might very well, once again, be confusing his own conscience with Kinkade's conversation. Chase was aware that his own weakness for one
woman in particular could have destroyed his career.
She had most definitely altered the path of it, and was
in fact the reason he sat across from his friend now.

But Kinkade couldn't possibly know this.

"Might one?" Chase asked idly. "Do *you* anticipate
being made or destroyed by a woman, Kinkade? Re-
formed, and etcetera, perhaps? Don't you see yourself
one day leg—" He stopped. *Leg-shackled* made him
think of the time Colin spent in prison, his younger
brother's legs dragging with the weight of the unjust
chains, and he shied away from the term. "—married?
You'll need heirs to fill up your houses."

"Oh, naturally, I shall take a wife one day. Someone
mild, unobservant, easy on the eyes, wide of the hips,
generous of the dowry. And thusly I shall continue to
live as I always have. Choosing my amusements. I lived
through a bloodbath, and I intend to ensure that the rest
of my life is a monument to comfort and indulgence."

"You're a romantic, Kinkade," Chase said wryly.

"It takes one to recognize one."

Chase did laugh at this.

"Speaking of marriage, how is Colin getting on?
One hears things."

"He gets on." He didn't want to talk about Colin. Or
cows.

Or, God help him, marriage.

He slipped his hand into his pocket just to feel the

garters. He imagined for an instant they were still warm from her skin, the satin of them reminiscent of that creamy satin between her thighs, and the thought made the muscles of his stomach tighten, not to mention what it did to his loins.

He might have been soundly rejected as a husband, but the issue of wanting Rosalind March—and of Rosalind March wanting *him*—remained . . .

It cannot happen again, she'd said.

He wondered how honorable it might be try to persuade her to want to go much, much further than the event in the library. And whether that would be at all wise for either of them.

He wouldn't talk about marriage or cows. But the garters reminded him of Rosalind, and he *would* talk about horses. For Rosalind's sake. He fingered those garters, and knew that a small fissure had opened up in his solid regard for Kinkade.

Chase succumbed to curiosity, and he knew a way to begin.

"Speaking of drawings, there's a painting of a horse above the hearth in your library, Kinkade—do you recall it? Tall chestnut, fine head. Is it Ward?"

"Aye. My father commissioned Ward to paint it. My father's favorite horse. Brandywine, his name was. Won a derby or two. Sired dozens of offspring. I suppose my father identified with him in that respect. The horse, that is, not the painter. Haven't the faintest idea about the number of *his* offspring."

Kinkade was blessed—or cursed—with innumerable siblings.

"My sister Genevieve—you met her last season, yes?—is the lover of art in our family. She's quite knowledgeable. Is capable of falling into raptures over paintings. I managed to avoid acquiring any education in art at all. I know what I like and what I don't."

"You always do, Eversea." A faint smile here. "Always did."

The barmaid ventured over to them.

"Have you anything that doesn't taste like pig piss?" Chase asked in all seriousness.

"No, luv. You might want to try the donkey piss."

"Bring me one of those, then." He smiled at her, and she looked as though she'd received a blow to her head. Her eyes filled with stars, and she basked and basked in it.

"Off you go, love," Kinkade said gently. He shook his head at Chase. She staggered off, happily dazed.

Chase turned back to Kinkade. "Have you ever *purchased* any art? I wouldn't know where to begin."

"One doesn't *buy* art, Eversea. One *inherits* it. It comes with the houses." Kinkade stretched out his legs and waved out a languid hand, like an orchestra conductor weary of bringing up the violins. The Kinkades had houses and property simply everywhere. Two town houses in London, an abandoned theater outside Covent Garden called Mezza Luna, estates in Northumberland, Wales, Plymouth. They didn't equal the value of Eversea holdings, as the Everseas had been property holders since the Conqueror set foot on English shores, but the scope of them was impressive nevertheless.

"What if you inherit a painting you can't abide? Do you keep it out of duty? Is one obliged to keep every horse, dog, and homely ancestor? Donate it to the British Museum?"

Kinkade looked amused. "Speak for yourself regarding the ancestors. But I cannot imagine feeling strongly one way or another about a picture. I haven't done a thing with any of the paintings; they're all welcome to stay, as far as I'm concerned. Now *houses*, one has little choice in the matter when they're entailed, is this not so? Or property. Damned expensive to keep all of it up."

So he hadn't donated a Rubinetto to the Montmorency.

Or . . . he was lying about it.

It occurred to Chase then that Kinkade had never felt strongly one way or another about much of anything, whereas *he* generally felt strongly one way or another about everything. And perhaps this was why they'd managed to tolerate each other for so long, and to call this tolerance friendship.

And perhaps this ability not to feel strongly was why Kinkade succeeded in his role in the Home Office. Yet despite his responsibility in determining the fates of so many, it occurred to Chase that his friend was strangely unmoored, and as such, as unpredictable as a comet heading toward earth: one never knew how or where it would land.

It might, of course, simply orbit randomly for eternity.

It struck him as a dreadful way to spend eternity.

But then, this probably described many a spoiled member of the aristocracy, untouched by the financial realities of their times, or by the struggles other soldiers endured in the wake of the war.

How could a girl just *disappear* from Newgate?

Was *Rosalind's* story true?

Of course it was. She would never prevaricate when it came to her sisters. She'd devoted her life to caring for them. She had *reasons* to care, unlike Kinkade.

The donkey piss arrived, and Chase raised it to his friend, who raised his dreg-filled glass in return.

"My mother wants our portraits painted by someone fashionable," Chase said. "Know of any portraitists in London?"

"I know everyone fashionable, and not one of them are portraitists. Or even painters."

"More's the pity. Speaking of the fashionable, is there anyone new and interesting I ought to meet, Kinkade?"

"I wonder who you might like."

"Begin with a list of intriguing females."

"Thought you were already captivated, Eversea."

"Who says I need to confine my interests to merely one woman?"

"Shame you needed to depart early the other evening, because there was a countess you ought to meet, because from experience I can tell you she can put her feet over her *head* . . . "

The list of intriguing females was long and detailed, because Kinkade had rather a broad definition of what constituted intriguing.

The prurient, trivial conversation rained down over him, allowing Chase to think and participate at the same time, and he kept his hand in his coat pocket, running the satin of two garters through his fingers.

The most fascinating thing in the room was the clock perched on the bar, because in two hours he could call upon Rosalind again.

He knew he now needed to take her straight to the Montmorency Museum.

Chapter 12

Rosalind wore a green dress, because it made her eyes greener, and because it made Chase's pupils flare when he saw her, as she'd known it would.

There was nothing in the *world*, she decided, looking at Chase's frame all but filling up her small parlor, that could possibly make his eyes bluer than they already were.

Apart from a certain solemnity of manner, he exhibited no signs of being shattered by the rejection of his proposal. He was all that was dignified and respectful. She was relieved.

But then a grayer mood settled when he told her about his visit with Kinkade.

"He won't help?"

"He says he *has* tried to help. He says there was no record of Lucy Locke ever being in Newgate. He also says he never donated a thing to a museum."

She felt her palms turn to ice. "I swear to you, Chase, she was there. I saw her, and she told me—"

"I believe you."

"She can't— She can't just be gone. *Someone* knows where she is. Someone must—"

"I agree."

"And the clerk at the Montmorency told me that a Mr. Kinkade donated that—"

"I believe you."

There was something so unutterably bracing about his voice. Calm, even, certain. She took a deep breath and breathed in strength from his presence.

Still, she was now left with nothing, or so it seemed. The weight of it settled on her chest, and it was suddenly a struggle to breathe. She *never* gave up without a fight. But all avenues seemed blocked.

"What can I do?" she asked. She tried to sound strong. She heard, however, a whiff of despair in her own voice.

Later, she would realize it was probably portentous that he'd waited until she'd swallowed her tea and replaced her cup in her saucer before he answered.

"I should like to take you to a brothel."

She went very, very still.

Had she . . . *heard* him correctly? Surely he hadn't said . . .

She could feel heat scrolling rapidly up her face. She laid her hands flat on her knees, an attempt to steady her nerves. She was certain Chase was now looking at a tomato-colored woman.

And yet . . . the very word "brothel" uttered in his voice touched the base of her spine with a long rough-tipped finger.

Coincidentally, the kind of fingers Chase had.

"But . . . " she began.

But? But *what*? The proper response was probably righteous indignation. Or at the very least, *Why?*

He added very seriously, and in a mock rush, "Not because, Rosalind, I think you should apply for a position there. No insult to your powers of attraction intended."

His wicked glinting eyes made a lie of his solemnity.

"None taken," she said faintly.

The bloody man deliberately allowed her to flounder in confusion for a moment longer.

Oh, for God's sake. She wasn't a child. She inhaled. "I assume this proposed jaunt has something to do with Lucy?"

Her voice was even and cool, which she was proud of, but quite threadbare, which she was not.

"Well, here is the thing: My sister Genevieve has never heard of a painter called Rubinetto. And I assure you she knows a tedious amount about every important painter and all of the unimportant ones, too, particularly the Italian ones. Which in and of itself may or may not be significant. But I happened to recall—"

Wait. "Is your sister in London?"

A hesitation. "My sister is in Sussex."

Which must mean he *urgently* wrote to his sister to inquire about the Rubinetto straight away, nearly the moment they'd met at the museum. He'd at the very least been very *curious*.

For his own sake, if not for hers.

Still, she smiled slowly at him.

He frowned darkly at her, disconcerted. Knowing what she was realizing.

Which only widened her smile, as she was delighted to disconcert him for a change.

"As I *said*, I happened to recall that there was something *very* familiar about that particular angel. And now I remember. I believe I saw that very same angel in a painting in a brothel, a painting in much the same style as that Rubinetto. At the Velvet Glove."

So matter-of-factly presented that the meaning of the words arrived whole moments after she'd heard them.

The Velvet Glove?

"'A strong nasty drink and a woman,'" she murmured, quoting Liam. Looking at him wryly.

"I beg your pardon?" he said politely.

She declined to elaborate. She cleared her throat. "And you . . . have visited this brothel?"

This seemed rather evident. She didn't know why she'd asked.

"A number of times." He eyed her with maddening equanimity.

She knew about men and brothels. Particularly *soldiers* and brothels. It was just that it was somehow tremendously uncomfortable imagining him selecting a woman the way *she* might pop into Madame Marceau's to discuss a new hat. Or visit the butcher to purchase a chop.

It was tremendously uncomfortable imagining him with anyone else at all.

"Rosalind?"

"Yes?" She was startled from her thoughts.

"You *were* aware that I'm a man?" he said gently. His eyes were full of unforgivable glints.

"One can hardly overlook the fact," she said dryly.

He was delighted with her: she'd earned herself a quick half smile.

"Very good," he said briskly. He was enjoying her discomfiture just a little too much. "I should warn you that the angel in this particular painting is engaged in behavior one doesn't normally associate with angels."

"She's engaged in a boxing match?" she said lightly.

She had the peculiar sensation she was observing this conversation rather than participating in it. A slightly out of the body feeling resulting, no doubt, from finding oneself dispassionately discussing a brothel.

Called, dear God, the Velvet Glove.

"The instrument she's playing is an organ, not a harp."

Her mind instantly exploded with thrilling and inappropriate wonderings and obliterated all rational thought.

He waited patiently for her to speak.

And when it became clear that she could not, he said crisply, "I shall allow you to decide whether you wish to view it. But I think you should. And now, I think we should pay another visit to the Montmorency Museum to ask some more questions. Shall we?"

A familiar small dirty boy was entertaining himself by leaping from step to step in front of the museum when they alighted from the Eversea carriage.

The courtyard bore no evidence that hoards of visitors might be inside. The slap of the boy's bare feet echoed throughout it.

He greeted the two of them with an extravagant wave of both arms. Boys, Chase reflected, are forever waving their limbs about as though they're still getting accustomed to possessing them.

"Liam, are you *always* in front of the museum?" Rosalind sounded a little wary.

Liam snorted, as if this was hilarious "No one is always *anywhere*, unless they're in the graveyard, aye?"

Chase and Rosalind exchanged glances. Street urchin philosophy.

"But 'tis where the rich coves, go, ain't it? I earn me a shillin' 'ere and there."

Puzzling answer, given that the Montmorency had seemed all but deserted the time he'd been there.

"Rich coves?"

"Callender, 'e pays most when I hold the carriage 'orses," Liam volunteered, swinging his arms as though they were pumping the words out of him. "*Ireton* nivver. No' even a ha'pence. Stingy! Others, too. I ken the ones wi' blunt. Ye're a rich cove," he said to Chase, demonstrating that he could indeed tell the ones with blunt. "I will be one day, too."

Said with such cocksureness that Chase could have been looking at his own ten-year-old self.

"How do you know these 'rich coves' are indeed Callender and Ireton?" Rosalind asked.

"The coats of arms on their carriages. Callender's a barouche, aye?" Liam addressed this to Chase, clearly thinking that Rosalind would be thick about such a thing because she was a girl. "Four bays?"

Rosalind looked at Chase for confirmation, eyebrow arched, lips folded in on themselves to keep from laughing.

Chase reflected for a moment on the male of their species: a man could be acquainted with another man for twenty years and not be able to remember the name of his wife, but he would probably know the names of the man's horses.

"He does have a barouche and four bays."

"'As a spear, like, on his coat of crest, and a lion,

like so?" Liam lifted his arms and made a roaring face, by way of illustration.

Callender did indeed have a spear and a shield and a lion on his crest.

"Yes."

"'As gray hair? Ancient? 'As a big dot 'ere on 'is cheek?" Liam pointed to his own cheek.

By "dot" Chase assumed he meant "mole," which, in fact, Lord Callender did have. Callender might be ten entire years older than he was, which would make him a bit past forty.

"But . . . when, Liam? Have any rich coves been into the Montmorency today?"

"Oh, aye. Callender 'isself went in. And one came out this morning right before sunup."

"You mean one *arrived*."

"I mean one *came out*."

Chase fixed Liam with a one of those truth-extracting stares.

"Sometimes they go in and dinna come out. Sometime they come out and dinna go in," the boy insisted stubbornly.

"Liam," Rosalind said gently, "why are you speaking in riddles?"

Liam was so indignant he stopped waving his arms about, planted his feet. "'Tis the *truth*!"

"But you're not *always* here to see them coming in and going out," she pointed out.

"Aye. But *sometimes* I am 'ere all day. And this morning I was 'ere. Earned an 'a'pence when the rich cove go' in the 'ack and left. Earned me an 'a'pence from Callender."

"Do you remember what the rich cove looked like?"

"Nivver seen 'im before. 'Is clothes were like yers, but 'e wore funny shoes. Wi' straps-like. 'Is toes they stuck right out! Why bother wearing anything at all?" Liam was amused. "Like shoes carved right up with a knife, they were."

"He was wearing *sandals*?" Extraordinary. Like an Italian peasant?

The boy frowned. "Sand . . . ?"

"Never mind."

"How long have the rich coves been coming and going like that?" Rosalind asked sharply.

"Always *some* coves wi' blunt comin' and goin'," Liam said philosophically. "Always 'ave been. But many more lately. We even paid *rent* on our room," he added proudly.

Who was "we"?

Pointedly, neither he nor Rosalind asked.

"Is it possible you simply didn't *see* anyone go in and out?"

"Two ways in and two ways out, Captain Eversea." Liam used both arms and simultaneously pointed at the great main doors and at the smaller door to the right, just around the corner of the building—the service entrance, from the looks of things—stairs down into it, surrounded by a short fence, backing out onto a mews. Anyone exiting it could be seen from the courtyard. "I knows because me sister works but one day a week inside. She dusts and whatnot."

If Callender was inside now, they would certainly be able to find him.

"Thank you, Liam."

Liam's bony shoulders went up and down in a modest shrug and he put out his hand, since as far as he was concerned, "Thank you" generally meant that he ought to be paid for something, even if he hadn't the faintest idea how he'd just been helpful.

Chase frowned at the boy long enough to cause the small face to begin to twitch with worry. And then he produced a ha'pence.

"My thanks," Liam said, in an almost flawless imitation of Chase's accent, and shoved the coin into his dirty trouser pocket.

"What fine manners you have, Liam," Chase said dryly as he took Rosalind's arms and led her up the steps.

"Aye, that I do," the boy agreed reflectively, and resumed leaping from step to step, and waiting, they supposed, for the next rich cove. "That I do."

"Good morning."

The clerk bolted to his feet again. "MacGregor, *sir*!"

Chase tried not to smile. He'd inadvertently made the greeting sound like an order again.

Mr. MacGregor looked up at Chase, and then glanced at Rosalind, and . . . blinked.

And then . . . well, Chase would have thought it admiration, but MacGregor froze and went decidedly pale. Unless he'd *begun* the morning pale.

"Which regiment, MacGregor?" he asked softly.

MacGregor's eyes flared in surprise. "The Fifty-first Foot, sir."

Chase didn't ask MacGregor what he was doing working in a museum. He was fortunate to have a job at all, regardless of the nature of it: so many soldiers from classes other than his own were unemployed in the wake of the war. Lost and at loose ends, impoverished.

"Did you know Sergeant Beresford? Good man."

"Aye, I knew Beresford well, sir. I would agree wholeheartedly. And a friend—Percy Emry—served under you. Said it was an honor, indeed. Said he shouldn't like to get on the wrong side of you."

Chase ducked his head, accepting the compliment. Such as it was. "And 'tis an honor to have been spoken of with distinction by a fine soldier."

Both Beresford and Sergeant Emry had died at Waterloo.

Great swells of fatigue curved beneath the clerk's eyes, which were pale blue and swimming in pink, rather than white.

"Late night, Sergeant?" he asked suddenly.

The eyes widened in surprise. "Er . . ."

"It's just that you look a little pale."

A hesitation. "I've a new baby, Captain."

There was nothing Chase wanted to hear *less* about than a new baby.

"My felicitations."

"Thank you," MacGregor said somewhat faintly.

"I have a question for you, Mr. MacGregor. Our family—the Everseas—wishes to make a bequest of a few family artifacts to one of London's fine museums. I've found the Montmorency quite interesting."

"A bequest!" MacGregor seemed genuinely surprised. "That would be kind of you, sir. The British Museum, as you might well know, is usually the recipient of such gifts. We were outbid by the British Museum for the noose meant to hang Mr. Colin Eversea," he said sadly. "Your brother," he clarified needlessly.

"Er . . . well, that wasn't quite the sort of artifact we had in mind for donating."

"We invariably are outbid for things," MacGregor said morosely. "The Montmorency is."

Chase redirected the subject. "The Everseas thought perhaps we'd donate a painting—we've quite a number of some historical interest to the British public—or a suit of armor, as we've more than a dozen in the house in Sussex. I understand your collection here at the Montmorency was not solely the result of the Earl of Bavelock's death?"

"Aye, sir. We've had a few additions since he died."

"How are acquisitions assessed and accepted?"

Another hesitation from MacGregor. "We could always do with a fine suit of armor."

It wasn't quite an answer. Was it evasion? The grains of Chase's finite patience were sifting away.

"If someone were to drive a wagon up to the front of the building and deposit a few chairs, a spinning wheel, and a sketch of their grandmother on the steps, would you find a place for all of it inside? Near the puppets, perhaps?"

"Certainly not, sir! The decision of worthiness is made by committee. Mind you, if you were to deposit the suit of clothes Mr. Eversea the younger were wearing on that fateful day—"

Enough was enough. "Who donated the Rubinetto in the East Wing?" he barked.

Sergeant MacGregor took a moment to recover from the barked question. He braced himself. "I fear I cannot recall, sir."

Chase carefully didn't look at Rosalind, who'd been told by the man in front of him that all the Italian paintings had been donated by the Kinkade family.

"A pity about your memory, MacGregor."

"I've always thought so, too, sir."

He stared evenly at Chase, but the white around his mouth had taken on rather a green cast. His pale eyelashes twitched nervously. The tip of his nose was pink. Chase was reminded of the time he'd held a soft little rat in his fist, its nose twitching, pink eyes frightened.

"How long has the painting hung on the wall there?"

"Some months."

Bloody unspecific answer for a man who likely had an encyclopedic knowledge of the entire museum.

"You see, MacGregor, the reason I ask is that I thought I recalled another painting hanging on that wall, and I came in hoping to see it. But I could well be confusing the Montmorency with the British Museum." It was useful to mention a rival, he decided. "Perhaps you've moved paintings within the museum? We've— the Eversesas—an Italian painting or two we might wish to share with the art-loving British public."

"I cannot recall moving paintings, sir. We're simply happy to have a painting the . . . caliber of the Rubinetto to hang on that wall."

Another answer that wasn't an answer.

Which in itself, as far as Chase was concerned, was an answer. Of sorts.

He suspected MacGregor had been instructed by someone to be less forthcoming. If not to everyone, then specifically to him.

"The reason I asked about the Rubinetto is that it's

hung in such a fine location. The room is snug, protected from too much light that might fade the paintings. Our donation might be contingent upon hanging our painting on that very wall." This had the faintest hint of regretful warning. "I saw no other location quite so appealing. The painting I had in mind would beautifully suit the room."

"Such things are decided by committee, sir," MacGregor said cautiously. "But I shall share your preferences with the museum board."

"Perhaps I have friends on your board who might be amenable to a bit of influence. Would you mind sharing a few of their names with me?"

"Oh, I'm not privy to the names of the board members, sir. I'm merely a clerk."

In just two days, a very helpful man had become vaguely and politely obstructive.

Chase scowled at him.

The clerk flinched. But said nothing more.

Information. Chase sifted through fragments of it. Perhaps connected, perhaps not. A bit like an archeological dig. It added up to very little as of yet.

"May I visit the wing once again? To ascertain whether it would suit our bequest?"

"You're always welcome to visit the wing during visiting hours, sir," said MacGregor bravely.

And yet he of course knew how to parlay his limp as a lever, and it led him to the next question, and made him feel *brilliant*. "Perhaps there is another, more convenient exit from the museum closer to the East Wing?" Chase suggested delicately.

He looked speakingly at his walking stick. Then back at the former soldier. Shameless of him.

"We've only the tradesmen's entrance—perhaps you've noticed it to the right of the building, near the front?—but it's kept locked at all times except when we're expecting a delivery, of coal or cleaning supplies, or when we allow in our cleaning staff in the morning. I fear the tradesmen's entrance is no closer to the East Wing than to this exit, sir."

"You must have a veritable battalion of cleaning staff. Silent as mice, and unobtrusive. I haven't seen a member of it yet."

"We appreciate your appreciation, sir. It is not so much a battalion as a dozen or so efficient and very careful individuals who dust and polish the entire place but once every Tuesday, so if you have not yet been in on a Tuesday, you would not have seen them. Occasionally we've craftsmen in for repairs and maintenance. We've someone who sees to the candles every morning and evening."

Chase glanced over at the open page in the book. Only four names were scrawled on it, and none were names he knew, and none were Callender.

"I don't suppose you require the staff to sign the book?"

"Oh no, sir. That's only for our guests."

Some go in and dinna come out. Some go out and dinna come in.

Chase made a great show of signing his name in the book.

And then Rosalind leaned forward to sign hers, and stumbled forward with an "Oh! Goodness!"

And swept the big book from the table. It crashed to the floor, barely missed landing on Chase's boot. "I am *so* clumsy. I'm terribly sorry!"

The clerk dove for it, but Chase was faster. "Allow me, Mrs. Smithson."

Chase took his time lifting it up, and as he did, he casually, nosily—surreptitiously, he hoped—once again rifled through the pages of the book.

His eyes were quick.

He hadn't seen Callender's or Ireton's names in the Montmorency Museum's book when he had his first flip through it. And he didn't see them now.

Nor did he see the names of any other "rich coves," for that matter, at least none with whom he was acquainted. London circles, and the circles that encompassed the Everseas, were simply riddled with rich coves.

Was Liam lying to them? But *why*? To impress them with his knowledge of rich coves?

He heaved the great book back up onto the desk and spread it back open to the page of the day.

"Thank you, Sergeant MacGregor."

Rosalind paused to finish signing her name in the book: *Mrs. Smithson*. She beamed at MacGregor, who could not seem to smile in return, and followed Chase into the museum.

A quick circuit of the museum revealed only one other guest, a young man who appeared to be a scholar or a painter, seated before a Renaissance painting, sketching busily with his tongue between his teeth.

They saw Callender nowhere.

And they were now before the Rubinetto once more.

Chase looked about, just in case someone was watching, and surreptitiously lifted the edge of the frame.

The wall beneath it was the same color as the wall surrounding it.

If the painting had indeed hung for some months,
the wall behind it would have been brighter, untouched
by dust or elements that might dull it.

Which meant the painting hadn't hung for very long
in that particular spot.

He glanced at Rosalind, who glanced back at him.
She understood why he'd done it.

"All right, Rosalind. Look very closely at the
angel."

The great bovine stared out at them from the middle
of the painting with soulful eyes, its swishing tail
upraised. Up in the corner, the angel was still strumming her harp, her body arched so that her white toes
pointed skyward, her toga slipping down around her
plump calves, her bosom spilling forward, pink nipples
exposed. Her lips were curved in a smile of dozy contentment; a pair of fluffy white wings held her aloft.
She was a brunette.

"She would plummet to earth and land face first in
a cow pat with wings like those." Chase was irritated.
"They would need to be at least three feet wider to get
her airborne at all. She would never be able to fly, let
alone be able to hold a *harp* while flying."

"Thank you, Icarus," Rosalind said. "That's
fascinating."

He turned slowly to her and smiled with pure
pleasure. She smiled back: it was impossible not to.
They beamed at each other for perhaps longer than
necessary.

"All right. Rosalind, if you saw this angel again in a
different context, would you recognize her? If she were

painted in the same colors, with the same . . . physique . . . in a . . . well, similar pose?"

She hesitated. "She's rather distinctive, isn't she?"

"Distinctive is certainly one way to describe her."

She carefully did not look at Chase.

As the context in question was of course a painting in a brothel in which the angel was likely doing something much less innocent than strumming a harp.

She suddenly felt very shy, very green again, and she half resented him for it. It brought back the early days of her marriage to Colonel March, when she'd been so in the dark about nearly everything, from proper etiquette at a formal dinner to what precisely would happen to her on her wedding night.

She could not pretend to sophistication. She knew Chase wouldn't have to *pretend* at all. About any of it. She sensed the sheer magnitude of the man's sensual knowledge every time he touched her.

Involuntarily her thoughts steered her gaze to the room next to her, the room where she thought she'd seen a ghost, and lingered upon that grand, arrogant, sensual, curtained bed. She sucked in a short sharp breath, as desire and memory pierced.

It cannot happen again, she'd told him last night. Because in Callender's library she'd begun to sense that there would be no end to the pleasure that could be had from him. And she knew it was because the man's very presence—exhilarating and unnerving—even now, tempted her to do anything at all he might ask of her. She didn't dare.

Chase, inscrutably, followed the direction of her gaze. They lingered on the bed speculatively, too. Returned to her face.

Rosalind jerked her eyes—and a warmer face—back to the angel. Who still looked pleased with the world. But she didn't seem to have any answers, either. About anything.

Rosalind gazed at her. And then turned to Chase with a rueful, almost apologetic smile.

Her breath caught at the expression fleeing from his eyes.

It occurred to her then that her very presence was a constant razor strop to his desire, and perhaps an unfair test of his own control.

How had she come to play this role in his life—the woman who must ever be at arm's length? The woman who lured him into trouble? It seemed unfair. She knew how badly he wanted her.

But then life, she thought ruefully, was seldom about "fair," or about what we wanted.

Chase was once again all composure, as if the expression in his eyes had never been.

"I probably would recognize her," Rosalind said softly. "The angel."

He nodded shortly. "If you should like to see the angel at the Velvet Glove, send for me tomorrow morning, Rosalind. Keep in mind, if it's the same angel, we might be able to discover who Rubinetto is and why this painting is here, and if it has anything at all to do with Lucy's disappearance."

The forceful Captain Eversea, despite his formidable powers of persuasion, was giving her a gift: he was patiently leaving the decision in her hands.

Chapter 13

When they emerged from the museum, Liam was standing on the steps holding in one grubby hand a piece of bread folded over what appeared to be a wedge of cheese and was bringing it to his mouth.

Chase asked, "Liam, can you count beyond ten?"

He tucked the sandwich into his pocket, much to the mutual dismay of Rosalind and Chase.

"Aye, I can count. But not on me fingers. Only wi' shillings and pence. I can add them and subtract them, and the like. I'll show ye now. *If* ye've shillings and pence."

He thrust his hands into his pockets and rocked back on his dirty heels. And grinned. He directed most of the radiance of his grin at Rosalind, perhaps thinking she would be a softer touch.

"Very witty, Liam," Chase said. "How many apples are stacked on the bottom row of the costermonger's cart?" He swung up his walking stick and pointed out into the street.

"Five of them." Almost instantly said.

"How many pigeons are currently eating . . . whatever that might be?" He gestured to a group of pigeons, who were doing what pigeons do best, clustering about a great puddle of something and having the pigeon version of a luncheon party.

With a flourish, Liam's finger stabbed the air eight times in the direction of the pigeons. The boy ought to have been on stage.

"Eight pigeons."

"Very well. I've an assignment for you."

"Assi . . . ?"

"A job."

The boy's eyes lit. A job meant money.

"Can I trust you with an important job?"

"Aye, Captain Eversea."

"I should like to know how many people go into and how many men go out of the Montmorency Museum while you are here. Can you write?"

"Nay!" Liam snorted. Why *would* he be able to write?

"How is your memory for detail?"

" 'Detail' is . . . "

Rosalind surprised Chase by taking his arm and turning him abruptly away from the boy. "Liam, what color are Captain Eversea's eyes?"

"Blue" came instantly from the boy.

"What color are Mrs. March's eyes?" Chase countered. Rosalind closed her eyes immediately.

"Green. 'Er 'air is brownlike. Soft voice, 'cept when she's stern. Tall fer a girl. Smells nice, like roses. Is that what ye mean by detail?"

Was the urchin mocking them? Chase wondered. Or reading his mind?

He was definitely grinning, the little devil.

Rosalind opened her eyes then. But her cheeks had gone the color of the aforementioned roses.

They both studiously avoided looking at each other.

The boy was still grinning at them.

Chase cleared his throat. "Very well. I think we've established you've an eye for detail, Liam. So I should like you to count how many men you see today and remember anything of significance, and report it to me."

"I know only so many words, Captain Eversea, and signiwhatsit isna one of 'em."

He wasn't going to humor this bright bugger.

" 'Significant' means 'important,' or in this instance, 'unusual.' Remember the word, as I may use it again. Remember anything that seems unusual and then tell me tomorrow in the morning."

"But the puppets might be in the square tomorrow if the weather is fine. I *love* puppets!"

Dear God. Did *everyone* love puppets? What was wrong with the world?

He sighed. "Then we shall discuss it after the puppet show."

Anticipation was like a gong. It woke Chase early for a change. He all but bounded downstairs, nearly frightening the staff to death by being awake so early and by the bounding, which seemed an inordinately sprightly thing for the lately dour, limping Captain Eversea. If he'd told them it was because he was waiting for a message from a woman he hoped to take to a brothel, doubtless they would have all crossed themselves.

Or perhaps not. Most of them had worked for Everseas for decades now and had come to expect nearly anything.

But no message from Rosalind had yet arrived.

Resigned, he took himself outside.

* * *

The day was indeed fine—if "fine" meant dense heat, nary a rain cloud in sight, a breeze like a fetid breath, and a generous layer of coal smut once again jaundicing the London sky. Dull *yellow*—now that was a proper London color. Blue was for Sussex, when the sky wasn't washed with fog or filled with thick rain clouds.

He wished he could tell Rosalind what a sacrifice he was making on her behalf by attending a puppet show. He hadn't had the nerve to tell Rosalind that he thought the *puppets* might be speaking directly to him, possibly about the painting in the Montmorency.

Nevertheless.

Delighted people were already clustered in the square. Chase craned his head: sure enough, the marionettes were already twitching on strings on their miniature stage. He stared in something like disbelief. He'd seen a man convulse after being struck by a bolt of lightning once.

Watching the marionettes was *just* that pleasant.

Only a need to grasp upon anything that might help Rosalind could drag him closer. He didn't see Liam in the crowd, but then again, the boy had a talent for blending into his surroundings, especially if the surroundings were grimy.

He could hear the squeaky puppety voices rise up in a crescendo—delivering the joke, no doubt—and then they were drowned out in a roar of laughter.

He saw a friend in the audience and shouldered his way over, employing the gold horse muzzle head of his walking stick once to prod someone in the arse when they refused to shift. He shrugged one shoulder som-

berly when the arse shifted and a head turned to aim
a glare at him, and continued to maneuver through the
crowd, exaggerating his limp.

Shameless. But he had an objective.

He was close enough to see the puppet's painted
eyes flash turquoise as they turned this way and that.
He could have *sworn* they were seeking him out.

He wondered if this line of thinking meant he ought
to drink more or drink less.

"Mr. Charles!"

"Why, Mr. Martin." Chase touched the brim of his
hat. Martin, hatless, nodded pleasantly and held out an
apple. It was an early one—small, pale yellow, exquisitely shaped, and covered all over in a flush of red.
Chase thought of Rosalind and her earlobes turning
pink with fury and her face flushing with desire and
her sweet, smooth, small apple arse and how neatly it
fit into his hands, and he took the thing with pleasure,
closed his fingers over it slowly.

He was tempted to close his eyes for just a moment,
just to allow himself again the imaginings that had
kept him awake much of the night. The feel of her
peach-firm arse, for one, the smooth tautness of her
skin.

Ah, Rosalind.

He suspected he was doomed to see her metaphori-
cally in everything from now on. Apples. The backs of
women in crowds. The shapes of clouds. Bad paintings.
The color green.

Probably not marionettes.

"Gets 'em from a costermonger up Black Cat Lane.
Worcester, they come in from."

Chase finally took the apple out of bonhomie. Mr.

Martin watched until he took a polite bite. Admittedly, it was a very fine apple. A pearmain. Later in the fall the flavor would be too cloying, but now it had a near perfect balance of sweet and tart.

And there it was again: another way of thinking of Rosalind.

Chase held the apple in his mouth, savoring it, and felt the slightest twinge of competition; an ancient apple orchard stretched out over Eversea land and on the farm that Colin was running now; it fluffed into bloom in early autumn, and then wagons of harvested russets headed to London to sell to the likes of Mr. Martin. He could hardly grow up in Pennyroyal Green without knowing a bit about farming.

Granted, not nearly as much about farming as Colin seemed to want to know. But Everseas had farming in their blood along with roguery.

He wondered what kind of farmer he'd be if ever took it up.

He nodded appreciatively. "Thank you. Fine apple, indeed."

He handed it back to Martin, who looked flattered and then made the rest of the apple disappear with one bite and flung the core indiscriminately over his shoulder.

"Ow!" they heard distantly.

Good arm, had Martin.

"Soldier, was ye?" Martin asked without looking at Chase, fortunately spraying juice toward the rest of the crowd, as he didn't want to miss a moment of his entertainment.

"Was," Chase said shortly. It was an easy enough conclusion to draw, given his limp and his age.

"I works down 't the docks. Unloading ships when they come in from America and India and the like."

"I'll be off to India in a week or so."

"Ye dinna say!" Martin was intrigued.

"I'm on assignment with East India Company."

"I've seen them come an' go o'er the years. Ship's in the dock now."

"The Courage, I'll sail on."

"That's the one," Martin confirmed. "Best of luck to ye then, lad."

"Have they done the song yet?" Chase didn't need to explain *which* song.

"Nay." Mr. Martin looked up at the sky, perhaps gauging the time of day. "They sang it but the one time I've 'eard. Aye, and see, now 'ere come the hat through the crowd." Mr. Martin got up on his toes and peered. "They've done their bit for th' day, and then they be off. Canna stay all day, I wager. Need to find a fresh crowd. I've 'eard it said they set up in Covent Garden now and agin and over t' Grays Inn."

It had been a fluke, perhaps: the singing of the Colin song while he stood on the outskirts listening.

Chase was relieved.

Suddenly, excitement rustled through the crowd, and all around him audience members murmured and gripped each other's arms in sheer anticipation—sure enough, the puppets had decided upon an encore.

> *"And if you thought ye'd never see*
> *The likes of Colin Eversea*
> *Well, just take a look at the lot of them, boys!*
> *Sing along with me*
> *From their heads to their toes*

> *They're all of them rogues*
> *And have been through history!"*

A song about Colin was one thing; insulting his entire clan was another thing altogether. Despite whether their musical assertions had any merit or not.

Which, inarguably, they did.

Chase flung eye daggers at the stage while marionettes happily disparaged his family and the crowd enjoyed it.

"*Love* me a good rogue!" Mr. Martin enthused, rising up on the balls of his feet in enthusiasm. "The Everseas, they sound a right good time!"

"Encore!" The crowd cried, predictably. Hands slapping together thunderously.

The puppeteers obliged, and another squeaky song rang out, and this time the dance was a more languid one.

> *"Georgie porgie puddin' pie*
> *Kiss the girls and make them cry*
> *And while the world is fast asleep*
> *The lords are all in their cups deep*
> *The angel looks the other way*
> *When they come and take the girls away."*

Chase froze.

Come and take the girls away?

Cryptic and chilling as hell, calculated to intrigue . . . and once again, a bloody *angel*.

He *loathed* being intrigued by puppets.

He turned on his heel and stormed in the opposite

direction, with a cursory tip of the hat to Martin, who looked startled by his abrupt departure.

It was as difficult, however, to swim against the tide of the crowd here as it was to move through Callender's crush. The masses did gulp down their free entertainment, and were resentful when someone thought to deprive them of a moment of it, even if they took that moment just to budge their arses.

"Captain Eversea!" came a sharp little cockney voice from somewhere near his hip.

"Christ!"

Liam was delighted to have startled him.

"How did you know I was a captain, anyway?" Chase said testily.

"The liedy. Mrs. March. She told me to call ye 'Captain.' Or *else*," he added admiringly.

"Did she really add the 'or else'?" He was fascinated by this.

"Nay, but she might *well* as 'ave. Sounds just like ye, she does." Liam was all admiration.

"What did you call me *instead* before that?"

Liam's jaw dropped. He was clearly full of awe for how clever Chase was. But he wasn't about to tattle on *himself.*

"You might as well give up, Liam, Not only was I in the army, but I was once a boy and I have three brothers. I have the advantage over you in every regard."

"Mayhap ye do."

Chase found himself smiling at this guarded concession. "Did you enjoy the puppets?"

"Are you the person they're singing about?" he

asked shrewdly. He opened his mouth to bellow. *"Oh, if ye thought ye'd nivver see—"*

Chase frowned at him so blackly Liam clapped his mouth shut instantly.

"Have you a report for me, Liam?" he demanded.

"Aye, Captain. Six men went in. No liedies. Three men came out. But the same what went in weren't the same what went out."

What the devil was going *on* in there?

"You're absolutely certain?" he asked sternly.

He'd been in that museum. It was more like a mausol*eum*, in some ways, in terms of its silence. Not exactly thronged with the fashionable set. They needed to go inside and take a look around to see what might be going on there. After *dark*.

Doing anything at all with Rosalind after dark started a frisson of pleasure up his spine.

"Did you recognize any of the men today, Liam? Callender? Ireton?"

"Nay, and came away with ha'pence only," Liam said regretfully and meaningfully. "From a man 'oo went away in an 'ack.

"Good work, Liam."

Liam glowed. "Thank you, Captain Eversea," he said gravely.

Chase produced a shilling, and tipped his hat to Liam, half sardonically. Chase thought he would walk as far as Black Cat Lane and try to find a hack.

Liam apparently didn't think "Thank you" was synonymous with "Good-bye," which was what Chase had hoped.

The boy trailed behind him.

"My sister, she didna return 'ome last night." He said it casually.

A peculiar cold sensation plucked at the back of Chase's neck. "Where is home?" he asked offhandedly.

"Rooms o'er the shop there." Liam pointed so vaguely past the square that Chase was certain he was lying.

Chase kept walking. Strangely panicked. He didn't want to know more about the boy. Liam continued to walk behind him.

"Does she always return home at night?" He began to worry that Liam's sister was a prostitute.

He was irritated that he was worried at all.

The boy shrugged. Chase stared at him, not wanting to ask and yet suddenly unable not to. Which made the question come out more sharply than he'd intended.

"What is your sister's name?"

"'Ortensia."

Chase sighed. "It's not."

"It is!" Liam insisted, planting his feet three feet apart as though bracing himself against the gale force of Chase's certainty.

Chase stared him down.

"'Er name is Meggie," Liam confessed. "But I *wish* it was 'ortensia. 'Tis a right pleasure to say, ain't it? ''Ortensia, 'ortensia, 'ortensia.' " He hopped a hop for every syllable of the name on the cobblestones as he sang out the name.

"Liam." Chase needed to interrupt before he went mad.

"Aye, Captain Eversea."

"Are you worried about your sister?"

"Nay. She's fat and cruel."

"Is she?"

He was silent. Hopping over the cobblestones thoughtfully. "She looks like me mum."

"And your mum?"

"Well, she's dead, ain't she?" Liam said with some resignation.

"Is she? I'm sorry."

Liam said nothing. He did one more halfhearted Hortensia hop, just for rebellion's sake.

"Your father?"

Another of those shrugs.

"Have you a surname?"

"'Tis Plum."

Which meant it might be and might not be.

"Is Meggie truly fat and cruel?"

"Nay," Liam admitted after a moment. "Quite nice, actually. Pretty. Pretty as Mrs. March."

Chase doubted this very much, but Mrs. March was most definitely his own standard of pretty, so he didn't debate the point.

"Where do you suppose Meggie is?"

A hesitation. Something haunted flickered over Liam's face.

"She'll come 'ome." He said this with confidence, as though speaking to himself. With a little smile. As though he were the only one in the world who could reassure himself in Meggie's absence.

Chase felt an impatience, a pressure rising in his chest. And he was rendered absolutely, coldly silent.

His impatience wasn't with the boy, but with the world as it was, and what passed for justice, and for the complications it seemed to be laying in his path two weeks before he would leave this boy, and Rosalind, and his family, and his country, behind.

He didn't want to care. It was uncomfortable; his soul ached, creaking, like a muscle unused too long.

"Is that a new shirt?"

"Ye've an eye for detail, too, Captain Eversea. Mrs. Bandycross. Bought fer a penny. I wanted one like yers."

It was much too big for him, but it was a decent shirt and clean, and he supposed it could be considered "like his" in that regard. And Chase knew it had probably been stolen before Liam bought it, since *everything* in London was capital and could be stolen, bartered, sold and resold, and he didn't even bother inquiring who Mrs. Bandycross might be. A fence, doubtless.

If the shirt was clean, the face was not. "Liam, wouldn't you rather be clean?"

"Ain't I?" He sounded surprised.

How to answer *that* question? "To an extent."

Liam sussed out the meaning of this. "Jus' get dirty again, wouldn't I? The water from the wells is fer drinkin', not bathin'. And fer tea, *when* there's tea. Fer when Meggie comes 'ome wi' enough money."

What if Meggie didn't come home?

Chase watched Liam and felt the terror of this possibility, and knew that Liam must, too. But children had a gift for imagining the impossible and for hope, and this one was irrepressible. But he was small, and the world indifferent to the likes of him and Meggie, and if there was no one else between Liam and the world, he could still be crushed.

A hackney was clopping by.

Chase needed to hail it, desperate to know if a message from Rosalind awaited him at home, to know if he could help *her*, at least. To be of use to someone.

To take the worry from her eyes.

"Goin' to see Mrs. March?" the boy said slyly, dragging his dirty toes up and down one dirty calf.

"Ah, so she introduced *herself* to you, did she? Gave her name to you?"

"We 'ad a fine chin-wagging a few nights ago," Liam said as Chase boarded the hack. "About you!" He leaped on the hackney footboard momentarily for the sheer pleasure of being a rascal.

Then hopped down again, and he and his grin became smaller and smaller and smaller as the hack took Chase home.

Chapter 14

❦

I t was with a sense of unreality that Rosalind found herself climbing the steep, judgmentally squeaking stairs of a brothel.

Waaanton, the stairs seemed to squeak. *Waaanton.*

Chase was behind her. Doubtless watching the sway of her arse.

Within two days of seeing Charles Eversea again, she'd obligingly parted her legs just a liiittle bit more so he could fondle her more explicitly behind a bookcase, and rejected a marriage proposal, which might have very well saved her honor in his eyes and her own.

She supposed climbing the creaking, steep stairs of a brothel while ten pairs of curious female eyes bored into her was a natural progression. She'd even been introduced to a woman whose first name seemed to be "The." As in The Duchess.

Mortifyingly, the Duchess had looked at Rosalind, then at Chase, and said, "It's the men who have been somewhat scarce of late, not the girls, so you needn't have brought your own."

Brought his own! As if she were a picnic lunch!

Chase was all aplomb and ease in the place. "I fear we're paying a social call today. I have a question about your paintings. I wondered if you owned any Rubinettos?"

"Who the devil is Rubinetto?" The Duchess was amused. "I'm afraid our paintings do not precisely come with pedigrees. I'm not even certain any of them are signed. We owe their presence to a number of artists, but one in particular. He occasionally takes it out in trade, and none of the girls here object, as he's quite a charming devil and not at all objectionable."

"Bartering is a fine English tradition," Chase humored. "Now . . . Duchess . . . this might sound . . . untoward . . . "

"We pride ourselves on the untoward, Captain."

"But may I bring my friend up to look at the painting?"

"To . . . 'look' at the painting?" The Duchess was all arched brows and insinuating incredulity. And Rosalind's face heated about ten degrees.

"Yes. Is the room occupied at the moment?"

"Not at the moment, but from the look of things between Amanda and Mr. Lavay, you might want to be quick about . . . looking at the painting."

So up the stairs they went.

The very first thing Rosalind noticed, of course, was the bed. A pink velvet counterpane was stretched over a plump mattress, and a heap of fat pillows were mounded at the head of it.

The sight of it made her swallow.

"It's there," Chase said softly.

She didn't need to follow the casual gesture he made. She found it—the painting—over the bed.

She was riveted.

A gentleman—presumably he was a gentleman, to have the money to pay for such a thing—was sprawling on a settee, knees up, great hairy white legs spread wide-open, arms flung behind him, his eyes rolled back in all appearance of bliss. He possessed Byronic curls.

Kneeling between his legs was the angel, quite nude apart from some superfluous gossamer scraps clinging to her, not covering any parts typically covered by clothing, and she was leaning over him attentively.

His enormous cock was in her mouth.

Rosalind suspected she stopped breathing.

She stopped being aware of the functioning of her lungs anyhow. But she *could* suddenly feel every inch of her skin, feverish, alert as though every cell had its own lively consciousness.

"Rosalind."

She gave a start. But she didn't turn. Low, soft. God. That voice. He might as well have just licked the back of her neck.

"I—" she croaked.

She couldn't speak. She couldn't stop staring. She did manage to tear her eyes away for a moment to inspect for a signature: there was none. But her eyes went back to the interesting portion of the painting immediately.

"Rosalind."

Since she couldn't seem to turn around, because the sight of him would likely further overwhelm her senses and she might very well swoon, which had never done in her life. She closed her eyes.

"Are you shocked?" he asked softly. He sounded concerned.

She was fairly certain she'd find his eyes devilishly

glinting when she mustered the nerve to look into them.

'Of . . . of course not.' Her voice was still very weak, but she managed a semblance of indignation. "I've of course seen that sort of thing before."

Dear God. Why on earth had she said *that*?

She instantly wished again for her invisibility shawl. He *had* warned her about the painting.

He was struggling to keep his voice solemn. The bloody man. "Oh. Have you, then?"

She swallowed. She still couldn't bring herself to turn around. "Does it really . . . " She faltered.

"Does it really . . . what?"

She turned, as if the rush of words spun her around. "Does it really feel as good as the painting makes it seem?"

And now *he* was speechless. He stared at her a moment, drop-jawed.

He closed his jaw. And then his words emerged in stumbling disbelief. "The colonel never asked you to . . . that is . . . you didn't . . . "

How would she ever survive the conflagration that was her cheeks at the moment? She said nothing.

"He *didn't*?" Chase was well and truly shocked.

Which seemed a funny thing to be shocked about.

She knew her continued silence was answering all manner of questions for him.

"Yes," he said finally, quite evenly, in clear bemusement. "It feels every bit as extraordinary as the painting would have you believe."

A beat of silence.

"Oh." She tried to say it casually; the word emerged

a cracked squeak. It was difficult to be casual when he was looking at her like that, and he possessed those eyes, those hands, that body, that mouth, that mouth, that mouth . . .

Curiosity and helpless arousal were overriding good sense and embarrassment: "But do *married* men and women—"

"Oh, dear God. Without a doubt, Rosalind," he said instantly. "It is *not* an activity confined to brothels." He didn't add, *It's quite commonplace, you poor sheltered ninny,* but she thought she detected the flavor of that sentiment between the words.

She absorbed this enormity for a moment.

"Shall I describe the pleasure to you, Rosalind?" His voice felt like it was coming from *inside* her. She felt it on her skin, as surely as hands.

No, is what she ought to have said.

Her head moved up and down and without her conscious permission.

"Well, it's well-nigh *indescribable*. The snug, wet heat of a woman's mouth over one's . . . ahem . . . and sucking . . . and licking . . . " He said this slowly. Torturously slowly. Apparently, thoughtfully allowing her time to picture all of it. "It makes one mindless with . . . well, bliss. As the poets say," he added with a diabolical amount of cheer.

He was watching her rather fixedly.

Mesmerized, she watched his mouth form the words "snug" and "wet" and "heat" and "sucking," and felt faint with fascination, and the snug and wet parts of her throbbed as though he'd called them by name.

"I didn't know," she said finally, almost sadly.

"And Rosalind . . . " His voice had become velvety with sympathy. "Imagine the positions of the angel and the gentleman there . . . reversed."

She looked at them again. Then looked quickly away.

Back to the man in front of her, who was far more erotic than the painting by virtue of his mere existence.

"One can . . . " Her voice was squeaky gravel from nerves. She cleared her throat. " . . . do that, too?" She bravely met his eyes. "I mean, a man can . . . to a woman . . . "

He became far more specific.

"Nothing is more erotic than kneeling between the legs of a woman one desires and . . . tasting her . . . licking her . . . until she writhes and screams with pleasure. The warmth, and wet, and heat . . . "

He said this with the absolute conviction with which she was so familiar, and in the tone with which he might recite a requisitions list.

Her skin had acquired a fresh coat of fever. *Do that to me.*

"S-Screams?" She was fairly certain she'd never once *screamed* in the throes of passion.

Was he telling her the truth?

Of course he was. She knew, simply based upon how she felt when he'd simply kissed her. Or when he was even *near*.

Her knees were suddenly made of butter. She began to put her hands up to her face. Then brought them down again, out of pride. Though she was certain the color of her face, and her threadbare voice, and the way her bodice was moving, gave away everything she felt.

It was difficult to breathe through this onslaught of erotic education.

There was a silence.

She threw another sidelong glance at the angel.

"Rosalind . . . " he said gently. He gave her name the intonation of a question. As though something had occurred to him.

She looked up miserably. She was afraid of what he was going to ask next.

His turn to clear his throat. His face was carefully expressionless now. "He did . . . make you come?"

It took her a moment to realize to whom he was referring.

"Of course!" she said with indignant loyalty. "At *least* five times that I can recall!"

Chase froze.

"Five times . . . in one *go*?" He sounded significantly subdued.

She frowned, puzzled by the question.

And then his eyes widened, his face lit, and his head went back a bit and came down again in comprehension. *"Ohhhhh."*

He looked briefly troubled, and inscrutability swept all other expression from his face.

Her own comprehension set in with a cold shock. "Can it—can *I* . . . ?"

"Every . . . single. . . . time," he said firmly. "Well, if done properly. Sometimes more than once per . . . well, per. And there are so many, many, many ways to . . . "

Stop stop stop stop *stop*.

"How?" The word forced its way out, though it sounded a little strangled. *"How* can you . . . what are the . . . "

She knew of but one way.

So, apparently, had her husband.

"I hardly know where to begin. Right side up, upside down, vertically, horizontally, backward, forward, wrong side out, diagonally, nude, partially clothed—"

"Wrong side *out*?"

"I wanted to see if you were listening. You can even do it for yourself."

She'd guessed this, as she had rather participated— at his prompting—in her own near seduction behind a bookcase.

"I . . . "

"Rosalind . . . "

She looked up at him.

"I would be happy to show you all of it. Any time at all. You deserve to know."

The words were smoky soft, a sensual lullaby. Her knees were tempted to buckle, her body to stretch out on the bed he tellingly glanced toward.

There was a silence, dense as those velvet curtains on the bed in the Montmorency.

"If you wish, you can imagine this bed is the Henry VIII bed in the Montmorency, Rosalind. For fantasy plays a role, too. And I'll show you now."

"How . . . how did you know?" she whispered it, awestruck.

"You'd be surprised by what I know." He was whispering now, too.

"I doubt that."

His smile was all lazy wickedness.

She closed her eyes tightly. It was too much. It wasn't that she hadn't overheard soldiers discussing coarse and sexual things, and it wasn't as though she'd been unduly troubled by it, as she wasn't a fragile flower. But all of those things had been rather . . . *straightforward*. Conversation riddled with cant for breasts and penises and the act of sex, and the like. The army was a decidedly earthy place.

But *this* . . . this was like stumbling across a world parallel to the one she lived in, with its own rules and laws and landscape and language. It had become clear to her that there were endless angles and depths of sensuality to explore, and that Chase could likely lead her through each one. She was unnerved and dizzy, and *angry*. She knew he'd been purposefully explicit: to dissolve her resolve. Very unfair, as he knew by now what he could do to her with a single touch.

But in truth, she appreciated being enlightened.

Because now she understood what she'd missed. And what she would sacrifice if she never experienced it.

And what he truly wanted from her.

She took in a deep fortifying breath.

"Thank you for being so forthcoming," she managed coolly.

She was gratified when he blinked.

She turned for the door, and over her shoulder said firmly, "And that's definitely the same angel."

The Duchess looked up as the creaking stairs announced their descent.

"Did you learn what you came to learn?" she asked.

"And then some," Chase confirmed, noticing that Rosalind was narrowing her eyes at him. "The angel upstairs is compelling."

He followed her down the stairs, watching the lovely

sway of her sweet peach arse, and regretted what he'd just done to her. He'd done it in part deliberately, and it hadn't at all been cricket, and he'd timed it badly.

A man may time things badly when he wants something badly, he thought.

"Ah, yes. I can see why," the Duchess said. "That particular angel has inspired many a gentleman to feats of endurance, and I do believe her very presence helps to awaken slumbering appendages, given what she's doing to a gentleman's appendage in the painting. Though not always, I should say," she added.

God. Marie-Claude had obviously said something to the Duchess about him.

"That painting," she added, "and the one over the settee of the sprawling girl, would be the work of a Mr. Wyndham."

Wyndham? He'd never heard of a painter named Wyndham in his life.

"Are you interested in investing in erotic art, Captain?"

"I might well be," Chase said smoothly. "Do you know Mr. Wyndham's direction? We should like to have a word with him about his work."

"He lives and works in Bethel Street—above a cobbler's, I believe. I shouldn't think there are many cobblers on Bethel Street."

"My sincere thanks. How is business for you now?"

"Well, livelier since an American ship as well as *The Courage* pulled into port. I understand we'll be losing you soon to that fine vessel? The stocky gentleman standing near the hearth is the first mate of the American ship. A Mr. Lavay. Determined to spend all his money here, and we're happy to encourage it."

"And I'm happy to hear that commerce is alive and well. I sent Mr. Kinkade regards from you, and from Marie-Claude in particular."

"Thank you for the thought, Captain Eversea. We're still awaiting his return."

If she noticed that Kinkade hadn't sent his regards in return, she didn't say a word about it.

"You're certain we can't tempt you into lingering, Captain Eversea?" Her eyes darted from Chase to Rosalind and back again so quickly they called to mind billiard balls.

"You can certainly tempt me, Duchess," he said gallantly, "but I fear we cannot linger today."

They agreed to call upon Mr. Wyndham straight-away.

From what he understood of artists, they typically lived in garrets because the rent was cheap. But this one lived in a fairly respectable part of town, and he was indeed above a cobbler. As they climbed his stairs, they heard the steady *thwack thwack thwack* of a shoe being built or repaired.

A woman with a thunderous, fleshy face, hair wrapped up in a rag, wielding a broom the way one might clutch a pike, answered the door.

"'Es up there." She used her chin to point.

The first thing they saw in this blazingly sunny room was a much larger than life-size painting featuring almost nothing but miles of rose and cream flesh. It was notable primarily for the artist's enthusiasm for its subject—a nude woman reclining—rather than its finesse.

"Commissioned by an earl. It's not a very good paint-

ing, all in all," the artist who must have been Wyndham
called over his shoulder with cheerful candor. His back
was to them; he was rifling among a row of jarred pigments lined on a shelf, each labeled neatly with their
names, ready for crushing and mixing. He came away
with OCHRE.

"Aye, but she's pretty." Chase was appreciative.

Rosalind was regarding the painting bravely, without blinking. The woman truly *was* imposing: twice
the size of a usual woman, sprawling lazily and round
everywhere—round white thighs, round tum, round
arms, enormous breasts, lush curls atop her head and
between her thighs. A quite obvious brunette. A very
earthy painting. Not painstaking, and not the least
sentimental.

Wyndham looked amused by the fact that Chase
hadn't disagreed with his own assessment of the painting. "A rich man's mistress."

"A fortunate man."

They shared a manly grin while Rosalind struggled
to appear sophisticated.

"My job is no hardship. I do make a fair living, current appearances notwithstanding. There are times of
lean and times of fat. And so it goes."

"As it so happens, I'd like to speak to you about
commissioning a painting."

"Commissioning *me*? You must frequent brothels.
Or perhaps you're contemplating opening your own,
Mister . . . ?"

"Charles."

Mr. Wyndham turned fully around and took a good
look at the two of them.

He was a lean chap, pale from a life lived indoors

and, from the looks of him, gleeful nights of debauchery. He was decorated in vivid streaks of paint; his shirt was linen, loose and old, two buttons open at the throat, rolled up at the sleeves. Hair clipped short, the better to keep paint out of it, Chase supposed, and just a shade darker than a fox pelt. His eyes were sherry-colored, narrow, and glittered in the broad light of the room, mischievous, a bit jaded. It appeared that his nose had been broken once.

Wyndham's eyes widened. "Please accept my apologies. My questions were asked in all seriousness— I'd wondered where you happened upon my work, or where you might have heard of me. I didn't notice you had brought"—he studied Rosalind for a moment, then decided upon—"a lady with you. Though I doubt I'd be any less blunt in her presence."

He smiled at her, and bowed, and Rosalind smiled, too. Chase could *feel* her tamping her flirting impulses. It was virtually the only way any woman could communicate with this man, he decided.

"But perhaps this is a social call? *Mrs. Pomfrey!*" Wyndham suddenly turned and bellowed down the stairs, "Will you please bring up tea for three?" Flirting.

"Ye didna gi' me the *blunt* fer market, ye stingy bugger!" The feminine snarl came from somewhere in the bowels of the house. "Canna buy tea wi' *air*! Drink *paint* if ye're thirsty!"

"I fear I cannot offer you any tea," Wyndham confirmed gravely. "But I've . . . " He looked around the room. "Brandy!" He'd located it on a shelf beneath the window, tucked between jars of oil. "It was a gift from a friend. And he's an earl, so it's drinkable." He rubbed his hands on a cloth tucked into the waistband of his splattered trousers and looked about, apparently for glasses, saw none, shrugged, dashed the bottle up to his mouth, took a slug, passed the bottle to Chase, who also shrugged, threw back a gulp, then held it out to Rosalind.

Who stared at him with burning incredulity.

He handed the bottle back to Wyndham, who settled it back on the table. Which wobbled, as one leg was clearly shorter than the other, or the loft itself slanted somewhat downward.

"You know of my work, sir? Where would you have seen it?"

"At the Velvet Glove."

"Of course, of course. There's the one over the settee, and several up in the rooms," the painter confirmed.

"One of an angel . . . " Chase paused.

"Well, she isn't *quite* an angel," Wyndham modified. "Given what she's doing."

While the two men shared another manly grin, Rosalind was desperately seeking a safe place to land her eyes. Everywhere, there were naked things or bawdily smiling men.

"If you see my angels, like as not you're in a brothel," Wyndham agreed complacently. And then he turned to admire Rosalind quite baldly.

She returned his gaze evenly, taking his measure.

"I take it you don't mean to explain your friend, sir. Fear not. I number among my favorite acquaintances all manner of unexplainable men and women. Did you wish me to paint her? Perhaps she'd like some modeling work? Or . . . perhaps I'll be quiet and you can explain to me why a man of obvious means is here with a beautiful well-bred woman."

"You might direct those questions to me, Mr. Wyndham. I am standing right before you." Rosalind could be stern, too.

He looked genuinely startled.

"I beg your pardon, madam. The sort of women accompanied by men to my loft generally leave the talking to the men. I'd be delighted to address *anything* at all to you."

A leading statement to be sure—"the sort of women," indeed—but he said it so disarmingly that the rays of his charm were surely felt as far away as the banks of the Thames. Surely people were basking in them even now.

Mr. Wyndham could likely get away with nearly anything.

Chase liked him for no particular reason except that he seemed entirely himself.

He was also certain he would never allow Wyndham anywhere near any of his sisters.

"We do admire your technique, Mr. Wyndham," he said smoothly. "Have you ever painted anything other than bordello art? We thought we'd like something a bit . . . pastoral. For a country home. The Duchess was certain your skills extended beyond . . . "

"Togas and tits?"

"Precisely."

"Pastoral, hmmm?" Wyndham studied them with his sharp eyes. Intrigued. Amused.

"I'm fond of cows," Rosalind offered brightly.

"She's fond of cows," Chase reiterated.

"I *have*, in fact, painted cows," Wyndham admitted. He said nothing more.

Rosalind was rigid with anticipation.

A few days ago, when he was listening to Colin, Chase had never dreamed that talk of cows would fill him with such anticipation. But he realized he would have to tread carefully here. Mr. Wyndham was nobody's fool, and he had the air of someone who cared not the least what anyone thought of him. Which made him a man not easily frightened or swayed.

"Perhaps I can view this pastoral painting or something like it to ascertain whether you can paint what we wish to purchase?"

He'd just done a wonderful imitation of a prig. Genevieve would have been proud.

"Well, in truth, I've painted landscapes for the Earl of Rawden, who does God only knows what with them, as I haven't yet seen them hanging in his home. I painted another, a much larger and more complex work featuring cows, though never met the gentleman who commissioned it, in truth. Though I was happy enough to take his money. A gentleman approached me and asked me to paint something that could be mistaken for an Italian Renaissance painting. Ha! Was I amused! I was informed that it was for a wealthy client whose mistress was a bit of a snob but wasn't particularly educated and wouldn't know the difference. And I was told that more commissions would be forthcoming if I were discreet about it, as he didn't want anyone to know he'd learned of me from the Velvet Glove. A married man, I imagine. So I painted cows and horses and cherubs and I threw in an angel because I can paint them easily enough and he wanted one. He wanted me to add a moon, too, and moons are quite easy, too. Just a . . . " He made a sweeping, curving motion in the air. "Is that the sort of thing you had in mind?"

He'd just neatly described the Rubinetto painting at the Montmorency.

But Chase knew he couldn't ask Wyndham whether he painted under a different name without revealing what he already knew.

It was also entirely possible Mr. Wyndham hadn't even signed the painting himself. That *Rubinetto* had been added later.

So he asked a question Mr. Wyndham was certain to understand.

"Does your threshold of discretion come with a price?"

Mr. Wyndham's head went back in appreciation of this gambit. He smiled slowly. "What did you have in mind, sir?"

"Ten pounds."

"It was commissioned by a Mr. Welland-Dowd."

Chase stared.

Wyndham grinned. "I've the morals and loyalty of a cat," he confessed. "And I need to pay my housekeeper."

"Bleedin' *right* ye need to pay yer 'ousekeeper!" The voice was unnervingly close. The sound of a broom being violently applied to a corner was heard at the foot of the stairs. *Slam, slam, slam.*

"A time of lean?" Rosalind inquired sweetly.

"She's merely expressing her frustrated love for me via the broom," Mr. Wyndham explained, sotto voce.

"Do you know Mr. Welland-Dowd's direction, perchance? Or anything else about him? I should like to see the painting. I'm wondering if I'm acquainted with him or can affect an introduction, as his name sounds familiar."

"Hmm. Cannot say where he lives, but I can tell you he's a nondescript chap. Thin, a bit pointy in the nose, but that describes half of the men in England. Had a squint, but it was bright in here the two times I saw him, so I'm not certain it's a defining characteristic. Not dressed expensively. Or interestingly. Blue coat, boots of no discernible pedigree. A bit diffident, all in all. My favorite of his characteristics were his deep pockets." Wyndham winked.

There was a ring of the bell down below, the sound of a broom flung aside, stomping feet and a door flung open. *Bam*.

"A *hoor* is 'ere to see ye, ye useless benighted malodorous codpiece!" his housekeeper bellowed up the stairs.

"Benighted!" Chase mused, impressed. "An underused word, to be sure."

"She's positively Shakespearean when she's had enough liquor. She can cook adequately when there's food in the house, and she does keep the place clean. It's as if she can't help it—the cleaning—even when she isn't paid."

He turned to bellow in return.

"*Which* hoor, Mrs. Palf— Oh, good afternoon, Minette," he said as a woman's head appeared at the top of the stair. "She isn't *actually* a whore," he explained to Chase and Rosalind. "She's a model."

Minette nodded her head rapidly in agreement, and beamed at them, ducking a curtsy.

Upon closer inspection, it became clear they beheld the angel from the Velvet Glove, and, as fate would have it, from the Rubinetto painting.

He wondered if Rosalind recognized her, too. He

thought he saw her sneaking a glance at her bosom, and then at her face, and—yes, yes, there it was: the dawning of recognition.

And a not entirely warm fascination.

"Pay the angels, or pay the housekeeper? How is one to choose, Mr. Charles?" Wyndham said, coming forward to bow to Minette and escort her forward by the arm. He brought with him an interesting smell of debauchery: oil and beeswax, the kinds of things artists mix into pigments to create paint, brandy, a bit of old sweat, lingering cigar smoke.

"I'm on the side of the angels, Mr. Wyndham."

"I thought you might be."

Minette dimpled at Chase.

Rosalind seemed disinclined to take sides regarding angels and housekeepers, but she'd gone rigid as a cat ready to attack.

Which Chase found gratifying, somehow.

He found ten pounds—a fortune indeed for the painter—in his coat and handed it over to him.

"I thank you for your consultation, Mr. Wyndham."

"Do let me know what you decide about the cows, sir." Wyndham was quite ironic. "Now, Minette, my dear, today you'll be posing as a mermaid . . . "

Chapter 15

❧

They dodged the housekeeper and her viciously applied broom and saw themselves out. She spared them a withering glance.

"Good day," she said with some dignity. But slammed the door behind her.

"The house *was* spotless," Chase conceded as they made their way down the steps.

"You noticed?"

"I was a soldier. We were trained to keep things quite neat and to notice when they were not. Ironic, when one also learns to sleep in the mud and dirt. But it's the little things that hold our worlds together. Old habits die very hard."

Rosalind knew this to be true, particularly when it came to Chase.

"Do you think Kinkade is Welland-Dowd?" she wondered.

Chase burst into laughter so booming that every head on the street rotated, startled.

Oh, God. She'd just understood when she'd said it aloud.

Welland-Dowd.

Well-endowed.

"Well, I'm not one to judge, and when compared to *me*, of course, no one *is*, but I have gone swimming in the same swimming hole with the man, and I can tell you he has nothing at all to be ashamed of—"

"Don't don't don't *don't*." She covered her ears.

He was still laughing. He was *gorgeous* when he laughed. Bloody bawdy soldier.

She couldn't hold it against him: his laughter was glorious, and it struck her that he did it so seldom these days. Her heart became a kite and sailed, sailed away. Unfamiliar and a bit frightening to feel so light, so unmoored, so tempted to give away control at every turn. With an effort she furled her heart back to the concern that kept her anchored:

Lucy.

With every clue, with luck, they would be led closer to Lucy.

"We know the painting was commissioned for a purpose," he said, "a purpose about which Mr. Wyndham seems to have been kept in the dark. If he was trying to hide something from us, he would have lied. So the Rubinetto was painted by a brothel artist and hung in a museum from which men seem to go and not come out, or go out but not come in. We need to have a look around the museum in the dark. Tonight. Something is definitely amiss."

"A look 'round the museum tonight? After it's *locked* for the evening?"

"We can likely get in through the service door. My guess is I can easily pick the lock or otherwise force the door. Failing that, I shall try a window."

He noticed she was regarding him with mystification. "When on earth did you learn to pick *locks*?"

"My brothers. Unless you'd prefer not to accompany me?" he added, reconsidering the wisdom of taking her.

But she was not a wilting flower. "I'll accompany you," she agreed.

"What does it mean?" she asked. "*Not* his name," when he whirled with shining eyes to begin to explain it to her in what she was certain would be an abundance of physiological detail.

He hesitated. "I'm uncertain what it means, if anything. The man he described doesn't sound a bit like Kinkade. You know what Kinkade looks like."

She did indeed. "Why would someone commission it and then donate it to the museum? And why would the museum *hang* it?"

"Because it's a genuine Rubinetto, and I understand they're quite rare."

Rosalind laughed. "I should like to own one."

"Would you?" Chase made it sound as though she'd revealed a disturbing new aspect of her character.

She smiled. She wondered if he realized how very much he *cared* about everything. "It looks so . . . peaceful." Not quite the word she wanted. She, like the mistress Wyndham had described, knew nothing of art. But Mr. Wyndham's contentment with his lot showed in his work.

"Peaceful?" Only Chase could make that word sound distasteful. "It looks unlike anything in this world or the next."

He made this sound like treason. Which made her smile again. She was about to ask him what *he* knew of the next world, but stopped herself immediately. She'd listened to the ravings of men thrashing in the midst of their fevers when they were wounded; she knew they saw visions of torment and of bliss. She'd heard them conduct conversations with loved ones just before they died. She didn't want to know what Chase had seen in that world between life and death, because she would be reminded of all the possible different outcomes to Waterloo.

And in none of them would he be walking next to her now. The chill of that possibility touched the back of her neck.

"Precisely," was all she said.

He was watching her, a furrow between his brows; she'd puzzled him. She didn't care. She'd thankfully jettisoned the need to explain herself years ago, along with that girl she'd been. She was content enough just to walk down a slightly disreputable street right now alongside a slightly disreputable man who had just a bit of a limp. The gold head of his stick flashed almost cheerfully in the sun.

"Isn't it peaceful in Derbyshire?" He wanted to know.

She was tempted to tell him of the terrain, and the little flowers growing by the brook near her home, and her neighbors, who were nosy and talkative but only intermittently interesting, and the house that was now hers thanks to her late husband but never actually felt like hers. Just to torture him with details. To see how long he could endure it.

And then she realized that details weren't necessary and had nothing at all do with her answer.

"It isn't my kind of peace." She hadn't realized this was true until she'd said it aloud.

"Your kind of peace?" It was, she realized, an invitation to expound.

She wasn't sure how to do it. "It's just that . . . even though the painting is desperately odd and whimsical, every creature in it looks quite pleased with its circumstances and very accepting and a little . . . a little dreamy. As though they know all is well and will always be well. It's lively and strange and a bit . . . well, supernatural. And it's very colorful."

Chase was unaccountably charmed to the marrow by this singular list of reasons for liking a painting.

His sister Genevieve would have heard them, and stared at Rosalind for a dumbstruck instant before laying a gentle hand on her arm and issuing a gently appalled, "Oh no. Oh no no no no. Good heavens, my dear. No." Genevieve would have explained the precise critical reasons for the painting's hideousness, whereas Chase's instincts told him it was hideous. Even Mr. Wyndham had no illusions about his own talents.

And then Chase began to understand. *Everyone in it was content*, she'd said.

Rosalind's life had been hectic and colorful and violent and she'd seen more of the world than either of his sisters had. *She'd done what she'd needed to do*, she'd told him. And now she wanted to be able to *choose* what came next.

He understood afresh how much she'd been forced to surrender to circumstances, none of them of her choosing. But he also understood the great satisfaction that could be had in doing one's duty. Her path to maturity hadn't been entirely graceful, but she had navigated it, and all because of an innate courage. She hadn't shied away from the blood and death of war.

She was as dutiful as he was.

Dutiful, he thought, rhymes with beautiful.

It was the only poetic impulse he'd ever had in his life. He decided it would be his last, because it made him feel foolish.

If only he didn't admire her as much as he desired her. And he suddenly felt something entirely new: he was afraid to seduce her as much as he wanted to seduce her, and as much as he suspected she could be seduced.

For then he would have to leave her. He honestly didn't think he'd be able to give her up.

And he didn't think he could make love to her without possessing her.

She'd made it very clear that it wasn't what she wanted. And he still wanted her to choose.

So he knew a strange happiness, a simple pleasure in being with her cut through with a strange desolation. Like those sunbeams pushing through rain clouds on the day he was attacked, his first day back in London.

It was an oddly peaceful sensation, for all that.

"It *is* colorful," he allowed gently. "The painting."

"Why are you smiling?" She was suspicious of the gentleness.

He shrugged innocently. They walked on.

"Is it peaceful in Sussex?" she asked. "In Pennyroyal Green?"

"It is *never* peaceful in Pennyroyal Green," he said grimly. "Don't let anyone tell you otherwise."

"Doubtless because *you* live there." It was her turn to smile.

Her eyes disappeared with her smile, her cheeks rounded, her face luminous; her mouth made a sort of vee. Her smile was entirely unselfconscious, and it transformed her from delicately, sensually, beautiful into plain but joyously lit.

He felt restless watching her.

"Which is why you can't wait to return," she added.

He ignored this. "I'm certain India will be significantly more peaceful by contrast."

"Why isn't it peaceful in Sussex? Apart from the fact that the benighted Redmond family lives there."

"Ah! Very good use of 'benighted.' "

She shrugged modestly.

"Well, the Redmonds live in Pennyroyal Green. For a beginning. You might know how our family feels about the Redmonds. And my brother Colin lives there, whom you may have heard a thing or two about—and now that he's married he's become an insufferable livestock authority. There's Miss Marietta Endicott's Academy for Girls, which we all call the School for Recalcitrant Girls, and indeed it is—all the girls in England who make rather a habit of misbehavior get sent there, which means all the boys in town can scarcely stay away. Ned Hawthorne's daughter Polly—his family has run the Pig & Thistle for centuries—cannot seem to forgive Colin for marrying at all and she's but seventeen, which is the age when such things are taken quite seriously and most painful. Sometimes it's hard to get served in the Pig & Thistle for that reason!"

"You don't say!"

"My sister Olivia pretends she isn't becoming a spinster simply because that bastard Lyon Redmond took it upon himself to disappear some years ago, but she becomes thinner and more glittery-eyed every day."

"You worry."

He shrugged. "And Ian seems to be following in

Colin's footsteps. Back when he was dangling from the balconies of married countesses, that is."

"Sounds colorful."

He smiled again. "It gets better. I was banished to London to ascertain the suitability of a distant cousin for the role of the new vicar of Pennyroyal Green because in fact my family can no longer stand my company. I haven't yet seen him."

She turned to him in surprise. "Your family owns the living in Pennyroyal Green?"

He was amused that she didn't leap to disabuse him of the notion that his family could no longer stand him.

"Yes. As unlikely as that seems. He's a cousin, allegedly. Dozens of times removed, but possesses the surname Sylvaine, as did my mother. A Mr. Adam Sylvaine. It's my second given name."

She stopped and stared at him incredulously. Well, it was more of a glare, really.

He stopped, too. "What is it?" he asked, irritated.

"Chase, you must go see him straightaway! He'll want to know whether he'll be able to feed himself or start a family or move to a new home. Perhaps he'll be offered a living elsewhere if you don't find him suitable." She sounded appalled at his lack of consideration.

He, in truth, wasn't proud of it, either.

It was her fault. He'd been thinking entirely of *her*.

Still, he fixed his captain's glare upon her, haughty and affronted.

She gave him cool green implacable command in return.

"How on earth will I know whether he'll make a suitable vicar? Deciding such a thing is an enormous responsibility. My father was clearly not in his right mind when he entrusted this godforsaken task—yes, I realize that sounds like a contradiction in terms—to me. Now why are *you* smiling?"

"Your definition of an enormous responsibility. Truly. Remind me again: *how* many men were under your command?"

He was silent.

She began walking again. "No one expects you to know *everything*, Captain Eversea."

She was smiling to herself.

He studiously did not look at her. It was outrageously disconcerting to be understood.

What was odd was that he didn't mind being shamed into going to see his cousin, necessarily. It could have something to do with the fact that Rosalind was doing the shaming.

He'd sent a note round to his cousin, apologizing for being remiss in seeing him, saying he'd been unavoidably detained, which was not strictly a lie, and in response his cousin issued an invitation to call upon him straightaway.

How on earth was he supposed to ascertain the "suitability" of a new vicar?

He knew his Bible; his parents had insisted the whole brood attend church every Sunday in Pennyroyal Green, despite the fact that he was absolutely certain he'd seen his father sleeping with his eyes open more than once. In fact, a fly had once done precisely six aerial figure eights—Chase had counted them—before it settled on his father's nose during one summer service, whereupon his father shot bolt upright with a grunt, kicking the pew in front of him and jarring Mrs. Notterley's hat from her head. Despite the fact that his eyes were open and that *everyone* could see where the fly was about to land.

A good skill when one has a slew of mischievous brothers: sleeping with one's eyes open.

He wondered if this vicar could keep the congregation awake, and how on earth he would determine whether he would. Perhaps he would ask him to orate, and he would sit like an Oxford don, unsmilingly judgmental, tapping a rule against his palm. Or glare blankly like a captain inspecting a subaltern.

He could always challenge his cousin to a card game for the living. If he was any sort of respectable family member, then gaming would be in his blood.

Unsurprisingly, given the neighborhood and the accommodations, Adam Sylvaine answered his own door.

A wedge of lamplight lit his first glimpse of his cousin, who could nearly look him in the eye. Tall. Blond. Surprising. He'd never before met a blond family member. He did have the elegant long-boned face and pale eyes, vivid against his fair coloring. In all likelihood they were blue.

"Charles Eversea," Chase said, and bowed.

"Captain Eversea—cousin," Adam said pleasantly, establishing their relationship straightaway. "Very good to meet you, indeed."

Good voice. Good bow. Not obsequious. He would not have been able to abide obsequious. Not too hale-fellow-well-met. *Did* sound genuinely pleased to meet him.

Adam stepped aside and ushered Chase in, taking

in his own hands Chase's coat and hat. Chase did not proffer his walking stick.

"I must apologize for . . . " Adam waved a hand at the simplicity of the room.

Chase saw a small sitting room; a fire burning low, which served as a place to toast bread in the morning; doubtless the bedroom was a tiny cell off the short, narrow hallway.

"I only intended to be in London for a few days, and these rooms were close to the library. I take my meals at the pub across the road."

Chase hated it when people felt the need to apologize for what they couldn't help, though he realized it was all part of social niceties. The room was perfectly adequate for a cousin begging for a living from another much wealthier cousin, and perfectly adequate for temporary lodgings, and perfectly adequate for a man who'd slept in the mud before—as he had. Irritation must have shown on his face, because one of his cousin's eyebrows leaped into a steeple. His mother could do that. Interesting skill.

"That is to say, I would have received you at Whitehall, but the King was using his antechambers."

Chase laughed. It was a decent attempt at a joke, but Cousin Adam was nervous.

A silence followed. It suited Chase, for the moment, to allow the silence. People tended to reveal things about themselves during silences.

Adam did. He had long scholarly fingers that drummed in intervals on his knees, as though they would have been preferring to turn the pages of a book. He was thin—his shirt hung a little too loosely on him—which was to be expected of someone who likely read a good deal and forgot to eat while he was doing it. His boots were old, creased at the toes, but had been recently polished. Broad shoulders ran in the family, Chase noted; Adam had them.

Chase seldom knew how to talk to scholars. Miles Redmond would have known, as he was an eccentric intellectual, too. He spent a good deal of time hunched over the chessboard in front of the fire at the Pig & Thistle with Mr. Culpepper and Mr. Cooke, and was planning another trip to the South Seas. He'd gone and married someone no one ever heard of before, a lovely woman of the sort Chase had never dreamed would look twice at Miles Redmond, and brought her to church, which caused necks to tremble with the effort of not craning to stare.

Marriage was an *epidemic* in Pennyroyal Green these days.

Perhaps his impulse to propose to Rosalind had stemmed in part from that: the contagion.

He shunted the thought away and looked about the room hopefully. Saw only a teapot and two cups of tea nicely arranged on a tray in preparation for pouring, a few slices of purchased lemon seedcake arranged on a plate, and no brandy decanter. Not even any sherry.

He turned his head slowly back to his cousin and looked at him incredulously.

Adam cleared his throat. "I imagine you've come to inspect me for suitability and the like."

"Why the Church?" Out the question came without preamble.

"Why the military?"

Well. Point to cousin Adam, because he hadn't expected to be lobbed a question as an answer to a question. Unless it was the sort meant to answer his question, a typically irritating scholar trick.

"Because it's the thing that suits me best," he said. "It came quite naturally to me."

He had never in his life been asked that question, or considered the reason.

As for vicars, in his experience, men became vicars as a result of having no choice in the matter.

"Why do you suppose that's true?" his cousin asked.

So conversationally asked that the answer eased right out of him before he even thought about it. "It's what I do best. Serving and commanding men in the service of good purpose. Fighting to protect things that matter—family and country. Maintaining peace and freedom. Order and discipline and loyalty and camaraderie in honor of all those things."

Unlike his brothers Colin and Ian, the military had literally and figuratively left its mark upon him. And now, unlike Colin and Ian, he seemed not to fit anywhere anymore.

"I think the Church is what I'm best at. For oddly enough, very similar reasons."

He stared at his cousin.

Who stared back. Then helped himself to a slice of seedcake.

"So, Cousin Adam . . . "

Adam sat up alertly at Chase's tone. Challenging.

There was something Chase wanted to know. "You've rules, yes, in your profession? Love thy neighbor, and so forth? Rules that you're honor bound to drill into your parishioners and to live by?"

"I suppose that's one way to look at it. Soooo . . . I'll

say yes," Adam said, waiting expectantly, thinking this might be a test. He also looked a little amused, Chase noticed.

"What if you don't see how the rules apply in a given circumstance? What if doing right in one way means you must do wrong in another? And does a grave wrong take anything away from a good deal of right?"

He was of course thinking of Rosalind, and Kinkade, and Colonel March.

"When the rules as you understand them—when your *own* rules—don't fit your circumstance," his cousin said, "you must trust your instincts to guide you toward the higher good. You must trust that your own innate good will lead you to do the right thing, to do what you believe is the right thing, which is the best any of us can do. None of us ever truly knows the ultimate consequence of any of our actions."

Chase stared at his cousin.

Adam Sylvaine gazed evenly back.

And then finally Chase sighed. "Oh, I think you'll do, Adam." He said this sourly.

Adam grinned at him. Chase noticed that it was his mother's grin, around the edges anyhow.

"My thanks, Captain—"

"Please do call me Chase."

They chatted about family for a while longer, and then Chase decided he must take his leave. "Feel free to call upon me if you intend to stay in town longer, Adam."

"I will be here for another week or so, cousin, and then I'll return for my belongings and move into the vicarage. I shall look forward to meeting the rest of my family."

It occurred to Chase that he would need to warn Adam Sylvaine about the Redmonds. An interesting position for an Eversea relative to be in: tending to a flock containing Redmonds was rather like asking a cat to look after the spiritual welfare of dogs. It might pose an interesting moral dilemma for his cousin, and this cheered Chase, who loved presenting anyone with a good challenge.

He clasped his cousin's hand—Adam had a good shake, as he'd had brothers to wrestle with, too—and turned to leave.

It was when he'd reached the door of the small room that he noticed his leg didn't hurt. At *all*.

That he'd walked holding, but not using, his stick.

He went utterly still.

Chase had seldom known true fear.

Oh, there were different kinds of fear. The fear of confronting a heavily armed enemy, for instance, which was familiar. Tolerable. He knew how to behave in those circumstances. There was a known within an unknown.

This was *entirely* different. It was a fear that he'd gone mad.

His heart leaped into his throat. He felt again uncertain as a child, and it was a feeling he loathed, because he'd never, never felt that sense of uncertainty these days.

That was, apart from when he spent time with Rosalind, of course.

He paused at the door and turned slowly to look at Cousin Adam.

He might have imagined it. It might have been a trick of the light.

But he thought Adam looked terrified.

Whatever expression Chase had caught on his cousin's face transformed quickly into a smile.

Chase lifted his hand by way of farewell. Adam lifted a hand by way of farewell.

And Chase's leg ached again by the time he'd arrived home.

Chapter 16

The next day—another sticky, appropriately lemon-skied London summer day—he fetched Rosalind to go back to the Montmorency, which was, as usual, not precisely bustling with activity.

At least of the sort visible to anyone outside of it.

Liam was, unsurprisingly, sitting on the steps. For some reason today he seemed dwarfed by the museum facade, as he'd never been before. And Chase realized this was because he was ever in motion: he had never seen the boy truly still.

Liam looked up as though his head suddenly weighed twice what it once had. His arms were extended out in front of him, resting on his knees.

When they approached, he splayed five fingers without lifting his arms, as though the effort was simply more than he could endure.

"Care to interpret that, young man?"

Liam finally looked all the way up, and Rosalind's breath caught.

His eyes were utterly lightless. His face was blank, stunned. As though he'd taken a blow.

"Interp . . . ?" And then he stopped. As though he didn't care whether he spoke another word again.

"Interpret means please tell me what *this* means." And Chase fanned out his fingers in imitation of Liam. She could hear the subtle tension in Chase's voice, even if Liam did not.

Chase, despite himself, was worried.

Liam straightened a little at the tone of Chase's voice; one could use that tone as a spine, in a pinch, she thought.

"Five men went into the museum yesterday, Captain Eversea. Two came out."

Chase exchanged a look with Rosalind.

"Liam." Chase said it with low command, but tension thrummed in his voice. Careful not to be too gentle, because he sensed the boy would balk. "Please look at me."

The head went up. Those bleak eyes were intolerable. Rosalind was unaccountably frightened.

"Are you ill?" Chase kept his voice even.

And that's when she knew Chase was frightened, too. The two of them carefully did not meet each other's eyes, for in this moment they understood something irrevocable had happened to the two of them: they'd allowed Liam to matter.

Liam appeared to be biting the inside of his lip. Finally he spoke.

"Said she'd nicked a loaf of bread. Called the Charley's. Took 'er away."

Oh, God. They knew he meant Meggie.

The very worst part was that he wasn't crying. He had the look of someone far beyond tears. Dazed, and yet stoic, and Rosalind could scarcely breathe for the plummeting panic she felt on his behalf.

No ten-year-old boy should ever look like that. And

yet here he was, absorbing another loss, overwhelmed by the fact that life was stripping away from him the very few things he could call his own. And now he was entirely alone.

So little remains between *any* of us and this kind of desolation, she thought. What holds the world together for us are the people we love.

"Are you talking about Meggie?" Chase was all sharp questions. "Who told you this?"

Liam seemed not to be fully listening. "She willna be comin' 'ome after all," he confessed shamefacedly.

"Liam. Answer me. Who told you this? *Might* she have nicked a loaf of bread? Where did they take her? *Who* took her?"

Liam shrugged. "She might 'ave done. She 'as before, I ken. When we dinna earn enough to buy food. I 'eard it from everyone in the boardinghouse."

He was right. It didn't matter. Theft was theft, and theft was wrong, and the justice system all too frequently seemed unjust. Hanging was seen as a deterrent; the English preferred to eliminate their criminals by sending them away or killing them, as he and Kinkade had discussed.

And soldiers were routinely flogged for petty theft in the army. Chase had found himself needing to order more than one flogging for various transgressions.

But this wasn't war.

And starvation was wrong, too.

And vanishing sisters were wrong.

And suddenly right and wrong were superfluous, and he thought of his cousin's words, and was fiercely glad he'd heard them.

"Where did this happen? And do you know the name of this Charley?"

"Aye. 'E walks o'er t' Covent Garden most nights. Name o' Buckthwaite. Everyone knows him. But she isna in the stone pitcher. No one has seen her. I tried to find her. I tried . . . " His voice trailed off.

The "stone pitcher" meant Newgate, they knew.

Chase and Rosalind exchanged a look. Chase's eyes were nearly black with anger, but something stoic and determined hardened his features.

Rosalind sent him a beseeching look. He met it inscrutably.

And they looked away from each other.

Each understood their reluctance to do what they did next, but there was never a question that they would do it.

"Come, Liam."

The boy looked up at Chase in dull surprise. As though words were taking longer to penetrate his mind today.

Chase swooped down, picked him up under one arm, barely allowing him time to squeak, and swung him back into the carriage.

They took him to Rosalind's borrowed home, as it was closer, and she had no servants other than her maid who would be scandalized by the presence of a filthy boy, and because, in truth, neither of them could bear the smell of Liam for a much longer trip. The memory of him would likely linger in the carriage's upholstery until it was cleaned and aired.

On the way there it became increasingly clear that

Liam would need to be scrubbed in order to be tolerated in close quarters, and would likely leave a lingering memento behind in the way of his own singular odor in any place he visited until then.

So Rosalind heated four kettles worth of steaming water and dumped them into a large copper tub, then pumped in cold to make a perfect broth for bathing a boy.

And then she beckoned Chase and Liam into the kitchen.

She produced a bar of soap—Liam was going to smell of lavender whether he wanted to or not—and slapped it into Chase's hand.

He stared back at her in mute appeal.

"It has to be you, and you know it. Just . . . show him how it's done, if he doesn't know."

Chase sighed heavily. Man and boy vanished into the kitchen.

Much splashing and rude swearing, and then, mercifully, magically, laughter ensued while Rosalind listened from the parlor, sitting in the chair, curtains parted slightly to allow sun in to warm her face. She felt unaccountably exhausted, unaccountably light, strangely borderless. She was entirely uncertain how to feel about anything at all in this moment, but missed Lucy profoundly and felt glad to have both Chase and Liam there, though they represented nothing to her but uncertainty and possibly heartache and she was too weary to care about that for now. It was sweet and bittersweet, and much better than if they hadn't been there at all.

They would not have been if Lucy hadn't been missing.

She nearly dozed off to the low tones of Chase's

voice, oddly soothing, though he was no doubt telling Liam more gory stories of battle.

It was the sound, oddly enough, both of safety and a fear she could not articulate.

A half hour or so later Chase half carried, half herded a blanket-wrapped somewhat abashed Liam out of the kitchen and deposited him unceremoniously in front of the fire, for all the world as if he were a pile of wet clothing or kindling.

Liam spent a minute struggling to keep his eyelids aloft. They watched him nod off and begin to tip, sit bolt upright with surprise to find himself nodding off and tipping, then nodding off and tipping again.

He did this a good five times before he finally toppled completely over.

In an instant he was in the deep, twitching throes of the kind of sleep available only to the very young.

Rosalind watched him, almost regretting the bath. Without his layer of dirt for armor, for necessary street camouflage, he looked like any other boy: small, vulnerable, ordinary, pale. The sort that could be hurt and abandoned and forgotten.

She knew a quiet terror, a quiet sense of possession, that she recognized was part and parcel of caring about anyone.

Bloody hell.

It wreaked havoc on the heart and nerves, caring for someone. No wonder she'd learned not to do it indiscriminately. There was such a cost.

When the boy began to snore, Chase scooped him up wordlessly and carried him straight back to her bedchamber.

He returned moments later, lowered his body into the chair across from her and carefully stretched out his leg.

"He weighs nothing at all." He said it nearly tonelessly.

They sat in silence. Knowing they'd both just irretrievably given up the safety of ambivalence toward the boy. They'd allowed him to mean something. Neither of them were pleased about it, but neither would they give him up for the world now.

The fire popped loudly. Rosalind jumped.

Chase didn't. He was somewhere else entirely, in the grip of a black, black mood. He sat in the chair, his face grim as granite, his mouth a forbidding line, eyes dark as black ice, *thump . . . thump . . . thumping* his walking stick at maddeningly even intervals.

"You look cleaner, too," she tried.

He still didn't look at her. "If I'm cleaner, it was inadvertent." *Thump . . . thump . . . thump* went the walking stick.

"And you smell pretty," she added helpfully.

He looked up at her then. "So do you. You always do."

The bald compliment shocked her.

He smiled faintly, pleased to have surprised her speechless.

"Roses," he added softly. Holding her eyes with his own.

"Yes," she said softly after a stunned moment. *Utterly* disarmed.

"It's how I think of you. Roses."

Well.

How else do you think of me now, Captain Eversea?

It occurred to her that despite his impatience with details, Chase Eversea noticed the details that mattered. He listened far more than he let on. He cared about what was truly important.

And he'd been so utterly, unnaturally patient with her, and all that was *gentlemanly*, damn him and bless him, all smoldering looks and carefulness and arm's length after that moment in the brothel. The front of his shirt was soaked to transparency. Through it she could see the hard planes of his chest, the dark damp hair curling against it, the smooth tanned column of his throat rising up out of it. The sleeves were rolled to the elbow, and his forearms, thick, corded, covered in more manly dark hair, seemed inordinately fascinating. His hair was plastered to his forehead with water.

He noticed her looking at it and his hand went up and pushed it back, where it stayed. Somewhat sideways.

"Better?"

"I suppose it depends on how you define 'better.'"

In truth, she wasn't looking at his forehead. She was mentally peeling the shirt from him and purring, *Oughtn't we to get out of your wet clothes?* and then rubbing his chest slowly dry in front of the fire. Or perhaps she could lick him dry, like a kitten. And he could then return the favor, as she would most certainly be wet by then, too.

In places.

Their silence acquired a crackling density.

She noticed that neither of them had looked away even once, and once again she suspected he could read the content of her thoughts, because his eyes had gone fiercely dark and *tremendously* interested.

She willed him to come to her.

And then her breath caught, because she was suddenly afraid that he would.

He stood. Somewhat awkwardly.

And then slowly, slowly, he moved toward her, the way one might approach a frightened animal. She rose out of her chair, breathlessly, slowly, as though his motion dictated hers.

Still, somewhere in her mind, she was uncertain whether to meet him halfway or to bolt.

He paused and looked down at her. His hands seemed unnaturally still at his sides, but she was certain it was because he was willing them not to touch her. Or could not quite decide where to begin if he did touch her.

Or was uncertain whether she would truly welcome his touch.

After all, she'd soundly and in detail rejected a proposal of marriage, which would have meant access to his body for the rest of her life.

He took a deep breath. "I'm going to go speak to that Charley now," he said. "Buckthwaite."

She blinked. For a second she was mute with a grave disappointment.

She found her voice. "But I want to be there when you do."

"You are certainly not coming with me."

"But. . . . it might be dangerous."

"Good God! I best not go, then! Danger is *scary*."

And now she was irritated because he was amused at her expense. "Don't jest."

"Rosalind, danger is in the eye of the beholder. He's just a Charley. An officer of the law. We're just going to have a . . . conversation."

She didn't like the way he said "conversation." He drawled it a little too darkly and with a little too much pleasure.

"But—"

"First Lucy, and now Meggie Plum. He's the same Charley, Rosalind, who walks the Covent Garden neighborhood where Lucy was arrested. I know it. Something is amiss. I need to do it tonight. We'll visit the Montmorency later as we planned, and you'll experience your measure of danger then. Will that do?" he said dryly. "I'll send for my cousin Adam to stay with Liam when we do—he might as well make himself useful as part of the family. But *you* will stay here until I return, and you'll keep the door barred until I do."

Briskly planning, shouldering responsibility without complaint in an instant, making decisions for everyone, sweeping up everyone in his certainty. That was Captain Eversea.

"Very well," she said softly.

"How dare," he said almost to himself, "how dare anyone do harm to you, or to Liam, or to Lucy?"

He smiled a small, unnerving smile. He made the statement sound not indignant, but like a blackly amused question. Inherent in it was retribution. As though he almost pitied anyone who attempted to hurt someone he cared about.

Suddenly, subtly, swiftly, without her realizing it, he was so close to her that the damp of his shirt touched her breasts. She was instantly, incongruously enveloped in lavender and sweat and a hint of what might be Bay Rum. Wet linen. Man. Chase. So close now that she was surprised steam didn't rise from her bodice from the sheer *nearness* of him.

Still, his hands remained at his sides.

Slowly, slowly, his face came down toward her. She tried: she could not keep her eyes from fluttering closed. It was sweetly difficult to breathe; anticipation did that to lungs.

Just slightly, he brushed his cheek along hers, and she felt the heat of his skin, the start of whiskers, the hard plane of his jaw. His breath, hot, soft, brushed the lobe of her ear, and then his firm lips were there, just scarcely brushing the whorls of it, and gooseflesh danced over her arms and legs and spine and, for all she knew, her very soul.

"God, how I want you," he whispered.

Her knees nearly buckled.

And then, slowly, slowly, he drew his cheek away.

He stood back to look at her of-a-certainty dazed face, his expression thoughtful.

And then he nodded once, some sort of conclusion drawn or decision made, gave her one of those half smiles, the devil, and was gone.

Covent Garden was its typical mayhem, as it was payday. Men were often paid for their jobs in public houses which made it easy for them to drink their pay, then started fights that spilled into the streets, where prostitutes cheered them on or issued invitations to those still standing when it was all over.

Prostitutes called out to Chase with cheerful prurient suggestions he could scarcely understand, given that he was a little behind on his cockney. But he knew that asking a prostitute was exactly how he'd find Buckthwaite, so that's what he did, because prostitutes always knew where to find the Charleys.

"Ye'll find 'im in the Queen of Bohemia, luv. 'Urry back t' me when ye're done there, now."

A noisy crowd, to be sure, was in the Queen of Bohemia, swigging gin in unconscionable quantities. The place stank of bodies determinedly unwashed for a good long time, of spilled spirits and smoke of every variety; the floors were scuffed and scarred from fights and centuries of chairs and tables scraped over them and stomped by boots. The ceilings were low. One of the pillars was charred black all along its north side from a long-ago fire. The Queen of Bohemia was hundreds of years old, and had endurance.

He found Buckthwaite by asking another prostitute who was draped over another customer whose gin fumes brought tears to Chase's eyes.

Buckthwaite, as it turned out, had a table to himself, a little island of cynical law enforcement in the center of chaos, prepared only to intervene if weapons were drawn or if death seemed imminent, as his job was an uphill battle and he chose the skirmishes involved in that battle. He was a solidly built man with a seen-everything air to him, and like the clientele, he was not entirely clean, either. His hair was sparse and greasy; his shirt was gray and ought to have been white. Perhaps his way of blending into his surroundings.

He turned unimpressed eyes and a smirk up at Chase when he paused by his table.

And then took a second look.

His gaze fixed. It became clear he couldn't immediately decide who or what Chase might be, but was certain he didn't belong in the Queen of Bohemia and wasn't there to be paid for labor and drink gin. His ale-and-sun-reddened face became stony and guarded. He ironically lifted his tankard of ale by way of salute. Interestingly, he appeared to be just about the only person in the place not riotously drunk.

"Are you Mr. Buckthwaite?" Chase asked politely.

Buckthwaite didn't rise. "Aye, sir," he drawled with mock gravity. "And who might you be?"

"Captain Charles Eversea."

"Trouble outside, Captain?" This was ironically said, given that there was, of course, *nothing* but trouble outside. "Need my help?"

"I'm here to inquire about Meggie Plum and Lucy Locke."

The hesitation was infinitesimal. As was the fleeting dart of his eye, the stiffening of posture. Casually, Buckthwaite reached for his tankard and lifted it to his lips. And drank down half of it while Chase watched.

Buckthwaite wiped his mouth and said, "I fear I don't know of a Meggie Plum or a Lucy Locke, Captain Eversea."

Chase looked down at him for a moment longer, thoughtfully. His lips curled into a faint smile.

Buckthwaite began to reflexively smile in return.

Chase shot out a hand, clutched a fistful of the man's shirtfront and yanked him roughly to his feet. The chair went toppling backward.

He pulled Buckthwaite's ear level with his mouth and bit the words off, slow, low and venomous, right into the Charley's ear.

"Don't. Lie. To. Me. Buckthwaite."

He was close enough to see the veins hatching the man's cheeks, the gray at his temples, the lines at the corners of his eyes, the once broken nose. The man's nostrils flared in fear. His pupils turned his eye black.

The pulse beat in his throat. His gaze remained steady enough.

"I'm the law, sir," Buckthwaite said with no apparent menace and little conviction. "Perhaps you oughtn't cross me." It sounded like he was testing Chase.

Chase released him from the choke hold, and Buckthwaite nearly lost his balance. He took a step back and smoothed down his shirtfront almost reflexively. He regarded Chase.

"Who are you more afraid of right now, Buckthwaite? Which of us do you think is the most dispensable? Which of us do you think is more believable? Who do you think most able to buy themselves credibility?"

And at that Buckthwaite barked a laugh. Decidedly bitter. He shook his head. "We've witnesses, Captain."

"Then don't bother reaching for your pistol. Mine is trained on you."

And it was, from beneath his coat.

Buckthwaite took a deep breath, and released it in resignation.

"We'll talk outside," Chase said.

It was scarcely quieter outside the Queen of Bohemia than inside.

A roar of phlegmy laughter went up in the street, where men seemed to be comparing the legs of one prostitute to another; both prostitutes helpfully had their dresses hiked. Across the street stood the empty, boarded-up theater owned by Kinkade, the Mezza Luna.

Buckthwaite and Chase leaned against the side of the building and watched dispassionately. One night here was much like another.

"You arrested Meggie Plum for stealing bread," Chase said, "but she seems to have vanished. Lucy Locke went to Newgate for allegedly stealing a bracelet and hasn't been seen in a week. Everyone denies she was ever there. But she was indeed, there, because someone whose honesty is without question—someone unfamiliar with our particularly labyrinthine and chaotic and corrupt system of law—saw and spoke to her. Someone who cares about her. You were the last person to see these women before they disappeared."

"Lucy should not have made it as far as Newgate," Buckthwaite said absently after a moment. "That was a mistake."

Chase turned his head slowly. "Explain."

Buckthwaite pushed a wad of tobacco extracted from a box in his coat into his lower lip. He waited before speaking, apparently allowing it to fortify him.

"Captain. I think you and I can both agree that I am required to uphold the law. The laws are clear about theft. So when someone makes an accusation of a crime and there is some basis for it, my job is to make that arrest. Both women were accused of crimes by reputable men. I arrested both women."

"Where are they now? Why aren't they in prison?"

"Oh, did you *want* them in prison? A great believer in English justice, are you, Captain Eversea? Seems quite . . . *exacting* of you. Funny, isn't there a jaunty ditty about your brother? 'Oh, if you thought you'd never see—'"

Christ. The bitterest version of the Colin song he'd ever heard.

"Just tell me where the girls are."

The Charley hesitated. His face was blank with the

burden of carrying too many conflicting emotions and motives.

In front of them, a drunk took a very slow swing at another drunk and missed by miles, toppling himself over in the process.

"Here is the thing, Captain." Buckthwaite turned to Chase and yanked up his shirt. His chest was a shocking hatch of thick white scars, as though someone had attempted to carve their way into him. "You've your share of scars, no doubt. You didn't come by that limp accidentally, aye? Do you know how I came by mine? I was attacked bringing in two felons. Murderers, as it were. Just doing me job. They came at me with knives. I near bled to death and was months recovering me health. Everyone is surprised I'm still alive, not the least of all me. Do you know how much I was paid for my trouble during that time?" Another of those ironic smiles. "Naught. Did me job, and was nearly destitute for dying for it. And such is law enforcement valued in London. 'Tis Sisyphus, I am."

Chase was a quick study. "So someone is paying you to do something with these girls. Which is why you do it. You need the money."

Buckthwaite's silence confirmed it.

"To do *what* with these girls?" Chase's patience was ready to snap its tether.

"It's more than my life is worth to tell you, Captain Eversea."

"Are you under the impression, Mr. Buckthwaite, that you have nothing to fear from *me*?"

"Ah, but you're a man of honor . . . Captain Eversea." Ironically said. As though he found honor subjective and even contemptible.

"Oh, yes," Chase said. "Your tale of woe is quite, *quite* moving. I've an appreciation of a man who does his job in the face of danger and ingratitude. But I won't leave you without the information, and if I discover you've misled me in any way . . . well." Chase watched with interest as the man in front of them argued the price with an indignant prostitute, who shook her fist at him. "I shouldn't like to be you tomorrow," he said easily.

And he turned and smiled a slow, mad smile that left the Charley looking decidedly shaken.

"Where are they, Buckthwaite? Are they alive?"

Buckthwaite was silent for a moment. "I don't know, Captain. I was told they wouldn't be harmed. Better off, likely, than if the courts got to them, is what I was told. I'm not by nature a corrupt man, sir, but the job has a way . . . " He trailed off. "They'd be strung up or dying on a ship on the way to Botany Bay by now, and you know it. They had no one, aye? They *were* no one. No connections."

No one.

"They. Have. Me."

Chase had never known such black, black rage. It was nearly a miasma; a haze floated over his eyes. It must have done something to his face, lit him like a death's head.

For Buckthwaite looked rattled; the whites of his eyes momentarily brightened the darkness.

The fury nearly prevented Chase from breathing, and made him quieter and quieter. "How many of them? What are their names? What is your mandate? Where *are* the *girls*?" He hissed it.

Buckthwaite, maddeningly, hesitated again. "I'd be obliged, Captain, if you would—"

"Take my hand," Chase said coldly.

Buckthwaite stared at the fist Chase had extended abruptly, startled.

"I said, take my fecking *hand*."

Buckthwaite did, and came away with pound notes Chase had extracted from his pocket.

"Included in the price is keeping my name from it, aye?" Buckthwaite smiled, ironically, and spat toward the ankles of a prostitute passing by, who cursed him. "My mandate is to find the prettiest of the petty criminals, Captain, and make sure they don't go to prison."

"Where do they go instead?"

"I quite honestly don't know. I can tell you I'm charged with making the choice, and I've an eye for the pretty ones, if I do say so myself. And I'm paid for each one found acceptable. I don't turn them over to the magistrate. There was a witness to Lucy's arrest, so she ended up with the magistrate, and then in the Stone Pitcher."

"How many so far have you 'found acceptable'?"

"Three. Lucy Locke, Meggie Plum, and Cora Myrtleberry."

Chase hadn't the faintest idea who Cora Myrtleberry might be.

"Are they alive?"

"I cannot say, Captain. I would imagine so."

"Who do you turn the girls over to? I want a name."

Buckthwaite seemed to be struggling with the decision. "I've never seen him. I've only heard of him."

"A *name*, Buckthwaite, or so help me God . . ."

His pistol was already cocked, and he made sure Buckthwaite saw it.

"Oh, my cock is big."

Buckthwaite said this with such grim resolve that for a disorienting instant Chase thought he was simply volunteering personal information. *Rather* a non sequitur, if so. Or much, much worse: commenting on a current condition. A prostitute was grappling with a customer a few yards off, after all, and he'd had her bodice pulled down and a breast out, and she seemed to wish to charge him additional for this peek.

But one second later Chase understood it.

The Charley clarified it for him anyway.

"That's the name, Captain Eversea. O. McCaucus-Bigg."

Chapter 17

C hase told her everything he'd learned from the Charley; he told her about McCaucus-Bigg and Kinkade and the drawings.

All was tense, musing silence in the Eversea carriage. As usual, Chase refused to waste time on speculation or to draw conclusions until he knew for certain.

The lamps dimmed by the driver at his command, Chase thumped the ceiling on the outskirts of the square, and when the carriage stopped, helped her out.

She and Chase walked the rest of the way, laying their feet down as quietly as possible, hugging the walls of the museum gate to take advantage of any deep shadows thrown.

Rosalind was breathless with fear.

The muffled strike of Chase's stick against the cobblestones was scarcely a tap; in the dark, it seemed to echo like something hurled down an empty well. The voice of the watch was carried to them on the night air, but the time he marked was indistinct. All Rosalind could hear was the "o'clock."

At night the museum courtyard fairly yawned behinds its bars—far too large and empty, offering nothing by way camouflage, no movement, no other people, no trees or shadows. Clouds milled nervously about a bright half-moon.

The spiked fence could have skewered them, indeed, had they intended to climb it. And the journey to the mews seemed endless, with nothing to break the silence but breathing, which took on far greater volume and meaning in that silence. That, and the careful tread of their feet. Measured as clock ticks.

A shorter gate surrounded a small, neglected garden—one very large old mulberry tree presided over overgrown shrubs that could have hidden all manner of attackers.

She seemed to be all heartbeat: the hammer blows of it rang everywhere in her body, and it made her blood whine in her ears. *Never* in her life did she dream she'd be breaking into a building brandishing a pistol.

But Chase was there, and her own pistol was cocked, and she wasn't certain she wouldn't shoot the very first thing that stirred other than Chase.

It was a very good thing nothing else stirred.

She was able to scale the small gate with a decidedly inelegant hike of her gown, exposing her stockinged legs to the night air and, of course, to Chase. She avoided tearing her stocking, of which she was absurdly glad in the moment.

She fumbled for the latch in the dark, and it gave easily in her hand. She jubilantly gave the little gate a push.

The hinge screamed as though she'd plunged a knife into its heart.

Sweet Christ.

Her heart stopped for a painful instant. Keeled over with a thud, truly, like a stone.

She closed her eyes, her breath dangerously shallow with terror. From the other side of the gate Chase seized her hand; hers was all ice, his all heat and strength.

He clung to her for a breathless moment, pulling her close to him across that gate, and together, wordlessly, they listened hard, and he willed heat into her.

At night, sounds carried oddly, and she thought she imagined hoofbeats off in the distance. She thought she heard the rant of a drunk somewhere, and two voices raised in a fruitless shouting match. The watch had better things to do than watch the museum, it seemed, which after all was surrounded by a spiked metal gate.

She opened her eyes again, still clinging to Chase's hand. She could feel his pulse: it was hard and steady and remarkably normal. It soothed her.

He was very still, simply watching her. Arrested by her face. Or perhaps his long, long view of her long legs. His blue eyes glittering as surely as stars in that starless night.

And his face—hard, fierce, uncompromising, enthralled—made her heart leap again with a primal anticipation. *I want you*, he'd said earlier this evening.

She didn't doubt for an instant that he always got what he wanted.

She wondered how he would go about getting it.

And whether she did indeed intend to give it to him.

He gave her hand a quick squeeze; it was a query. It broke the spell.

She nodded: *I'm all right now.*

He edged through the gap in the short gate, lifting up his coat to avoid catching it. They forbore to close it, lest the bloody thing screech again.

She spared it a disgusted look as they passed, as though it were a traitor.

Five feet later they were on the threshold of the service entrance, and Chase spent long moments kneeling, the lock pick inserted. His ear to the door. A quiet click later the lock tumbled. He turned and made a "voilà!" gesture.

He gave the door a poke with just one finger. It gave just a little. He poked it again. It swung wider by inches.

Bless the maids who make a point of oiling hinges, Rosalind thought.

And then Chase drew in an audible breath and pushed it all the way open. Silence and darkness and stale air rushed out at them.

Instantly, it seemed to rob them of their voices the way a vacuum might.

Delicately, they closed the door behind them, slowly, slowly.

The door eased shut with a click.

Blackness engulfed them.

She fumbled for him; a stray shred of moonbeam caught the gleam of his cocked pistol, and she held onto his coat.

She heard a *snick*. A spark flared against the glint of a blade—Chase had struck a flint against his knife to light a nub of candle scarcely as high as his thumb. It flared weakly. It was a wholly inadequate light, but was the only light that wouldn't cast shadows up to the ceiling, which could then be seen, if someone were to look, through the arch of those great windows. The candle could light an inch or so in front of them, and so they would creep along.

As agreed, they each drew their already unlocked pistols. The sound of unlocking could crack like a gun-shot itself in a place this quiet.

He gave her the candle to hold and motioned her ahead. He wanted to protect her from anything that might creep upon them, and so she would determine the path of their reconnaissance of the place.

The service hallway allowed them out into a hall lined with Renaissance paintings, lush colors washed on canvases hung in frames surely unnecessarily heavy and luxurious. The candle lit fragments of faces, hands, horses, angels, trees, as they passed. The hallway poured them out into the museum proper.

Chase following her, his gait uneven, his walking stick touched down delicately, one hand at all times lightly touching her waist. And despite the delicacy of his touch, she could *feel* his angry, focused determina-tion. In the heat of his body. In the staccato breaths that fell softly against the back of her neck.

He wanted to make things right for her, for Liam, for everyone ever wronged, for himself.

And *she* wanted to pay attention, to look for clues to what the museum might have to do with Lucy or any of the other girls being gone. But she saw nothing. And the scent of Chase behind her began to drug her senses. The floral of the lavender soap had faded to as-tringency; now she smelled man, and the cigar smoke clinging to his coat, and perhaps a bit of horse . . . and the musk of desire.

Around a corner they stumbled upon a room full of insects.

It was a large room, and it featured one of the high, half-moon windows that would have shed light had other buildings and clouds not interfered. A cloud scudded clear of the moon for a moment, and the insects were particularly dreadful in the moonlight that found the windows: enormous motionless butterflies still iridescent in death, fragile wings spread out for everyone to admire. Great dark scarab beetles, their spiky legs looking like towering thorns and their antennas many feet long, thanks to the magic of shadows. The tiny hairs at the back of her neck tingled as though a beetle were actually crawling about there.

The smell of snuffed candles lingered here, caught in the dense and near motionless air. She thought she detected smoke from a cigar, separate from the scent that clung to Chase. It smelled, in fact, nearly like her late husband's cigar.

She stopped. She frowned.

He paused, alertly, radiating a silent question to her: *why had she paused?*

They listened. For what could very well have been eternity. It seemed to Rosalind that they would never have known, for time itself seemed literally embalmed inside the museum.

They heard nothing at all but their own breathing. She fancied she could hear her *hair* growing. She prayed she wouldn't need to sneeze, and then of course she nearly needed to, and her eyes poured water from the effort of holding it back.

She shrugged. Soundlessly, of course. They moved on.

Through the Egyptian rooms now, with their solemn-faced sarcophagi looking gray and tired and somehow not at all frightening in shadow. They peered behind them; saw nothing but wall. No mummies emerged from cases.

Past the stone slabs of ancient words. Someone's shopping list? A poem? Regardless, it was forever profound now that it had been etched in stone.

Still they saw nothing at all of any interest.

She stopped suddenly again. But this time it was purely for the pleasure of feeling Chase's hard body bump into hers. And this time he lingered, touching her. As though he couldn't bear to move away.

For a moment they stood in mutual, helpless, motionless thrall. His fingers still only lightly brushed her waist. Any other man might have attempted at the very least a throat nuzzle. Odd, but just when she decided patience was not Chase Eversea's long suit, she remembered that war was half waiting for something to happen, and that control comprised a goodly portion of his character.

And honor, too. She knew he wanted her to come to *him*. To decisively choose.

I want to decide what I want, she'd told him.

He would be leaving soon. The thought of this opened up a gulf of peculiar panic.

She moved on.

They inched down the hallway toward the room of gleaming suits of armor and pikes. None of the suits of armor suddenly sprang at them; no eyes glittered through the visors.

Still, she slowed. And stopped again.

In . . . out. In . . . out. The sound of their breathing. It could just as easily have been the sound of the night, because she felt indistinguishable from it now. And the nature of the tension in him had shifted, like a wave, into a different kind of tension altogether. With a great, great effort—it was like combating gravity, for her body knew precisely where it wanted to linger—she moved on.

From the armor, they found their way down the hall lined with the hideous puppets—their garish faces caught in erratic moonlight crossbeams. Rosalind noticed she was urged along a trifle more swiftly by Chase here.

And at last they arrived before the Italian pastoral paintings.

Beyond that was the room with the vast, velvet-hung bed, the mirror, and the ghostly man.

She didn't want to look in there. It had taken on too much meaning.

The painting, as usual, told them nothing.

It began to seem as if it wouldn't have mattered whether they'd merrily jigged through the entire building with clogs on. Apart from whatever ghosts might linger, they were alone, for all intents, in the museum. They would leave no further edified than when they'd entered it.

The quiet cocooned them, then held them fast. And in some instinctive agreement, they came to a stop. And then Chase dragged in a long breath.

The sound might as well have been a thunderclap. It signaled a change in atmosphere. He exhaled with enough force to flutter the fine hairs on the back of her neck. Gooseflesh raced up her nape and arms in portent.

Which was borne out when moments later his hands closed decisively over her shoulders. She went as still as a kitten seized by the scruff.

He turned her slowly around to face him. Not gently. Not abruptly. *Purposefully.* Like someone who had decided it was time to solve a problem and knew precisely how to do it. In short: the way Captain Chase Eversea did everything.

He held her at elbow's length, his hands epaulets on her shoulders, the grip almost accusing, as if he'd captured her in the midst of a crime.

She risked a look up to find his eyes as glitters barely distinguishable from the shadows. The semilight made a harlequin mask of the planes of his face. She couldn't read his expression. It didn't matter. The tremble in his fingers betrayed the drawn-bow tension in his body.

And in seconds the heat of his body, still inches away from her, had induced torpor. They stood like that, staring at each other, until their breathing syncopated.

And then . . . and then his thumb tentatively broke ranks from his disciplined grip.

And once, twice, again, he drew slow feathery strokes over the sharp fine edge of her collarbone. Tenderly reacquainting itself with the texture of her skin. Uncertain of his welcome.

Devastating.

A long breath dragged itself shuddering up of the furnace her lungs had become, and she needed for an instant to close her eyes. She felt almost literally on *fire*. This would have seemed a comical thing to think only days earlier. Such a *purple* phrase.

Then again, she supposed all clichés began as profundity. They *were* clichés because they were universal unassailable truths. So be it: she was on fire for Captain Charles Eversea.

He was watching her. She knew he was waiting for an answer.

And so she breathed in. And exhaled.

And gave a short nod.

His face came down hard.

The kiss was rough—the scrape of his short whiskers against her cheek, a collision of lips and teeth and then, and then sweet merciful God, the dark sweet hot incomparable taste of him. She moaned into his mouth. It was almost more a devouring, in truth, than a kiss; she tasted him, dueled with him equally. They feasted. They'd waited long, long years, and it seemed they could not taste each other enough.

The taking would be rough, too, she knew, when he pressed her swiftly, inexorably, back against an ancient polished bureau. Every bit of him was so implacably hard and immeasurably strong and wall-like, it occurred to her that she could not have escaped if she tried. A tiny part of her wondered whether he would allow it if she *did* try, such force and momentum he suddenly had, the momentum of years of wanting behind them.

And all of this ought to have frightened her.

Instead she helped him.

Her breath came in impatient puffs as she yanked her skirts upward in shaking hands as his hands were busily dragging her skirt up the back. His arms were around her back, his hands sliding hard down the length of her spine to her arse to lift her up and press her closer to the hard swell of his cock, so hard already it nearly hurt, and yet a silvery shiver sliced through her and she knew she would come sooner than she wanted and not soon enough.

He was shaking, awkward with his need, and for a moment paused, to tuck his chin against her throat as she pushed her fingers up hard through his soft hair, stroking, gentling him, though it was futile. This man contained battles, carried in him violence endured for the people and country he loved, fury over the injustices of life, at his own inability to right everything for everyone. And this could simply be release for him, but why he wanted her mattered not at all. It only mattered that she could give him what he wanted, because it was precisely what she wanted, too.

Need boiled in her.

He opened his lips, touched his tongue to where her heart was thudding in her throat, placed a molten kiss there: lips, tongue, breath, tongue. Finesse, but Rosalind didn't require finesse of him at the moment. She dragged her own efficient hand down to the bulge of his cock and claimed it with a bold hard stroke.

His head went back hard in a shock of pleasure and he hissed air in through his teeth. He brushed her hand away from his trousers, as always, a man of economy and purpose: he could get his own buttons open more quickly, and with impressive speed moments later they were.

She did momentary graceless battle with the furlongs of his linen shirt, and it began to feel like a cruel magician's trick, the one where scarves were pulled for an eternity out of a false-bottomed hat, and he choked a laugh.

At last the shirt was clear of him and she was able to slip her hands into his open trousers and push them down.

His muscles contracted as her palms and fingertips landed first to trace the sharp contours of his narrow hips, the hard plane of his belly, the fine hair trailing from the dip of his navel and hot, soft skin beneath— getting her bearings, the lay of the land—before she took his swollen cock in her palm and dragged her hand over it, relishing the heat and power of it.

He ducked his chin abruptly into his chest, and the sigh might have held the shape of her name or might have been a profane oath of pleasure, but it was impossible to know. Her dress was now fisted in his hands and together they'd managed to gather it above her waist so that all she now wore below it was the hot motionless air of the museum.

She hadn't even realized this sort of thing could be done from a standing position until he'd told her, but Chase's certainty and confidence was as usual contagious, and became her own, made it seem right and even sensible. She felt his hands, hard and hot on the vulnerable skin of her arse, his fingers sliding along her tender skin, soothing and arousing her, then teasing with one slip of his finger between her cleft, testing and finding her wet and ready, as he'd found her two nights before, and her body pulsed, leaped to his touch.

And then his cock was there, the head of it smooth and swollen and hot. She whispered needlessly, desperately, *"Now now, God now."*

He at first eased . . . then thrust hard into her.

The force of it rocked her backward, then forward. She stifled a gasp against his skin.

Locked together, he paused. He angled his head, leaned forward to kiss her.

She turned her head. Whispered adamantly, *"Now."* She said it for his sake as well as her own: she didn't need to be kissed. She wanted to be fucked.

Too long too long it had been too long.

And Captain Eversea, so accustomed to giving commands, obeyed hers.

And when he moved, the slide of him inside blind-sided her.

Her release struck like lightning; she immolated, became light and flame. She stifled a sob of incredulous, embarrassed bliss against his throat as her body pulsed with his; her bones were perhaps incinerated, because she nearly lost her grip around his neck, because they were both hot now, sweat slicking their skin, her hands sliding from each other around his neck.

But he had her. He had her.

He would never release her because he was intent on his own pleasure. His hands held her fast, and her hands found each other again and laced tightly round his neck, and his sweat-dampened hair brushed the backs of them. His breath gusted in her ear as his hips drummed his cock into her with the ferocity born of a need to vanquish all that had happened in the war, all that had happened between them, all of his fury and want. She felt him everywhere in her body.

And she hadn't thought it possible, but nothing was impossible now, in this museum and moment: rushing with bonfire speed upon her until every cell was a lit fuse, another release. She thumped a fist once against one of his hard shoulders, in mad joy and fury that he could move her to this, make her do anything, make her want him more and more even as he was inside her. The rhythm of his hips grew frantic; the smack of his skin against hers was unbearably erotic.

And then it rippled through her, seismically deep, soul deep, wracking her with pleasure. Her head fell hard against him.

The ragged roar of his breath stuttered, and his head rocked back; he bit his lip to keep from shouting. Her vision was peculiarly hazed; through it she could see the gleam of sweat on the taut cords of his neck.

His body went still. She felt it tremor through him; her body felt his tremors as surely as her own as he spilled hotly into her.

Just breathing now.

There ought to be peace, and completion, satisfaction.

But Rosalind had never felt wholly peaceful in Chase's presence. She didn't now.

Despite the fact that her body still seemed boneless, warm and pliant as wax, and she remained upright only because he held her.

The very *fact* of him demanded so much from her.

She'd gotten her breathing under control and looked up. He was frowning a little, studying her. Then slowly he lowered her leg, slid his hands from her thighs. He hesitated.

And his hands came up to her face.

To her astonishment, he thumbed tears from beneath her eyes.

Well, then. That would explain the haze of her vision.

She was surprised and yet not surprised: he'd shaken her to the core, after all, and she was a woman, and had not given her life over to the practice of stoicism the way he did, the way men did.

She gave a dismissive one-shouldered shrug. For some reason the corner of his mouth twitched up.

And then he looked down at his hand, and rubbed his thumb and forefinger gently, slowly, together. Rubbing her tears into his skin.

There followed a long moment of silence.

"Well, there's that done, then," he whispered.

She stared at him. *Not* precisely the words *she* would have chosen. Not remotely close to a declaration of love. But what had she expected? Of all the impossible things taking place this evening, she considered that loving him might turn out to be the most impossible.

Love. She shied from the thought as though it had suddenly flown at her out of the dark.

"Come," he whispered next.

And they crept out of the museum much the way they'd crept into it. And the journey out seemed to take an eternity and only seconds. Her body was still not her own. It was his. She felt him everywhere still, and she welcomed the silence and dark to unabashedly savor this, to hoard every sensation.

And as they passed through the Italian room once again, Rosalind thought that she smelled the smoke of her dead husband's cigar.

She wondered if it was the smell of guilt or of absolution.

As instructed, Chase's driver, Phillips, arrived for them just an hour after they'd gone in—had it really been only an hour?—and they'd all but leaped into the carriage while it was still moving.

And inside the beautifully sprung and maintained vehicle—which, Rosalind noted, still smelled a bit the way Liam had before he'd been cleaned—the distance between them was marked, as if each needed a distinct bubble in which to indulge their thoughts.

To recover their equilibrium.

It was as though they had exhausted conversation, she thought, after greedily, violently breaking a fast together. And indeed, she *had* broken a fast.

"I'm sorry we found nothing."

He was thinking about his failure to find answers—
he who always had answers—and not about her.

She smiled a little, ruefully. "Did you . . . did you
smell a cigar when you were in the museum?" she
asked him.

He shook his head. "Why?"

"I thought I smelled one the last time we were in.
When no one was about."

Perhaps it really is just my conscience speaking to
me, she thought.

Chapter 18

S he was nearly nodding off in a haze of fatigue when the driver pulled the horses to a halt before her little red-doored house. Chase stepped down, then reached up for her hand to help her down, too.

"Go ahead and light the lamps now, Phillips." His voice was just above a murmur. "My thanks."

The driver climbed down to do just that, and in moments the carriage seemed to sprout glowing eyes. Chase reached up a hand for Rosalind, and—her body, deliciously aching, humming from being treated the way a woman's body *ought* to be treated—she took his hand and stepped down.

The sky was pearl gray. Dawn, she thought drowsily.

"I should like to speak to you privately for just a moment, Rosalind. May I come inside?"

So terribly formal, given that they had been climbing each other's bodies just moments earlier.

It felt odd to speak in a normal voice after the long hush of the evening.

She was peculiarly relieved that he would be leaving. She wanted to be alone to review those shattering moments. To try to ascertain whether her curiosity had been satisfied. If the need had been sated. If it had been merely curiosity and need.

And she was worried she would hear a reprise of his proposal.

Perhaps his sense of honor demanded he issue one every time he touched her. She didn't relish refusing him again.

"Very well," she said softly.

Chase followed her inside.

He stood and watched while for a few moments she busied herself with little domestic things. The fire had burned low; she poked it up, coaxing a bit more heat from the weary coals. She moved to light two lamps. The softly swelling circle of light they created was like the rising sun by contrast to their hour of unrelieved darkness and quiet.

He waited quietly as she did all of this.

And then she turned toward him and gave a start. He was standing very still, his face white, his mouth a tight line. Her heart lurched. She recognized pain when she saw it.

"Chase, sit down," she ordered quietly.

She brought the old softly upholstered chair closer to him with one swift pull.

He lowered himself into it and stretched out his leg, and she watched him quietly endure whatever pain he'd been left with in Belgium. They had done what they could, she knew, the battlefield surgeons. They had sewn up Charles Eversea with utilitarian hands and they hadn't taken his leg. But they'd left him with this.

She took the chair next to him. A moment later she

tentatively laid her hands on his leg, offering him the warmth of her hands. As much for her sake as his own. She couldn't bear the whiteness around his mouth.

He peered out at her through lowered lids, his breathing a little unsteady. "Perhaps if you dug your fingers in just a little . . . "

She dug in her fingers a little and kneaded the heavy muscle there.

And after a few moment Chase exhaled, some of the whiteness around his mouth easing.

"Better," he murmured. "My thanks."

She slid her hand away from him. In the moment, they both seemed to have retreated into themselves, abashed at this intimacy that seemed somehow more intimate than lovemaking.

"Do you know, Rosalind . . . " He stopped, considering what he was about to say. "I felt no pain when I left my cousin's company last evening."

She might as well give up anticipating what this man was about to say next. She hadn't gotten it right yet.

"You . . . drank with the vicar?" Seems as though Chase drank with everyone these days.

"It wasn't meant as a euphemism. I wasn't offered a drink other than tea. The man hadn't even a brandy decanter visible anywhere in the room." Chase made this sound like the height of incivility. "I spoke with him, enjoyed his company as much as I could the company of someone who is related distantly by blood but is still a stranger. And literally—for a moment—I felt no pain at all when I left."

He was trying to tell her something important, something he had no real words for.

But suddenly her mind froze on his last words and her stomach tightened. "Are you in pain . . . all the time?"

She was careful to keep her tone as easy and neutrally investigative as a surgeon's. But she could feel the precise aching contours of her heart in her chest.

When did his pain become her pain?

She shied away from this thought.

There was a hesitation, which she disliked.

"Not *all* of the time." Said wryly enough for her to believe him, and she eased out the breath she realized she'd been holding. "It varies. From . . . " He paused and shook his head sharply once, an eloquent substitute for the word "unbearable." " . . . to hardly present. But this was different. It was as if . . . as if it had never even been at all. It was gone." For some reason he sounded grim. "And I assure you there's a significant difference."

He was not a fanciful man. He was not one to idly interpret something as a religious experience. She felt as disoriented as he must have felt.

"Did he . . . touch you?"

"Yes." He said it with dark amusement.

She didn't know what to say. She shared in his wonderment and skepticism. She, like he, wasn't given over to fancy.

"It wasn't a laying on of hands, or anything of the sort. Just a hand clasp as I went to leave. I turned around, was about four steps toward the door when I noticed that . . . well, when I noticed. I confess I was thunderstruck. I turned and looked back at him . . . He looked *frightened*. It might have been a trick of the light, but somehow I don't think so. But I think he knew what I felt. Which was . . . nothing at all."

This was entirely beyond anything in Rosalind's experience, and clearly beyond anything in Chase's, too. She imagined it wreaked havoc with his sense of what was possible and what was not. His sense of the absolute.

"Did you like him?" she asked.

"He's well-spoken. Will be popular with the ladies of the village. I anticipate they'll be flinging themselves at him in very genteel and strategic ways via dinners and village fairs and the like. He'll be fat from all the suppers he's invited to. The pews will groan under the sheer capacity of the Sunday audiences. Genevieve will swoon."

"Handsome?"

"Yes," he said, with the matter-of-fact confidence of a man who knew his own appeal was matchless.

"Charming?"

"He'll do."

She smiled. "Did you like him?"

"I suppose I did. He is a relative, on my mother's side." He paused. "I hope I was imagining it. For his sake."

She knew he hoped he was imagining it for his own sake.

"Do you really think he can . . . "

"I have no idea what to think." And he said it so conclusively that she knew he dreaded thinking any one person could take away his pain, because thinking this possible would haunt anyone who lived with lingering pain.

It did seem an awfully immense power—the power to heal. And a humbling one. Possibly, strangely, a dangerous one, too. *Surely* it wasn't true. Perhaps Chase had simply entirely lost himself in conversation to the vicar; perhaps, somehow, miraculously, he'd forgotten the pain entirely.

"But it's interesting. Some of us walk about with the burden of old wounds. What must it be like to have the burden of . . . healing? If that is indeed the case?"

"I think in a way we *all* walk about with the burden of old wounds. And in some ways, we all possess the power to heal them." She said this carefully.

His head came up sharply.

He stared at her through narrowed eyes.

Not a stupid man. He knew an oblique reference to their indiscretion of years ago when he heard one. Obliquely was apparently the only way they would ever discuss it.

"I know, Rosalind, that you think I'm rigid and unyielding and so forth. No, don't protest."

She hadn't been going to. Which made him smile, though there was little humor in the smile.

"But it's *necessary* in times of war. Lives hinge on order, discipline, and certainty, and unwavering decisions. Weakness, poor judgment, in that context is unforgivable, especially when you possess the choice *not* to be weak. Especially when lives—*countries*— depend on the soundness, the consistency, of your judgment."

"Sometimes we're not able to choose not to be weak. Weakness chooses us. And everyone has a different definition of weakness."

He snorted. There was a silence.

"You're not at war anymore, Chase." Quite softly.

He looked at her hard a moment longer. Then sighed. It could have been exasperation. Or fatigue. Or anything, really.

"It seems the Montmorency rarely has many visitors at all," he said.

A subject change, is what it was.

"I saw only three people there the day I first visited," she said. "And one of them was you."

His head went up sharply. "Who were the others?" he demanded. "It wasn't a Tuesday, so they were not the cleaning staff. MacGregor said the cleaning staff came in only on Tuesdays. Did you recognize any of them?"

"No one I knew. And one—well, to be honest, I still think I imagined him. I thought I saw a man dressed like King Henry VIII. Wearing stuffed hose and a great hat. Scurrying through that room with the . . . the big bed."

Chase said nothing for a moment. He frowned at her, his eyes wry. She could virtually hear the whir of his thoughts.

"And the other?"

"The other was a strange little craftsman, a puppeteer, who was messing about with that hideous marionette."

Chase went very still.

Frighteningly still.

And then slowly he began to lean forward, as if urging her words on. Or tipping out of his chair.

She eyed him nervously

"Go on," he commanded oddly.

"He'd noticed I was looking at the Rubinetto. He

asked why; I told him it reminded me of my sister. He told me the painting reminded him of his daughter. He also said . . . he didn't like it."

Chase remained frozen at a lean. His eyes were ablaze with a peculiar triumph.

"Rosalind?"

His voice was so strange that her heart stuttered.

A pause, during which she began to worry about his health and sanity.

"I should like to take you to a puppet show tomorrow morning. If the weather is fine."

Again, she never would have guessed what he was about to say.

"Very well," she agreed. With a certain amount of relief.

He leaned back in his chair. He spread his own big hand over his leg, soothing it.

"And so the pain has returned?" It was less a question than something to say.

"I can't feel it at all when I make love."

And just like that her face all but went up in flame.

She stared at him, thunderstruck. Bloody man was so very *direct* and so very good at ambushing her.

He watched her, his face rueful. Softly, in that smoke voice of his, he said, evenly: "Perhaps we can be lovers until I leave for India."

He was a planner, was Captain Eversea. Always wanted to know what would happen next.

"I . . . " It was a stammer.

Lovers. What would this entail? It sounded so sophisticated. Would she need peignoirs? Would she need to enlist her modiste, Madame Marceau's, assistance in preparing for this?

Tonight had seemed . . . necessary to both of them, inevitable. A culmination and a release. She didn't know how to think beyond it, but she needed to do it out of his presence.

And she wanted to think about Lucy. She *ought* to think about Lucy.

"You're entitled to pleasure, Rosalind," he said quietly. His voice so soft. "Even in the midst of duty. And I promise . . . I can give you extraordinary pleasure. It would be my honor."

Her turn to jerk her head up. He, once again, had sussed out the run of her thoughts. But not quite all of them.

She bit her lip and looked down at her knees for an instant.

Then looked up at him, a plea in her eyes. Willing him to understand what she couldn't articulate.

He gave a shake of his head, absolving her of the need to answer.

And stabbing his walking stick into the floor, he drove himself to a stand with a grace that belied he'd ever known pain at all.

She knew better.

"We will find Lucy," he said firmly.

"I know we will."

She wanted to trust in his certainty, and she knew he needed to hear it from her.

"Thank you for this evening," he said.

She knew he meant, *Thank you for making shameless love against a three hundred year old bureau with me.*

Again, his voice was so formal.

The kiss was not. He leaned down toward her. Their

lips merely touched, lingered softly: it was a chaste kiss.

In seconds it had turned her blood into molten honey.

He leaned his forehead against hers briefly. Closed his eyes. And so did she.

And a moment later he drew in a breath and sighed it out softly.

Then backed away from her, his face once again tense and expressionless.

"Dream about it, Rosalind," he said softly.

Then he bowed a good-night.

The next day, Chase fetched Liam from his cousin's boardinghouse in the Eversea carriage, which had been scrubbed and aired and left to dry in the mews overnight.

"I saw yer," Liam said slyly. "Last night."

"Saw me what?" Chase said.

"Kissin' Mrs. March."

When would he have . . . ?

"In 'er 'ouse. Afore you left. Afore Cousin Adam came to take me to his house for the night."

Cheeky bugger. He must have been up after he'd put him down to sleep. "I wasn't kissing Mrs. March." He hadn't, then.

"You wanted to."

He'd wanted to do much, much more to Mrs. March, and then, sweet merciful God, so he had in the museum. He'd never known such shredding pleasure in his entire life, and he still wasn't certain it hadn't been a mistake. Still, it was worth whatever it cost him in sleep and memories for the rest of his life, or so he told himself. Whether or not he ever took her again.

But he knew precisely where he wanted to take her next, and he knew where she wanted to be taken. He knew how he wanted to make love to her.

And he *would* take her again, at least one more time before he left, because he was all but certain he knew what Rosalind March wanted better than she did.

And she wanted him. At least in her bed.

"You shouldn't spy, Liam."

"I should spy only when ye tell me to, is what you mean."

"You should spy only when I *pay* you to."

Liam laughed, amused with himself and with Chase, which was much better than how he was the day before. The reason was that he'd transferred his faith and hopes in finding his sister to Chase, and the child's cheerful mood brought home to Chase the enormity of his responsibility to find her for him.

And if he didn't find his sister, what in God's name would he do with Liam?

How on *earth* had this happened to him? Just a week ago he'd been drinking himself into stupors and resentfully listening to monologues about cows.

"I was up to use the chamber pot, and I saw ye, is all," Liam volunteered.

"So kind of you to leave a full chamber pot for Mrs. March," Chase said dryly.

Liam laughed delightedly.

The boy was almost comically clean. Clean enough for Chase to notice that he almost could have passed for an Eversea, what with the brilliant eyes and the hard little chin with the dimple pressed into it. The ears were unfortunate. Quite large. The hair was decidedly tow and straight as straw, the eyebrows and lashes so fair they were nearly white, and no one on his side of the family had that coloring. Then again, his cousin, Adam Sylvaine, came very close.

"Hush, Liam. We're here to fetch Mrs. March now."

The little crowd, as usual, had massed in the square, clustered around the pink and gold striped tent. Marionettes were already patting their little wood feet on the stage, bouncing in that marionette way that made them seem only partially subject to gravity.

The tune abruptly changed as Chase dove into the crowd, startling both Rosalind and Liam. And as usual, the crowd didn't precisely part like the Red Sea.

He ruthlessly prodded, poked, elbowed, stomped, leaving in his wake squeaks of righteous indignation, clearing a path for Rosalind and Liam to trail him, until he was for the very first time right in front of the stage.

There, in gold letters, it read: THE MYRTLEBERRY THEATER.

He whirled on Rosalind. "The puppets *have* been speaking to me!" he crowed in triumph.

He briefly registered her grave concern for his sanity as he dove toward the theater.

> *"And if ye thought ye'd nivver see*
> *A saintly man called Evers—ack!"*

Chase snatched the puppeteer by the shirt collar and dragged him backward. Myrtleberry went, trailing puppets and strings, and a chorus of frightened "Ohs!" went up from the crowd.

Chase roughly released the puppeteer.

"Drop those puppets, Myrtleberry—"

"You mean *marionettes*," Myrtleberry squeaked.

"—and stuff them into their little *coffins*—"

"They're called cases," the puppeteer corrected, faintly.

"—and 'come along with me,'" Chase mimicked snidely. "We're going to have a little chat. And don't bother passing the hat. There won't be a show today. It's over."

Rude whistling and shouting and general tumult had taken over the crowd. A few apple cores were hurled in their direction when it became clear that someone had interrupted their entertainment.

"Move from that spot upon pain of death," he snarled at a blanched Myrtleberry.

He strode to the front and bellowed: "Myrtleberry will return with his theater next time the weather's fine. *With a new* repertoire," he added conciliatorily to the crowd.

And *warningly* to the puppeteer.

This seemed to placate everyone well enough. They filed away, grumbling and murmuring in speculation about what that repertoire might be.

He'd told Liam to amuse himself for an hour, marched Myrtleberry into the Mumford Arms, cleared a table of the people sitting at it with a single black scowl—they'd scrambled to get away—and now he and Rosalind and the puppeteer were seated together.

He quickly told Rosalind of the songs he'd heard and his suspicions, to reassure her as to the state of his sanity. And she quite understood why he hadn't said anything earlier.

"Myrtleberry sounds more like the name of a puppet than a man," Chase said testily. He threw back half a pint in a mighty swallow that widened Rosalind's eyes. He winced and wiped his mouth.

Donkey piss, he mouthed to her. He pushed it over to her, and she sipped at it.

Less confusing when she actually tasted it.

"It's me real name." Myrtleberry was a bit defensive. The theater, as it turned out, could be bundled into a bulky but portable trunk along with the puppets, and the trunk now rested at his feet beneath the table. Chase looked down at it askance. Gave it a nudge with his toe as if all the puppets might come springing out of it, and if they dared, he'd stomp them to splinters.

"Why do you feel the need to mock my family in song every time you see me? What the devil are you trying to tell me, old man? How do you *see* me in the crowd?"

"You're quite distinctive, Captain Eversea. You're very tall, your features are quite pronounced, your eyes are very bright, you look quite wealthy and haughty, and the top of your walking stick is quite distinctive, too. It shines in the sun, and in the type of crowd we get in the square, you rather stand out as a character. That's how I see you." He peered more closely at Chase. "You'd make a wonderful marionette."

"Bite. Your. *Tongue*. Myrtleberry."

He felt Rosalind press a restraining knee against his at the pub table.

"What do you know about that painting? What are you trying to tell me? And why couldn't you have just told me *directly*? Instead of this cryptic nonsense?"

"Because they said they'd kill my Cora. And me."

The man was trembling now.

Rosalind touched him very lightly, and just that touch induced calm.

Chase inhaled. "Start at the beginning, Myrtleberry."

Rosalind noticed that he seemed to be enjoying saying the name "Myrtleberry."

"I knew you would help, if you could. I overheard you speaking with Mrs. March by that painting in the museum, you see. And I've heard about you, Captain Eversea. A friend of mine served under you in the war. Clackham."

"Good man, Clackham."

All of his men had been good men, Rosalind noticed. Likely thanks to him. Chase sounded warily conciliatory.

"And I thought that if I could only draw your attention," Myrtleberry went on, "you might pay attention to the songs, and they might strike a chord, as it were, and you'd be inspired for yourself to discover . . . what is going on. Since Mrs. March's sister is missing, too."

"What do you know about Lucy?" Rosalind's voice was taut now.

It was Chase's turn to press a restraining knee.

Myrtleberry sighed. "Cora made a mistake, aye? She was arrested by a Charley who said she nicked fruit from a costermonger wagon, and she may have done. She's nay a saint, my girl, though she's a good heart. And then she disappeared. I couldn't find her anywhere, the magistrate said he hadn't seen her, and my heart was near to breaking—she's all I had in the world."

This was quite a familiar theme, a dastardly one, and Chase's fist closed tightly around his pint.

"And then I was sent a letter saying that Cora was safe, that she was enduring a different but easier sort of punishment. And that she would not be harmed *if* I were to build a few things to specifications. I'm a carpenter, aye? In addition to being a puppeteer."

It took a moment for this to register, because they weren't expecting to hear anything of the sort.

Chase asked, "*Build* a few things? What kind of things?"

"I built a pirate ship. I built a small forest—a stage set, really—featuring miniature toadstools, a rainbow, and a pot of gold. I was asked to build something resembling a large rock surrounded by sea."

More astounded silence.

"But where did all of this take *place*?" Rosalind asked.

"Start at the beginning as best you can, Mr. Myrtleberry," Chase ordered evenly.

Myrtleberry looked up hopefully at the brisk, dispassionate question. Bracing, as always, Chase's tone.

"I was told to come to the museum alone one night, very late, if I would do the work for them. I was worried about me Cora, aye? So I did. I was met by a masked man in front of it—he had a pistol drawn, and he was much taller than I—who was I to resist? He blindfolded me and marched me—with the pistol in my back—well, I still cannot tell you precisely where. Though I *know*—I would swear it—we walked through the museum. I could *smell* it. The linseed oil. The candles.

I could *feel* the air. I know the museum, you see. And so we walked for—ten minutes or so. Went through a door of some kind—I heard it open. The air changed from close to musty and cool . . . "

He paused. Rosalind pushed over the rest of Chase's pint, and Myrtleberry drank it thankfully.

"When they removed my blindfold, I found myself in a very large room, grand, mind you, with a high ceiling and a marble floor, but with naught in it. The walls were painted pink, and there was molding all around, and a hearth. Like a bedchamber, aye, only much larger? And the materials I needed to build these things were in the room. Hammers and nails and a saw and an awl and the like; wood and paint. They knew as a puppeteer I could build sets; I'd built sets for stage shows in Covent Garden once or twice. I was given specifications, told to begin, and then they locked the door behind me."

He paused. And drew in a shaky breath.

"Go on," Chase urged.

Rosalind put a hand over the puppeteer's big gnarled hand.

"A few hours later a masked man would return— same man, same voice, very aristocratic—and I was blindfolded again and led back out. Always at pistol point. Each day, for a few weeks, this very same thing happened, until everything was built to satisfaction. If I told him there was something—a tool, or some such—I needed to get the work done, it always appeared. If he wanted something I'd built altered, I was told to alter it. And then at last I was told I no longer needed to go to the museum. But that Cora wasn't yet free to go, because they might need me again, aye?"

"What do you remember about this man? His voice, anything distinctive about it?"

"He seemed tall. Voice came from a great height over me. Very aristocratic. I would know it anywhere again."

"When was the last time you were marched at pistol point, Mr. Myrtleberry?"

"It's been well nigh a month now. And me Cora . . . she's still gone."

Rosalind felt the ache in the man's voice squarely in her chest.

"And why . . . but why are you singing about the painting in the museum? The Rubinetto? Angels and so forth?"

"Well, I look after the puppets at the Montmorency, aye? And sometimes . . . " He inhaled. "Sometimes I think can hear me Cora laughing when I'm in the museum. But distant like. Like a memory, not a real laugh. And when I hear it, it's always when I'm in that room with the Slovakian marionette. And each time I was marched through to the room where I worked, I could smell the oil I use on the puppets. It's much stronger in that room.

"And Captain Eversea . . . once, when I was locked in the room, when I stopped hammering, and the like, I heard through the walls, too: men laughing. And one of them . . . well, one of them said something about girls on their backs."

The three of them were suddenly chilled silent.

"I'm afraid, Captain Eversea. I want my Cora back, what e'r she done."

All the lords laugh at the girls on their backs.

Rosalind looked at Chase, and he was looking at her, and the kaleidoscope of clues began to solidify into one awful suspicion.

What felt like an iceberg mounded in Rosalind's stomach.

She felt Chase's knee against hers again.

It struck her that they'd scarce spent a moment without subtly touching each other the entire time they'd sat in the Mumford Arms. He knew, she thought. *He knows what his presence does to me, and how unable I am to think when he touches me, and he wants both to reassure me . . . and to ensure that we become lovers.*

If you see my angels, like as not you're in a brothel, Mr. Wyndham had said.

"Do you think the museum is being used as a brothel?" Chase said this quite evenly.

But Rosalind glanced at his hand. His knuckles had gone white around the tankard of . . . donkey piss, apparently.

Mr. Myrtleberry's hard, round, red cheeks blanched.

"I could not say, sir," he said faintly. "But to hear them laugh about girls on their backs . . . I cannot say what else it might mean. I swear to you it's those are the very words I heard."

"We've had a look around the museum during the day," Chase mused. "We've had a look 'round it at night. We didn't see any additional rooms."

Mr. Myrtleberry gave a start, perhaps at the idea of them creeping around the museum at night. And regarded them both with great interest.

"A brothel would certainly explain why the Velvet Glove had seen a certain amount of *attrition* in its clientele in recent weeks," Chase continued thought-fully. "It's been quiet, the Duchess said. I found it so. Very odd." Rosalind didn't think she'd ever grow ac-customed to offhand references to brothels. Even Mr. Myrtleberry's hard round cheeks blushed rosier.

But Chase was oblivious to the discomfort of his companions and quite clearly still thinking aloud.

"I suspect the painting must be an indication of the presence of a brothel, or at the very least a place for ar-ranged assignations with . . . indentured women."

She recognized the almost dangerous calm in his voice. The thread of dark glee. He *did* like a challenge. He did like righting wrongs. And as usual, he seemed happiest in the presence of contrariness.

"Chase . . . I know I mentioned it, but the cigar smoke I thought I smelled that evening was fresh. Not stale smoke. As though someone had just passed through with a cigar."

He drained the donkey piss, plunked town the tan-kard, and said to her, "Well, I think you and I will be visiting the Montmorency again tonight with a more specific plan."

Chapter 19

After promising Mr. Myrtleberry he would do what he could to find his daughter, Chase brought Rosalind home.

He walked her from the carriage all the way up to the bright red door.

"Rosalind . . ."

She looked up expectantly, thinking perhaps he'd had another inspiration regarding the whereabouts of the girls.

"I should like to make love to you again soon."

The sudden words gave her vertigo, and he seemed to know, the devil. He casually reached out a hand and with two fingers braced her from toppling from the top step.

"You need only say yes when next I ask you. You'll know the moment. I'll fetch you at dawn."

What could a woman say to that?

He took a step down. And turned back.

"And Rosalind . . . think back to the Velvet Glove, and a certain painting, and all of the things I told you were possible, and you'll know precisely what I have in mind for us. In case that helps your decisions."

He waited to ensure that she was properly scarlet

and breathless from picturing it, for she could not have
prevented it if she tried.

He took the final step down.

"And Rosalind . . . I leave for India in one week, but
I'm leaving for Sussex to say good-bye to my family
tomorrow, and I don't know how soon I'll return."

He stopped at the foot of the stairs and those blue
eyes burned into her. Stripped her as surely as knowing hands. They were dark with intent but not with en-
treaty; he was a gentleman, but he had pride.

Whatever they finally learned tonight, whatever
they discovered, he still wanted her to choose what she
wanted.

He tipped his hat, and nodded, and boarded the carriage, and was gone.

She was fetched by the Eversea carriage two hours
before dawn.

Rosalind had dressed herself in shadow-colored
clothing in honor of their plans.

Once she was in the carriage, she pressed herself
against the seat, folded her hands in her lap, held her
body still, and wondered when he would say the word.
It was all she could do, frankly, not to spring at Chase—
his eyes burning into hers in the dark, shadows making
a harlequin of his face—but anticipation was a potent
aphrodisiac.

You're entitled to pleasure, Rosalind.

It was all very similar to the first time: the silent
journey to the service entrance, the opening of the
little gate (Chase had brought oil for the hinge); the
deft *scritch-scritch-scritch* as he picked open the lock;
the lighting of a tiny candle, the stealthy creep through

the museum hall, unlocked pistols in hand, until they entered the open museum proper. With a pace, of necessity, excruciatingly slow yet nevertheless direct, he led her to the sixteenth century bedroom.

He settled the tiny candle in the ancient candleholder on the writing desk with some ceremony, and she watched with a sense of time slowing to a lava pace.

"Here," he whispered.

One second . . . two seconds . . . three seconds . . .

She knew how to build suspense, too. She wanted to hear his breathing escalate to a soft roar.

It did.

. . . four seconds . . . five seconds . . . six seconds . . .

"Yes," she said softly.

So swiftly, so matter-of-factly she scarcely had time to know what he was about, he spun her and had her laces undone and loosened so the shoulders of her dress began to sag. His hands traveled up and with quick, gentle precision found and plucked the pins from her hair, and he put them neatly somewhere; she heard the whispering clink of them stacking on polished sixteenth-century wood. His fingers combed, savoring the heavy satiny length of her hair. And then he had her stays unfastened, and it seemed as though everything that bound her fell away from her nearly at once, and he swept them into his arms and folded them on the bed with his soldier's neatness.

He gently, deftly, peeled off her dress with his hands, folding that efficiently, too, and she stepped out of it into his arms, stifling an astonished laugh over the fact that she was suddenly entirely nude and utterly vulnerable and he was entirely clothed and in command.

He swept aside the curtains, tipped her backward onto the bed, and a cloud of disturbed dust glittered in the candlelight and then disappeared when he yanked the curtains closed again, enclosing the two of them in dark and as dense and soft as the velvet coverlet beneath her back. A dark so thorough the pale contours of her own body took a moment to come into focus, leaving her feeling strangely formless and disconnected again, needing him for an anchor.

She could just sense the heat and shape of Chase as the bed shifted beneath his weight. There was a rustling sound, which she fervently hoped was some article of his clothing being loosened and removed—far be it for her to be the only nude one—and an instant later his warm hands began a journey over her skin: landing tentatively at first before wrapping around her ankles to get his bearings, gliding up the curves of her calves with his fingertips, fanning over her thighs, brushing up the short hairs there, skimming over the curve of her belly, discovering her the way a blind man might and leaving behind a trail of gooseflesh and heat and shivers of sensation that fanned through her body.

His palms were on her breasts, cupping their soft weight, skimming over the tight peaks of her nipples, and she arched them with a stifled whimper. His mouth found and settled lightly on hers. She threaded her fingers up through his hair to impose her will, to hold him to her, to make the kiss last, wondering if every kiss with him could feel entirely new. Because this one was different than the others. A soft feinting of lips at first—a bump, a slide, a teasing pull of her lower lip between his—then the leisurely meeting, twining of tongues, the sweet heat and wet, as their fingers knit through each other's hair. He was dark and endless, and she fell into the kiss as one would plummet down a volcano.

But Chase had an objective.

He began a return journey of sorts: he moved the kiss to her chin, slid it to the beating pulse in her arched throat, settled one into the valley between her breasts and visited each of her nipples, stopped midway along the seam between her ribs to kiss her there, whimsically, deliciously, dipped his tongue into her navel. His hands were on her thighs now, deliciously brushing over short hairs, then her calves, coaxing her knees apart.

Her breathing was rushed now.

She felt his breath there, hot between her legs, where she was soaked and deliciously aching: his exhale built her anticipation. And was followed by a startling coolness; this time he blew softly.

She knew, could sense, what was coming next.

It was—*dear God*—the stroke of his tongue.

Sinewy, hot, velvety, wet. Very, very deliberate. Even in the near perfect blackness of the curtained bed, the man knew his way about a woman's body. She shuddered.

She could not have described the sensation unless it was with one word: *more*. Which was hardly a description. She didn't know yet whether she even liked it because it was too acute and too new and the things it did to her body were total: sent threads of breath-stealing flame through her veins.

But he did it again.

Softly this time, and this time she whimpered and arched into it. And he did it again, and her hands curled into the old velvet counterpane.

And again he tasted her, a persistent and deliberate caress, and she surrendered. Surrounded by velvet dark and with velvet pressed against her back and with the most hedonistic imaginable activity between her legs, she floated, disembodied, her consciousness narrowed to a point of acute and ramping pleasure, and she accepted with greed, as her due.

But he paused.

No, no, no. She wanted to protest, she wanted it to continue until her release shattered her, but couldn't speak, so drugged with pleasure and darkness she was. He shifted, deftly, quietly, and turned so his thighs straddled her torso, and he bent to kiss her again, a promise, a vow, that he intended to continue, but that he wanted something from her, too. She opened her eyes to see the pale muscular curves of his buttocks, and he dipped so his swollen cock touched her lips.

She knew a moment of shock that nearly jolted her from her torpor of pleasure.

And then she touched her tongue tentatively to him, and then traced the rim of it, lingeringly, and his shoulders bunched; he muttered a hoarse approving oath, so Chaselike, so satisfying: she knew now the wild power she had to please him. And she knew instinctively to take him all the way into her mouth: first, the slippery, silken dome of his cock, then the warm, living, nearly muscular shaft, swelling even as she closed her lips over him.

She felt the pleasure shudder through him, and his hot breath, his deliberate tongue, were once again where she wanted them to be.

In the dark cave of the bed, in this peculiar museum, in this carnal world they'd created together, it seemed once again a *sensible*, a right thing, to do, to share in this feast of pleasure. To taste and suck and tantalize. She mimicked him; he stroked her hard with his tongue; she stroked him hard with her tongue; he gently sucked, she gently sucked, achieving a rhythm of power and pleasure so primal and instinctive she knew every woman must somehow be born with the knowledge, this *right*. And yet, had her husband lived, she might never have realized this. And so odd that an act so intensely furtive and intimate, that a pleasure she knew would be cataclysmic should be so *quiet*.

His thick cock slipped from her lips, but her skin was alight now, and she was arching against him in unconscious demand. She could no longer be in service to his pleasure; she was at the mercy of her own.

Her head thrashed back. A whisper: "I'm sorry—I need—"

"It's all right, love."

Love?

No matter what, she knew she would be safe with him. He'd always been there when she needed him, and he was there now.

He turned himself around. His warm body covered her; she reached up, sliding her hands over the delicious hard planes of his chest, the crisp hair tangled with sweat. His cock was in his hand, and then he was brushing it against her, hard, seeking his way into her, and that was all she needed to shatter into glittering, gasping fragments of bliss.

He braced his arms stiffly above her and thrust in.

She clung, watching the primal dive and thrust of his pale narrow hips, that hard race toward his own pleasure, reveling in the savage fact of their coupling, the feel of him deeply inside her, so deep it nearly hurt.

He bit his lip on a gasp, and went still, trembling over her, his release wracking his body as he spilled and spilled hotly into her.

"Rosalind." He murmured it.

She'd never heard her name said in quite that way. In her name she heard everything he felt. And such a mix of things it was.

Her body was thoroughly pleasured, her mind adrift. It was likely hardly safe to do so for long, she knew, but they lay alongside each other for a moment.

Together and separate. Their bodies touching, but only just.

Love. He'd said it. But it was one of those big words, used in moments when control was lost. It was either *that*, or some raw oath.

Rosalind dragged her hand over the slick hard surface of his arm, over his shoulder, over the muscles of his chest, as though searching for the yield anywhere in him. There was tension in him, even now. Her hand rose and fell with the rise and fall of his chest. His warrior's heart thumped in there. She rested her hand, allowed the steady beat of it to lull her, to reassure her. So many times that heart could have been stopped. She greedily allowed it to beat against her palm.

She wished she could tell him he didn't have to fight anymore.

She wished she were certain this was true.

She wished he understood that true strength sometimes had to do with the ability to simply surrender. To life, to circumstances, to uncertainty, to his own humanity and fallibility.

To a desire that didn't require anything of him apart from the giving and receiving of pleasure, which is what he had given her.

She slipped her hands over his broad back, hands sliding over hot satiny skin, skin that could tear and bleed like the skin of any other human. There was too much proof of how he'd nearly died: her wandering fingers encountered the rise of scars, different shapes and textures. Violent hieroglyphics left upon him by the events of his life, some in play, no doubt, most in battle.

She turned her head into him, rested her cheek between the valley of his shoulder blades, and breathed in: sweat, musk, sex, Chase.

For a moment nothing changed: he lay quietly next to her, breathing. Spent, but not entirely at rest. Pausing between bouts of being his stubborn, irritating, fascinating, astonishingly sexually sophisticated self. His cock at ease now between those thick hard thighs, looking humble.

Until their breathing swayed now in and out, in and out. Together now.

And then he shifted a little, tucking his arse into her groin. She smiled, her lips curving against his hot skin. Little by little she felt tension ebbing from him, and their bodies blended together.

A moment later his hand found her hand where it had wrapped his waist. He tentatively touched the tips of his fingers to her palm, as though he'd never felt a hand before.

Then slowly, deliberately, threaded his fingers through hers, and held her fast.

She knew she was as strong as he was, perhaps stronger in some ways, and in some ways just as brave.

There was so little she could give to him. Just this moment, before he left for India. And more memories of her, of the woman who had turned his life upside down more than once and given him pleasure in return.

So she held him.

And he allowed himself to be held.

Seconds later he jerked upright, away from her. Put one hand over her mouth and a finger on his lips. And put his hand to his ear.

She listened carefully and heard . . .

Was that a *giggle*?

It wasn't *her* giggle. There was a heartbeat's worth of silence.

And then they heard it again. It came from everywhere and nowhere. Muffled and faint.

They needed to scramble upright. He did.

And then a horrible realization: he had *his* clothes. He only need pull up his trousers and slick down his hair and he could set out. *Her* clothes were folded neatly, her hairpins stacked, on a bureau once owned by King Henry VIII.

A good, oh, eight feet or so away.

Not counting the seventeen miles of bed she needed to cross to get to them.

Another ghostly hint of sound, musical and cascading and flirtatious: it was indeed feminine laughter. So distant, so muffled, it surely was reaching them from another century.

Her hand still lingered over his heart, which was thumping swiftly now. He pressed her hand hard against him, in reassurance.

She didn't feel entirely nude while he remained close to her.

"Ghosts," she whispered into his ear.

He turned his head toward her and scowled so insultingly she practically *heard* it.

He withdrew his hand from hers, slowly, slowly, and eased away from her slowly, slowly, until his body no longer touched her. She felt chilled and bereft. He turned his head, held his finger up to his lips.

As if she was about to start shrieking *now*.

It was her turn to scowl.

Which made him smile. A reassuring little half-moon of white in the dark. An odd moment, certainly, but something about it made her heart give a tiny, sweet kick. She knew then she couldn't bear it if anything happened to him, and was somehow certain it couldn't, it wouldn't.

For a man so large, he managed to slink toward the end of the bed without causing undue squeaks in the ancient mattress. She watched him go, feeling a trifle desperate, tempted to begin fashioning a toga of sorts from the elderly, velvet counterpane so she could make a graceful escape.

And then she saw why Chase was still wearing his boots: that's where his pistol lived. He slipped his hand into it, and out slid the glinting, shining muzzle.

Another moment of utter motionlessness. Of listening. To . . . dust falling?

There were no other sounds at all. He took one finger and slid it along the seam of the curtains just enough to peer out.

More silent listening. They didn't hear any more giggling.

It was all growing rather dull, in fact.

Ghosts, she felt like insisting in reiteration. Regardless of its source—through the ether, or in some other sixteenth-century bed somewhere in the museum—surely there was nothing sinister about a giggle?

And then Chase slipped all the way out of the curtains, and she was left alone in that big bed.

Quiet for a tick or so. The in-out of her own breathing was suddenly deafening, and then unnerving.

A hand burst in through the curtain.

She sucked back the shriek so quickly she nearly choked on it. Then the hand beckoned impatiently.

Chase was telling her it was safe to exit.

She tried to do it as gracefully as he had, without causing the bed to heave or squeak unduly, or any more than it already had. She'd begun to creep across on all fours toward him when he poked his head in through the curtain so he could watch her crawl, nude, across the velvet counterpane.

Another of those white grins flashed in the dark. He was enjoying himself.

If he was a gentleman at all, he would hand her the clothes and she would get to the business of dressing in the safety of the curtained bed.

Otherwise she would be forced to dress while he watched.

Though dressing while he watched—and this was evidence of his effect upon her—held a certain amount of appeal. Regardless of whatever peril they might be in at the moment.

She'd been well and truly corrupted, obviously. Somehow she couldn't find it in her to regret the loss of her morals, if indeed this was what she'd lost to him.

He handed her clothes to her then, and rudely, delightfully, refused to turn his back as she dressed, as quickly as was possible. With his eyes upon her, getting dressed was nearly as pleasurable as getting undressed, and he helped her, swiftly, his hand leaving hot places behind on her skin.

Chase relit the candle using knife and flint and nursed the spark of lit wick until it swelled and gained strength and officially became a flame. He tucked his unlocked pistol into his coat pocket within quick reach, grasped her hand, brought it to the waist of his coat and folded her fingers over it. They inched from the room, Rosalind clinging to him.

There was the giggle again. Faint, unearthly.

The nub of the lit candle turned his fingers into a grid of light, almost but not quite burning them. And in this fashion they crept quietly, just a few feet, until they stood once again before that painting. They paused and listened and felt: he could indeed smell linseed oil powerfully here. Myrtleberry had said the laughter was louder in this room.

And suddenly the candle flame swayed and twitched, slightly singeing his fingers.

Suspicion touched a cold, fine arrow point to the base of Chase's spine.

He slowed his breaths to near silence.

He thought back to the first day he'd seen Rosalind staring at that painting. He'd studied her from behind, fascinated by just the back of her, of course, but there had been a moment when he thought she must have turned to look at him. And in a split second turned away from him again. It had seemed impossible—for why wouldn't he have noticed?

But the plume in her hat had been quivering. Ever . . . so . . . slightly. As though she *had* moved. As though someone had sighed over it, he'd thought then.

Or as if . . . as if . . .

Tentatively he lifted the candle again, level with the middle of the painting. He could see the big dark bovine.

And one by one uncurled the fingers of his hand until it burned unsheltered, tiny but shocking as a lantern in contrast to the previous moment.

He waited.

He heard the thud of his own heart in his ears.

He heard Rosalind's breathing behind him, syncopating with his, her body tense with an unspoken question.

A second later the tiny flame gave a leap, then swayed like a tiny South Sea dancer.

With blinding speed he licked his fingers, pinched out the candle, and spun about to face Rosalind, covering her mouth with his hand to stifle her gasp.

Total dark bell-jarred them.

He held her fast, one arm wrapping her waist from behind, the other across her mouth. She was rigid with astonishment. For a worrying moment he thought she might have stopped breathing. He kept his hand firmly over her mouth for a communicative second before slowly lifting it. And then he dragged a finger over her soft lips, a luxury, a temptation, a caress, and a signal: remain utterly silent.

She understood. She complied. She trusted him now, and he felt the honor of the responsibility.

And her curiosity remained nearly as palpable and dense as the surrounding dark.

He lifted his hand from her lips.

He couldn't yet explain himself; he could only wait for the shadowy outlines of things to emerge from the blackness, which seemed tacked down around them.

And as luck would bloody have it, the first thing to materialize from the dark with any clarity—thanks to an unfortunately angled shaft of moonlight through one of the arched windows—was the hideous lumpy puppet. In the grayish light it was all leering red lips and bulging white eyes and impotently dangling limbs. Its head listed limply, like a man hauled from the water after an unfortunate diving accident.

Chase was riveted. The little hairs on his arms pricked up in revulsion.

Rosalind, perhaps sensing his tension, instinctively pressed her body even closer to him, gathering up a tighter grip on his coat. He almost smiled. She was protecting him from the puppet.

He jerked his gaze away and redirected it at the painting, willing it to come into something resembling focus.

In seconds he could make out the bosomy angel, because she was all in white, and then the cherubs, glowing in their flowing nappies and wings, and then the contours of the enormous blob of the cow.

He licked his finger again, held it up before him

and waved it with painstaking thoroughness, with something akin to ceremony, horizontally across the painting. Beginning at one end. Rather like a sorcerer conducting a ritual. He was distantly amused when he became aware that Rosalind was watching him with grave concern. Doubtless thinking he'd finally surrendered to lunacy.

He was midway across the painting, his finger level with the cow's haunches, when the tip of his finger chilled. He held it there for a moment, his scalp prickling again with confirmed suspicions.

A tiny but unmistakable breeze was blowing . . .

Right out of the cow's arse.

He spared an ironic thought for Colin in that moment.

As this was an entirely new dilemma in his experience, he allowed himself a moment of consideration.

If fresh—or *close* to fresh—air was blowing through the cow's arse into the dense, close air of the museum, there *was* something behind that wall. But what could it be? A windowed room? An alley? A passageway?

The muffled, ethereal giggle had originated there. He was certain of it.

This wing of the museum faced nothing but other buildings. Ah, but the English were clever, and history was riddled with stories of the need to hide or smuggle something: priests, gunpowder, women. Tunnels and passageways were seldom built whimsically. Inherent in their nature was the need to hide or flee.

But then he remembered the tunnel dug between Brighton Pavilion and the King's Arms—a brothel. Where would this tunnel lead?

Of course: just yesterday evening he had stood with Buckthwaite, staring at Mezza Luna, the old theater owned by the Kinkade family in the very worst part of Covent Garden, boarded shut, seemingly abandoned.

But *large*.

Large enough to accommodate a brothel.

And easily and quickly reachable from the museum . . . through a tunnel. Bypassing busy streets clotted with carriages and horses and prostitutes. And Kinkade had met him in the Queen of Bohemia, right near the theater.

Mezza Luna . . . meant half-moon in Italian. And there was a half-moon in that painting.

He turned and pressed his lips right against Rosalind's ear. "I think this might be a tunnel."

She understood. Her eyes flared whitely in the dark.

It occurred to Chase that the cow's arse was a peephole. Even now someone could be watching them.

Though if a human stood on the opposite side of the painting watching them, a breeze wouldn't have been able to exit it.

He rotated, wrapped his arms around Rosalind and swept her aside. Surely no one would be able to identify them in the dark.

Should he attempt to relight the candle and have a good peer up the cow's arse?

What would happen if the white of someone else's eye met his?

Christ.

He waited. He listened. He rotated slowly about and studied their surroundings once more, ensuring they were alone. His eyes, invariably, snagged on the bulging white eyes of that leering puppet.

"You might try pressing the brass plate beneath the frame," the puppet whispered helpfully.

"Fucking hell!"

Chase leaped straight upward and aimed to blow the thing to smithereens.

"Ack! Don't shoot! Don't shoot! Aye, it's me, ain't it?"

The puppet made a grating, shifting noise on the shelf, its head flopping first left, then right, then flopping forward as though it were casting its puppety accounts on the museum floor. It seemed to be attempting to lurch into a standing position.

It was horrible, horrible.

What felt like a million spiders with ice cold feet marched up Chase's spine.

Rosalind had a steady hold of his elbow, and she was aiming her pistol, too, with all evidence of steely determination. A restraining and yet reassuring grip. His heart was *slam slam slamming* in his chest.

"Hate puppets," he muttered.

"One would *never* have guessed," she whispered.

This almost made him smile.

Odd how the grip of her small hand on his elbow should make him feel as though nothing in the world, even demon puppets, could harm him. He still felt a little separate from his body. He'd *levitated* from horror.

Though he was proud of the fact that his pistol hand was steady, and it was cocked and aimed.

The thing made a shuffling sound, righted, then tipped over with a sickening *thunk* as though he really had shot it.

Rosalind gripped his elbow a bit more tightly.

And out from behind the toppled puppet stepped Mr. Myrtleberry, the puppeteer. "Come closer so I can kill you," Chase growled at him.

"You wouldn't kill me, aye, Captain Eversea. Just a puppeteer."

They glared at him, because his very presence had yet to make sense.

"You hopped like a spring lamb there, you did, Captain Eversea." Myrtleberry was whispering, but unconscionably amused.

"What the *devil* are you doing here? How long have you been there?"

"I just arrived, aye? I finally got hold of the plans for this building, Captain—and Montmorency built a tunnel between his house and the Mezza Luna. I once worked upon a great estate o'er Marbury way riddled with passage and doors and such like. This is a door, right here by this painting, I'm sure of it, and *something* will release this one, lad."

Chase spun back toward the painting. "Rosalind, would you—"

But she'd thought ahead. She put her finger over the cow's arse to block the peephole should anyone care to look through it.

He put his ear to the painting and heard nothing on the other side of the wall. No giggling, no footsteps, no thundering herds of armed men, no screams.

Chase began fumbling blindly at the edges of the frame. He lifted the frame up, looking for signs of a seam, a hinge, anything that might indicate this wall was anything apart from a wall sporting an ugly painting in a disreputable old museum.

He pressed the painting itself with delicate hands,

every inch of it. He slid his hands down to feel for the brass plate beneath it.

Mr. Myrtleberry spoke up. "Perhaps you ought to try the brass plate at the—"

There was a subtle grinding sound as the wall swung violently outward and swept Chase and Rosalind into blackness.

Chapter 20

⌒◯◯⌒

The wall *thunked* closed, and Rosalind heard a loud grunt and a sickening thud as she tumbled down a grade.

That thud, she knew, was the unmistakable and unpleasant sound of a body hitting the ground hard.

"Chase!"

She was surprised to find herself on her knees on what appeared to be a dirt floor, in a dimly lit chamber, very happy her pistol hadn't gone off.

"Chase!"

"I'm here."

He was standing, uninjured, unrattled, and he bent to grip her arm.

Her own head was still spinning, and her breath had been knocked from her.

She stared at the door in disbelief. It looked precisely like a *wall*.

"Are you injured? Can you stand?"

She shook her head; a mistake, as it was already swimming. "Just a bit dizzy. Breath knocked from me. Limbs intact. One moment."

She'd learned how to report just the facts.

"But I thought I heard someone fall," Chase said.

"So did I," she said.

"Then who—"

They were still for an astonished moment. He helped her to her feet when she nodded, her breath regained, and they looked about in wonderment.

The passageway—it was indeed a passageway—narrow, seemingly endless, was lit along its length by torches arrayed in sconces at the very top, throwing out flickering light and long leaping shadows. It smelled of earth and smoke.

A lovely draft came from somewhere down where the passage originated.

And terminated in the cow's arse, of course.

"But . . . I could have sworn I heard another pers—"

Something tickled Rosalind's ankles. She kicked out with a hoarse shriek and leaped backward.

A moment of focusing in the shadows revealed that she'd violently attacked a plume. A dark purple one. About as long as her arm.

She followed the length of it with her eyes. A moment of focusing on the ground revealed that the plume was attached to an enormous hat, which was lying upside down, like a creature gone belly up in death.

A hat rather like one King Henry VIII would have worn.

She gingerly followed that hat with her eyes.

Which is when they both saw the body.

It was man, and he was wearing a doublet, a cape . . .

And stuffed hose, à la sixteenth-century fashion.

The hat had obviously been knocked from his head when they'd inadvertently clubbed him unconscious with the museum door.

•

"He was clearly trying to exit as we came in and we knocked him out cold." Chase knelt down and reached for the limp hand, his thumb seeking out a pulse. "Still alive."

Rosalind stood on tiptoe and helped herself to one of the many torches, then crouched over the body, next to Chase, holding the torch low enough to illuminate the man's face. A round face, an unfashionable short beard, long lashes shut against his cheeks. Apart from the burgeoning bump on his head, he might have been peacefully asleep.

"Do you know who he is?" she asked.

"It's *Ireton*," Chase whispered in disbelief. "Friend of Kinkade's. What the *devil*—"

And suddenly, from out of the darkness, that damned flesh-crawling giggle floated, reverberating through the tunnel like a crazed thing swooping to attack them.

Chase scowled, looking irritated, not afraid. "I have to move him before anyone else comes down here. I wonder if he was the lookout? Or just trying to leave?"

"I saw *him* that day! Remember?"

Ireton was one of those men who packed a good deal of flesh and muscle into a compact frame, and he was remarkably difficult to budge. *Carrying* him gracefully out of the path of the passageway wasn't an option. Chase took the torch from Rosalind, replaced it in its sconce, and the two of them managed, gruntingly, to drag Ireton by the ankles over to the corner near the door. Chase propped him up against the wall.

Where he slumped. Like that damned puppet.

Rosalind retrieved the hat and gently placed the great plumed thing over his face. The feather extended vertically. Anyone stumbling across him would hopefully think he'd merely temporarily succumbed to an excess of drink.

And then they turned to stare down the baffling passage.

It seemed endless, but that could have been an illusion of the flickering leaping torches and the fact that the place was bloody dark.

Another giggle floated through. It seemed to come from nowhere and everywhere, the very product of darkness. There was an echo to it. A *hackle*-raising, gut-chilling echo.

Rosalind took in a shaky breath.

Chase reached out his hand and took hers in reassurance, but she could sense the impatience in him. She almost smiled.

King Henry VIII had *not* been a ghost. He had a name: Ireton.

The giggle was louder now, and was of a certainty originating in *this* world, not beyond it. Clearly, from the end of the tunnel.

They whirled then froze when they heard footsteps crunching toward them. Chase fingered his pistol.

Surely anyone can hear the beat of my heart, she thought. Banging like a bloody war drum.

How had Chase managed to acquire his aplomb?

The crunch became a blur of white. It was definitely moving directly toward them. Rosalind felt disembodied herself, suspended in that limbo between disbelief and terror, where the mind tries to convince the eyes that everything is quite, quite normal.

Because surely that white blur emerging from the shadows could only be a ghost.

Crunch, crunch, crunch. The footsteps came steadily, and then a man dressed in a toga came into focus.

"Well, good evening," said a cheery voice.

A wreath of gold leaves gleamed around his pearly bald head, and large hairy feet poked out of a pair of sandals that laced up his thick calves. What appeared to be a greatcoat was slung over one arm; he held his hat and a pair of boots in the other. He looked for all the world like a banker returning home from work.

Apart from the toga.

Not a ghost, in other words.

"Brought a new one?" He looked up at Chase with no apparent recognition and all evidence of bonhomie. He peered at Rosalind, who ducked her head bashfully and skillfully moved aside a fold of her skirt to hide her pistol.

"Yes! A new one!" Chase agreed brightly.

"She looks like a screamer," the man said encouragingly. "Cheerio."

He pulled his hat onto his head expressly, it seemed, so he could tip it to them, and crunched his way to the end of the passage.

They were utterly motionless, fascinated. They watched him closely as he pressed his eye to the peephole.

"Much more convenient, this way in and out, isn't it, than the Covent Garden exit?" he said over his shoulder conversationally. "This one is much closer to my home. Gets me there in time to get a good night's sleep and up to breakfast with the wife. One hates to be seen exiting in the Garden. Quite a dangerous place, that."

So there was *another* exit?

Which would explain the peculiarities of the men going in and coming out and vice versa. Liam had been *right*.

She oddly felt as proud as if her own son had done it.

The toga-draped man glanced down and noticed the man slumped beneath the great feather hat.

"Tsk tsk, Mr. Woodcock. A touch too much again?"

The toga-draped man reached up, pulled at a sconce not sporting a burning torch, and the wall spun out again, revealing the shadowy museum.

"Don't forget to blindfold her now, lad! You'll ruin everything if you don't!" Rosalind craned her head: she could even see that godforsaken lumpy puppet.

Then the man walked through the opening. He gave that hidden door a push, and it *thunked* softly back into place behind him in seconds, as though it had never been.

They stared, dumbstruck, for an instant.

"I'll . . . be . . . damned," Chase murmured.

The English had a long, fine history of hidden passageways and tunnels and the like, but this one was blindingly original.

This had once been Montmorency's actual residence. What could the passage have originally been used for? Smuggling goods? Hiding Catholics? Most likely Montmorency had used it for precisely what it was now being used for, since this tunnel likely terminated in Covent Garden and the Mezza Luna.

The only thing left to do was forge ahead or retreat the way they'd come. Neither one of them would dream of retreating, for at the other end of this tunnel there were answers, for good or ill.

Chase gifted her with a smile, brilliant with wickedness. Better than a torch, that smile. Better than the certainty of the sun rising tomorrow.

Bloody man was *elated* when things were at their most contrary, and he sensed he was about to win. And Rosalind simply couldn't find it in her to believe otherwise. As usual, his certainty became her own.

Rosalind returned the smile—how could she not?

He tentatively took her hand, the one not sweatily gripping a cocked pistol. He held it an instant, then raised it to his lips and kissed the tips of her fingers gently, by way of reassurance.

And then she realized the kiss was also an apology, because he pulled off his cravat and said, "We need to blindfold you. My guess is that they bring girls in blindfolded so they'll never know where they are or how they got there."

Bloody hell. She had sensed this was true, but she didn't relish the prospect.

She sighed. "Very well," she agreed softly.

"I'll be here, Rosalind, and I shan't let you go."

She stared up at him, and there was no one in the world she trusted more than him. She sighed again, and nodded.

He wound the cravat gently around her eyes. The dark became darker, and then all she saw was a dull black tinged with a reddish glow. It was fine silk, the cravat, and warm from his body and smelled like him, and it was like donning armor even as she relinquished her sight.

"I have you," he whispered reassuringly.

He always did.

"But keep your pistol in your hand," he added cheerfully, on a whisper.

He took her hand in his, and silently, pistols drawn, they moved deeper into the tunnel.

"If that gentleman was walking casually, we haven't far to go to reach the end," Chase murmured. "He wasn't precisely provisioned for a long journey."

The proper response to that hardly seemed "Hurrah!" given that they hadn't the faintest idea what might be on the other end of the tunnel. But if Lucy were safe and alive, a journey to anywhere would have been worthwhile.

The bright blobs of torches penetrated her blindfold as she walked. Dark, bright, dark, bright, was how she saw her journey now. One foot carefully placed in front of the other, her pace matched to Chase's. *Crunch. Crunch.* The ground inside the passage was packed and swept dirt, scattered with pebbles. Their footsteps echoed, no matter how carefully they stepped.

As she had when they crept toward the museum in the dark, she began to measure the world with her other senses. She counted her footsteps. She listened for breathing, hers and Chase's. She was conscious of the hot press of Chase's hand in hers.

She began to feel like a ghost herself.

On they walked; no one else approached them. But eerie fragments of disembodied voices reached them, bouncing from the walls, reverberating in the tunnel.

A burst of masculine laughter made her jump.

Chase squeezed her hand, but didn't indulge her nerves. He inexorably pulled her forward.

Once again that nervous giggle shrilled. It was louder still, less ethereal; clearly they were drawing closer to its source.

Another hearty burst of male laughter, followed by

a hoot, reverberated down the tunnel. Ricocheted, like a frightened bat.

Rosalind's breathing quickened. There was no way of knowing what would be at the end of this, and how could Chase know, armed with a pistol, two knives, a walking stick, and arrogance?

And then came the scream.

It blasted her nerves like lightning. Panic momentarily paralyzed her. Cold, then hot, then cold again with terror. She halted, sucking in a whimper. Her breath came in awful tattered gasps.

"Chase."

"*Listen*, Rosalind." He was stern.

And there it was again. The scream. Fainter, this time. A bit shorter in duration.

And this time she noticed that it somehow. . . . lacked conviction?

If such a thing could be said of a *scream*.

Her breathing began to ease a bit. She took in a deeper breath, feeling drained by fear.

Funny, but the sound in fact reminded her of the time she and her sisters had put on a play taken directly from a horrid novel she'd read aloud to them by the fire. Lucy, at first, had been elected to be the heroine, which would have required her to scream when she saw a ghost. But she'd been terrible at acting; she was unfortunately much too good at simply being herself, and struggled to be anything but.

Jenny, however, was very good at screaming, as she was the loudest.

But this sounded more like a Lucy scream. Not precisely terrified or accomplished or as a result of any particular trauma. Quite odd, really.

She had no choice but to take her cues from Chase's reaction. He wasn't charging toward the sound, pistol drawn.

Then, of course, he would never dream of endangering her, regardless of who else was being endangered at the moment.

God help them.

She'd never been suspended in a nightmare quite like this one. But if one needed to have a nightmare, she thought, it was lovely to share it with Charles Eversea.

On they walked, hands entwined, utterly silent. Forty steps into their journey the silence gradually took on texture: rather than intermittent ghostly bursts of sound, a distinct hum of masculine voices came toward them. The sort of hum that only a *group* of voices could make.

How on earth would she and Chase confront an entire group of men? What on earth would they *find*?

Chase pulled her to a halt. "Watch your step. Lift your feet up carefully," he murmured into her ear.

She knew why in a moment: the dirt beneath their feet had given way to hard floor. Marble, from the sound of it against her slippers.

Ten more steps she counted, and during those steps the dull red glow of the torchlit tunnel slowly gave way to a different sort of light: the warm pervasive light of a chandelier and fire and candle. Unwavering.

The hum was no longer a hum: distinct and separate conversations, loud though they were, could now be picked out.

" . . . what a splendid idea! I could barely scrape together the subscription, but I'm beyond delighted that I did."

The tunnel had been chilled and somehow filled with cool air, and now the familiar heat of a fire-heated room swept over her, and she knew the tunnel was behind them and whatever they were about to face was quite officially ahead of them.

Chapter 21

Two corded velvet curtains had opened directly onto a small domed, marble-floored foyer from which several hallways branched. A heavy crystal chandelier, tiered like a reverse pyramid to a single, long narrow drop, dangled over it, like a fancy Sword of Damocles.

Chase was bemused to find a man presiding over what appeared to be a reception desk, much like Sergeant MacGregor did at the Montmorency. He was young and still coltish of limb, but very briskly official looking and dressed in a uniform that elevated him above footman but not quite to gentleman: a long dark blue coat with gold braiding, pale blue stockings, and buttons that winked a little too brightly to be truly tasteful.

"Your first time, sir, isn't it?" he said pleasantly. With no apparent surprise.

The first time creeping through a tunnel from a museum to what might very well be a brothel? That would be a yes.

"Yes, as a matter of fact." Chase matched the jovial tone.

"Hmm. I wasn't told to expect anyone new this evening, but on occasion this has been the case. Would you mind sharing the name of your sponsor?"

This was brightly asked.

Bloody hell.

Chase thought quickly. The toga-wearing man in the tunnel had referred to Ireton as "Woodcock," another juvenile appellation in a series of juvenile appellations characterizing this entire misbegotten enterprise. The success of a clandestine operation such as this would utterly depend on anonymity, considering what was at stake. Mentioning Kinkade's name would likely be certain disaster and reveal him as an interloper.

"Mr. Welland-Dowd," he guessed.

Heart thumping hard, fingers gripped tightly in Rosalind's, getting and giving reassurance. Her soft hand was damp. He could feel the rapid tick of her pulse, too.

"I'll have a page fetch Mr. Welland-Dowd for you," he said, and Chase knew a surge of triumph.

The man paused to have a good look Rosalind. He frowned a little uncertainly. "I see you've brought a woman, and she looks to be the appropriate sort, but perhaps no one told you that a client bringing in their own woman is slightly irregular practice."

Irregular practice, indeed.

"Mister . . ."

"Wrexion," Chase supplied with great dignity. "Mr. Hugh G. Wrexion."

It took the man a moment.

"Oh, very good one, sir!" His face lit with delight.

"Thank you," Chase said somberly.

Rosalind squeezed his hand twice, which he liked

to imagine was her way of indicating incredulous hilarity.

"I agreed to pay a slightly higher subscription rate. Mr. Welland-Dowd will tell you as such. It strikes me as something you ought to have known. He did tell me he would share this information with you."

The sentence was etched in aristocratic condescension and accompanied by an obsidianlike stare.

The man looked up at him. Drummed his fingers once. Twice.

"Of course, sir," the man soothed crisply. "I'll just send a page for Mr. Welland-Dowd now. If you would sign our book . . . "

Chase bent and scratched out *Hugh G. Wrexion* in the guest book.

"Very good, sir. If you'd kindly wait right here, Mr. Welland-Dowd will arrive shortly and he'll show you around. There's a gaming room ahead of you— through the curtain—you can probably hear the gentlemen in there having a wonderful time, but from the looks of things"—by "things" he apparently meant Rosalind—"you'd like to get started straight away. If this is true, you'll find the Pleasure Rooms off to the left."

Chase followed the man's gesturing arm with his eyes. Black-and-white-checked marble hall lined with dark wood doors, rather like a hotel.

Or, of course, like a brothel.

Some of the doors were standing open. And from one of them, the closest, came the noncommittal scream.

The page was retrieved via a bellpull, much the way a servant was summoned.

The man at the reception desk regarded Chase and

Rosalind with bright hospitable eyes. He began to tap his quill and whistle soundlessly.

They heard footsteps on the marble and looked up as the voice preceded the appearance of the man.

"Mr. Twigenberry, what's this I hear about—"

He stopped cold when he saw them. As well he might.

For Mr. Welland-Dowd, as it turned out, was Sergeant MacGregor.

He reached for his pistol, but Chase and Rosalind were faster, and of course their pistols were already unlocked. Rosalind yanked off her blindfold.

"If you touch your pistol, MacGregor, I'm pulling the trigger," Chase said. "And what kind of soldier would I be if I didn't have more powder and shot? I could shoot all night."

It was an exaggeration, but it worked to blanch MacGregor.

Rosalind trained her pistol on Mr. Twiggenberry, who began to smirk. He refused to drop his pistol.

Chase whirled and drove his walking stick down into the man's foot. Mr. Twiggenberry howled in surprise, and Chase twisted the pistol from his hand with a snort of disdain.

And then he reached behind Twiggenberry and yanked the gold cord holding back the draperies.

"Rosalind, tie his hands behind his back and gag him with my cravat. And you'd best put your hands behind your back, sir, or I promise I shall hurt you if she doesn't do it first. She's quick on the trigger, this one, and unpredictable. You know how women can be." He winked at Rosalind.

He turned back to MacGregor.

"*Why*, MacGregor?" He meant . . . all of this.

The soldier was wavering. "McCaucus-Bigg needed my help. He paid me, and he threatened me. I've a family to feed."

"My heart weeps for your tribulations, truly. I *wish* I found them interesting. Where the hell *is* McCaucus-Bigg?"

MacGregor was silent.

"Where is Lucy Locke?"

MacGregor remained silent.

"Where is Meggie Plum?"

MacGregor remained silent.

"Where is Cora Myrtleberry?"

MacGregor remained silent.

"Oh, for Christ's sake, MacGregor, I will give you to the count of three to tell me, then I will shoot you and search for them myself."

"Shooting will make too much noise," he said hopefully.

Chase sighed. And from his sleeve slowly slid the knife into his palm. Those knives had been quite useful since he'd acquired them from his attackers.

MacGregor's bulging, watery blue eyes fixed upon it, mesmerized. They could all see MacGregor, quite terrified, reflected upside down in the blade. As though the knife had his name on it all along.

"Knives," Chase clarified evenly, "kill much, much more quietly than pistols."

"He'll hurt me. He'll hurt my family," the sergeant said in a choked rush. "I don't want to help him. Mrs. March, he made me write threatening letters. And I'm absolutely terrible at writing threatening letters!"

"I noticed," Rosalind sympathized.

"He won't hurt you or your family. I'll make very damn certain of it." This was Chase.

MacGregor hesitated, on the brink of decision.

"You *want* to help, don't you, MacGregor?"

The odor of the man's terror sweat rose up. His face was shiny and white and his pointy nose pink, and his Adam's apple rolled in his throat when he swallowed. He closed his eyes. And then opened them and sighed. "Yes, sir. I truly do."

"Good. Now tell me what the devil is going *on* here."

"The girls . . . well, they're arrested and the pretty ones are brought blindfolded through the tun—"

"I know how they get here," Chase interrupted curtly.

MacGregor didn't even blink. "This is how it works . . . They can buy their freedom faster on their backs. After a certain number of . . . assignations . . . they are allowed to leave." He darted a pained, imploring look at Rosalind, whose eyes were nearly black with temper. "Mr. McCaucus-Bigg is rather strict about that rule. There are rooms upstairs for that. The Pleasure Rooms. All the girls are locked into their rooms at night and when they are not administering to a fantasy. But Miss Locke and Miss Plum are locked in rooms on the floors above that. They've been given a week to decide whether they wish to . . . participate. Which is the usual way of things when girls are brought in. Miss Myrtleberry has at last agreed to be a mermaid, but she cannot seem to stop giggling. Mr. Kirkham has found it interferes with his fantasy," he added superfluously.

So it was indeed Cora Myrtleberry giggling all

along, Rosalind realized. An awful thought, knowing her father could hear her and not be able to find her.

"Take us to Lucy and Meggie. I'll take care of Cora now," Chase said restlessly, having the same thought.

"Only Mr. McCaucus-Bigg has the keys to the upper rooms."

Chase thought a moment.

"Perfect. I should very much like to speak to Mr. McCaucus-Bigg. Fetch him, and tell him that Lucy Locke has decided to earn her way out of here on her back, and she'd like him to be her very first."

"Chase!" Rosalind said softly. A warning. She wasn't certain he could trust MacGregor.

"I want to see him pay, too, Mrs. March," MacGregor said simply. "It's despicable, and I don't want to be a part of it any longer. You can trust me, sir."

While they waited for McCaucus-Bigg, they peered into the room where the desultory screams originated. A tableau had been set up: a lovingly crafted pirate ship, Mr. Myrtleberry's handiwork—complete with sails and a mast, to which was lashed a girl whose dress was torn at the shoulder.

A pirate—or rather, a man dressed as a pirate—was holding a sword to her throat. A fake one, as it turned out, carved from wood and painted to shine in the lamplight.

"Aaaaaah!" she screamed halfheartedly.

"I'll have you walk the plank for your insubordination, you filthy wench!"

"Aaaaah! Aaaaaah!" She thrashed her head to and fro. In truth, she looked rather bored. She brightened when she saw the little group standing in the doorway.

There was indeed a plank, Chase noted. Beneath it was a bed. Perhaps he did eventually force her to walk a plank.

The atmosphere in the room wasn't one of danger. It was, in fact, very nearly desultory.

"Are you lost, luv?" she called out. "I'll be free at quarter past. For *you* I'll take the upstairs rooms and work it all off in one night."

"Cora?" he said softly, hoping for the puppeteer's sake that it wasn't. Testing. "Meggie?"

"It's Cassandra," she spat. "We're all alike to you gents, I ken," she said bitterly.

"If you're planning to buy your freedom faster on your back, luv, *I'm* first in line!" said the faux pirate indignantly.

"Bugger off, Cox. There are rules and you know them."

Apparently everyone there had been apprised of the rules.

"One more 'Bugger off, Cox' out of you and I'll report you to McCaucus-Bigg." The words were fraught with menace.

There was a pause.

"You know you're supposed to say, 'Bugger off, *Captain Cook*!'" he growled.

"Right!" the woman said resignedly. "Bugger *off*, Captain Cook!"

"I *like* it when you talk that way to me, wench! What *else* would you like me to do to myself? You're not *thrashing* enough."

She thrashed her head obligingly, her red hair flying out moplike against the mast of the ship. "I'd like ye to take that sword and shove it up yer—"

Chase backed away from the door.

Cox. It seemed so strikingly obvious. He wondered why he hadn't thought of it.

They blazed down the hall a few more doors, following the giggling. She was wearing a mermaid tail and a long dark wig that covered the front of her. An irritated Kirkham was dressed as what appeared to be King Neptune. He was holding a trident.

"I don't know why it's so *funny*," he was saying to the girl.

"Cora?" Chase said carefully.

The mermaid looked up. She had her father's large round eyes, and a pleasant round face, and her face was pale with fear.

"Eversea!" Kirkham was startled. Even more so when he saw the pointed pistol. He looked at it, then back up at Chase in question.

Chase threw his coat over Cora. "Have you a room here?"

She nodded, puzzled.

"Go up to it and change and get into your clothes. We'll be leaving. And Kirkham—if I were you, I'd leave very, very quickly. The way you came in."

"Are we in danger of being discovered?"

"Yes, indeed," Chase agreed solemnly.

Kirkham fled out the door with his trident.

Rosalind and Chase turned, guns pointed upward, when they heard brisk footsteps coming toward them over the marble. They turned to see a familiar tall, elegant figure.

O. McCaucus-Bigg, as it turned out, was Kinkade.

He slowed when he saw them, his face gone hard and blank, inscrutable. He stopped. And Kinkade turned slowly to look at MacGregor with amused venom.

"Oh, well done, MacGregor," he said with soft, deadly irony. "*Et tu, Brute*, and all that."

Kinkade's hand made a move for his coat, so subtly one would have missed it. The butt end of the pistol in his hand came into view.

Chase aimed his own pistol between Kinkade's eyes. "Drop the pistol."

Silvery eyes, hot and enigmatic, fixed on Chase for long moments.

Then, with a disgusted oath, he dropped the pistol.

Chase kicked it over to Rosalind, who picked it up.

"Mr. McCaucus-Bigg. Such a pleasure to meet you. You'll take us to Lucy and Meggie now."

Kinkade led them up a flight of marble stairs. Three weapons and six pairs of eyes followed his every move.

"Now, Chase," Kinkade said conversationally over his shoulder, "what can you possibly find to object to in this endeavor? I mean, truly?"

"Kidnapping? Imprisonment? Prostitution?" Chase suggested with black irony.

Kinkade snorted. "Most of the girls are perfectly willing to participate once they learn what's involved. Those that can't decide to cooperate within two weeks—which is as long as I'm willing to feed and house a petty criminal—go right back into prison through the same Charley that arrested them in the first place. And those that talk about it . . . well, there was only the one. And she unfortunately hung straight away, didn't she, MacGregor? Was found guilty of her crime."

MacGregor looked ill. He declined to answer.

"I believe she did say a thing or two about a brothel, and captivity, and the like, to prison officials," Kinkade went on. "It was put down to ravings. She had no one—no family, no husband—and certainly no authorities believed her. She never once heard any of our real names, of course. She couldn't possibly know the location of his place, as all the girls are brought in blindfolded and kept here. She rather sealed her own fate."

"Why the devil do this at *all*?"

"Boredom, Eversea! It costs me very little, all in all. The men are carefully chosen, all known to me. They have a good deal to lose if word gets out, so they're all scrupulously discreet—and they pay an exorbitant subscription fee, which entitles them to unlimited fantasy enactments with the girl of their choice, and the girl has no choice but to act them out lest we cast her right back into the hands of the magistrate. They generally take on a sort of sexual nature, the fantasies. Only to be expected, mind you. But no servicing is required. The girls who wish to be released *sooner* must truly earn it. And there are plenty of pretty, petty criminals, Captain, who don't even blink at the thought of earning their freedom on their backs with their legs in the air, or wherever a gentleman might wish them to *put* their legs. The rules of conduct are clear, and I'm quite strict and fair, both with the gentlemen and the . . . ladies."

"You're depraved," Chase said tonelessly.

"You mean I'm *clever*." Kinkade was amused. "I

only meant to do it for a short time, you know. These things are only pleasurable in an ephemeral way. I would have been on to the next thing."

He led them to a door. With fumbling hands that betrayed his true state of mind, he inserted a key. Rosalind's heart pounded.

And then the door creaked open.

Sitting on a narrow bed, face pale, curly dark hair down around her shoulder, brown eyes wide, was Lucy.

"Rosalind?" she said querulously. She stared for a moment. Then frowned, puzzled. "What did *you* steal?"

Chapter 22

K inkade cast a long-suffering look at Chase.

"Lucy." Rosalind felt sick relief. Her voice shook with it. Chase gripped her arm to steady her. "Lucy, we're here to fetch you. You're free to go."

Lucy still looked puzzled. "But I haven't decided whether I'll be a merm—"

"Yes you have," Chase said quickly, firmly.

"Captain Eversea?" She looked very surprised to see him, as recognition dawned. Then began to smile a little, flirtation around the edges. She couldn't help it, bloody woman.

"You're going home with Rosalind, Lucy."

"I can *go*?" Lucy stood up cautiously and looked at Kinkade with some worry. "You're certain?"

Kinkade, grim-faced, said nothing.

Lucy inched past him through the door. And then she flung herself into Rosalind's arms and burst into tears.

"Are you going to *kill* him?" Lucy wanted to know between sobs. She'd noticed all the pistols, and she glanced from Chase to Kinkade with interest, and not without a measure of bloodthirstiness. "Rosalind, I thought he was lovely and handsome, but he's really quite *na-naaa-sty*!" She sobbed bitterly.

"We know, Lucy," Rosalind said patiently, patting her back.

Kinkade sent a look to Chase that seemed to say, *See what I mean? Bubbles in the head.*

Rosalind held her sister fast.

Her sister might be a featherbrain, but she was *her* featherbrain. And Lucy's tears made Rosalind feel savage. *She* would have happily killed Kinkade on the spot.

He sighed and said, "Well, so that's Lucy." He handed the ring of keys to Chase.

Who hesitated, then took them tentatively, surprised.

There was a silence, apart from Lucy's weeping on Rosalind's shoulder.

Everyone looked at Kinkade. He seemed to realize that everyone expected him to speak.

"Well, *are* you going to kill me, Eversea?" He sounded amused. "You certainly seem to have grounds for calling me out, if you're so hell-bent on protecting honor and so forth and doing things the right way. We're both excellent shots. We can probably do without swords, given that you're not exactly . . . quick on your pins. But you'd have to do an awful lot of killing if you intend to start with me. Every man in the place is armed. You'd like as not have trouble getting out again alive, you and Mrs. March and the lot."

Chase's head went back with amusement.

"Here is the wager *I'll* take, Kinkade. Every man in this place is *far* more interested in saving their own skin than avenging yours or protecting their right to his particular brand of entertainment. I warrant these men—at least some of them—have a great deal to lose should this be discovered. Am I right? You'll be dead, your brothel will close, and they'll lose the money they paid for your little secret venture, but not their reputations or livelihood. So I feel quite free to shoot you. I haven't decided yet whether I will." He turned to Rosalind's sister. "Lucy."

She was still sobbing noisily and rocking her head back and forth in her hands.

"Lucy!"

Chase and Rosalind simultaneously barked it.

It dried Lucy's tears as surely as the desert sun.

She looked between them in surprise.

"Are you whole? Are you sound? Did anyone at all hurt you? Answer me truthfully. If you don't, I shall know it. Tell me, in your words, what happened to you here." Chase's voice was the clear, dispassionate one of a judge.

It was impossible for anyone not to answer truthfully when Chase barked questions.

"Well, I was arrested. For stealing a bracelet. The bracelet was gold, with—"

A long, exasperated sound from Chase. As though he were attempting to siphon patience from the very air.

Rosalind nudged her sister sharply.

"Anyhow, I was taken before the magistrate. I wound up in prison very quickly. My goodness! So terrifying! So dirty! Everyone was so loud and unkempt. Billy heard about it, and he came to see me there. Just the once. He said it all looked very dire for me indeed, and that the trial could not have possibly gone my way, particularly since the bracelet was so very, very valuable and the merchant so angry. I swear to you I didn't take it!" She paused, perhaps remembering the caution about telling the truth. "Well, I didn't *mean* to take it. It all rather happened suddenly and I can scarcely recall," she said very airily and quickly. "It was just so pretty!"

Despite everything, Rosalind knew an impulse to turn her sister over her knee and spank her.

"But Billy said he could get me out if only I'd do a wee favor for him, and he told me all about . . . all about this place. The museum. The wall. The painting. He said he told me because I was a friend. He gave me but a week to decide what I wanted to do. He said I could . . . care to dress up as a fantasy, or, as he said, earn it . . . " She cleared her throat. " . . . earn my freedom faster on my back." She said it gingerly, and made it sound as though she was quoting someone. She did have the grace to flush and duck her head. "I was so afraid, Ros. But I cannot say truthfully that anyone physically hurt me. But my *feelings*!"

Rosalind sent a sizzling black look at Kinkade.

"If you were going to go *that* far, Kinkade," Chase said, sounding disgusted, "why in God's name didn't you just release her?"

Kinkade laughed. "God, Chase, I do believe you have me confused with *you*. The honor bit. You've entirely missed the point. I wanted a *go* at Lucy, don't you see? I would have been her very first. And sweet Mary, I have wanted a go at her ever since she allowed me into her bodice in the first place."

Lucy darted a guilty look at Rosalind. And then ducked her head again.

"She was *perfect* for this place. The gents would have

enjoyed her thoroughly and she would have helped to make my reputation. And, in all honesty . . . I mean . . . look at them."

The "them" in question was, of course, Lucy's bosom, because that's where his eyes went.

Lucy looked down, and Kinkade looked down.

Chase and Rosalind and the queasy looking MacGregor forbore to look.

"Do you think I'd miss an opportunity to indulge in *that*, Eversea? Are you mad? She was very close to capitulating, too, weren't you, Lucy?" He smiled a loose, sensuous smile that had Lucy clinging ever closer to Rosalind.

Chase sent Rosalind a warning look, as she appeared to be itching to slap Kinkade.

"Didn't precisely fight off my caresses, did you, Lucy? Chase told you to tell the truth, now."

"To Chase," Lucy said, in a rare and clever grasp of semantics. "Captain Eversea told me to tell the truth to *him*."

Which of course was tantamount to an admission from Lucy that she *had* rather liked it.

Kinkade sent another *See?* look to Chase.

"I cared for you!" Lucy wailed.

"Yes, yes, of course you did, darling." Kinkade sounded bored. "I like you, too. It would have been marvelous, dear, I promise you. But I'm not a *rapist*. Just very inventive and very persuasive, and I do happen to want what I want and generally get it.

"All in all, given her *tremendously* unfortunate circumstance—brought down upon her own head, I might add—Miss Lucy Locke was presented with a reasonable option," Kinkade went on, turning back to Chase.

"More than most women would have been presented with. I could not have prevented her from hanging or being transported if the jury decided this would be her fate, and such is the system of justice in our fine land that they would have sooner hung her than freed her. Once a thief, always a thief, and all that. England does like to rid itself of criminals. As we've discussed, Eversea."

"But I'm not like those other girls! I'm not!" Lucy burst out.

"Lucy," Kinkade explained with a horrible exaggerated patience, "*stealing* makes you like those other girls."

"It was just a bracelet!"

"Just a bracelet! Just bread! Just a button! Just a shirt off a line! My love, it matters not at all to the courts. Not really."

"For God's sake, Kinkade." Chase's voice was dark with contempt. "What the bloody hell is wrong with you?"

Kinkade whirled on him. "Do you think I *like* it, Eversea? It never, ever ends. Nothing helps, nothing saves them, nothing stops them. *Every single day* I see it happen. They're not saints. They're not evil. Some are quite hopelessly wicked, others unfortunate or victims of poor timing. But every single one of these girls could well be dead right now. They would have died at sea on their way to Botany Bay. There's naught I can do. I feed them and clothe them—"

"Like *pirates*!" Lucy said indignantly. "Like *leprechauns*!"

Chase fleetingly wondered which of his acquaintances liked seeing women dressed as leprechauns.

He didn't think there was such a *thing* as female leprechauns.

"—and in return for a little entertainment or a little leg spreading, they get a chance at freedom . . . *if* they please the clients. If we've complaints from the clients, well, they're out and they know it, and they know what their fate is likely to be when they go back to prison, for we can't have them talking. And I am, for the moment, temporarily quite amused by all of it and pleased with how things are going and profiting greatly from the whole endeavor. It isn't cheap to keep these buildings standing, you know, and I've finally found a use for this one."

Chase listened to this with a growing, weary incredulity.

His mouth quirked ironically. "Ah, yes, you're quite a savior, Kinkade. Do you remember the conversation we had about whether a woman could make or destroy you?"

"Are you laboring under the misapprehension that I've been *destroyed* by women, Eversea?" Kinkade was scornfully amused. "I'm making a fortune and having a splendid time. I contemplated asking you to participate, but no, no. I knew you'd be appalled. So upright, Captain Eversea. So . . . honorable. Right, Chase?"

All dark, insinuating irony.

"No, Kinkade," Chase said thoughtfully. "I don't think a woman can destroy you. You can't be destroyed because . . . there's nothing *to* destroy. I warrant that you just reflect whatever's near you. Like a puddle of mud. You reflect honor if you're near it. You reflect decay if you're near it. Left to your own devices, you've no moral center at all, no concern except for your own pleasure. This is the result."

Quietly, casually said.

Something poisonous and subtle and dangerous shimmered in the air between the two men, and frightened everyone into silence for a moment.

Kinkade's voice was lazy and very, very low.

"Very inspiring speech about honor from a man who cuckolded his commanding officer."

Rosalind sucked in a sharp breath.

Lucy looked at her sister in great interest.

Kinkade threw Rosalind a coldly disdainful look.

"So *you* told him," Chase said softly to Kinkade.

Despite everything, Rosalind could hear a hint of the pain of betrayal in his voice.

She wanted to kill Kinkade in that moment, too.

Kinkade gave a soft, disbelieving laugh. "I *had* to, Eversea."

Chase was motionless, absorbing the blow of a long withheld truth. "You had to hurt him, and hurt Rosalind, and possibly destroy me?" His voice was taut and flat.

"I had to *save* you, you fool." Kinkade was exasperated. "*And* the rest of our regiment. I'm *not* you. No one is. I knew how he—how all of us—relied on you. And I saw how you looked at her, Eversea. I saw how she looked at you. And then I saw . . . well, I saw you rather climbing each other that day. Your hands all over her. You *idiot*. She's just a woman! But I knew it would affect your judgment, and so help me God I wanted to live through that war. So I told Colonel March. And he reassigned you."

A long, complicated silence, broken only by Lucy's sniffles, followed.

And then MacGregor stifled a sneeze in his fist. "I beg your pardon," he whispered.

They all stared at him for a surprised instant.

And then Rosalind spoke and everyone stared at her.

"Mathew forgave me," she said with quiet contempt to Kinkade. "And Mathew forgave Chase. He *knew* Chase—and me—well enough to know that our own consciences would punish us more than he ever could. But he never forgave *you*, Kinkade. I never knew for certain it was you—he never told me the name of the person who betrayed us—but if there's one thing Mathew understood it was the difference between a good man and a weak one. He made certain Chase was reassigned for Chase's sake, too, and for the sake of his pride as a man. But in his eyes, your crime was the greater, because he understood your true reasons for doing it. He despised you for it."

Kinkade went still. He inhaled at length and pressed his palms to his eyes. He sighed out the breath.

And then he lowered his hands again, and his face was gray and weary, too.

"Kinkade . . . " Chase's voice was truly curious. "Did you . . . *hate* me?"

His friend gave a short laugh. "I never *hated* you Chase. There were times that I wished I was more like you, but I warrant it's rather more uncomfortable possessing a great overstuffed conscience than I should ever like to be. I prefer comfort to honor. I prefer pleasure to productivity. But you know this. The world is not quite the black-and-white place you need it to be. We cannot all be you—imagine how very dull it would be. Not to mention people like you would have no one to go about fixing and judging." He quirked his mouth bitterly.

"Aaaaaah!" They heard the desultory scream of the pirate wench below.

Chase stiffened in anger and resolve. "You will end all of this now." His tone was even and lethal.

"And you'll do what, Eversea? Unleash thieves upon London again? They're not all of them weeping bubbleheads like the one you see before you."

"I—" Lucy squeaked indignantly.

Rosalind pinched her arm.

"Petty, hardened criminals, the half of them," Kinkade continued. "None of them violent, mind you, or I wouldn't have them in with my clients. But they'll steal again. Prey on you, perhaps members of your family."

"No one preys on Everseas, Kinkade, and lives to tell about it."

This was rather supported by proof, and everyone in the room knew it.

Kinkade was silent, then said, "I thought you were a great believer in crime and punishment and all that, Eversea. How many subalterns were flogged for stealing?"

"This isn't war. If these girls steal again and are caught, then they'll have to contend with whatever brand of justice the English courts decide. Not yours."

"So you're judge and jury?"

"Why not? You've been."

"Dead. All of them will be dead, Chase," Kinkade said wearily. "If not by the noose, then suffering on a ship somewhere on the way across the ocean."

Everyone knew this was indeed a possibility.

Chase said, "It doesn't give you the right to use a flawed system to serve your pleasure, or to prey upon the powerless. You'll be leaving the country for Botany Bay on a ship that sets sail tomorrow."

Kinkade snorted. "You can't make me do anything of the sort."

"I can."

"Lucy will go to trial, if I do," Kinkade ground out. Whiter around the mouth now. Silvery eyes glittering with anger. "I'll see to it. Every witness called will testify that she stole."

"Lucy's accuser will find himself more than compensated for whatever grief he experienced when she stole a bracelet, and I shall make very sure he never makes that accusation about her again."

"But I *didn't*—" Lucy began to protest. Then sighed, as the truth was rather more complicated. In her eyes, anyhow.

"I have no faith that you'll do any good wherever you go, Kinkade. But as you said, England does like to rid itself of its criminals, and it will be ridding itself of you. You'll volunteer to go, in fact, which will make you look quite the hero. Turn around," he barked, a sound familiar to Rosalind: Captain Charles Eversea in command. "MacGregor?"

MacGregor knew what to do. He whipped off his cravat and Chase tied Kinkade's hands behind his back, shoved him in the room once occupied by Lucy, and locked the door.

"We'll escort him to that ship tomorrow," he said to MacGregor.

"Yes, sir," MacGregor said, color restored to his face. Honor restored to his life.

MacGregor was dispatched to tell the gentlemen downstairs to go home as quickly as possible through the Covent Garden exit—as luck would have it, another tunnel emptied out near the Final Curtain—as word had just reached them that they were in grave danger of being discovered.

They all abandoned their drinks and scrambled out in a sheepish panic, some still in fantasy costume. Then again, it *was* Covent Garden. Doubtless no one would look twice should an eighteenth-century pirate go staggering down the street.

And Chase and Rosalind, dragging Lucy with them, went one by one knocking on doors, interrupting "pleasure" in progress if necessary, until all the men were sorted out from all the women, and the surprised women—resentful pirate wench included—were ushered out through the Covent Garden exit, too, and told to leave, lest they risk arrest.

Not one of them needed to be told twice.

All, that was, except Meggie Plum, Lucy, and Cora Myrtleberry, who'd been restored to her own clothing ("Ye willna tell me da I dressed as a mermaid, will ye?" she asked anxiously, and she was assured they would not) and returned with Rosalind, Chase, and Sergeant MacGregor through the museum tunnel. Ireton had apparently regained consciousness and gone home. He was no longer slumped against the wall, anyway.

Though he'd forgotten his hat.

"Oh, Ireton was forever going out the wrong way," MacGregor explained. "He has a terrible sense of direction. He likely wanted the Covent Garden tunnel and ended up here."

Which explained why he'd been scurrying through the museum that day.

"Would you like a souvenir?" Chase asked Rosalind, holding out Ireton's hat to her, chucking her under the chin with the plume.

"Let's leave it here to confuse future generations when they excavate a bricked-in tunnel. They'll be puzzled, no doubt."

"Very good thought, indeed."

So they left the hat upside down, where it was, and he pulled the sconce, and for the very last time they all passed through the museum wall.

The wall *thunked* closed behind them.

As an afterthought, Chase lifted the Rubinetto down from the wall and took it with him. He had plans for it.

Cora Myrtleberry was restored to the arms of her joyous father, who was waiting in the museum breathlessly, and they dashed off to no doubt do puppety things.

Meggie Plum was delivered to a joyous Liam at the home of Cousin Adam Sylvaine, and Meggie dropped to her knees and squeezed her brother nearly blue and wept just a little.

"Girls," Liam said disdainfully over his sister's shoulder to Chase, though his eyes were suspiciously damp, too.

Rosalind decided to take Meggie and Liam to her town house.

* * *

So Rosalind's formerly quiet town house was suddenly filled with people: a chastened Lucy, who was packed off to bed with tea instantly, and Liam and Meggie, who were to share another room for at least the evening. It was rather nice but a bit overwhelming. She would need the maid to come in more frequently, she thought, if this was to be the shape of things.

Rosalind considered making tea, but her eyes would not stay open.

"I suppose I'll be off."

She looked up at Chase. It was something someone might say after they'd departed a dinner. It reminded her of his *There's that done, then,* after they'd made explosive love for the first time in the museum.

"Why are you smiling?" he wondered.

She just shook her head.

"Rosalind?"

"Mmm?"

He hesitated. "Did he really forgive us?"

"He did. The only person who hadn't forgiven you is you."

Chase's head went back at this. And then came down in realization.

And then he frowned at her a bit to punish her for being so insightful. Which made her smile.

"I was sorry to have to leave you alone with the consequences, Rosalind. I knew he must have known."

"Oh, I survived. It wasn't comfortable, but he was not as shredded as one might think. He was made unhappy, but I believe he understood. He loved us both, and he knew I was terribly sorry to hurt him. *I* never had any illusions about whether or not I was human; I am all too human. But Chase . . . I knew I ought to have been, but I was never sorry that you kissed me."

He hesitated. "Neither was I," he said softly.

Quite an admission of humanity from Captain Eversea.

And then they were quiet.

This had begun to feel very like good-bye.

He glanced at the door, as if to confirm this, and then hesitated.

"Am I doing the right thing?" he asked. "Allowing all those women to go? Letting Kinkade go to Botany Bay without a public humiliation?"

"What is right? What is wrong? You made a few people immeasurably happy. You righted a few wrongs. You can only follow your instincts when the rules fail, and I would trust the people I love to your instincts any day, Chase."

He gave her a half smile. "It's an honor to be trusted by you, Rosalind."

She looked into his blue, blue eyes. He was weary, too.

"I have a confession," he said. "I know I righted a few wrongs. But I mainly wanted to make things right for *you*."

It was a lovely confession. "You did."

In so many ways.

"Thank you for everything," she said softly.

She did mean everything. From Lucy to the brothel to exquisite pleasure in the huge curtained bed, which seemed an eternity ago. To making her feel more like a woman than she'd ever felt in her entire life. For resolution. For being the extraordinary person he was.

"Thank you for defending me against the puppet," he said.

She laughed.

He leaned down, cupped her face in one hand and kissed her gently, his mouth warm and open, his tongue touching her tongue just slightly, sweetly. Their lips clung, and once again all of her senses surged toward him. Her body began to melt into him.

But he ended the kiss before she did, with what appeared to be an effort. "I'm returning to Sussex tomorrow to say good-bye to my family."

She reared back suddenly and spent a moment in silent absorption.

"Will you . . . will say good-bye to me before you leave for India?" she finally said softly.

He went abruptly still.

"Yes." He smiled faintly, and it was a smile she didn't quite understand. Ironic. It didn't reach his eyes. "I will come to say good-bye."

Chapter 23

"What's this?" Colin was holding the Rubinetto and staring at in puzzlement.

"It reminded me of you. See? Air whistles right through a hole in the cow's arse." Chase demonstrated by holding it up and blowing through it.

"Splendid!" Colin was delighted with his gift.

Chase told him the entire story, counting, of course, on his brother's discretion in every regard, eliminating, for Rosalind's sake and the sake of his own pride, some of the more intimate details. And was that a twinge of . . . longing! Ah yes, indeed it was. Longing in Colin's eyes. Colin missed being a rascal. But not as much as he enjoyed being a farmer and a husband.

"I thought I ought to give it to you to remember me by. I might not have looked beneath the cow's tail at all if not for you."

This had made Colin nearly misty-eyed.

But it could have been because they'd just had a series of farewell pints at the Pig & Thistle, and were now lounging about the drawing room as his mother and father and all his brothers and sisters—Olivia and Genevieve, Ian and Marcus—went in and out, testing

Chase's mood and discovering him much improved. They hadn't taken kindly to his news that he was leaving for India, but if this was the cause of the much improved Chase, they would reluctantly embrace his decision.

Though they never said as much to him. Just to each other.

"I'm sorry I've been so insufferable." Apologizing was not Chase's long suit. He said this stiffly.

"*I* never thought you were insufferable," Colin lied.

Chase stared at him, waiting for it.

"We *all* thought you were insufferable." He grinned.

And they were worried about him, too, Chase realized now. As usual, they had known what was best for him by sending him to London, and to visit the vicar, and they'd been right. But it was far too girlish a thing for any of his brothers to say to him.

He was now quite touched he'd been sent off to see to the vicar, because he suspected he knew the reason why.

They'd been quite worried he'd meant *I cannot bear it any longer* literally, in another way entirely.

Perhaps, in a way, he had.

"Will we like the vicar?"

"Very much, I think." He didn't tell Colin his suspicions about the vicar or his odd moment of profundity. It was something he would share only with Rosalind. If nothing else, leading Adam Sylvaine to Pennyroyal Green would potentially ensure that the place didn't become dull in his absence.

"You look better."

"Better than what?" Chase said crossly.

"Peaceful." Colin often did that: said something so

surprisingly insightful one didn't have time to formulate a sarcastic response. Chase suspected his brother and the vicar would become fast friends.

He knew a regret, suddenly, that he wouldn't witness it. Though he'd begun training his thoughts away from regrets, from all regrets, and toward India, because India would be his life now.

"I'm doing what I'm made to do. It's *my* purpose. Somehow war shaped me; I seemed to have no say in the matter. You, and Ian . . . "

"We fought and came home. You were the real warrior, though. Born to it. And the country, and whomever and however you serve are luckier for it. I really think you ought to marry, though."

Chase gave Colin a dark look and surrendered to a moment of gloom. He contemplated telling Colin that he *had* proposed to someone, but didn't want to dim the glow of Colin's marital bliss by asking his brother to bear his disappointment along with him. And he understood now that Colin wasn't merely being insufferable: his brother truly wanted him to know the kind of happiness he had.

"Perhaps I ought to," he said gently.

And Colin's eyebrows went up in surprise.

And then Chase remembered something he'd meant to ask Colin.

"Do you still own the suit of clothes you wore to the gallows?"

"Oh, it's rather worse for wear now, but I can likely locate all the pieces."

"May I have them?"

"Consider them a parting gift, brother."

* * *

Rosalind paused between packing her trunk for her return to Derbyshire to arrange a tea tray: black tea, two cups. And then she waited.

The knock at the door made her heart jump, even as she knew whom it would be.

She led Chase, hat and walking stick in hand, into the parlor. As usual, he seemed to fill most of the place up.

She'd drawn the curtains mostly closed, but the afternoon light squeezing in through the many-paned windows wasn't the kindest or softest. He was stark in it. He looked weary; the lines raying from the corners of his eyes seemed a little deeper now, as did the hollows beneath. He could have done with a closer shave; a faint hint of blue remained beneath his chin. He looked exactly his age. He looked beautiful, in other words.

"You sail, then. In a few hours," she said softly.

Well, why not begin a conversation by stating the obvious? Since he hadn't seemed inclined to begin the conversation at all.

"I sail in a few hours." He nodded, confirming the obvious.

And then it seemed they'd exhausted conversation.

She motioned him to the settee, and they sat beside each other, knees not touching. Imposing a certain almost comical propriety, for all the world as though the presence of a porcelain teapot was a grim chaperon ensuring decorum.

"Lucy has been installed with Miss Marietta Endicott at her academy in Pennyroyal Green," he told her.

"Thank you for arranging that. She isn't a little old for the academy?"

"Miss Endicott has made an exception for her. And if *anyone* can do something about Lucy, Miss Endicott can."

They smiled together.

"Mr. Myrtleberry and MacGregor have disabled the museum wall so that it will no longer turn, and a proper painting hangs there now. No cows or angels in it, I might add. I've donated Colin's gallows suit to the Montmorency and allowed MacGregor to take all the credit for the donation, which inspired the museum board to give him a great raise in pay, and there was a line out the door for the first time in the museum's history to see it."

"Aren't you clever!"

He rewarded her wryness with a brisk nod. "Liam and Meggie are going to live in Pennyroyal Green. Seems there's a job for Meggie at the Pig & Thistle, and Liam will be allowed to help out at the vicarage. I've brought them to London with me. Meggie wanted to fetch some things from their rooms, and Liam wanted to see my ship off."

"And they all lived happily ever after."

He tried to smile at that, but it didn't quite happen.

There followed a silence. Rosalind filled it by pouring a cup of tea.

She made quite a ceremony of pouring a cup, in fact. Her hand didn't shake at all, astonishingly. She offered it to him with politely raised eyebrows.

He gave a short, ironic shake of his head.

She didn't want tea, either.

Absurdly, she settled it with a *clink* back into its saucer.

Say something, she wanted to shout at him.

He wasn't a man of words, however. He generally spoke with his body, whether he was using it in the service of love or war.

She remembered how he'd told her precisely how he felt about her all those years ago, all without saying a word.

She ought to just say good-bye and have done with it, she thought. It would be easier; the result would be the same. A lingering farewell would make nothing better and give her no memories she wanted beyond the ones she already had of him. She stared at tired Captain Eversea, imagined his things all packed in a trunk in preparation for boarding *The Courage*.

She couldn't imagine him growing older across the sea, away from her, where she wouldn't witness it. It was unthinkable. To not see gray hair at his temples, to see more lines in his face, to see *him*. Doubtless he would go on being his stubborn, incomparable self, perhaps marry an exotic dark-skinned girl or at least take one for a mistress. They were wanton and free, those girls, she'd heard, at least the ones in the South Seas were, the ones the likes of Miles Redmond wrote about.

Suddenly she found herself reaching over to lay her hand against his cheek. She'd surprised herself. She felt a little foolish, like a blind woman attempting to get her bearings.

But all those years ago when she'd touched him just as tentatively, she'd known, sensed, the power of the longing and need thrumming beneath his formidable control, and had wanted to see if he was real, if he was vulnerable, if she could reach the *man* in there. He'd always seemed afraid of nothing at all. Though she now knew this wasn't true. His need to do what was good and right had always given him courage, been stronger than fear. He was principled.

He was astonishing.

And now, just as then, she marveled at the bristle of whisker over his cheek, the clean edge of his jaw, the warmth of his skin, the thump of his pulse.

I'm touching Charles Eversea.

He turned his face into her hand again.

She held him for a moment, then slowly took her hand away. And then she hesitated, feinted, and tentatively touched his eyebrow. He went perfectly still, surprised to have his eyebrow touched. She couldn't blame him. She traced the arch of it, then followed the line of it to the bridge of his nose, then stopped and dropped her hand, along with her eyes, to her lap.

For God's sake.

He made a small sound. Almost a laugh. Surprised.

The truth was, she didn't know which of his features she'd choose to touch if she could touch him just one last time. He should just leave and be done with it. Say good-bye politely. Quickly, cleanly, briskly, the way he did most things.

Stay, she sternly told her hands. They lay there quietly in her lap. Reacquainting themselves with the way life used to be before Chase reappeared. Before her hands had become so wanton and knowledgeable about the terrain of his body and gone about touching it freely.

She could speculate and feel later, much later. She wanted this over and done, now.

He lunged forward suddenly. She gave a start and reared back.

Which made him smile. It was a faint one. But recognizable as a smile, nevertheless. Careful, she thought. You're doing it more and more easily these days, Captain Eversea.

He leaned back again, indecisively.

Oh, God. They were *comical*, the two of them.

A second later he shifted forward again, a trifle more gracefully, decisively. And this time he gently scooped her quiet hands from her lap, as though they were a delicate bowl, and raised them to his lips.

He placed a kiss—a soft, reverent kiss—in one palm, then gently folded her fingers over it. In her other palm, he placed another kiss—this one was hot, lingering, and answered by echoes of longing in her body.

And then he slowly closed her fingers over that one, too.

And he slipped his hands from hers. Leaving his kisses burning inside her closed fists.

Two different ways to remember him.

She would *not* cry.

She smiled the sort of smile one manages when fighting tears. A crooked one. She couldn't tell if her heart was breaking or was simply so full her body could no longer comfortably contain it. Regardless, it hurt. Everything inside her seemed to hurt.

The corner of *his* mouth twitched upward, providing the other half of her smile.

And then his expression drifted into thoughtfulness, and then resolve.

He inhaled deeply, exhaled extravagantly, and stood, stood, pushing himself to his feet with his walking stick.

She pretended not to see the hand he reached down

to help her to her feet. She was unwilling to offer her just-kissed hands up to him yet; she was hoarding that last feel of his lips.

She stood on her own.

Wordlessly, he turned to collect his hat and coat from the chair where they had sat for a mere five minutes. He turned back to her, framed in the window, his features washed in the mid-afternoon light, his eyes brilliant and burning.

"Good—"

She didn't let him say it. She couldn't help it. She slid her hands around his neck. Soft, soft hair, heartbreakingly soft, brushed the back of her hand. A man this hard had no business having hair so soft. They would say good-bye today the way they'd said good-bye during the war, with a kiss, though they hadn't known then that it would farewell.

And just like that day five years ago, somehow, their lips met.

He crushed her into his body, because of course their bodies scoffed at the very idea that their minds had any say over whether or not they touched each other for the last time. This time the kiss was sophisticated. It began gently, softly, just a bump of lips, but it had purpose, direction. As though they had all the time in the world, rather than a few hours more. They knew each other now. So slowly they kissed. Deliberately prolonging the moment when their tongues would meet.

And she moaned when they did.

She pulled his face closer to her, and his hands slid down to her arse and pulled her closer. And she freed her hands from behind his neck and slid them down instead to the buttons on his shirt.

She wanted Captain Eversea nude in her parlor.

He shook out of his coat, and her fingers worked open his buttons, and his broad chest was bare to her touch.

"Here," he said.

His coat and his hat went back on the settee. His shirt came off, and then his trousers were lowered, but not his boots because neither of them wanted to waste any time pulling them off, and Chase was standing in her parlor completely nude but for a pair of boots and his dropped trousers.

Her shaking hands had difficulty with the laces of her new dress, and then his hands were there to rescue her. *Her* clothes went in a disgraceful heap on the floor of her parlor. She gave them a little kick to clear them out of the way.

He settled back into a chair that creaked a bit, and she was a trifle concerned because he was so large.

"Come here."

She straddled his thighs, which were thick and hairy, one of them battered and scarred, and her hands slid over them, memorizing him. She pressed herself against his thick cock, not yet astride; his hands savored her breasts, thumbing the nipples into peaks. When she gasped, her eyes closing to slits, her breathing coming short—his hands on her breasts made her simply *wild*—he tipped her back in the hard cradle of his arms so he could bend his head and suck.

Hot bliss fanned through her body where his lips met her nipples.

His hands folded her to him closely, and she could watch the light play over his face, see the burning wonder in those eyes, then revel when he closed them, swallowing, the cords of his throat taut with pleasure. He raised her up, and she sank down on him until he filled her deeply.

And slowly she rode him. Slowly, slowly. But they could not remain slow: they soon bucked against each other, and in the end it was an inelegant coupling, their bodies coming together swiftly and hard, rhythm beyond their control. He came with a thrash of his head and raw gasp of her name as Rosalind shuddered.

For a silent moment longer they held each other. His head tucked into the crook of her shoulder. His breath lulling against her sweat-dampened skin.

Tacitly, silently, they disentangled. And silently they got him dressed again, and she dressed herself from the heap of clothes on the carpet.

He looked down at her solemnly, impossible to read. She'd begun to suspect that Charles Eversea's face revealed least when his mind was fullest.

He watched her, blue eyes glittering. His breath seemed to be held.

She offered up a rueful ghost of a smile.

Chase went very still. He gave a short nod, a faint twist of a smile, and with a gentle, almost formal touch of his hat, he really did leave.

Well.

As usual, Chase seemed to take half the light and air of the room with him when he'd gone.

For some reason, she was careful to hold herself very still. She felt peculiarly hollow.

A few silent seconds later she realized it was because she was *afraid* to move.

Much like a person who has taken a great fall. And

then she understood this was the moment of blessed numbness before the anguish set in. Before she understood just how injured she was. Just how complete and permanent the damage might be.

She felt oddly disconnected from her body, but some instinct made her raise her trembling arm up to her face: the smell of his skin was still on her skin.

She breathed in, and squeezed her eyes closed . . . ah, and *here* was the anguish. Along with the suffocating realization: it wasn't Charles Eversea who was hard and unyielding. It wasn't Chase who was afraid to be vulnerable.

She was.

She'd been the one unable to surrender to the possibility of love, and he'd known it. He protected himself from hurt even as he'd loved her in every way he knew how: with a patience with her that surely must have *killed* him, in his insight, in his protection, in his tenderness and passion, in his determination to see that she had what she wanted, that she was safe, that she was happy.

And she'd been so terrified of surrendering to the enormity of how she felt, so afraid was she of losing him yet again, so afraid of *loss* itself that she'd held herself carefully away from him for so long, even as she made love to his body. Afraid of a heartbreak that would surely kill her, since it would of course be equal to the magnitude of how much she loved him.

Because, oh God, she loved him.

She'd likely loved him from the moment she laid eyes on him five years ago.

So afraid that, like an ass, she'd let him go.

And like an ass, he'd *gone*.

That, she decided, in a sudden fury, was taking the idea of ensuring that she had what she wanted too far.

He still wanted her, and he'd left anyway.

And as she was resourceful, and as this time she was determined to get what she wanted, she bolted for the door and flung it open.

Only to run smack into the wall that was Chase Eversea's chest.

"Rosalind."

He looked very stern, very determined. He placed one not entirely gentle hand flat on her sternum to keep her from sending them both toppling down her steps. And then he eased her back into the house, his eyes never leaving hers.

Her heart was clanging like the bells of St. Mary Le Bow inside her chest, and surely he must have felt it through his palm.

They stared at each. His eyes seemed particularly brilliant, which was when she noticed just how pale he was.

Captain Eversea was *nervous*.

He planted his feet apart in a stance that led her to believe he was about to give a speech.

She folded her hands in front of her and waited, biting her tongue.

She had one of her own prepared, just in case.

"Rosalind . . . " his voice was quite steady. "I was wrong when I said what I do best is serving my country. I was wrong when I said it's what I was made for. I wasn't *far* wrong, of course, but I was wrong. What I was made for . . . " and here he stopped and took in a long, fortifying breath. And then he cleared his throat, and when he spoke again, his voice had gone husky.

"What I've learned is that what I was made for is to love and protect. *Specifically*, I was made to love and protect you."

He waited. She could not speak over the clanging of her heart, but something in her face must have encouraged him to continue.

"I know you wanted a chance to determine what you want. But what I want is this: I want to be wherever you are. Whatever that means. Wherever that might be. So if you want me, I will stay. For as long as you want me. *However* you want me. Because . . . " He sighed. " . . . I love you."

Said with such absolute certainty and finality. The way he said everything.

There passed a silence noisy with glorious unspoken things, during which they gazed at each other and she couldn't feel her hands or her toes. She was tempted to reach behind her to see whether perhaps she'd sprouted wings, like that prurient angel in the Rubinetto painting.

Imagine Captain Charles Eversea, offering up his grand, brave, scarred, difficult, beautiful heart to her.

She would die for the honor of protecting his heart forever.

"Chase?"

He waited, pale, his jaw taut, his eyes fiercely blue.

"I love you, too." His voice had been so bold. Hers emerged a whisper. *Damn*.

She reached up an impatient hand to knuckle away tears, because she didn't want a single second of this moment to be blurred.

Slowly, slowly, he simply smiled.

"And Chase?"

He waited. His breath appeared to be held.

She wanted to be the one to give the order this time.

"We ought to marry."

He went utterly still.

Something fierce and brilliant suffused his face. And then he closed his eyes and inhaled like a man taking his first ever breath.

He released it slowly.

When he opened his eyes again, he gave his head a disbelieving shake.

She knew how he felt: *How did I become so lucky*?

They beamed like ninnies, like besotted schoolchildren, and then Chase startled her by closing the distance between them with one long step.

Gently, as though she'd suddenly become breakable, tentatively, in acknowledgment to how new this was to both of them, he pulled her into his arms as though still uncertain she was his to keep. She reassured him; she went to him easily; she clung. He folded her tightly into him, and beneath her cheek his breath went out in a sigh, a very final sound, a sound of *home*.

She linked her arms around his neck, threaded her hand up through his hair, and her lips found his. The kiss began awkwardly, and became fierce, then deep, and then slow. A kiss that echoed the curve of the years they'd known each other, and they took their time about it. Because it was just the first kiss in what would be a lifetime's worth of kisses.

Unsurprisingly, Liam was waiting outside for him when Chase left a few minutes later to inform the captain of *The Courage* he would not be on board as scheduled after all. He was passionate, but he was dutiful, and Rosalind approved.

"Where did *you* come from?" he said to the boy.

"Followed ye," Liam said complacently.

"Ah," Chase said.

"Ye're walking like the blazes, Captain Eversea." He was gleefully sly about it. "Almost *dancin'* . . . ye might say."

"On air . . . you might say."

"D'yer see the liedy?" Shrewd little cove.

"Oh, I saw the liedy."

"Is she yer woman *now*?"

"Oh, aye, Liam. She's my woman now. Now . . . " He turned around, walked backward a few steps, the sea behind him, Rosalind in front of him, watching him go and waiting for him to return. " . . . and forever."

"Cor!" Liam said, and gave a hop. "Knew it all along!"

At Avon Books, we know your passion for romance—once you finish one of our novels, you find yourself wanting more.

May we tempt you with . . .

- **Excerpts** from our upcoming releases.

- Entertaining **extras**, including authors' personal photo albums and book lists.

- Behind-the-scenes **scoop** on your favorite characters and series.

- **Sweepstakes** for the chance to win free books, romantic getaways, and other fun prizes.

- Writing **tips** from our authors and editors.

- **Blog** with our authors and find out why they love to write romance.

- **Exclusive content** that's not contained within the pages of our novels.

Join us at
www.avonbooks.com

AVON

An Imprint of HarperCollins*Publishers*
www.avonromance.com